The Lady's Guide to Death and Deception

The Lady's Guide to Death and Deception

A Secret Life of Mary Bennet Mystery

Katherine Cowley

TULE
PUBLISHING

The Lady's Guide to Death and Deception
Copyright© 2022 Katherine Cowley
Tule Publishing First Printing, September 2022

The Tule Publishing, Inc.

ALL RIGHTS RESERVED

First Publication by Tule Publishing 2022

Cover design by Patrick Knowles

No part of this book may be used or reproduced in any manner whatsoever without written permission except in the case of brief quotations embodied in critical articles and reviews.

This is a work of fiction. Names, characters, places, and incidents are products of the author's imagination or are used fictitiously. Any resemblance to actual events, locales, organizations, or persons, living or dead, is entirely coincidental.

ISBN: 978-1-957748-56-6

Praise for *The Secret Life of Miss Mary Bennet*

"Beautifully written, masterfully plotted, meet a Mary Bennet every bit as fascinating and twice as daring as her more famous sisters."

—Gretchen Archer, USA Today bestselling author of the Davis Way Crime Capers

"Cowley's creative continuation of the story of one of literature's famous forgotten sisters into a world she could never have dreamed possible, broadens her horizons and ours. Following the pedantic Mary Bennet in her adventures after the conclusion of Pride and Prejudice was a delight that Jane Austen and mystery fans will embrace and cheer."

—Laurel Ann Nattress, editor of *Jane Austen Made Me Do It*, and Austenprose.com.

"In *The Secret Life of Miss Mary Bennet*, Katherine Cowley takes the least interesting sister from Jane Austen's *Pride and Prejudice* and turns her into the heroine of her own story. It's very fun to watch Mary transform into a competent spy, but the true delight is how Cowley masterfully keeps Mary true to her pedantic, socially awkward self from Austen's original while making her a whole person we can root for."

—Molly Greeley, author of *The Clergyman's Wife: A Pride and Prejudice Novel*

"A delightfully fresh take on Miss Mary Bennet. A story I didn't even realize I was waiting for until I read it."

—Jess Heileman, author of *A Well-Trained Lady*

"An intriguing historical mystery that fans of *Pride and Prejudice* will find compelling."

—Tina Kashian, author of the Kebab Kitchen Mysteries

Dedication

to my father,
Richard

Chapter One

"Bonaparte, tired with the weight of Sovereign cares at Elba, is represented as desirous of relinquishing his dominion of that island, for estates in England or Scotland!!"

—*The Oxford University and City Herald*, Oxford, England, February 1815

Miss Mary Bennet, the daughter of a gentleman, and, perhaps more relevant to this circumstance, a spy for the British government, cocked the trigger of her duelling pistol, aimed at the target, and fired.

The bullet entered the target just outside of the centre circle. Mary smiled. The target was only twenty paces away, yet she was pleased with her result. Her first time using a gun had been two weeks ago, but after some training and dozens of hours of practice on her part, she could now consistently hit near the centre of the target.

"Do not forget the stance of your feet," said Mr. Withrow.

From her mentor, Lady Trafford, Mary would have found this to be a worthwhile suggestion—she had forgotten, once again, that the manner in which she stood could impact the results. Yet the suggestion came from Lady Trafford's nephew Mr. Withrow, and his criticisms always managed to vex her.

Perhaps it was because he was only another spy, and not her superior. Perhaps it was because she still harboured a grudge from their initial meeting, though two years had passed. Or perhaps she would have found his criticism more palatable if he were a less handsome man.

Mary's younger sister Kitty, a new spy, stepped forward, aimed, and fired. Her bullet entered the target three inches farther from the centre than Mary's, but Mr. Withrow did not criticise her. Kitty twirled away from the firing line in a manner that made Mary grateful that most guns held only one bullet. Then Miss Tagore, the daughter of an important trader from the East Indies, stepped forward. Her bullet hit directly in the centre of the target.

"Well done, well done, Miss Tagore," said Lady Trafford, and everyone clapped.

It was Mr. Withrow's turn. He stepped forward and stood, shifting his feet into position.

It was not that Mr. Withrow was always disagreeable—he could be charming, whenever he wanted something—and sometimes he was even kind. Last year, after a rather disastrous incident that included the explosion of London's Custom House, Mary had spent four days in her room, unable and unwilling to leave, filled with despair. Mr. Withrow had come all the way from Worthing, not with the express purpose of calling on her, for he had other business in London, but he had visited her, convinced her to leave her room for a walk in the park, and lent a sympathetic ear. After the walk, she had felt like she could keep trying, even in the face of disaster.

Mr. Withrow aimed his pistol and fired. His bullet was only fractionally closer to the centre than hers, yet the difference still annoyed her.

"Let us pause now," said Lady Trafford. "My ears are ringing."

They set down their pistols and headed to a group of benches which had been placed in a circle. In addition to Mary, Kitty, Miss Tagore, and Mr. Withrow, there were four other spies in attendance. Three of them, Mary still did not know well: Mrs. Ford, a woman in her forties, Mr. Twamley, and Mr. Matthews. Mary knew the final spy, Mr. Stanley, a little too well. A little over a year before, they had worked together in London, and Mary had declined his offer of marriage. Her goal, over these weeks of training, was to avoid him as much as possible.

Mr. Stanley sat on an empty bench and gestured to the open space beside him. Mary pretended not to notice and squeezed in between Miss Tagore and Kitty. The bench was frigidly cold, and Mary hid her hands in her skirts. Why they had to train outside, in late February, was a mystery she had yet to solve.

"Let us reflect on this morning's activities," said Lady Trafford. "Defence team, what did we learn?"

Shortly after dawn, they had performed an exercise in an abandoned farm. Mary's team had been the defence and had consisted of herself, Mr. Withrow, Mrs. Ford, and Mr. Matthews. They had been assigned to protect and extract Lady Trafford's housekeeper and confidante, Mrs. Boughton, who had dressed as Napoleon Bonaparte. The offensive team had been tasked with performing the capture of the fake Bonaparte—or so she had thought.

Unfortunately, the offensive team's true mission had been a fake assassination, which Mary's team had failed to prevent.

No one else on her team seemed inclined to answer Lady Trafford's question, so Mary volunteered her reflections. "In many ways it is more difficult to defend than attack. You may hold the ground, but the offence may come at any angle, and with all sorts of trickery, which makes it difficult to plan."

"Good observation," said Lady Trafford. "There are many military commanders who prefer to attack than defend for that reason, and the principle can apply to spy work as well. What else?" She looked at Mr. Withrow and the two other members of their team in turn.

Mr. Withrow glared at Mary. "It is much harder to win if you have a turncoat in your midst."

Mary blinked her eyes rapidly and gritted her teeth. "Are you implying something?"

"It is clear that you were working for the other team."

How could he even think that? "I was not."

"You gave away our position. In essence, you signalled to them instead of to us."

She still felt embarrassed at her failure, but his accusation was unfounded. She tried to not raise her voice, but she failed at this as well. "I would never intentionally give away our position. I had no way of knowing that they would follow me through the barn or see and interpret the signal."

Lady Trafford cleared her throat. "Mr. Withrow is right that there was a turncoat. But it was not Miss Bennet. I assigned that role to Mrs. Ford."

Mrs. Ford gave them both a long, slow smile. It was unclear to Mary whether Mrs. Ford was married, a widow, or had simply taken on the title of "Mrs." because it suited her purposes.

"So you meant to help us," said Miss Tagore. "I was unsure."

Mary turned to Mr. Withrow. "You owe me an apology."

He crossed his arms. "The available evidence led me to a

false conclusion. There is no reason to apologise for that."

As they discussed the exercise in more detail, Mary tried to suppress the irritation she felt towards Mr. Withrow, but she could not. It was like an itch—you scratched it to relieve the pain, and a few minutes later the pain only grew, spreading until it felt as if your skin was covered by scurrying beetles.

"If you were assigned to assassinate Napoleon Bonaparte, what would you do?" asked Lady Trafford.

Ten months ago, Bonaparte had been defeated by the Allies, and the rule of France had been returned to the Bourbon monarchy. As part of the peace accords, Bonaparte had been made emperor of the isle of Elba. It was a small island located in the Mediterranean Sea, in between Italy and France. Yet despite the island's size, Bonaparte was not friendless; a number of members of his court had joined him on the island, along with over a thousand of his finest, most loyal troops.

"I would do better than the Corsican," said Mr. Matthews.

A few weeks before, a man from the island of Corsica, Theodore Ubaldi, had visited Elba and befriended Napoleon Bonaparte. While Bonaparte was reading a newspaper, Ubaldi attempted to assassinate him with a stiletto. After a short struggle, Bonaparte disarmed him and banished him from the island.

"Like the Corsican," said Miss Tagore, "I could not best Bonaparte in hand-to-hand combat. Befriending Bonaparte and getting him alone is a good strategy, but I would probably use a small Queen Anne pistol rather than a stiletto, and I would aim for his heart."

"Would you do it, given the order?"

"Yes," said Miss Tagore, "with no hesitation, though I would likely be killed by his allies after."

Miss Tagore treated the idea that she would willingly sacrifice her life as a given. It was not something Mary had considered, and it was a sober reminder of the consequences that could befall spies.

"What about if we were assigned the reverse, to protect Bonaparte from an attack?"

Mary had more to say on this subject, as it was the part she had played, and they had a hearty conversation about possible tactics. Much of it involved counterintelligence and learning which specific nation or group was targeting him, possibly neutralizing their agents, and moving Bonaparte to a safe location.

"None of this may be relevant," said Mr. Stanley, "if what the newspapers say is true and he is willing to trade Elba for an estate in England or Scotland."

"Do not trust everything you read," said Lady Trafford. "I doubt he would give up the title of emperor so easily. At least Europe is safe, as long as he stays on the isle."

During his time as leader of France, Bonaparte had caused, both directly and indirectly, the deaths of millions of people. Endless war and slaughter and subjugation, with crops and livelihoods and nations disrupted. It was no small comfort that Britain and her allies had finally put a stop to his rule.

"We have a little more time before we return to the castle for tea," said Lady Trafford. "Let us discuss, for a few moments, the art of finding and using informants."

Mary hoped the conversation truly only lasted a few moments. Every single one of her breaths was turning into a white fog in the cold.

"Informants fall under two general categories. First, there are unknowing informants—people from whom you can gather information that do not realise that they are providing, or do not realise your true purpose for gathering such information. Second, there are people who you can actively recruit to our cause, who realise, to some extent, what they are providing information for." Lady Trafford smiled. "How do you like to make informants comfortable with you?"

"I like to use my *feminine appeal*," said Mrs. Ford.

"What do you mean by feminine appeal?" asked Kitty, leaning in a little. "Because I'm rather adept at conversing with men, but if you have any specific approaches to extracting information…"

"Conversation is definitely a start," said Mrs. Ford. "Coupled with attraction, flirtation, meaningful glances, a touch of a finger on an arm, a quiet room, a kiss—" Mrs. Ford gave a demure look, lowering her eyes slowly and somehow managing to look scandalous as she did it.

"Kissing?" said Kitty. "That sounds like an intriguing proposition."

Mary had best say something before her sister was filled with ideas which might lead her to trouble. Their youngest sister, Lydia, had ran off with an officer named Mr. Wickham. She had lived in sin until her uncle, Mr. Gardiner, had forced them to marry. Lydia's actions had almost led not only to her own ruin, but to the ruin of the entire family.

"Kissing a man to gain information is immoral," said Mary. "Once lost, female virtue is irretrievable. One false step—one single kiss—can lead to her complete ruin." She felt herself warming up to her theme, and repeated statements she had made on the subject before. "A woman's reputation is as brittle as it is beautiful. It is impossible for a woman to be too guarded in her behaviour towards the undeserving of the other sex."

Mr. Withrow crossed his arms. "You must have a very refined sense of morals, Miss Bennet, yet your logic eludes me. How is it that you are willing to kill a man for our country, but you are not willing to kiss one?"

"It is not the same thing."

"Society's perceptions of an action do not make it wrong. Would you not agree that the act of killing is more egregious than kissing?"

"Strictly speaking, yes," said Mary. "But they are both condemned in the Ten Commandments."

"Thou shalt not kill may be mentioned, but kissing is not the same as committing adultery."

Mary turned to Lady Trafford. "Surely you cannot approve or condone this sort of…behaviour as a means to extract information."

"Do I require it? No. Is it the only method? No. Is it useful in every situation? No. Can it be used effectively? Yes."

"But—"

"It is a tool, one of many tools and techniques. Some spies might favour a particular tool," here she glanced at Mrs. Ford, "but the fact that you personally do not find a tool to your liking does not mean that it should never be used."

Mary bristled at Lady Trafford's rebuke. Accepting criticism was often useful, but this felt like an attack on her entire system of morality.

"We are not due to discuss ethics until tomorrow," said Lady Trafford, "but I invite all of you to consider the question of what actions are and are not appropriate for spies, as well as whether or not direction from a superior absolves you from any guilt or consequence. Now, in addition to those approaches used by Mrs. Ford, what other techniques can be used to gather information from informants?"

Mary swallowed. Despite the cold air, her entire body felt hot. She could not listen to this—she could not simply accept the idea that kissing for her work could be necessary or moral.

A few years ago, she would have stormed away to give herself time and space alone. But now, she knew better than that. She did not leave nor voice further objections, but rather she sat silently, observing the conversation until Lady Trafford declared that it was time to return to Castle Durrington.

Rather than joining the rest of the spies in carriages, Mr. Withrow mounted his horse.

Kitty grabbed the reins of his horse. "You should be nicer to my sister."

Despite being younger—Mary was the third of five daughters, and Kitty was the fourth—Kitty had recently become rather defensive of Mary, something that Mary found both endearing and entirely unnecessary.

"I think, Miss Catherine, that you have developed a false perception of our responsibilities. It is not our job to be nice to each other," said Mr. Withrow. "We are attempting to train against endless possible threats. The entire continent is holding its breath, watching the Congress of Vienna. Will Prussia insist on taking Poland, and if they do, will we have another war?"

"I am not talking about war," said Kitty. "I am talking about Mary, and how you are harsher with her than with anyone else. It is as if you are trying to prove something."

He paused for a moment. "I have never intended to be anything but congenial to your sister."

"Well, I think you could do better."

Mary climbed into a carriage and watched out the window as Mr. Withrow rode away. Kitty was correct—he did treat her more harshly than he treated everyone else. While at times he was respectful, he often ignored her or treated her with disdain. Not that this had any true impact on her personally. She did not need his good opinion or manners.

When they arrived at Castle Durrington, Mary did not join the others for tea. Instead, she entered a room that always made her feel comfortable: the library.

Yet today the library did not dispense comfort. As she passed Mr. Withrow's desk, she could hear the acerbic tone of his comments in her head, the way he had belittled her, the way he supposed her inferior simply because she actually cared about virtue.

The others had also dismissed her concerns, yet there were endless verses of scripture on the chastity of women.

Mary removed Lady Trafford's family Bible from a shelf and sat down with it. Since becoming a spy, Mary had not devoted nearly as much time to religious studies as she ought, but surely, she could find several verses on morality and use it to provide evidence of her position.

Unfortunately, no specific verses came to mind, so she flipped through the pages. She stopped on the book of Joshua and read a story that she had forgotten. The Israelites sent spies to Jericho to gather information preparatory to their invasion, and a harlot named Rahab hid them on her roof. Then Rahab helped them escape by letting them out of her window and gave them useful advice on avoiding detection.

Mary flipped ahead, reminding herself of the details of the story. Not long after, the Israelites had marched around the city, which was then destroyed. Only Rahab and her family were spared. A harlot, working with spies, had made victory possible and saved the people who mattered most to her.

Mary slammed the Bible shut. A story about a faithful harlot was *not* the moral message she had sought. She wanted something to shore up her views, not to discomfit her further.

What *was* she willing to do for her country? Since she had committed herself to working as a spy, she had worn disguises. She tried not to lie too often—sometimes she could gloss over the truth or omit details. Yet she had told lies as part of her work, sometimes even to her family. She had come to accept that this was, to an extent, justified.

Was she willing to kill? If there was an imminent threat to her country, if she was defending herself against a criminal, if it was under Lady Trafford's direction and she could save a number of lives, then perhaps she could do it.

Yet kissing a man was meant to be done after marriage. Not that any scriptures dictated that—clearly, even harlots were allowed in particular contexts—yet preachers such as Fordyce warned against this sort of behaviour.

If a genteel woman kissed a man and anyone found out, it would ruin her reputation. Of course, if much of her work as a spy were made public, it could also ruin her reputation.

Why then did kissing feel worse than killing?

She supposed that for a man it would not. Of course, a man could go off and have natural children left and right and it would not cripple his future prospects, while if a woman had a child out of wedlock…

But the subject at hand was not…relations…but rather, whether a spy should be willing to kiss if it led to useful information.

Here she was, engaged in a giant, but ultimately, rather unimportant dilemma, when there were real problems…corn shortages and unemployment and the question of what to do about Napoleon Bonaparte and disagreements at the Congress of Vienna. These were the problems at hand, not kissing.

Kissing a man for her work would require her to set aside propriety. Propriety—the accepted morals and norms of society—was a shield, one she had clung to. Without propriety, many would be directionless and fall into great error. Yet her internal sense of morals was stronger than that—she had maintained a clear conscience despite setting aside other societal norms.

Still, she hesitated. Perhaps her real problem was not propriety, but that she was afraid to do something so utterly outside of her experience.

Of course, inexperience had never stopped her before. Inexperience was one of the easiest faults to rectify.

She returned to the drawing room where the others were drinking their tea, and stood, lingering, in the doorway.

"Miss Bennet, please join us," said Lady Trafford.

Everyone silenced, and Mary decided to speak before she lost her nerve.

"I have realised that my assumptions were incorrect in our previous conversation, and I would like to make a request. I do not harbour any false delusions to my skills. I tend to perform much better at things if I have ample practice in advance." She realised that she was talking around her proposal, without addressing it specifically. "In the same way that we have practised with weapons, I would like to practise kissing, so I am prepared to use it in case it is ever necessary in the field."

Perhaps she should have made this proposal privately, with only Lady Trafford, rather than publicly with the entire group. Every single person in the room stared at her. Miss Tagore had a hint of a smile on her face, Mrs. Ford looked about to laugh, and Kitty had her head tilted to the side, as if

THE LADY'S GUIDE TO DEATH AND DECEPTION

she were considering Mary in a new light. Mary could not even bring herself to look at the men. Blood rushed to her cheeks, and she wished that she could blot out what she had said.

"An excellent proposal, Miss Bennet," said Lady Trafford, bringing her hands together. "In fact, we shall do it now. If anyone would prefer not to participate, they are welcome to abstain." There was silence. "Very well. But we should use a more spacious room." She turned to Mr. Withrow. "Henry, will you lead the other gentlemen to the ballroom?"

Mary stepped to the side, as each of the men walked past her into the hallway. She felt inexplicably nervous.

"Come, Miss Bennet, let us discuss."

Lady Trafford waited until Mary had taken a seat near her.

"I believe that the woman should choose their partners. Does anyone have a preference?"

"I think Mary should choose first," said Kitty, "as it was her proposal. And she likely needs the most practice."

"Do not be impertinent, Kitty," said Mary.

"It is not impertinent if it is the truth."

"I have no strong preference," said Miss Tagore.

"I would kiss anyone," said Mrs. Ford with a devious smile.

"Very well. Miss Bennet?" asked Lady Trafford.

Mary considered her options. If her goal was to avoid giving Mr. Stanley further encouragement, she could certainly not choose him. Mr. Twamley and Mr. Matthews were unknown quantities. Either would function, she supposed. Mr. Withrow, on the other hand, clearly despised her, so kissing him could be considered the most moral option.

"I choose Mr. Withrow," she said quietly.

Kitty gave her a knowing look but fortunately did not say anything.

Once Mary had chosen, it turned out that the others did have preferences. They divided up the men in the same manner in which they might divide a roast chicken, then Lady Trafford led them to the ballroom.

The curtains had been opened, exposing the windows on both ends of the long ballroom. Lady Trafford looked at each of the men. "I need you to commit to share not a word of this to anyone. If any of you choose, for any reason, to expose any of the women here or damage their future prospects, I will personally ensure that you regret the act."

Each of the men agreed. Lady Trafford was not a woman to be trifled with.

She listed off each of the partners for the exercise, leaving Mary and Mr. Withrow for last, so it was clear that they were partners even before she said it. Mr. Withrow looked at her with a certain wariness, and then took her arm and led her to the large windows at the far end of the ballroom. They stopped, and he released her arm. In the distance, Mary could see the ocean, or really, the English Channel. Mr. Withrow had been with her the first time she had touched the water, there, on that very shore.

"Miss Bennet," said Mr. Withrow, looking very solemn. His eyes were a deep brown. She had never noticed that before. Of course, she did not normally look at someone like this. She only noticed eye colour when drawing, and despite creating portraits of almost everyone else at Castle Durrington, she had never drawn Mr. Withrow.

"I know, as a spy, that there can be a great amount of pressure to conform to expectations," said Mr. Withrow. "However, if this is not something that you want to do, you should hold your ground and not do it."

"I have made up my mind," said Mary. "I am not unwilling."

"Not being unwilling is not the same as being willing."

"Do you truly want to have a debate of words?"

He considered this, but before he could respond, she stepped closer to him, and pressed her lips against his.

After a moment she pulled away. She had not expected such an abundance of physical sensation, and such a pleasant abundance at that.

It would be useful to catalogue the physical sensations associated with kissing, so she did so in her mind. Her lips tingled and felt warm. She was relatively certain that her cheeks had gone red, but she felt no embarrassment. And she felt very much alive, as if she was more awake.

"I suspect I need more practice than one kiss, if you are willing, Mr. Withrow."

"Yes, I am willing," he said.

This time he leaned into her, and the kiss was a little longer. Mr. Withrow smelled of leather-bound books. The fact that he was about her height was rather convenient for this sort of activity.

They pulled away again.

"That is not the sort of kiss that would cause someone to reveal secrets," said Lady Trafford before heading in the direction of the other couples who were positioned at other spots across the ballroom.

Frankly, Mary felt it had been a very good kiss, but as she had limited experience, she supposed Lady Trafford might be right.

"Do you have any suggestions, Mr. Withrow? I assume you have much more experience at this than I."

"I have no suggestions for you, Miss Bennet." This might be the first time he had not criticised her when given the opportunity. "However, we could try a more...French style of kiss. That may be what my aunt is suggesting."

"A French style?"

"Well, it involves the parting of the lips and, often, the incorporation of the tongue." He almost seemed embarrassed at this admission. She wondered how many women he had kissed before...how many French women.

"That sounds unusual," said Mary.

"We do not need to attempt it if you are not inclined." He adjusted his already straight cravat.

"I think it would benefit me to practise a full range of kissing styles."

He no longer looked solemn, but beyond that, she could not tell what he was thinking at all. She wondered if he was experiencing the same range of physical sensations. How strange to think that they might be sharing that.

She was unsure of what to do, so she waited for him to initiate the kiss.

He reached out his hand, took a lock of her hair, and tucked it behind her ear. And then he kissed her.

The kiss felt *very* French, and produced a whole ream of additional sensations, which, due to their number, were difficult to catalogue. Better to get lost in them than to attempt to sort them in her mind.

When they pulled away, Mary was not quite sure what to say, so she said, "*Merci*, Mr. Withrow. That was quite educational."

"For me as well, Miss Bennet."

What could he possibly mean by that? He had clearly kissed before; surely there was nothing she could teach him.

Lady Trafford approached. "Do something with your hands, Miss Bennet. You are as stiff as a board. And Henry, your posture is just as rigid."

"I do not know what to do with my hands," said Mary.

"Then improvise," said Lady Trafford.

Mary looked around the ballroom, hoping it would provide some sort of inspiration. Kitty had one hand on Mr. Stanley's chest, and one on the nape of his neck. Miss Tagore had her hands wrapped around Mr. Twamley's back. It was almost disturbing, but Mary reassured herself that everyone in this room was *only* kissing and doing nothing more. To her surprise, she rather liked kissing. It was a strange sort of admission.

"Shall we attempt?" said Mr. Withrow.

He held out his hand towards her, and she placed her hand in his. And then he smiled at her. Somehow, this felt more intimate than kissing him. After a moment, she placed her other hand on his chest. She could feel the sunlight on her face. They both initiated this kiss, and soon, Mr. Withrow had wrapped his arms around her and pulled her close. It was quite extraordinary, like being wrapped in a blanket next to a cosy fire.

She did not want to stop kissing him. Of course, that was a sure sign that she *should* stop. She pulled away and brushed imaginary dirt off her skirt.

"I think I have had sufficient practice," said Mary.

"Very well," said Mr. Withrow, as formally as ever. He bowed to her, and then he left the room. An irresponsible part of Mary wanted to call him back.

That evening, Mary agreed to walk with Kitty, Miss Tagore, and Mrs. Ford through the garden. Unfortunately, the subject turned to the very topic that she wanted to avoid.

"What did everyone think of their kissing partner?" asked Mrs. Ford. "I found Mr. Matthews to be surprisingly inexperienced."

"Mr. Stanley was charming, but a little repetitive," said Kitty.

"Mr. Twamley is not really my type," said Miss Tagore, "but he served the purpose."

"What about you, Mary?" asked Kitty.

Mary shrugged her shoulders.

"Surely you must have some sort of reaction," said Miss Tagore. "After all, you did choose to kiss him."

Everyone's eyes were on her, and it was beholden for her to say something. Yet she did not want to talk about Mr. Withrow specifically, to treat him as if some sort of object, or a new tea she had tried and now was expected to judge. It would be more proper to give some sort of overall response on kissing rather than comment on him specifically.

"Well," she said, "I had never before understood why women fall so easily into temptation, which has resulted in so many hastily arranged marriages. Now, however, I have more sympathy towards these women, for it is apparent that even a kiss can create powerful and unavoidable physical sensations and internal emotions."

At this, everyone laughed. Yet she had not meant it as a joke.

At that very moment, Mr. Withrow stepped out from a tall hedge. He had probably overheard the entire conversation.

"Miss Bennet, will you walk with me?"

Kitty burst out laughing and pushed Mary forward. For the first time in Mary's life, she wanted to commit sororicide.

She and Mr. Withrow were quiet as they walked. He gestured for her to lead, so she chose a path that led towards the front of the house, away from the others. The last thing she needed was Kitty listening in on their conversation. It was too dark to see far, but the moon and the stars provided enough light for their immediate path.

Mary did not regret kissing Mr. Withrow—as Lady Trafford had said, it was simply another tool that she could have at her disposal, albeit one she did not intend to use. She was glad she had practised kissing with someone like Withrow, someone who was not a stranger, who she knew adequately and who was, to her knowledge, a good man.

Yet clearly, there were good reasons for the numerous sermons preached to women about maintaining virtue. Kissing a man…well, it was the sort of act that could lead to dangerous sensations, dangerous thoughts.

It was Mr. Withrow who broke the silence. "I had not realised that the women selected their partners."

"Your aunt thought it best."

"Why did you choose me?" He looked at her as if her answer to the question was the most important thing in the world. Of course, he always asked questions in this manner, to anyone from whom he needed information. It was one of the things that made him effective as a spy.

And despite herself, she always found herself answering his questions.

"I thought kissing you would be the most moral option, seeing as you despise me."

"I do not despise you, Miss Bennet," said Mr. Withrow.

"You have made your dislike for me clear, many a time."

"That was never my intent. Miss Bennet—"

A horse galloped off the main road, and up the approach towards Castle Durrington. What could be the meaning of such high speed, at this time of night?

They hurried down the lawn, meeting the rider as he dismounted.

"Napoleon Bonaparte has escaped from the isle of Elba! He has escaped."

Mr. Withrow cursed, the first time Mary had ever heard him do so, and a sudden fear gripped Mary's heart.

If Bonaparte had truly escaped from Elba, there would be another war.

Chapter Two

"Peace be to France, if France in Peace permit
The just and lineal entrance to our own;
If not, bleed France—and Peace ascend to Heaven."
—Shakespeare's *King John*, as quoted in *The Antigallican Monitor*, May 28, 1815

MARY KNEW THAT she should look ahead, out over the water towards the continent, but instead she looked back, her eyes fixed on England's retreating shores. Her home was an island. It had never felt that way to her—circumscribed, alone and separate in the vast sea of humanity—and yet it was. Life must contain a thousand possibilities she had never considered.

They had boarded the ship at Dover, and the white cliffs were more spectacular from the water than they had been on land. She had never been to Dover before this trip, and now she had only been to it for a single night before leaving it behind. The cool sea breeze hit her cheeks, the smell of the sea filled her nose, and a little salt water splashed from the waves and landed on her arm.

It was strange, to say goodbye to everything she had known, and yet hope that what she knew would still be useful to her in some way. She moved to the bow of the ship, to stand next to Lady Trafford and Mr. Withrow. She stood next to Lady Trafford's left rather than Mr. Withrow's right. Withrow had been decidedly more cordial to her in the past few weeks, but that did not mean she desired to seek out his company.

From this position on the boat, she could see a glimmer of France on the horizon. But they were not headed to France, now in the complete possession of Bonaparte, who had somehow retaken his country from the Bourbons without firing a single bullet. This boat sailed to Ostend, and from there they would journey by land to Brussels, a central point for the Allied opposition, and a location where Lady Trafford and her superiors thought it would be useful to situate a number of spies. No one knew what Bonaparte would do next, but the Allies had already signed an agreement declaring their opposition.

Miss Tagore and Mr. Matthews had been sent—separately—to the heart of the enemy, Paris itself. They had both arrived five or six weeks ago. Mr. Stanley was in Italy, staying with cousins and monitoring France's southeastern border. A number of other spies, who Mary did not know, had been deployed across the continent, to bolster the number of those already in various cities and countries.

Yet not everyone was headed to the continent: Kitty had been sent to London. She had been, as she had put it, "extremely forlorn" to miss the opportunity to travel to the continent, but Lady Trafford said she was not ready, and besides, they still needed spies within their own borders, particularly with the riots over the price of corn. Mary's friend Fanny Cramer, a spy and dressmaker who had not attended the training because of her busy schedule, was in London as well.

Lady Trafford seemed deep in thought, and Withrow had his face turned away, so Mary watched the water until it all started to look the same and then withdrew a letter from her youngest sister, Lydia.

Lydia and her husband, Captain Wickham, were arriving in Brussels this very day; Wickham and many of the British forces were gathering there to prepare for the expected hostilities. Before Mary's journey, and Lydia's own, Mary had written to her sister, and to Mary's astonishment, Lydia had replied.

Lydia wrote regularly to their oldest sisters, Jane and Elizabeth, likely because Jane and Elizabeth regularly sent her money. But she rarely wrote to Kitty, despite how close they had once been, and she had never once written to Mary, despite the quarterly letters Mary wrote to her. As such, Mary had no way to compare this letter to others from her sister, yet something about the letter struck her as peculiar.

My Dear Mary,

I appreciated receiving your letter. Yes, I will be going to Brussels, along with many other officers' wives.

I do not understand your desire to visit Brussels. Mr. Wickham says that we will not be available for welcoming visitors, and if you do come, it would be best if you spent your time with Lady Trafford.

Your sister,
Lydia

The shortness and the terseness did not surprise Mary, as they had never shared any real connection. Yet the line about not being available for welcoming visitors—what else did Lydia plan to do in Brussels, if not enjoying the social opportunities?

Lady Trafford peered at the letter. "We shall have to invite your sister and her husband to dinner. They will not turn me down."

"I am sure they would appreciate that, but it is not necessary for you to put yourself out for my family."

"I value all of your family, because I value you," said Lady Trafford. "Besides, any connection to officers or to women who might observe useful information is to be cultivated."

"My sister Lydia cannot be trusted with secrets of any sort and could not be relied upon to gather any information." It was one thing for her sister Kitty to assist in the cause, and quite another for Lydia to do so.

"I apologise, Miss Bennet. I did not realise my statement would receive such a strong reaction from you. I trust your judgment on your sister's skills and usefulness, but I was not, in fact, proposing, that we use her in any large way. We need dozens and dozens of unknowing informants, people who will unintentionally give us useful information. In this, your sister may or may not be of any use, but it is impossible to know who will be of use in advance, and so cultivating a number of relationships is of great importance."

"I understand," said Mary.

Lady Trafford turned to her nephew, who was leaning over the rail, clutching his stomach with his other hand. "You look quite unwell, Henry."

"I am sorry, my dear aunt, I am sorry, Miss Bennet, but I must—"

He hurried off without finishing his sentence, looking very ill indeed.

"Does he need assistance?" asked Mary.

Lady Trafford thought for a moment. "If only there was something we could do for him. It is a pity boats do this to him, as he very much loves the ocean, at least on the shore."

He felt indisposed in carriages, especially for long rides,

but this seemed much worse. Mary's stomach felt nothing out of the ordinary.

"We should get to work," said Lady Trafford.

"But what can be done before we reach Brussels?"

"We can cultivate relationships with possible unknowing informants." She looked around. "Ah, I see Lady Dawson and her daughters. I will introduce you." She paused, and a cunning look crossed her face. "Actually, I will converse with them, and I will introduce you later, but first, I want you to cultivate new connections. Before we reach Brussels, you need to turn three strangers into people who would feel comfortable sharing information with you. Start with…that woman sitting over there, by herself."

"Who is she?"

"I have no idea, but she looks lonely. Endear yourself to her—either be useful to her in some way or find something distinct that you share."

"Must all three connections I make be with complete strangers, with whom I do not have the ability to gain a proper introduction?"

"After her, I will allow you to receive introductions through people you already know. But this will be a good experience for you."

Mary considered the woman for a moment. She looked older than Mary, but likely not yet thirty. She wore a smart blue bonnet, under which her brownish-blond hair caught and reflected the sunlight. She sat in her chair, looking out at the water, in a manner that suggested that she wanted everyone to assume she felt comfortable. But something about the way she looked around, as if she hoped to see someone she knew, and then settled back into her chair, made Mary think she was not at ease.

Rather than barge up to this unknown woman, Mary thought it best if she at least attempted some form of a proper introduction. Swallowing her nervousness, she approached the steward who had welcomed them aboard. "That woman over there—is she alone?"

"Yes, Miss Bennet, she is."

"It appears that she could use some company. Could you introduce us?"

"Of course, Miss Bennet."

He led the way across the deck. "Sorry to intrude, Mrs. Graham."

"Not at all," said the woman, sitting more upright and looking at Mary. "I see you have brought me someone to talk to? I have never been on a boat with such spectacular service."

"Yes, indeed, this is Miss Bennet, Miss Bennet this is Mrs. Graham." He beckoned to another one of the stewards, who brought Mary a chair and placed it next to Mrs. Graham's. "Can I be of any further assistance?"

"Thank you, but no," said Mrs. Graham. "You truly have excellent service. I shall recommend you to all of my friends." As he left, Mrs. Graham lowered her voice and leaned closer to Mary. "Do not tell the steward, but I have never been on a boat before. I would not want him to think I only believe his boat is the best because of my lack of experience."

Mrs. Graham laughed at her own statement. She seemed the sort of woman who liked to find herself and everything else amusing.

"I will not say a word on the matter," said Mary. "It is my first time on a boat as well." And now, to her task at hand—to cultivate useful connections. "I assume that you are also headed to Brussels?"

"Yes, I am to stay with some friends there, the Capels. Do

you know them?"

"Unfortunately no, but I hope to meet many people in Brussels."

"I suspect everyone travelling there does. Dukes and princes and military generals—it should be quite the affair. Much more interesting than dreary old London." She smiled to herself. "But enough about me. Are you travelling with someone?"

"Yes, with Lady Trafford." Mary gestured in her direction.

"Are you her travelling companion?" asked Mrs. Graham.

Travelling companions were typically hard pressed for money and were basically glorified servants, often impoverished upper class women.

"Not exactly," said Mary. "Lady Trafford is a distant relation and a friend, and she thought I might enjoy visiting the continent with her. My sister will be in Brussels as well." She worried that Mrs. Graham would lose interest in the conversation—not that she had anywhere to go—but she needed to establish a deeper connection. Lady Trafford always said that people loved to talk about themselves, if asked the right questions. "Is your husband travelling with you to Brussels, or is he already there?"

For a brief moment, Mrs. Graham seemed to lose her composure, but then quickly she returned her mask. "I am actually a widow." Her right hand went to a large mourning ring on her left. Mary had noticed the mourning ring on Mrs. Graham's finger, but so many people wore mourning rings, and it had not occurred to Mary that it could be for Mrs. Graham's husband.

"I am sorry for presuming, I—"

"No, it is my fault. It would be easier, with new acquaintances, if I could proclaim it without needing to talk about it. Maybe I should carry a banner to the next ball I attend."

This was at least partially in jest, thought Mary. "I understand." She extended her own hand towards Mrs. Graham. "This ring is to remember my father. He died almost two years ago, and I still mourn him deeply."

"I see that we understand each other," said Mrs. Graham. "It has been three years for me. My family wanted me to remarry last summer, but I was not ready to attend balls and social functions." She adjusted her bonnet. "I think I am ready now, to socialize and perhaps find a new husband."

As sometimes happened, Mary did not know what to say.

"Do not think me in competition with you," said Mrs. Graham, "but a widow does have a competitive edge when it comes to finding a husband." She lowered her voice to a whisper. "Some men prefer a woman with a bit of…experience."

Mary felt her face flush with embarrassment at Mrs. Graham's words. This was not the sort of thing that was *ever* spoken about in polite society.

"And now I have scandalized you. I apologise, Miss Bennet."

"No apology is necessary," said Mary, reminding herself that Lady Trafford had assigned her to speak to Mrs. Graham, and that she must not flee from her assignment now. Of course, it was probably best to move to a more comfortable topic. "What are you looking forward to most about Brussels?"

"All the officers, of course, and the balls and the parks and the ramparts. And I have heard the baths are quite good. What are you looking forward to?"

"The same." Or at least, she must pretend to simply be a

woman visiting Brussels for the social life. "Also, I hope to find at least one good bookseller."

"Do you speak French?"

"Adequately."

"I used to speak French well. I hope I can still manage."

Lady Trafford had not specified, but Mary thought it would be useful to accustom Mrs. Graham to conversing with her about more serious matters. "Are you worried at all, about the upcoming war? Do you think it will be safe in Brussels?"

"No, I am not worried. The Duke of Wellington is the brightest general of our time, besides, perhaps, Bonaparte himself. After what he accomplished in India and then in Spain and Portugal—well, I do not believe we have anything to worry about. He has only ever lost one battle."

"I read that he is rather aloof," said Mary. "But despite that, he cares immensely for his men."

"I heard that last year, when the Duke of Wellington was ambassador to France, he took as his mistress the same singer who had been Bonaparte's mistress. I see I have shocked you again, Miss Bennet. My goal shall be to scandalize you twice every single time that we meet."

"It will not be very hard, I suspect, and I am afraid that I will not have the ability to return the favour."

Mrs. Graham smiled. "It is a favour, is not it? Do not worry, I do not engage in any sort of scandalous behaviour myself. But I do so enjoy a scandalous tale."

If befriending Mrs. Graham were not part of an assignment, Mary would feel quite uncomfortable. Yet with her propensity for gossip, Mrs. Graham would make an ideal informant.

"Where in Brussels do your friends live?" asked Mary.

"Unfortunately, my friends just moved a few miles outside of the city, which will make spending time in Brussels more inconvenient. Were you able to find a place to stay? I have heard that housing is quite difficult to come by."

"Yes. Lady Trafford is renting a house two blocks from the Hôtel de Ville."

"So close to the main square! Has Lady Trafford been to Brussels before?"

"No, not at all."

"That is most impressive that she managed to obtain something downtown, at this time. I shall have to call on you, though do not feel any obligation to call upon me, as I will not be in the city itself."

"It would be a pleasure to have you call upon me, and I will try to call upon you as well," said Mary.

"You are too kind."

After a few more minutes, they said their farewells, and Mrs. Graham left the deck. Mary felt very pleased at her new, unknowing informant. She wished that she too could retire to her cabin—exerting herself to converse with strangers was downright exhausting. But she would not let herself rest. She had two more people to forge connections with before they reached Brussels.

AFTER TEN AND a half hours on the boat, they neared Ostend. Fortunately, the trip had been a short one; the crossing from Dover could take up to twenty-four hours. As they approached, she again removed her pad of paper and attempted to sketch her first impressions of the continent: a beach with sandy hills, and in the distance the town of Ostend itself, with its grey buildings.

The steward explained that boats could only enter the harbour at high tide. This created great congestion with dozens of boats entering the harbour at once. Their boat and a few other boats went directly to the dock. Lady Trafford's horses and carriage were removed from their place at the bottom of the boat; she had brought her own due to the shortage of both on the continent—over a decade of war had lowered the population of horses significantly, and the upcoming war meant that they were particularly difficult to acquire, especially for private usage.

Mr. Parker and Mrs. Boughton, two of Lady Trafford's employees who had accompanied them, made the process of disembarking easy and pleasant for Mary, Lady Trafford, and Mr. Withrow, who at this point looked very unkempt and pale. Yet those in the military disembarking at Ostend did not receive the same treatment.

A number of the two dozen boats carrying British soldiers made their way as close to the shore as possible and began to disembark without use of the dock. Soldiers unceremoniously threw everything overboard: luggage and saddles and horses. The horses swam and walked towards the shore, soldiers chasing after them.

"Can you not take more care?" one of the disembarking officers shouted.

"We've been doing it this way for weeks," said one of the men directing the procedure.

"What losses will we sustain by treating our resources in such a manner?"

"I can't help it. It's no business of mine—the duke's orders are clear. Speed is *the* most important thing. We can't unload twenty-four boats in less than three hours using any other method, and these boats have got to get back to England so they can bring more soldiers."

The complaining officer accepted defeat and wearily assisted his men. The soldiers looked greasy and hot, and some of their shirts appeared stained by vomit.

What a mad scramble to prepare for war. If the Duke of Wellington did not have enough troops, or did not position them in the right places, they would lose the war before it was even begun.

One high-ranking officer—perhaps a general—stood aloof from the others. After a few minutes, he hailed a younger-looking officer who had recently disembarked. Mary stepped a little away from Lady Trafford and Mr. Withrow so she could better see their interaction, which seemed unusual, somehow. The general handed the other officer something—papers or banknotes, perhaps. The younger officer saluted and then returned to one of the boats.

Mary and the others managed to escape the chaos of the beach, and they spent the night in Ostend. The one inn owned by English speakers, the Rose, was full, so they stayed at the Great St. Michael, which made communicating more difficult as none of their party spoke a single word of Dutch. Early in the morning, they again climbed into the carriage. It was seventy miles to Brussels, one of the most important cities in the new United Kingdom of the Netherlands, and it would take several days to make the journey.

Leaving Ostend was not easy, what with the glut of troops and horses and even cannons and artillery of all sizes. They ended up taking their carriage through the middle of an outdoor market, where soldiers haggled for fruit and fresh bread.

"At least our troops pay for what they take," said Lady Trafford. "I have heard that the Prussians and our other allies are not so kind."

"We are still invaders," said Mr. Withrow. "We are simply more polite about it."

"We are not invaders," said Mary. "We are helping them."

"So we like to think," said Mr. Withrow. "But we are helping them because it helps us as a nation, politically and financially. It is all a matter of profit."

As always, Mr. Withrow possessed a cynical view of all humanity—he truly was the most cynical person she had ever known, seeing always the worst possible motive in others.

A boy working at one of the stalls bumped a display, and suddenly, hundreds of apples fell, bouncing onto the ground.

"Stop the carriage," said Mr. Withrow, but their driver, Mr. Parker, did not stop.

A woman, likely the woman who owned the stand, began berating the boy.

"I said, stop the carriage," said Mr. Withrow, raising his voice.

"It is not a good spot," said Mr. Parker.

Mr. Withrow pushed open the door, and, while the carriage was still in motion, jumped from it into the market below. He was lucky not to land on anyone or twist an ankle.

Lady Trafford shook her head. "He can be very foolish."

Mr. Parker stopped the carriage, and Mary leaned out to close the door but stopped as she looked back at the fruit stand.

The woman was beating the boy with a stick. Why would she do so in public? Mr. Withrow thrust his body between the boy's and the woman's and took the next blow. Then he removed the stick from her hand, broke it, and tossed it away.

Lady Trafford leaned out the window, clucked her tongue

and shook her head, then sat back comfortably in her chair. "Prepare to wait."

"Has Mr. Withrow done this before?"

"Yes," said Lady Trafford and Mrs. Boughton simultaneously.

"But why?" asked Mary. "As has oft been said, 'Spare the rod, spoil the child.'" If her parents had been more willing to discipline, it would have greatly benefitted her younger sisters, especially Lydia.

"My nephew often responds too strongly when individuals he sees as defenceless are threatened. Take, for instance, the time when you brandished a fire poker at me. He tackled you to the floor, which was quite unwarranted. *I* knew that you were not going to actually attack me with the poker."

"Of course," said Mrs. Boughton, "in today's case, Mr. Withrow saw more than a threat: the woman was *in fact* beating the boy. There are situations when parents and other caregivers go too far, in which cruelty rather than discipline determines the amount of punishment."

Mary had to agree with this statement—she had read in the paper, once, of a lad being beaten to death by a caregiver.

"Yet even if that is the case here," said Lady Trafford, "it is unlikely that Henry's interference will make any lasting impact."

Mary rubbed her forehead. In the hypothetical, ethics and morality always seemed so clear, yet in practice, things often became murkier.

After about fifteen minutes, Mr. Withrow returned to the carriage. Yet before entering, he proceeded to lecture Mr. Parker. "If you had stopped the carriage the first time I asked, I could have prevented the beating before it happened."

"I am sorry, sir," said Mr. Parker.

"Sorry is not enough," said Mr. Withrow. "If I ask you to the stop, I have a good reason for it. Do you understand?"

"Of course, sir," said Mr. Parker.

Mr. Withrow entered the carriage, slamming the door shut behind him. His facial expression was sullen and dour, and Mary did not dare say a single word to him. As they left Ostend, he examined a red welt that was forming on his arm.

"So did you lecture the woman, or give her money?" asked Lady Trafford.

"I lectured her, and then I encouraged the boy."

Lady Trafford raised her eyebrows. "Is that all?"

"I gave the boy money," he admitted.

"Yet you left the boy in the same situation?"

"It was his mother," said Mr. Withrow. "The boy wanted to stay, and he would not take any suggestions otherwise."

"If it was his mother, it was well within her rights to beat him," said Mary.

"Legally," said Mr. Withrow angrily. "But I do not believe any adult *should* have a right to lay their hands on a child. There are better ways to teach and motivate and discipline children."

It was a rather radical notion.

"You know that your interference will not change anything," said Lady Trafford. "She will beat him again tomorrow."

"Would you have me do nothing?" Mr. Withrow's voice sounded raw and a little hoarse. "Yes, I accept that everything and everyone in this world is ugly and brutal—life has taught me that too many times. But can I not try to do something, anything to prevent it?"

Lady Trafford reached across the carriage and patted him on the knee. "I am glad you still keep trying."

Mary wanted to say something to him as well, to say that she appreciated his sentiments and the fact that he bestowed his concerns to even strangers, but her words became stuck in her mouth, and she did not manage to say anything. She did give him a brief smile, but he turned and looked out the window.

As the carriage drove into the countryside, Mary herself became arrested by the view outside the window. The rye was beautiful, the way it glinted in the sun. The corn seemed double Mary's height, despite it not being the end of the season. She had seen plenty of crops before, yet she had never, in all her life, seen land that was so fertile. It did not appear like a place for war. War was meant to happen in dry, barren places, bereft of life. The Netherlands was so idyllic, that an approaching war seemed impossible.

Yet perhaps it was its idyllic nature that made this country so desirable—perhaps that was why this land had been taken by conquest dozens of times over the centuries. And it would be overtaken by war once again, or at least, such was the fear of Britain and her allies.

Chapter Three

An extract from a Parisian newspaper:

"In the evening, there will be a general illumination, and [a] concert at the Tuileries at eight o'clock. Fireworks will be displayed on the Place de la Concorde at 9 o'clock the same day."

—*The Times*, London, June 2, 1815

From the moment they arrived, Mary liked Brussels. It was a quaint city, a fraction of the size of London, with less than a hundred thousand people while London possessed about a million. As soon as they arrived and settled into their rented house, they received half a dozen invitations to parties and balls and all manner of festivities.

"Social events are as essential to the war preparations as the gathering of troops," Lady Trafford informed them. "In them is manoeuvring, planning, and diplomacy, and they also act as a sleight of hand, a distraction so the enemy thinks we are focused only on trivialities."

Their first social event was held at the Hôtel de Ville. Despite the name, it was not a hotel, but a public building located in the Grand Place, which was the central square in Brussels. The Hôtel de Ville was a white stone building, built in a Gothic style, with a black roof. Its most salient feature was a grand, elegant tower, hundreds of feet high, not centred, but positioned near the middle of the building.

"That is St. Michael, the patron saint of Brussels," said Mary, pointing at the statue on top of the tower.

"How do you know that?" asked Mr. Withrow.

"I made the effort of reading a book about Brussels before we left England." Clearly, Mr. Withrow had not.

They entered the doors at the base of the tower, where they were greeted by Mrs. Watson, the wife of an important officer. "Ah yes, the Duke of Wellington requested I add you to the guest list."

"We do appreciate you obliging," said Lady Trafford. "It must be difficult to accommodate such last-minute changes." The Duke of Wellington had included a personal note with their invitation, requesting that they attend so he could speak to them.

Mrs. Watson smiled. "Half of the people here are those he requested I add to the guest list. But I do not mind at all—so many interesting people, of *all sorts*."

"What did she mean by *all sorts*?" asked Mary once they had stepped farther into the open gallery.

"Typical British sense of superiority," said Mr. Withrow. "I do not mean to denigrate our country or our people's accomplishments. However, when many of our countrymen travel abroad, they dismiss and judge and belittle the local populace, and act as if anything different is inherently inferior."

"That is very insightful, Mr. Withrow. As I encounter new experiences and people of various cultures, I will try to not assume I know best or that my ways are superior."

"I was not implying, Miss Bennet, that you need to modify your behaviour," said Mr. Withrow, turning to her. Lady

Trafford subtly moved forward, so it was just the two of them, facing each other, without her in between.

"I know," said Mary. "I just thought it was very well spoken, like one of my books."

"From you, that is a great compliment. I—" and then he stopped, as if he did not know what more to say.

She wanted him to keep talking—she did not like her curiosity to be left unsatisfied, and clearly he had meant to say more. "Is this your first time abroad, or have you travelled before?"

"I have travelled before, but it may not be the best time to discuss it."

"Of course." He must not be interested in further conversation.

"Perhaps another time," he said, and it seemed genuine. "For now, shall we join my aunt?"

She nodded, and they stepped forward to join Lady Trafford. They followed the instruction of attendants and turned to the right, passing between two lion statues guarding a grand staircase which they climbed to reach the second floor. What must Lady Trafford think of their private conversation? Hopefully she did not assume that there was any interest between them, for there certainly was not. Fortunately, Lady Trafford was not a matchmaking sort, and even if she was, Mary was not the sort of woman she would want for her nephew and heir. Mary had no fortune, after all.

They entered the Grand Hall. The hangings and the carpet and the benches were all made of green fabric. Those present were an exhibition of all those who had gathered against Bonaparte: Prussian officers; others from various German-speaking principalities; Russian and Austrian ambassadors, but no officers—their armies were gathering elsewhere; numerous Englishman; officers from Ireland; and Scottish Highlanders dressed in traditional garb. And then there were those from the Netherlands itself, the Dutch and the Flemish and the French-speaking Belgians.

People were eating, drinking, socializing, flirting. Normally, at social events, there were more women than men, but today there were more men than women, which advantaged the women. Mary suspected that Mrs. Graham was not the only person in Brussels with the intent of securing a spouse.

Despite some mixing of people of diverse origins, there still seemed to be a subtle segregation. In general, people congregated with those of the same origin, perhaps because if you did not speak the same language, it was difficult to have a conversation.

Mary looked for Lydia and her husband amongst the British officers and their families. Lydia was very tall, for a woman, and should be easy to see, but Mary did not see her anywhere. Then she realised that, as only a captain, Wickham might not have a high enough rank to be invited to the present occasion.

A distinguished-looking British officer approached them and bowed. He had brown skin, and more medals pinned to his uniform than Mary had thought possible. "Lady Trafford, you may not remember me, but I have not forgotten you. I am Major General Leon."

A major general—he must be very close in the command structure to the Duke of Wellington.

"Of course I remember you," said Lady Trafford with a smile. "We met…thirteen years ago, was it not? This is my nephew, Mr. Withrow, and a dear friend and relation, Miss Bennet."

"A pleasure," he said, and he gave Mary an additional

bow. He was truly quite charming. "If it is not inconvenient, the Duke of Wellington would like to meet with you now."

"We are at his disposal."

Major General Leon led them out of the Grand Hall and past a number of portraits. "Is it your first time in Brussels?"

"Yes," said Lady Trafford.

"I recommend the Baths on the Senne, at the entrance of the River Senne to the city. Pirlet's Baths also has an excellent selection of baths, and next to their garden you can partake of tea and chocolate."

"It sounds quite pleasant," said Lady Trafford.

"Are you a gambling man?" Major General Leon asked Mr. Withrow.

"I take plenty of gambles in life, but typically not with money."

"If you change your mind, Brussels is much more exciting than London. Not only are there races, but there are several very selective establishments—for gentlemen only—that you would enjoy."

"Thank you," said Mr. Withrow. "I do appreciate it."

Major General Leon knocked on a door. The door opened slightly. "Wait one moment," said Leon, stepping inside and closing the door behind him.

"If anyone asks why we met with Wellington, we will say it is because he knew my husband. Lord Trafford did a favour for Wellington once—put in a good word for him in India. No one will press us because of my unfortunate history of struggling to talk about the loss of my husband."

Lord Trafford had died several years before Mary had met the family. The loss still weighed heavily on Lady Trafford. Mary could understand this. It had been almost two years since the loss of her father, and while many times the loss was a constant ache, sometimes it flared up into overwhelming grief, making it feel as if she had lost him only yesterday.

Mr. Withrow took his aunt's arm, and she seemed to straighten at this comforting gesture.

Major General Leon opened the door and led them into the room.

Seated at the centre of a large table was the Duke of Wellington himself. He had a defined nose and eyes that were both perceptive and kind. He was surrounded by a number of other officers. One of the men appeared quite young, and rather thin, yet despite his age, his suit seemed of finer material and cut than anyone else's in the present company.

"I asked," said Wellington with a bit of bite to his tone, "for the number of troops stationed there."

"One thousand five hundred, sir," said a grey-haired aide.

Wellington shook his head in frustration. "It is not enough. And Sir Frederick does not know how to lead them. We will have the right people if I must write to London until my hand falls off." He looked up at them abruptly, then stretched out his hand to Lady Trafford, as if she were a man. She did not appear surprised and shook his hand firmly.

"The Duke of Wellington," he said.

"Lady Trafford."

"I remember your husband." He paused, considering them again. "I understand that the Office of Foreign Affairs has sent you to assist me."

"Yes, this is my nephew, Mr. Withrow, and this is Miss Bennet. Two of our agents arrived in Paris close to a month ago. You will have received word from them."

"I already have my own trusted spies spread throughout France, but I did receive one letter from Miss Tagore. I informed her, as I will inform you, that even should the opportunity present itself, under *no* conditions are any of our operatives to assassinate or cause any physical harm to Bonaparte or anyone else of import. That is not justice—that will not serve our purposes, and I will *not* accept any deviation from this order."

"Of course," said Lady Trafford. "Is there anything specifically that you would like us to focus on while we are here in Brussels?"

"I have no specific tasks for you—"

"If you are given a tool, you would do well to use it," interrupted a rather handsome man, about Wellington's age, who wore a finely tailored uniform covered with medals.

"Thank you, Lord Uxbridge," said the duke, an edge of anger to his voice. Then his voice calmed. "As I was about to say, while I have no specific tasks, it is of the utmost importance that general observation be applied to anything and everything of import, including the sentiments of French-speaking citizens of Brussels, societal gossip which has political or strategic importance, and complaints or unrest among the officers. I trust you will be able to decide what is useful, and I would like you to report any key details directly to me. And, of course, to the Prince of Orange."

The young man in fine clothing smiled and inclined his head towards them. So this was the heir to the throne of the United Netherlands. It had only been a few months before, at the Congress of Vienna, that Britain and the continental powers had decided to rewrite the maps. They agreed to make the older Willem King of the Netherlands, giving him not only Holland, but also Flanders, as well as the more French regions, including Brussels and Antwerp. He had been officially crowned king on the seventeenth of May, only two weeks ago. His son, also named Willem, was now the Prince of Orange and the heir to this newly formed nation.

"It was a pleasure to meet each of you." The Duke of Wellington nodded to each of them in turn. "Mr. Withrow, Lady Trafford, Miss Bennet." Then he began to speak to his fellow officers, as if his former conversation had not been interrupted.

Major General Leon mouthed the words "Thank you" to them, but he made no move to escort them from the room.

Instead, Lady Trafford turned, and Mary—and Mr. Withrow—followed her out of the room and back down the hall towards the party.

"That was not quite what I expected," said Mary. Not that she thought Wellington would greet them with open arms or lavish them with praises. But he *had* specifically requested they come so he could meet with them, and while the welcome had not been cold, it had not been warm either. Then she realised what her words might imply. "I apologise, I should not have spoken in such a manner. It was a great honour to meet with the Duke of Wellington."

"Do not apologise, my dear, but do consider his situation," said Lady Trafford. "An impossible task has been asked of Wellington—to gather back together his armies, when many of his best officers are months away, in the Americas, to combine dozens of national forces into a single Allied army, and to prepare to attack Napoleon Bonaparte, one of the most brilliant military minds this world has known. Anyone else would buckle under the pressure."

"All of Europe's hopes are upon him," said Mr. Withrow, nodding. "And even if he does not see a direct need for us, I am certain that we can still be of service."

They entered the Grand Hall, and Mr. Withrow looked over the gathered crowd. "I think I will begin." He gave a slight bow to them, his eyes pausing, very deliberately, first on Lady Trafford, then on Mary, and then he was gone.

"What do you propose *your* first task be?" asked Lady Trafford.

Mary considered.

"I will check in with the connections I already have and attempt to make new ones."

"Good," said Lady Trafford. "I will join you, for the time being."

Mary decided to begin with Mrs. Graham, who appeared to be just finishing a conversation with a British officer.

Mary and Lady Trafford walked in her direction, a little slower than Mary would have liked, but Lady Trafford was not a woman to be rushed.

Suddenly, a nearby officer tripped and fell into Lady Trafford. Lady Trafford managed to stay upright, but the officer landed on the floor.

The middle-aged woman accompanying the officer spoke quickly, her eyes not quite meeting Lady Trafford's. "I apologise for my brother."

The man stood. He was not a tall man, but he had broad shoulders and a thick neck and arms. He had three scars on his chin, each which could have been acquired from shaving, though if he had once lacked skills with the blade, he had since gained them, for his skin was perfectly smooth.

He gave a gallant bow to Lady Trafford, then took her hand and kissed it. "My extreme apologies, my lady. I hope that I have not caused you any injury."

"I am fine," said Lady Trafford, though she seemed a little ruffled. "Are you—are you a Kitsell?" she asked the woman.

"Yes, Lady Trafford," said the woman, her eyes finally meeting Lady Trafford's. Her voice was dry and devoid of warmth. "Miss Caroline Kitsell. We met, almost twenty years ago. This is my brother, Colonel Kitsell. And who is your lovely companion?"

"This is Miss Bennet."

Mary curtsied.

"How is your sister?" asked Lady Trafford.

"She died," said Colonel Kitsell curtly, before Miss Kitsell could respond. "Not long after our parents."

"I am sorry for your loss," said Lady Trafford, still addressing Miss Kitsell. "I know that you were very close to Susan."

"Yes, I was."

"Caroline has still not recovered," said Colonel Kitsell, patting her arm. He smiled at Lady Trafford. "If you need assistance of any sort while you are in Brussels, please let me know. That includes moving furniture or other hard labour—I can assign soldiers to assist you."

"Thank you for the kind offer," said Lady Trafford, and the Kitsells said their farewells and moved on.

"Why would he offer men to move furniture?" asked Mary. "That seems far outside the purview of a soldier's assignment."

"Rules are always bent for the well-connected or those with enough wealth."

"But that does not mean it *should* happen."

"True, very true."

Mary noticed Lady Trafford's face. "Something is troubling you."

"I did not know the Kitsells had a son. I must have forgotten. No matter."

But Lady Trafford still seemed a little troubled, even as they finished their original objective: walking to Mrs. Graham.

"Mrs. Graham," said Mary.

Mrs. Graham's face lit with a large, genuine smile. "Miss Bennet, what a pleasure to see you."

"This is Lady Trafford. Lady Trafford, this is my friend, Mrs. Graham."

"Are you a relation of General Graham?" asked Lady Trafford.

"Unfortunately not," said Mrs. Graham. "My connections are much more lowly than that, though members of my family have served our country."

"Mrs. Graham is staying with the Capels," said Mary.

"I see," said Lady Trafford. "It appears you underrepresent yourself."

Mrs. Graham gave a little laugh. "Is that not the task of all fashionable females? False modesty is, to use military parlance, both shield and sword."

It was clever, but a rather outdated metaphor. "Neither sword nor shield are very useful against a musket." As soon as she said it, Mary worried that Mrs. Graham would take it as criticism, rather than wit; sometimes Mary's wit was less than witty.

"You are right, Miss Bennet. False modesty is rather old-fashioned. Then truth shall be our musket, but we shall save it for use against our enemies, lest we accidentally injure our friends."

"Then we shall take everything you say with a grain of salt," said Lady Trafford lightly.

"As you should." Mrs. Graham gestured around the room. "I have already come to the conclusion that Brussels is as full of posturing and deceit as London. It is quite stimulating."

"How so?" asked Mary.

Mrs. Graham spared the briefest of glances to Lady Trafford. "There is plenty of scandal—gambling and not-so-solitary walks in the park...none of which would interest your ladyship." It seemed that Mrs. Graham did not feel as comfortable gossiping with Lady Trafford present. "There are a number of angry Germans," she said as if it was of no import. "The Prince of Orange and his father, the king, have dismissed almost all of the German officers from the Dutch army, yet many of their remaining officers are Belgian and were trained in Napoleon's army. In terms of news, it is rather dull, I am afraid."

To Mrs. Graham this might seem dull, but not to Mary. Bonaparte's own officers serving in the Dutch and Belgian portion of the Allied armies—they would understand Bonaparte's tactics, which could help in the fight against him, but where did their sympathies lie?

"Excuse me," said the Prince of Orange, suddenly at their side. "I am sorry to interrupt."

"Prince Willem," said Mary as she curtsied. Lady Trafford inclined her head, and Mrs. Graham's curtsy was so low that Mary was surprised she did not fall to the ground.

"Prince Willem," said Lady Trafford. "Have you met Mrs. Graham?"

"I have not yet had the pleasure," said the Prince of Orange, "but Lady Capel has told me so much about you, her dear friend." He took Mrs. Graham's hand and lifted her from the curtsy. "How do you find my country?" He gave her a smile that would melt any woman's heart, and it seemed to have this effect on Mrs. Graham.

"I just arrived, but so far it is absolutely delightful."

"I hope you will be attending the upcoming balls and

other events." He spoke English as if he were British, without even a trace of an accent, and he always used the precise word that a native speaker would use.

"Of course," said Mrs. Graham.

"I will call upon you and the Capels soon."

"That would be delightful."

He must know that she was a widow, and while clearly older than him, not that much older. Of course, a prince would never be seriously interested in someone without political connections. It was not long ago that Prince Willem had been engaged to Princess Charlotte of England, but she had broken off the engagement. While that political marriage was clearly not meant to be, it was guaranteed that another political marriage would be in the works. A small, new country like the United Netherlands needed strong allies, and what better way to create strong allies than by making them family?

The prince gestured to one of his countrymen, who was standing nearby.

"This is my friend, Colonel Johnson. Colonel Johnson, this is Mrs. Graham. I see that they have started up some music, and there will be some attempt at a dance, though it seems like they may need encouragement. Would the two of you lead the way? If that is acceptable to you, Mrs. Graham."

"Of course," she said.

Before leaving with her partner, Mrs. Graham leaned and whispered in Mary's ear, "I do have some stories…for you only. Later."

Mrs. Graham and her partner left to the improvised dance floor.

"Now I have you to myself," said the Prince of Orange, rather pleased. "Lady Trafford, Miss Bennet, will you walk with me?" He extended both arms, one for Lady Trafford, and one for Mary. If only Lydia were here. She would be quite jealous that Mary was holding the arm of a prince and would probably talk of nothing else for a week.

"I heard you were disappointed," said Lady Trafford, "that you were forced to give up command of the Allied armies to Wellington."

Mary was almost as shocked as if Mrs. Graham had told her something scandalous. Lady Trafford was practically interrogating a foreign royal.

"Disappointed?" said Prince Willem. "I know that I am no brilliant military commander. Maybe I will be in fifteen years—I do hope so. I served under Wellington on the peninsula, and I served well, but I simply do not have the experience."

"They say that the king was quite opposed to the shift in command."

"I was only in command because I was the officer here, in Brussels. I begged my father to give the Allied command to Wellington. If anyone can save our country, it is he. I am proud to serve under him again."

"You still maintain command of the Dutch and Belgian forces," said Lady Trafford.

"I may not have the strategy to win a war, but I do have the skill to lead my own men." His voice was a little stiff. "I am quite capable of defending my cities and my people's land." He softened. "You are direct for an Englishwoman, which I quite like, Lady Trafford. And so I suppose that I should be direct as well." He gave a quick look around, to make sure they were sufficiently isolated from the others. "Wellington asked that you report to me on your discoveries as well as to him, and I would appreciate it if you did so. I have my own network, in all of my border towns, as well as here, in Antwerp, and in other cities, and I also have a number of loyal spies in France. It is natural, of course, that Wellington means to rely primarily on intelligence gathered by those with whom he has a history, but I believe that my people and your people have much to offer as well."

He looked almost furtive, like he was afraid that he had betrayed his master. Yet Wellington *had* directed them to report to him as well. And of course, Mary would like to believe herself just as capable as Wellington's spies.

"A map drawn from only one viewpoint is much less likely to be rendered correctly than a map which draws from the viewpoints of many."

"Precisely, Miss Bennet," said the Prince of Orange.

Mary felt a warmth in her chest—not only had she spoken to a prince, but he had complimented her expression.

"We will do as the duke requested, and keep you apprised," said Lady Trafford, though Mary thought she seemed a little reserved.

"Wonderful," said Prince Willem. "I would like to introduce you to one of my favourite people. She has spent the past two decades recruiting some of the best men in my army, and she has also provided me with the best of my network of spies."

Lady Trafford's eyes narrowed. "Do not keep us in suspense. Of whom do you speak?"

"Why, the most important revolutionary of our age. My grandmother, of course. You probably do not speak German, her native tongue, but I assume you speak French?"

"Yes, we do," said Lady Trafford.

They approached the prince's grandmother. She was a stately woman in fine apparel, probably around sixty-five years of age.

Lady Trafford bowed, and Mary followed suit.

"Presenting Princess Wilhelmina of Prussia," said the Prince of Orange, then switching to French. "*Ma chère grand-mère, these two women are...friends of Wellington. They may need your assistance in order to be useful to us.*"

The princess considered them carefully. She paid particularly close attention to Lady Trafford, leaning in close to her, and then said, in French, "*You and I are very similar, I think. You have the same fire.*" She took her hand and lifted Mary's chin. The gesture was both intimate and strange, and Mary found that suddenly she feared this great woman. "*And you are full of promise.*"

She said something in German to her grandson that Mary did not understand in the slightest. From the tone it sounded like a reprimand—or maybe that was just the sharpness of the German language in comparison to French—but regardless of the actual intended tone, it made the prince blush.

"*I will give you one of my best,*" said the stately princess, and then gave directions on how to contact a woman of her acquaintance. She smiled at them benevolently, and then without another word, turned and walked away.

"Now that was helpful," said the Prince of Orange, with no trace of sarcasm. "I do not know where we would be without her, so if I were you, I would follow her directions. Come, now let us—"

But they never did find out where the Prince of Orange planned to lead them next, for a commotion broke out not thirty feet from where they stood.

The Prince or Orange immediately moved to the sound, as did Mary and Lady Trafford, and, seemingly, almost everyone else at the gathering.

A man—a British officer, by the look of his uniform—was yelling at an officer in a rather Napoleonic uniform, so probably one of the Belgian officers. "Apologise, you bastard."

The Belgian officer raised his fist, but then a German officer rushed forward and pulled him away. Two other officers joined the fray, and suddenly there was yelling in English, French, German, and Dutch. It was not clear who would throw the first blow, but it was clear that this would soon occur.

The whole room felt like a bubbling pot, about to boil. It was as if everyone suddenly realised that they stood next to individuals whose countries had fought with their own at some point in the not-so-distant past.

The Prince of Orange rushed into the central conflict. "Stop, please! *Ophouden! Calmez-vous! Hören Sie jetzt auf!*" Apparently, he spoke four different languages.

Major General Leon also rushed into the central conflict. "By order of the Duke of Wellington, I command all of you to desist."

The prince and Major General Leon spoke with each of the men, calming and separating them. A Dutchman raised his voice, in French, at Leon, and Leon gave him a stiff reprimand in English.

Finally, the conflict seemed to be at an end.

Lady Trafford went to gather information from those who had been closer to the scene. Not knowing what else to do, Mary walked, and as she did so she watched everyone, watched as the tensions eased but did not fully dissolve.

She passed near to Major General Leon and the Prince of Orange and caught just a part of their conversation. In this context, neither of them seemed polite or charming.

"I can handle my own people," said the Prince of Orange.

"Then handle them," said Major General Leon, not a little roughly.

Mary found Lady Trafford a few minutes later.

"What caused the fight?" asked Mary.

"One man bumped another man's cup of tea, causing it to spill."

They had almost come to blows over such a small matter.

How was the Allied army expected to fight together, if even a cup of spilled tea was enough to turn allies into enemies?

Chapter Four

*"Forget not, man, amidst thy joy,
The Pow'r that gives and can destroy."*

—"Ode on the present beautiful appearance of Spring," *The Ipswich Journal*, Suffolk, England, June 3, 1815

Mr. Withrow interrupted Mary's dream.

"Miss Bennet, Miss Bennet," he said urgently, as if she were the only person that mattered to him. She smiled.

"Miss Bennet, wake up! Miss Bennet."

Mary opened her eyes. Mr. Withrow was standing in Mary's room, holding a candle. Judging by the light, it was still the middle of the night.

She stumbled out of bed, almost falling to the ground, and Mr. Withrow caught her arm with the hand not holding the candle.

"Thank you," said Mary, looking up at him. For a moment, their eyes remained locked. The candle illuminated his face in a very pleasing way; it was the sort of scene Mary would like to draw. Withrow released her arm, and she straightened and looked away, as if the moment had not occurred.

"What has happened?" asked Mary.

"Someone has been murdered," said Mr. Withrow. "I do not know any details, but the Duke of Wellington has requested us. Forgive me for intruding upon you—Mrs.

Boughton would have come to wake you, but she is assisting my aunt."

Mary rubbed her hands together. The night was a little cool now that she was out of her bed.

"You should dress," he said.

She realised that she should probably feel uncomfortable, alone, with a man in her room, while she wore only a light summer nightgown. Her hair was down, falling past her shoulders. Yet she did not feel uncomfortable at all.

"You should also dress." He wore only a loose shirt and trousers, which certainly did not appear like his normal attire.

He stepped towards the door but then he paused. "I should add that time is of the essence."

"I am quite skilled at dressing quickly, without the assistance of a maid." Mrs. Boughton and Mr. Parker were the only servants who had come with them from England. They had hired other local servants, each of whom returned home every night to their families: it was easier to keep secrets if there were fewer people to constantly keep secrets from.

He took another step towards the door, but then he stopped again. "Can I light your candle?"

"Yes, thank you."

He lit the candle on the table, looked as if he was about to say something more, and then left the room, closing the door behind him. She banished thoughts about the way it had felt when he caught her arm as she stumbled—she would consider it later, when she had more time.

Mary was true to her word. She dressed and arranged her hair so quickly that she was ready, according to her pocket watch, three entire minutes before Mr. Withrow and seven minutes before Lady Trafford.

They descended the stairs of the townhouse to the waiting

carriage. Mr. Parker assisted Lady Trafford into the carriage. She took a little longer than usual to settle herself, and after thanking Mr. Parker said, "There are parts of growing older that I do not enjoy."

Mr. Withrow gestured for Mary to enter the carriage next. Lady Trafford had spread her skirts across the entire bench on one side of the carriage, which left the other bench for Mary and Mr. Withrow to share. Her habit, which she had developed when she first met Mr. Withrow, was to sit on the very edge to leave as much space between them as possible. Yet tonight Mary felt strangely—perhaps regrettably— compulsive. She did not sit in the very centre of the bench, for that would be both illogical and rude, but she did sit near the centre. If Mr. Withrow wanted space between them, he could provide it.

As Mr. Withrow sat down next to Mary, his knee bumped into Mary's. She pretended she did not notice. He left a few inches between them, but he could have sat farther away. Of course, he had probably given absolutely no consideration to where he had sat or that anyone might attempt to interpret his positioning.

Where she had sat, and Mr. Withrow's proximity, meant nothing. Yet it was strange to be so physically aware of him, the way he held himself, the angle of his face as he looked out the darkened window, and the manner in which he had tied his cravat. Even though it was three in the morning and hardly anyone would see him, he had taken the care to tie his cravat in a very presentable style. Mary almost regretted not doing more with her hair. However, their task was related to murder. She did not need a fine coiffure for the deceased—or the living.

She wondered if they were simply meeting with the Duke

of Wellington about a murder, or if they would be expected to view the murder victim.

Mary banished a sudden fear. She would be cold and rational about this. She would *not* experience the same difficulties as the last time she had examined a body—and fled from said inanimate body. She had not eaten anything in hours, so hopefully she would not feel sick to her stomach.

"It must be a person of at least some significance who has been killed," mused Lady Trafford. "Probably someone British."

"It is a pity that he did not provide more details in the message," said Mr. Withrow.

"We will find out soon enough," said Lady Trafford.

And indeed, they soon arrived at St. Catherine's, a church about half a mile from the Grand Place and the Hôtel de Ville. Portions of the church looked to be very old—perhaps from the 14th or 15th century. Abutting the church was the Bassin de St. Catherine—a large basin which felt like a harbour in the heart of the city, with mid-sized merchant vessels tied to its docks. This basin and the others in Brussels were located at the end of the Canal de Willebroek, which was the canal that connected Brussels to Willebroek, and from Willebroek through other canals and rivers all the way to the sea.

Next to St. Catherine's was a small adjoining cemetery with a sign, in French, stating that it was closed after dark. A British officer stood next to the gate, and after ascertaining their identities, let them in. They walked through the packed cemetery, which did not have space for even one additional grave. The lamp caught on the headstones and Mary read the names and the dates, none of which seemed recent. They must have established newer cemeteries in Brussels, or, perhaps, outside of the city. They reached a small stone building.

"It is my understanding that this is where they identify the bodies of any who drown in the canal," said Lady Trafford.

"They have that many people drown?" asked Mary.

Lady Trafford did not respond. Instead, she knocked.

The Prince of Orange opened the door, and suddenly Mary felt the weight of death. "They are here," said the prince to the others in the room. He had a grim look on his face, and while he still looked so very young, there was a weight around his eyes.

"Finally," said Wellington, gesturing them into the room. Besides the prince and Wellington, there were four other men in the room, none of whom Mary recognized. There was also a body, lying on a large grey slab of stone. Wellington gestured them towards it with no words, no introduction, except the stark, final introduction of death.

Mary felt like she was choking on her own saliva, but she forced her feet forward and kept her eyes on the body.

It was a man, that much was clear, and half of his face had been destroyed—taken apart, mushed together, shattered. There was a gaping hole, and she could see what must be parts of his brain. There was bile in her throat, and she forced herself to swallow. This was not her preferred approach for learning about human anatomy.

"Two bullet wounds," said Mr. Withrow.

This injury had been caused by two bullets? In all the training with a pistol, she had never truly considered what it would be like to shoot someone, what the consequences would be on a human body. She had practised to the point where she could load and fire a pistol two times in a minute.

She could destroy a man's body in this way in a minute. Would there ever be a circumstance where she felt it necessary to shoot someone? Could she really end someone's life, and in such a way?

This would require hours of reflection, hours she did not have at the moment, so she looked instead for the second bullet wound Mr. Withrow had mentioned. Her eyes took in, for the first time, the man's entire body—her eyes had been so fixated by the injury on the face that she had failed to notice any other details, had failed to take in anything about the whole. The second bullet wound was in his side, maybe six or seven inches below his heart. This wound was not as grotesque to look at. The corpse wore a fine tailored suit, marking him as a gentleman. His cravat was still tied. And his clothes were wet.

Then Mary realised that she knew him. She recognized his nose, his chin, his brown skin, the thin scar along his neck.

"It is Major General Leon, is it not?" asked Lady Trafford.

"Yes," said the Duke of Wellington.

Major General Leon. Mary looked at the half of his face that had not been marred by the bullet wound. And indeed it was Leon, the man who had introduced them to the Duke of Wellington just a few hours before, at the Hôtel de Ville. Major General Leon, one of Wellington's most trusted officers.

"What happened, as far as you know?" asked Lady Trafford.

"To me, it seems clear, and our field doctor confirms," Wellington glanced briefly at one of the other men, "that Leon was first shot in the side, from a short distance, maybe ten or fifteen feet. When that did not kill him, he was shot in the head, this time from a closer distance. His body was then thrown in the Bassin de Marchands."

"Time of death?" asked Mr. Withrow.

"We cannot be certain," said the doctor. "But it seems likely that it was after nightfall."

"We will need to confirm who saw him last, to establish a better sense of the time of death." Wellington tugged his hair, turning to the Prince of Orange. "I wish I could devote myself to this. I owe it to Leon. But I must do my duty to the Allies—I must focus on preparing for the assault."

"Then do as you proposed earlier," said Prince Willem. "We already agreed that it would not make sense for one of the constables of Bruxelles to lead the investigation, as it was a British officer, and many of your other officers must be interviewed."

Wellington nodded and then gestured towards them. "Examine the body more if you would like." He sat down at a worktable and gestured at someone to hand him paper, a quill, and ink.

Lady Trafford stepped closer to the body for a moment, staring intently at the man's face, and then she stepped away to talk to the Prince of Orange.

"Has anyone examined his pockets?" asked Mary, stepping closer. The corpse did not smell like rotting meat like last time—it had not yet had time to decompose enough for that. But still, it was not pleasant—it was the aroma of fetid water.

"Not yet," said the British military doctor.

"Did you bring gloves for me, Mr. Withrow?"

He gave her a quizzical look. "I did bring an extra pair."

She held out her hand, and, after a moment, he handed her a pair of work gloves.

The last time she had attempted to examine a body, she

had fled from the violence and the smell and her churning stomach. Mr. Withrow had remained. But she *could* do this work, even the parts that were not balls and purloining letters and prying secrets over tea. Her stomach felt a little uneasy, but she ignored it, pulling on the gloves and immediately opening the man's pockets.

Do not look at the face, do not look at the face, she told herself.

Withrow put on his own gloves. "What are you trying to prove?" he whispered. "Who are you trying to impress?" He glanced, for a fraction of a moment, at the Prince of Orange.

Did he really think she was trying to impress a prince by digging in a dead man's pockets? Is that what he thought motivated her? "I am not trying to impress *anyone*. I simply want to be useful in fulfilling my duties."

Mary managed to extract a pocketbook from one of the pockets. Mr. Withrow found a knife and a pocket watch with an inset diamond. There was nothing else inside any of the other pockets. She went through the pocketbook, but it contained only normal items—some money and some papers, all saturated with water.

She looked again at the body. The toes of the shoes were scuffed, and the fabric along the front of the clothes was worn in an unusual way, like it had been rubbed against a hard surface. There were also several rips, where the clothes must have snagged on rocks or other materials.

She pointed out the parts to Mr. Withrow. "I think the body was dragged, after it was shot."

He nodded. "That should make the location of the murder a little easier to find. There should be blood stains or other residue next to the basin." He turned to the doctor. "Have you extracted one of the bullets? That should give some indication as to the type of gun."

"I have not," said the doctor. He spoke to the Prince of Orange and the duke, and they instructed him to do so.

The doctor prepared his tools and approached the body, and Mary realised that if she watched, she would probably be physically ill.

"I do not think it is necessary for me to witness this part," said Mary, and she stepped away from the body and turned to the wall. She felt no guilt as she had no expertise or knowledge that would assist with a bullet extraction.

After a minute, Mr. Withrow joined her. "I have decided that I am of no use, and I do not particularly want to see this either." His lips turned upward, almost into a smile.

"Is it dreadful?" asked Mary.

"Quite so."

Mr. Withrow was not the sort to miss out on part of an investigation in an attempt to console her feelings—if he even thought they needed consoling. Whatever the doctor was doing, it must be dreadful indeed, which made Mary feel, even more than before, that she had made the right decision.

They did not talk more, but Mary felt very aware of Mr. Withrow's presence. She thought of the way he had taken her hand in the ballroom at Castle Durrington, the way he had pulled her close and wrapped his arms around her. She wondered what it would be like if he were to do so again—would it have the same thrill, the same warmth, as the first time?

But it would not happen again, she was certain. He had no interest in her, and even if he had, he was due to inherit Castle Durrington and Lady Trafford's entire estate. While she was a gentleman's daughter, he would want to marry someone with a fortune of her own.

Besides, she did not know that she was interested in him in *that* way either. Clearly she experienced a strong level of physical attraction to him—unreasonably strong, if she were honest with herself—but that did not mean she wanted to pursue him. For that matter, she would not know how to pursue a man if she desired to do so.

"I've got it," said the doctor. Mary and Withrow turned. The doctor held out a small circular ball, covered in blood and other residue.

The Duke of Wellington stood, interested, and then gestured to one of his other officers.

The man picked up the ball and rolled it between his fingers. "It is the standard size, what would be used in most duelling pistols, but smaller than is used in a military musket."

"There are a few pistols that can hold more than one bullet," said one of the other officers, "but they are rare. Either the attacker reloaded the gun with a new bullet before taking the second shot, or the attacker had a pair of pistols and used one and then the other."

"Good observations, all," said the Duke of Wellington. "And now, I have a task for Lady Trafford, Mr. Withrow, and Miss Bennet. I need you to find the murderer."

"I assumed that was why you had brought us here," said Lady Trafford.

"Who are the military or civil investigators we will be working with?" asked Mr. Withrow.

"There are none. The three of you will be the only investigators on this case," said the Duke of Wellington. "I will alert my officers with troops along the borders, to be watchful in case it was an assassin sent from France."

"No public investigators on the case?" asked Mr.

Withrow.

"I can provide a local investigator to assist, and his team can perform any necessary low-level work," said the Prince of Orange.

Mr. Withrow did not acknowledge Prince Willem's response, instead waiting for the duke.

"I am short-staffed," said Wellington. "Half the men I need were sent to fight the Americans, and most have yet to return. All of those who would be capable of carrying out this investigation are already overtaxed as we prepare to invade France, and all of them risk being blinded by their history with Leon and his associates. Yet even though I cannot assign it to them, this is an essential work: Major General Leon was one of the most important men in my command structure, and his skills were a key component of my strategy. Even though we are about to embark on another war, justice must be done. I need it investigated, and I need it investigated well." He looked at each of them in turn, and Mary felt the strength of his gaze. "I know that if I give this investigation to the three of you, it will be in good hands. I need you to do this, not just for me, but for our nation, for all of the Allies, for peace and freedom everywhere."

Mary could see why men would follow him into battle.

"I do understand your concern, Mr. Withrow, for keeping your identity a secret, so you may maintain your role as a spy. I assume, with your skill set, that you would be able to transform yourself, and create an alternate identity who I could appoint officially to this position."

"Yes, I am capable of doing that," said Mr. Withrow, but Mary thought she heard a touch of resignation in his voice.

"Good," said Wellington. "I have already written out and signed a paper giving you authority to do so. I simply need you to choose a fake name. Visit the spot where the body was found, interview relevant parties, find a motive…You know how investigations work. Lady Trafford and Miss Bennet, both of you will continue your undercover work to gather information that will coordinate with Mr. Withrow's more public efforts."

Mary felt like she and Lady Trafford had been relegated to a secondary role. She wanted to be gathering information, not waiting for Mr. Withrow to gather it so she could then commence with something useful. It was not prideful to admit that she was rather good at unofficially interviewing suspects and witnesses. Imagine what she could accomplish in an official capacity.

"Excuse me, Your Grace," said Mary, feeling a little intimidated but committed to plunge forward with her request, "but I would like to participate in the interviews and other more public investigations."

"A woman cannot be an official investigator," said the duke.

Lady Trafford laughed. "And a woman cannot be an effective spy. No one would ever tell their secrets to a woman."

"I do not mean to offend, Lady Trafford. There are plenty of women who would make brilliant investigators, but it has not been done before. It would draw too much attention."

"Miss Bennet can dress as a man," said Mr. Withrow. "No one will know."

That possibility had not occurred to Mary, and it seemed that it had not occurred to the Duke of Wellington either.

"I can think of at least three newspaper articles in the last few years about women dressing as men in order to work as soldiers and sailors," said Mr. Withrow. "They went undetected for years. How many women do you think there are in the Allied armies, acting the part of men? Women who are patriots and skilled fighters have surely found a place for themselves in your ranks."

"I do not actively seek to root them out," admitted Wellington. "It is only if their identity is revealed that I am forced to do something about it. What do you think, Miss Bennet?"

She had not had a chance to consider the full implications, and she could not fathom why Mr. Withrow had taken the effort to convince the duke, but she knew she was being offered a chance to take a more direct role in investigations. "I will ensure that I am not discovered."

"And you, Lady Trafford?" asked the duke.

"Mr. Withrow and Miss Bennet will both perform their roles admirably. As for myself, I would prefer to remain in the shadows."

"Very well," said the Duke of Wellington. "Now what shall be your fake names?"

"I shall be Mr. Pike," said Mr. Withrow.

"Good, and you?" asked the duke.

This was not the sort of activity Mary had prepared for; each time in the past when she had constructed a fake identity, she had considered the name at length. Yet now, with the Duke of Wellington staring at her, she did not have that luxury.

"I will be Mr. Fothergill," she said, stating the first surname that came to mind.

"Pike and Fothergill," said the Prince of Orange. "That has a nice sound to it."

Wellington arranged additional details and gave them an official writ of authority for the case. Then, accompanied by the Prince of Orange, he turned to leave. He stopped at the door and looked back at Leon's body.

"How in damnation am I supposed to build an army if I cannot keep the people that I have?" And with that, the man who held the hopes of the Allies stepped into the night.

Chapter Five

"A general and simultaneous movement appears to have lately taken place in all the French armies. They are condensing their masses; and most of the Generals are already at their posts. The army of the North has placed itself in connection with that of the Moselle. They both appear to form the chief strength of the military force of the country, and will probably be commanded by Bonaparte in person."

—*The Ipswich Journal*, Suffolk, England, June 3, 1815

MEN'S TROUSERS WERE officially scandalous, or at least that is what Mary was forced to conclude now that she wore them. Just a thin layer of fabric between yourself and the outside world, a layer of fabric that held rather closely to the human body.

The shirt was better, partly because she could wear a men's coat over it. However, she missed wearing a corset, with the structure it gave to assist posture and the support it provided for her female parts. Lady Trafford had helped her wrap a length of white fabric tightly over her chest to flatten it, and the result was somewhat painful. While she was not amply endowed, she was not minimally endowed either, which made dressing as a man more difficult.

"Henry!" called Lady Trafford, summoning Mr. Withrow into her bedroom.

He stepped into the room, stopping short when he saw Mary. "This will never work. Your face is much too pretty."

"She is fine," said Lady Trafford, adjusting the men's wig which Mary wore on her head.

Mary felt an unusual flutter in her stomach. Had Mr. Withrow called her pretty?

Mary examined his words. "Much too pretty." But the context meant that he had really said "much too pretty for a man," which was not necessarily a compliment.

"She will draw attention," said Mr. Withrow. "Maybe a moustache would help."

"A moustache?" said Mary. "I do not know that that is necessary." The thought of wearing someone else's hair underneath her nose did not hold any appeal.

"It could work," said Lady Trafford, agreeing, of course, with her nephew. "Let me find something. Meanwhile, help Miss Bennet with her cravat. It has been years since I have tied one."

Mr. Withrow approached. In his disguise, he also looked rather different. For one, he wore a blond wig. Mary preferred his natural brown hair, not that she had preferences for how he dressed or looked. His clothes were a little large for his frame, rather than being custom fit. He had also managed to change the appearance of his facial structure and had done something to make his nose look bigger.

"How did you do it?"

"Do what, Miss Bennet?" He managed to make the statement sound oddly formal.

"Your face."

"Oh, that. I put a pliable mould on my nose, and I placed

wads of fabric inside my cheeks."

"Is it uncomfortable?"

"A little. What sort of cravat would you like?"

"I do not have a strong preference, though it is probably best if it does not look exactly like yours."

He stepped closer and picked up the ends of the white fabric that was draped around her neck. And then he stood there, unmoving. A part of Mary—a very dangerous part—wanted to lean forward and kiss him. But she was Mary Bennet and had no intention of obliging the newly discovered more dangerous inclinations of her personality.

"Come on, then, are you going to tie it or not?" she said rather brusquely.

"Yes," said Mr. Withrow. "Of course."

He adjusted the fabric around the back of her neck. As his fingers brushed her skin, it felt as if she were on fire. Not in the sense of an actual fire which burned with an intense heat and caused pain and affliction—actually, that was the exact sense that she meant. Her skin felt heat, and perhaps even desire, which caused her pain, for she did not want to feel this way for Mr. Withrow—Mr. Withrow who had never thought she would make a good spy, Mr. Withrow who had resented her from their very first meeting.

Mr. Withrow began to fold and arrange the fabric in complicated patterns. "I have a book on different methods of tying cravats which I would lend you, were it not in England." His hand brushed against the fabric on top of her collarbone. Apparently even the collarbone could feel like it was on fire. "It is more difficult to tie a cravat on someone else. Everything is reversed."

His hands brushed her neck again and, when the expected fiery sensation resulted, she rolled her eyes. The human body was ridiculous. What sort of biological mechanism forced one to have this sort of physical reaction to a simple touch? It was preposterous, distracting, and wildly unnecessary.

He stepped back and nodded. "I will teach you how to tie a cravat when we have more time."

"That would be much appreciated." She did not need to experience these sensations every single time she had to dress the part of a man.

"Have you practised how you plan to speak?" said Mr. Withrow, with a touch of a Scottish accent.

"No," said Mary. "Is that how you are going to speak?"

"Yes," he said, and, continuing with his new accent, "I would not recommend an accent for you—layering too many things is difficult. You could try lowering your voice."

"What about this?" said Mary.

"Maybe a little lower."

"Is this better?" she said, lowering her voice lower still, to the point that it sounded rather gravelly.

"Say a few more words," said Lady Trafford, stepping into the room.

"My name is Mr. Fothergill," said Mary, "and I have been tasked with investigating the murder of Major General Leon."

"I think it works," said Lady Trafford.

"I agree," said Mr. Withrow, "though I still cannot believe that you chose the name Mr. Fothergill."

"The Duke of Wellington gave us—"

"If you are in the costume, speak in the character," said Lady Trafford.

Mary began again, pitching her voice low and gravelly. "The Duke of Wellington gave us only a few seconds to decide."

"But still—Fothergill?"

"Are you mocking me?"

"No."

"Are you teasing me?" asked Mary, her voice croaking a little.

"Yes." He sighed.

"Oh. Ha." Mr. Withrow had never teased her before, at least not that she had noticed. She supposed she should attempt to reciprocate. "Well, yours is a very normal sounding name. Almost too normal."

"Pike is not that common."

"In a way, our names are opposites. Does not Pike mean 'sharp hill'?"

He nodded.

"I believe the 'gill' in my name means 'steep ravine.'"

"I am sure you are correct," said Mr. Withrow. "Did you do that intentionally, when you chose your name?"

"No."

Mary pulled on a pair of men's gloves. The cut was different than for women's gloves, but they fit well.

"Time for your moustache," said Lady Trafford, and then she yawned. "Once I am finished, I am going back to bed. There must be time for rumours of the death to spread before I can collect the gossip."

After viewing the body and returning to their rented house, they had only slept for two hours before again waking to prepare their disguises. Withrow had arranged to be shown where the body had been found at seven in the morning. The time itself would have been in the normal range of when Mary awoke, if Mary had not had to wake up earlier still for a disguise, and if she had not been awake for hours in the middle of the night. Yet she would not complain about the hour he had proposed when he had advocated for her to be part of the investigation. The fact that he had done so still surprised her.

Lady Trafford directed Mary to sit in a chair and applied a sort of glue to Mary's face and adhered a fake moustache. It itched a little, and it was a strange sensation to have little pieces of hair above her lip, but Mary knew better than to scratch it.

Mary had worn disguises before—she had dressed as a peasant woman, and as Miss Levena Kendall, a woman newly out in society—but it felt different to disguise herself as a man, perhaps because so many societal expectations and rules were tied to being a woman.

They left via a servants' door into a back alleyway, and then walked the brief distance to the Hôtel de Ville where they were met by a man named Monsieur Jacobs, a constable in his fifties who had been tasked by the Prince of Orange to assist them.

"Monsieur Pike, Monsieur Fothergill, je suis désolé, mais je ne parle pas anglais." Monsieur Jacobs seemed quite apologetic that he did not speak any English.

"Nous pouvons parler en français," said Mr. Withrow, and he continued to speak in French. *"Can you show us where the body was found?"*

"Mais oui," said Monsieur Jacobs. He gestured them into his carriage, and the carriage made its way in the same general direction as their carriage last night, when they visited St. Catherine's. *"Dreadful affair, no?"*

"It is. Has the news of Leon's death already circulated?" asked Mr. Withrow.

"I was not the one to announce it," said Jacobs.

"I am sure the royal family would not trust you if you were the sort to spread rumours," said Mr. Withrow.

This touch of flattery loosened his tongue. *"The rumours have just started—it is still early yet—but already some are speaking about a British officer who got himself killed. Some say he was in a fight. Some are worried that Wellington will be angry and leave our city defenceless."*

Mary found herself afraid to speak, afraid that if she did, Monsieur Jacobs would instantly see through her disguise. Besides, Withrow was doing quite well on his own.

"Any anti-British sentiment?" asked Mr. Withrow.

The man shrugged. *"There always is a bit."*

"Do people think he deserved his death?" Even in French, his questions were asked with deep intent.

"Not him specifically. He was not well-known by those in Brussels."

"But more generally?" He leaned slightly towards Jacobs.

"There are those who wish that our city was not so…crowded, that you could walk a block without hearing any English."

"I imagine that some feel like we are occupiers rather than protectors."

"That has been said. Of course, I do not feel that myself."

"I have confidence in you, Monsieur Jacobs."

And then Withrow turned the conversation to Jacobs's preferred recreational activities. Mary was impressed, not just at Mr. Withrow's fluency—he sounded like a native speaker—but also at what he had already managed to achieve. She had never worked closely with him as a spy, at least not for any significant period of time, so she had not realised how very good he was at this occupation. He did not waste a moment. He had managed to have a deep, meaningful conversation within five minutes of meeting someone. This was something she could admire and respect on an intellectual level. She tried to banish that thought from her mind. It was bad enough to find him physically attractive; she did not need to find him as intellectually attractive as well, for in that lay a greater danger, a greater temptation. Yet, if she was honest, even from their first meeting she had admired his skills and found value in his perspective and insights.

Workers were sweeping the pavement in front of the houses. Some of the fancier town homes, their plaster painted a fresh tea green, were on the smaller streets, or tucked into lanes, while on the principal roads stood more weathered shops and cabarets and public houses. On one of the streets, a large dog pulled a small cart on which sat a woman with metal jugs of milk, ready to deliver to the inhabitants of the city.

The carriage stopped next to the canal—no, it was a wider section of the canal, so one of the basins. Monsieur Jacobs exited the carriage first, followed by Mr. Withrow. She was almost surprised when no one attempted to hold the door for her or help her out. Of course, she no longer had a dress to interfere with entering or exiting carriages, and she descended by herself with a certain relish.

She could see St. Catherine's in the distance, and this basin appeared to be connected via a waterway under a bridge to its basin, the Bassin de St. Catherine. She consulted her map. This meant she stood next to the Bassin de Marchands. While de Marchands connected to St. Catherine on one side, on the other side, it was connected to the Bassin de Barques. The de Barques in turn connected to the Grand Basin, which connected to the main portion of the Canal de Willebroek, which led all the way to the city of Willebroek.

Despite the early hour, the area already bustled with activity, people and dogs running this way and that. On the other side of the basin, workers used a metal crane with a hook to load crates onto a merchant vessel, and on this side, a man cleaned a boat with comfortable, cushioned seats—perhaps it was used for pleasure rides up and down the canals.

Monsieur Jacobs went to fetch the woman who had found the body, and Mary and Mr. Withrow looked out at the water. A few sections around the basin had a chain or a rail, but here nothing separated them from the drop to the water below. According to her book on Brussels, construction on the Willebroek Canal had begun in 1550 and had lasted about a decade: a decade of work to turn Brussels into an economic centre for the region. There had been talk of building another canal, to connect Brussels to Charleroi in the south, but no one had had the means or political willpower to build it, and with Bonaparte once again in control of France, it might never be built.

She wanted to say something to Mr. Withrow, to start a conversation with him, but she did not know how, and by the time she had formulated a topic, Monsieur Jacobs had returned with the woman. She did not wear a bonnet or a hat, despite the fact that they were outside on a city street, and the fact that the clouds foretold rain.

"*This is Madame Claes. She lives in a house a few doors down the street.*"

Mr. Withrow bowed to her, and Mary almost curtsied but caught herself and turned it into a bow.

"*Je m'appelle Monsieur Pike,*" said Mr. Withrow, but he did not introduce Mary, which forced her to speak.

"*Je m'appelle Monsieur Fothergill,*" said Mary. She breathed in deeply. It was better to not be afraid of her disguise. She would attempt to sound like a man, and hopefully she would not fail, but even if she did fail, at least she would not spend the entire day shirking her responsibilities. "*Tell us about when you found the body, and where.*"

The woman looked a little uncomfortable, but Monsieur Jacobs nodded at her encouragingly.

"*I could not sleep, and I came out to the canal. I was looking* at the water as I always do, and then I saw something stuck on this boat right here. I realised it was a body."

The boat in question was medium sized with sails, tied to the edge of the basin. Crates of goods were strapped on to the deck.

"*Was it clear that it was a body at first?*" asked Mr. Withrow.

"*No, it took a little time.*"

"*How could you tell?*"

"*It was the light, the way it struck it, and then I realised what the shape meant.*"

"We need you to show us precisely where on the boat the body was stuck," said Mr. Withrow.

The woman did so. The body had been face down in the water and had been caught on a metal sort of bumper at the front of the boat.

"*What did you do?*" asked Mary, her voice scratching like a growing boy's.

"*I screamed. And then they came out of the inn, and then the constable was summoned, and not long after, Monsieur Jacobs arrived.*"

"*Do you often have trouble sleeping?*" asked Mr. Withrow.

"*Yes.*"

"*Is it normal for you to wander the streets when you cannot sleep?*" he asked.

"*This is a good neighbourhood,*" she said, bristling a little. This proved that Mr. Withrow did not *always* ask questions in a way that drew out an ideal response.

"*It is a very picturesque view,*" added Mary, quite pleased that she had remembered the word picturesque—*pittoresque*. In some ways it was cheating, because it came from the same root as the English equivalent, but to use it so naturally made her feel a little more confident.

"*Oui,*" said the woman, appeased. *"I always like looking at the canal, especially in the summer."*

Mary felt a strange inclination to suspect everyone. Anyone could be lying: Monsieur Jacobs could be the killer, Madame Claes could be the killer, the innkeeper could be the killer. When you knew very little, anyone and anything connected to the events in any way could feel suspicious. Yet if Madame Claes were the murderer, why would she report the body rather than leave it for someone else to find?

"Do you have any more questions for her?" asked Withrow quietly, in English.

"No."

"Thank you for your time, madame," said Mr. Withrow. *"We will let you know if we need further assistance."*

Madame Claes left, and Mary considered, again, the front of the ship.

"We need to find the exact spot where the murder occurred," she said.

"Yes," said Mr. Withrow. "It is quite obvious that doing so should be the next step."

She gritted her teeth. The step might be obvious, but that did not make it any less essential.

"It is my understanding," said Mr. Withrow, "based on my readings about engineering, that these basins should have almost no water movement. They are basically pools—there is no flow, which would be caused by the water entering from one side and exiting from the other."

He turned to Monsieur Jacobs to confirm the matter in French. Jacobs agreed with him, explaining that the movement of a boat sometimes caused small waves, but not enough to significantly move a body.

Meanwhile, Mary found a long stick on the cobblestones. She lowered it into the water, holding the top of the stick only lightly, and indeed, there was no tug on the stick, no real movement of the water.

"Do you believe me now?" asked Mr. Withrow.

"I believed you before," said Mary. "I simply like to understand things in my own way."

"That is fair," said Mr. Withrow, and then he switched back to French for the benefit of Monsieur Jacobs. *"When a dead body is placed in the water, the lungs fill with water and it takes only a few minutes for it to sink. Several days later, it floats to the surface, but as Leon was alive yesterday we know this did not occur. This fact, combined with the lack of water movement within the basin, means that Leon must have been killed close to this spot, dragged to the canal, and thrown in the water where he caught on the boat."*

It was a rather neat and tidy conclusion, but it was logical, and they began to scour the basin and the street and the surrounding roads. However, they found no blood residue or any signs of struggle. They spoke to those at the inn, at a warehouse, and at nearby houses, but no one had heard a gunshot or anything else.

"Leon must have been killed elsewhere and wrapped in something so that his body did not leave remnants as it was brought here," said Monsieur Jacobs.

"The body showed clear marks of being dragged across a hard surface," said Mary.

"Perhaps it was dragged a little, and then wrapped in a protective covering," said Monsieur Jacobs.

"Regardless of how the body reached this spot, it is clear that we will not find evidence," said Mr. Withrow in English. "We would be better served to start interviewing. Someone will know when he was last seen, or where he was going."

"The interviews will take hours," said Mary. "If not days. It is going to rain, and if we do not find the location of the murder before then, evidence will be lost."

"But there is nothing. We have searched around this entire basin." Mr. Withrow's voice raised a little. "We have already established that there is no tide, no current, no way for the body to move from one basin to another. And even if there was a current, the body would sink to the bottom of the canal before reaching this spot."

"Monsieur Pike is correct," said Monsieur Jacobs. Apparently he understood English even if he did not speak it. Fortunately, they had not said anything out of character.

Mary looked at the passage between this basin and the next. It was narrow, barely large enough to fit one of the boats with the drawbridge raised.

"There has to be a way for it to have moved from one of the other basins to here," said Mary.

"I am sorry, Mis—Mr. Fothergill, but I assure you that there is not," said Mr. Withrow.

Mary ignored his objections and looked again at the boat on which the body had been caught.

"Who owns this boat?" she asked Monsieur Jacobs in French.

"I do not know."

"How is that not as essential as speaking to Madame Claes? And why is this boat loaded with cargo? If it was loaded yesterday, why did it not depart yesterday, or why has it not already left this morning?"

Monsieur Jacobs hurried off to learn about the boat's ownership, and Mary, feeling daring, leaped from the edge of the basin onto the boat. Jumping was certainly easier to do in trousers than in a dress.

She studied the crates but could not understand the markings. She then peered between a crack in one of the crates. She could not see anything, but the crate was cold, as if it contained ice, and it smelled strongly of fish.

"This appears to be fish," she said, for Mr. Withrow's benefit. "Brussels exports a number of items, including linens, lace, hats, porcelain, tobacco, soap, and blankets. They *import* their fish from the Dutch cities on the coast. Thus, this ship has not been unloaded."

Mr. Withrow nodded, understanding her argument. "Even kept cold, fish will not keep for long. So it must have arrived recently."

"Which I am certain Monsieur Jacobs will confirm. However, why wait?"

She marched along the side of the basin, Mr. Withrow following not far behind as she crossed the drawbridge over the passage that connected their basin, the Bassin de Marchands, with the one closer to the canal, the Bassin de Barques. There was a tall red building with gold trim that probably served as the office and home for those who cared for the drawbridge.

As she was about to knock on the door, it was opened by a tall woman whose expression could either signal anger or fatigue.

"Who are you? What do you want?" asked the woman in French.

Mary explained their credentials and then asked, as she pointed across the basin, *"Do you know when that boat arrived?"*

"Well yes, I know. It was ten thirty or eleven at night. My husband was not home—he never is, the lazy dormouse—so I had to haul the bridge up by myself."

She gestured at a metal wheel with spokes. It was about four feet in diameter, and when it turned, it locked into the teeth of a large partial gear that raised the drawbridge.

"It must be heavy," said Mary.

"I'm plenty strong," said the woman with pride.

"Last night, when you raised the—" For a moment, she forgot the word for *bridge*, even though it has just been said. "When you raised the bridge, did you notice anything unusual about the boat?"

The woman's eyes narrowed. "What do you mean?"

"Was anything attached to the front of the boat, or stuck on, or—" She could not think of quite the correct word.

"I didn't notice anything. It was too dark to tell. But there could have been."

"Thank you for your assistance. We may have more questions for you later."

Monsieur Jacobs returned. He had yet to find the owner of the boat, and he found it odd that they had not left a boy to watch the crates.

"What do you propose we do?" Mr. Withrow asked Mary.

She appreciated that he was now treating her opinions with more respect.

"I think Monsieur Jacobs should stay with the boat, in case the owner returns, and I think we should investigate possible spots where the body could have been lowered into the water and caught on the boat."

They all agreed. Mr. Withrow suggested that they examine the drawbridges between the other basins—if the body had been placed in the canal from a bridge, it was more likely to have become caught on the front of the boat, which would pass only through the centre of the basins.

Monsieur Jacobs stayed at the scene, and Mary and Mr. Withrow gave directions to the driver and entered the carriage.

"Thank you for voicing your dissent," said Mr. Withrow. "At times I become fixed on a path and struggle to see alternatives."

"If you had not been so obstinate in your views, it might have been easier," said Mary.

"I am sorry if I have ever not listened to you."

They stopped and searched the drawbridge between the Bassin de Barques and the Grand Bassin, and then they continued on, to the drawbridge between the Grand Bassin and the main canal which led to Willebroek. It was there that they found dried blood near the edge of the drawbridge, and they walked, side by side, following the trail of blood and ripped fibres to a treed promenade, which was inside the rampart walls which surrounded much of the city.

"There," said Mary, pointing at a splatter of blood—no, two separate splatters of blood—on one of the trees at the edge of the promenade.

"The promenade is a common location for meetings of business or sociality," said Mr. Withrow. "Perhaps Leon and his walking partner had a disagreement, which led to the shots being fired."

"It is unusual to take such a walk at that time of night, rather than during the day."

Withrow nodded.

Mary drew several detailed sketches of the area as Mr. Withrow spoke to the couple who oversaw this drawbridge. Yes, they had heard loud noises that might have been gunshots, but they had not investigated—loud noises were common in this area of town. Yes, the boat had come in late and they had raised the drawbridge. No, they had not seen a body or anything else in the water, yet they had not looked. However, they had seen a person in a cloak hurry off the bridge as the boat approached, just before they raised the drawbridge. It had been dark, they had been drinking, and they could not give a description of the individual's height or build.

Just as Mary finished her sketches, it began to rain.

She covered the sketchbook with her body as they rushed back into the carriage. Once she was safe from the rain, she looked back out and watched as the water erased most of the evidence.

"You were right about the rain," said Mr. Withrow.

"With the state of the clouds and the sky, it was not a very difficult prediction."

"Can I see what you drew?" asked Mr. Withrow.

Mary passed them to him, and he studied her drawings: the shape of the blood on the drawbridge, the tree's location, and the patterns of the blood splatter. After a minute he passed them back without saying another word. He looked out the window, which was rather pointless, as you could see nothing clearly through it, what with water pouring down the sides.

"Why did you stand up for me last night?" asked Mary. She used her normal voice instead of lowering it—it was just her and Mr. Withrow, and the carriage driver, outside in the rain, could not possibly hear.

"What do you mean?"

"Wellington did not think a woman could do this. But you supported me. Why?"

He was quiet for a moment. "I did it for selfish reasons."

"I know you claim that everyone does everything for money or self-interest, but I refuse to believe it."

"It *was* selfish. First, this is not the sort of investigative work I prefer and having another intelligent mind can compensate for my weaknesses and mistakes. Second, I enjoy your company."

That was absolutely the last thing she had expected to hear. "You enjoy my company?"

"Yes, Miss Bennet. Is that so hard to believe?"

"Despite my personality, there are a number of people who *do* enjoy my company. Yet you have never seemed to be one of them."

"I know that I am sometimes abrasive, especially when I have strong opinions or am tired of wearing a facade, but I do not understand what I have done to make you feel that I disliked your company, or, as you assumed a few weeks ago, that I despise you."

"Do you actually want to know?" There were dozens of circumstances that she could cite.

"Of course."

"The first time I stayed at Castle Durrington, almost everything you did or said seemed calculated to show your dislike. I also overheard a conversation between you and Lady Trafford." Mary's cheeks reddened at the admission. "She was telling you that you needed to train me, despite the fact that you did not find me attractive or agreeable. Lady Trafford would never have said such a thing unless you had directly expressed those sentiments to her."

Mr. Withrow slumped into his seat. He closed his eyes and rubbed his temples.

Mary thought she had moved past what she had overheard, but clearly she had not, for though nearly two years had passed, she again felt the sting. She had never intended to tell him, but now that she had said it…well, it would not change anything between them.

Mr. Withrow opened his eyes. He leaned forward and spoke. "My original sentiments towards you seem so foreign to me now…I had almost forgotten them. I was terrible to you, Miss Bennet, and that is inexcusable, unforgivable."

His manner of speaking made it feel like he valued her

opinion above all else, but she would not delude herself into believing that his sentiments actually matched his expression: he would speak that way to anyone, if there was something he wanted from them. Yet despite knowing that he must have ulterior motives, she did not want him to think her an unforgiving person.

"Do not be ridiculous, Mr. Withrow," said Mary. "There are a number of things I would consider unforgivable—murder and adultery and the like—but your behaviour is not one of them."

"I am glad," said Mr. Withrow. "I hope we can find a way to be friends."

"I hope so too," said Mary, though the thought saddened her a little, because part of her yearned for something more. She wanted to lean forward, to reach out her hands to him, to tell him that she might have feelings for him. But that was not a very English thing to do. A lady was not meant to venture her heart in such a manner.

"I think we work well together, as a team," said Mr. Withrow.

"Yes, we do." Mary crossed her arms and looked out the window, splattered with rain. She needed to focus, not on Mr. Withrow, but on the man who had been killed. That was the *only* reason she was here, in a carriage, wearing a moustache. She was here for nothing else.

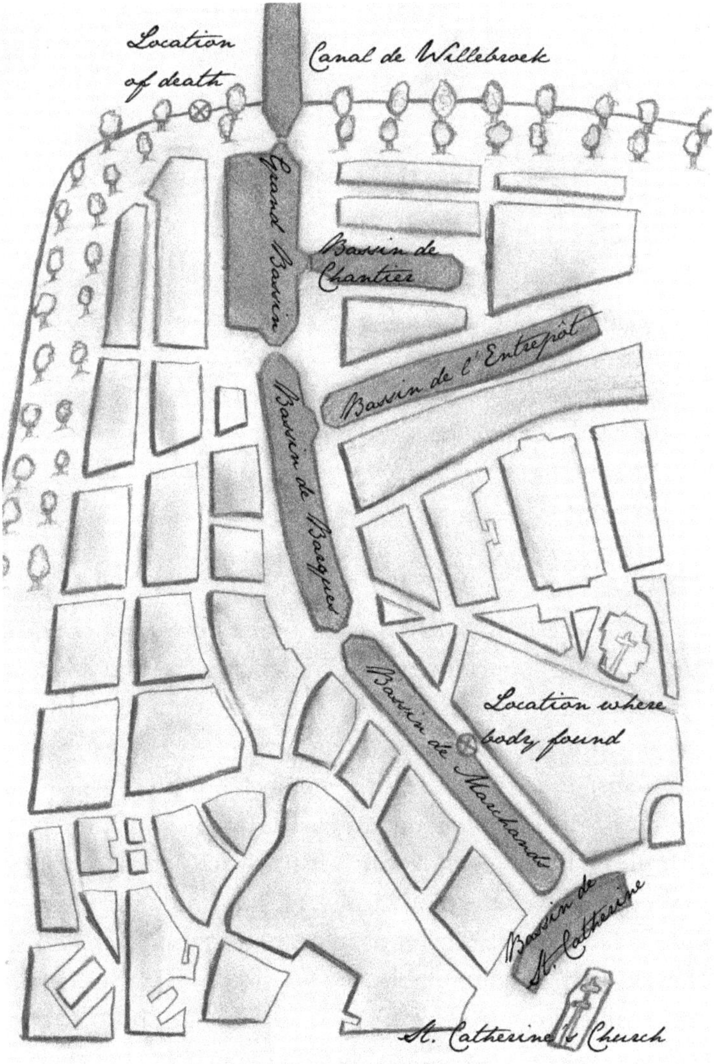
Location of death
Canal de Willebroek
Grand Bassin
Bassin de Chantier
Bassin de l'Entrepôt
Bassin de Barques
Bassin de Marchands
Location where body found
Bassin de St. Catherine
St. Catherine's Church

Chapter Six

"FASHIONS FOR JUNE. Carriage Dress—White satin pelisse, richly ornamented at the feet with clusters of leaves made in white twilled sarsnet headed with tulle…Hat composed of white satin and tulle, with a plume of feathers of the Pomona green. Half boots of similar colour."

—*Bristol Mirror*, Bristol, England, June 3, 1815

THEY SPENT AN hour interrogating the owner of the boat and three hours interviewing associates of Major General Leon—three hours gathering information about his final day and attempting to identify the strongest suspects. As soon as they returned to the house, Mary removed the wig, which was beginning to emit a foul odour, caused by the pomatum—the bear grease or lard—with which it had been styled. She then carefully removed the moustache. Her skin above her lip was a little red and irritated from the glue, but not unreasonably so. She put on a comfortable brown dress—not particularly fashionable, but after a long morning investigating, fashion was not her priority. Then she took out her investigative journal and attempted to formulate her thoughts on what she had learned.

THE LADY'S GUIDE TO DEATH AND DECEPTION

1. *A Sketch of Major General Leon*
   - *Born in Bristol, second son of Sir Frederick Leon. Forty-two years old. Joined military at age fifteen as a low-ranking officer and made his way up the ranks. Wife and three children in Bristol.*
   - *Helped Wellington with the transfers. Wellington did not want many of the existing commanding officers—he wanted those he had served with in the Peninsular Wars (in Spain and Portugal). General Swern and Lord Buckley already back in England. General Tippert has been transferred but is still in Brussels.*
   - *Organised many of the logistics (including food and housing) for tens of thousands of troops.*

2. *Timeline of Leon's Final Day*
   - *Morning meeting*
   - *Visited the troops*
   - *Belgian bakery*
   - *Hôtel de Ville (including breaking apart the fight between the Belgian and British officers)*
   - *Another confrontation with the Belgian officer*
   - *Another meeting*
   - *Two-hour gap that no one can account for*
   - *Dinner/dance with the Oldfield family (in attendance: two families; Lord Uxbridge; Colonel Kitsell—Miss Kitsell not present)*
   - *First person to leave the Oldfields*
   - *Body found dead hours later*

3. *Current Suspects*
   - *The owner of the boat. He did not know Leon, has no*

motive and may not have had opportunity, yet this is only his second time in Brussels and his entire behaviour in these events is unusual. He did admit that he had heard the boat bump into something when passing into the first basin, but he did not check what it was.

- *The Belgian officer who was in two confrontations with Leon (who is he?)*
- *General Tippert (upset at being transferred)*
- *People at the dinner?*
- *Other?*

Mary paused with her quill above the page, and a drop of ink fell, splattering on the page. Finally, she added one more name to the list of suspects.

- *Colonel Kitsell (Leon's aide. Insisted Leon had no enemies. At the Oldfield dinner. Defensive when asked where he went after dinner.)*

Mary found Mr. Withrow and Lady Trafford in the sitting room. Lady Trafford was combing over the list which she had acquired of those who had attended the event at the Hôtel de Ville in an attempt to identify the Belgian officer. Lady Trafford called Mary to her side and handed her a calling card.

"Your sister tried to visit," she said.

The card was handwritten, rather than printed on a printing press, which was more fashionable but also more expensive. Lydia simply gave her address and her name, Lydia Wickham—omitting the customary "Mrs.," but of course, Lydia had never been one for the proper formalities. There was no note, not even a hastily scribbled phrase. Yet even without a personalization, receiving the calling card created a positive emotion inside of her. Lydia must have changed her mind, after the original letter had been sent, and decided that she could receive visitors in Brussels. Lydia might be Lydia, with all her many follies, but still, she had attempted to call upon her. And while it was too late to save Lydia from her past sins, it was never too late to provide a good example for someone's future behaviour.

"I will need to find a time when it is not inconvenient to call upon my sister," said Mary. "Perhaps once we are finished with our investigation."

"The investigation could take days or weeks," said Lady Trafford. "It is more proper to return her visit sooner rather than later. You are welcome to go now."

"I do not want to abandon my duties." And truly, her duties as an investigator were more compelling than a possible visit with Lydia.

"We do not want you to lose an opportunity to visit your sister," said Mr. Withrow. "We will largely be organising information and reflecting on it, and while we appreciate your perspective, you can provide it when you return."

"You must go, Miss Bennet," said Lady Trafford. "I have never once regretted taking the time to prioritize familial relations."

Lady Trafford and Mr. Withrow possessed a stronger desire for Mary to see Lydia than Mary possessed herself, but she had no remaining arguments against visiting her sister, so she prepared to call upon Lydia.

Mary consulted a map of the city and found Lydia's address. It was only a mile away, and as it was no longer raining, she thought she would prefer walking rather than taking a carriage for that distance.

As she stepped outside the house, she was greeted by a carriage—not Lady Trafford's carriage, but one being used by Mrs. Graham. Mrs. Graham must be here to call upon Mary, for it seemed unlikely that she would call upon Lady Trafford. Yet while she liked Mrs. Graham, Mary wished she had not chosen this very moment to call upon her.

Lady Trafford had often extolled the virtue of flexibility with one's plans, however, for Mary, this was not an easy virtue. When Mary had begun to execute a plan, she found it difficult to shift to an entirely new one, for this required not simply changing one's schedule, but abandoning all the reasons and underlying principles on which one had made the plan in the first place.

"Miss Bennet," said Mrs. Graham, raising her arms as if Mary were a prize pony. She wore a fashionable white dress and a white hat with green feathers that matched her green boots. "I have come to call on you."

"It is good to see you, I just—" Should she tell Mrs. Graham that it would be better for her to visit another time? Yet Mrs. Graham lived several miles outside the city, and it was not fair to ask her to return to Brussels again. Would Lady Trafford be disappointed if Mary did not visit Lydia? Perhaps not, if Mary had a reasonable justification for her behaviour. "We can return to the house."

"It is clear that you were going out, and I would not dream of interfering with your plans." She smiled. "However, I would love to accompany you. It will be the perfect opportunity to tell you scandalous stories."

"That is very kind of you," said Mary. "I mean, the allowing me to continue with my plans and the accompanying me part, not the scandalous stories part."

Mrs. Graham laughed gaily. "Even if you do not admit it,

I know that you appreciate my stories. Will you join me in my carriage?"

"Thank you, I will." She did not feel that she could properly decline, so she gave the address to the carriage driver. As the carriage began to make its way down the streets, she discovered that this choice of conveyance was, in fact, beneficial. The streets were wet from the morning's rain and would have soaked her skirts, and most of Brussels did not have separate walks reserved for people, so the people and horses and carts mingled on the road together, with people pressed to the sides of the road and the horses and carts infringing on their space. The roads were quite crowded, and the carriage moved at a slow pace.

Mrs. Graham was in quite a lively mood. Brussels must be providing the stimulus and entertainment she sought.

"I was quite disappointed that I did not have the opportunity to tell you anything scandalous at the Hôtel de Ville."

"Honestly, I do not need to—"

"But I am afraid you do. Are you prepared for today's first item of scandalous knowledge?"

"I am prepared," said Mary, trying to school her face against whatever inappropriate thing Mrs. Graham was about to say.

"I am certain you have heard of the Richmonds. They are only the most important family here, besides the military officers."

Mary had not heard of the Richmonds, but she did not say so.

"The Duke of Richmond has been having an affair, and his mistress has been sending him quite bawdy letters. One was delivered to their house, and the servant accidentally gave it to the Duchess of Richmond instead of the Duke of

Richmond. I have it on good authority that you could hear her shrieking all the way down the street. Can you imagine her, such a staid, stuffy woman, reading all those details? Of course, maybe it will give her ideas of how to liven things up a little."

Mary's entire face flushed what she suspected was a bright red. She opened her mouth in an attempt to chastise Mrs. Graham or change the subject, but she could not manage to utter a single syllable, so she shut her lips.

Mrs. Graham burst out laughing. "Ah, you are such fun, Miss Bennet."

"I am glad that someone is enjoying this."

Mrs. Graham removed an ornamented fan and fanned herself. "I shall educate you, whether you like it or not. Now the second scandalous thing concerns your Prince of Orange."

"*My* Prince of Orange?"

"Yes, he gave you marked attention at the gathering. Everyone has been talking of it, and everyone wants to know more about you. Do not fear—you are my friend. I only said good things."

"I appreciate it," said Mary. "Yet given your penchant for storytelling, I suspect if you knew something scandalous about me, you would have shared it."

"You know me well. But there *is* something I must know. What did the prince want with you *alone*? He got rid of me quite quickly—in a very gentlemanly way, but he did it all the same."

"He did not want much, to be honest. He wanted to make sure Lady Trafford felt properly situated in Brussels." Mrs. Graham did not seem satisfied, so Mary continued. "And he thought that I might enjoy meeting his grandmother, due to the history of what she has done for the people of the

Netherlands, something I find inherently interesting."

"Meeting his grandmother!" She raised her left eyebrow. "How remarkable. Be careful, or he might decide to introduce you to the king and the queen."

"I rather suspect it will not come to that."

"Unfortunately, you are probably right." Mrs. Graham sighed dramatically. "As a prince, any entanglements he enters must give him great political advantage. But enough of this depressing matter! Let me tell you the things the prince may not have told you about himself. In the army, his nickname is Slender Billy. He is quite slender, you must admit, though in the *best* way.

"Now on to the scandal. He very much likes his parties, his races, and his drinks. Once, after a race, he was stone drunk, and he was hanging off the back of the carriage all the way back to London. It is said to be one of the reasons Princess Charlotte broke off their engagement."

It was not, truth be told, as scandalous as Mary had expected. Yet because it was the behaviour of a prince, it was under intense scrutiny—one of the burdens, perhaps, of being royal.

"We all have things we regret," said Mary. "Times when we have improperly exposed ourselves in front of society."

"And when have you done so?" asked Mrs. Graham. "I absolutely must know."

Mary thought for a moment. There were plenty of things she regretted, plenty of moments that had caused embarrassment and shame. But as for times when she had improperly exposed herself—there was one that she could share.

"I was attending a private ball with my family, and I played the pianoforte and sang, apparently very poorly. I did not recognize the cues that I should desist, and my father very loudly, in front of the entire company, asked me if I would stop playing."

Mrs. Graham laughed for almost fifteen seconds, yet although Mary was being laughed at, because it was Mrs. Graham, Mary did not feel like she was being mocked or belittled.

"That is the worst that you have exposed yourself?" said Mrs. Graham. "You are a much better woman than I, Miss Bennet. I do not think I could make your story sound scandalous if I tried."

"It felt very significant at the time."

"Things often do," said Mrs. Graham, patting Mary's hand with her own.

There was quiet for a moment, and Mary wondered if she could bring the subject from scandal to murder.

"It is not exactly scandal in the way you like, but I did hear some very serious news," said Mary. "Did you hear that Major General Leon was murdered?"

Mrs. Graham's face fell. "You are right. That is not the type of scandal I like. Everyone is talking about it, but nobody has any real facts. What did you hear?"

"I heard he was shot and then found in the river." Sometimes you had to give information to a gossip, and while doing so was risky, this was information Mrs. Graham had probably already heard.

"That is what I heard as well. It is so disturbing, and so tragic," said Mrs. Graham. "Do you know if he had any family?"

"Lady Trafford said that he had a wife and several children." It had actually been Colonel Kitsell who had told her that, but it was better to not mention that. "They are in England, so they have not yet heard."

Mrs. Graham was silent, and her left hand shook as it gripped the seat of the carriage. "They will be in such pain when the news reaches them," she said quietly. "Pain that is unquantifiable, unchecked."

It seemed now that Mrs. Graham was talking about her own pain, her own loss.

"Yes, it will surely cause them great pain," agreed Mary.

"Lady Capel told me that Major General Leon broke up the fight yesterday," said Mrs. Graham, her voice returning to normal.

"Yes, I saw it."

"You saw it yourself? You seem to be everywhere and anywhere important…speaking with the Duke of Wellington and the Prince of Orange, and right next to the fight. You are quite the interesting character, Miss Bennet."

Mary swallowed. Mrs. Graham suspected something, of that Mary was certain. It was a risk to use someone as an unknowing informant when they were as sharp as Mrs. Graham. If Mary took one wrong move, Mrs. Graham would uncover Mary's secrets and surely would not hesitate to share them.

"I myself did not witness the fight—I was still dancing with the prince's friend. But I wonder… No, I should leave speculations to those qualified to make them. Of course, a lack of qualifications has never stopped me before."

"What is your speculation?" said Mary, preferring that Mrs. Graham focused her speculations on the murder, rather than Mary.

"Simply that he may have caused hard feelings in one of the men."

Mary nodded. It was nothing more or less than what they had already considered.

"I wonder, though," said Mary, hopeful that Mrs. Graham might have some relevant gossip, "if it could have been a social connection. I have read that many murders are caused by individuals in the same social circle. Have you heard any stories about Leon?"

"Nothing scandalous, and if there was something scandalous, I hope that I would have heard of it. Oh, how dreadful. Poor Mrs. Leon." She shook her head, as if she could shake off the tragedy. "Come, let us talk of something else."

If there had been interesting or useful gossip about Major General Leon, Mrs. Graham would have shared it willingly. Which made it less likely that he had been killed for a social reason, though Mary could not eliminate that possibility entirely.

"Have you met anyone that interests you in Brussels?" said Mary, thinking of Mrs. Graham's earlier exuberance.

"I have met plenty of interesting people, Miss Bennet."

"I meant have you met any men. Purportedly, you are here to find a husband."

"I have not been here long enough to even form any inclinations," said Mrs. Graham, a little sharply, but then her tone softened. "What about you, Miss Bennet?"

"Not particularly."

"You paused slightly. There is someone."

"No, I truly am not interested in anyone I have met here in Brussels."

"Then it is not the Prince of Orange. It must be someone from home." Mrs. Graham paused. "Mrs. Capel said that Lady Trafford's nephew, Mr. Withrow, came with you both to Brussels. I wonder…" Mrs. Graham leaned a little closer to Mary, as if to examine her, and Mary could not prevent a bit of a smile. "I knew it! You are in love with Mr. Withrow. And staying in the same house with him—that is entirely too convenient."

"I do...like him." It felt strange to admit this aloud, but as she said it, she knew with absolute certainty that it was true. "But he does not feel anything towards me."

"You never know—men can be so opaque in these matters. But if he is interested in you, you should be careful, my dear. Do not marry for love. All it does is create future heartbreak."

"You loved your own husband deeply."

"Yes." Mrs. Graham looked down at her hands, and her face twisted a little, as if she was trying to keep control of her emotions.

Mary reached out and put her hands on top of Mrs. Graham's. "I am sorry that you are in so much pain and—" She paused, suddenly understanding why Mrs. Graham had snapped at her a few minutes before. "It was very stupid of me, to bring up whether you were interested in a man, when we were just talking about how painful it will be for Leon's widow, and you are a widow yourself."

"At least you recognize it," said Mrs. Graham. "Apology accepted. And I apologise for my anger."

"The way you spoke hardly qualifies as anger," said Mary. "Anger in the face of loss may not be considered ladylike, but in my opinion, it is quite understandable, particularly in the face of great loss. I was sad, but also, at times, angry, after my father died. Often I was even angry at myself."

"I never really understood anger as an emotion before my husband died. But then a family friend, Frank Hubbard, came and told me of my husband's death. At first I did not believe him, but then, instead of feeling sad, I was angry. It is always incredible to me that some people claim that women should not or cannot experience certain emotions. Should we not also have access to the full breadth of experience?"

"Yes, yes we should."

They sat there in quiet for a moment, and then Mrs. Graham said, "Thank you. And thank you for not trying to fix me or tell me I should move on or behave as a perfect lady, as everyone else does." She used a handkerchief to delicately dab the moisture next to her eyes. "I know I can be too brash and forward, but thank you for being my friend, Miss Bennet. I think you are the only person who truly sees me, as I am."

Mary was not used to such intimacy with a new friend, but it felt right, and although she had little experience with this, she knew what her oldest sister Jane would say in such a situation, so she said it herself. "Please, you may call me Mary."

"Mary." Mrs. Graham smiled. "It is so refreshing to be given someone's given name—it is like receiving a key that no one else is allowed to use, even if they know it. And now I will give you mine, and I insist that you use it. Are you prepared?"

Mary chuckled, and then attempted to tell a bit of a joke. "Yes, though I do hope it is a good name."

"Oh, it is." Mrs. Graham shifted to Mary's side of the carriage and leaned to whisper in her ear, as if she were about to reveal a grand secret. She smelled of lavender, a floral scent, almost heady. "My name is Clara."

Mrs. Graham—Clara—returned to her own seat, once again appearing happy and serene.

"Thank you, Clara."

"No, thank you, Mary."

The carriage came to a stop.

"Now, you gave the driver the address," said Mrs. Graham, "but you did not tell me where we were going, so I have no idea where we are."

"I am calling on my sister, Mrs. Wickham. She is also in Brussels, and I have not yet had the opportunity to see her."

"How long has it been since you last spent time with her?"

"Over two and a half years."

"I suspect, then, that you would prefer to see her alone. I will not join you, and I will not allow you to be a polite Englishwoman and insist that I do."

"Then I shall not." Mary was grateful that Mrs. Graham was so perceptive and considerate. "Thank you for the carriage ride, Clara."

"Thank you, Mary. It is hard to be strong, all the time, but you make it easier."

They said their farewells, and then Mary stood, for a moment, outside of Lydia's building. It was three stories and rather old and dilapidated. She did not know what to expect, really, of her reunion with her sister, yet spending time with Mrs. Graham was good preparation. Both she and Lydia possessed a similar level of energy and exuberance. Like Mrs. Graham, Lydia was wont to say things simply for the reaction, and like Mrs. Graham, Lydia seemed to always dress in the height of style.

Mary opened the door to the building—there was no servant or attendant, despite the fact that the building housed dozens of separate apartments. The halls were dimly lit, with only a few candles and no windows for sunlight. She made her way up to the second floor, found the number marking Lydia's door, and rapped on it with her hand.

The door opened almost instantly, revealing Lydia.

"Mary! You came to call on me? Please come in."

Lydia looked older than she did in Mary's memories, and

had lost her girlish appearance. This should not surprise Mary, yet surprise her it did. Her dress was quite fashionable, a well-tailored cream colour with lace and an angled hemline, but there were several spots where the fabric had been repaired. Her hair was arranged as perfectly as ever and was adorned with several ribbons, something Mary avoided whenever possible.

Mary followed Lydia into the apartment and took a seat in the rather small sitting room. The chair was frayed and stained, but Mary would not allow that to bother her.

"I apologise for missing your visit this morning," said Mary.

"You do not need to apologise to me," said Lydia. "I was the one who was thoughtless—I should have sent a note ahead in order to schedule a visit."

Sending a note in advance of a visit was not expected, so there was no reason for Lydia to apologise.

"It has been so long since we have seen each other. Has life treated you well?"

"Quite well, of course. How could it be anything but well with Wickham? There is always something interesting happening when you are married to an officer. To think, that you and I are the very first sisters in our family to visit the continent. Anyone would have thought it would be Elizabeth or Jane, since they are the ones with all the money, but it is us."

"While money can serve as a gateway to opportunity, money itself is no guarantee of better experiences, and is no substitute for a curious spirit or an ability to choose opportunities which will allow for the expansions of one's mind and understanding."

By the end of Mary's statement, it seemed that Lydia had

stopped listening. Apparently that habit had not changed in the intervening years.

They sat in silence, but it was not a comfortable one. They had so little between them. It had been years since they had spoken, and before—well, Lydia had been fifteen years old, and Mary had always found her sister spoiled and immature. Most of their actions had consisted of Lydia criticizing or taunting her. Lydia had spent years focused on making Mary miserable; for Lydia, it had practically been a sport, and her influence had often led Kitty, their mother, and other girls in Meryton to join in the torment.

Of course, to be entirely fair, Mary had also criticised Lydia, and not infrequently. She had been prone to make moralizing pronouncements to Lydia, which could hardly have been appreciated at that age. It was little wonder they did not know what to say to each other now. They had no basis on which to start.

Perhaps small talk could save the visit.

"How was your arrival in Brussels?" asked Mary.

"I loved the journey on the boat," said Lydia. "I spent as much time as possible on deck. Some of the officer's wives are very clever. I spoke to Colonel Carter's wife, and to Mrs. Williams, who was quite the character and has so many connections in London and in Brussels."

"Did you choose this apartment?" It was not what Mary would have chosen.

"No. Wickham was already here in Brussels, two days before I arrived. The officers travelled on their own boats with their men, and he chose our home. It is too small to keep a servant, but a woman comes and assists me once a week. I do not require a large and grand place to be happy."

The Lydia of old would have, so this was a positive

change.

There was a noise in the hall, perhaps footsteps near the door. Lydia's hands clenched around the arms of her chair, but after a moment, they relaxed.

"Is anything the matter?" asked Mary.

"No, I was simply startled." Lydia looked again at the door, and then jumped up. "I should have asked if you would like tea. I am a terrible hostess."

"Not at all. I do not need tea."

"No, I can do this right. I will not make any more mistakes." In an instant, Lydia had gone from comfortable to a near panic. This was not like her at all. She rushed out of the sitting room, which held no fire or teapot. Mary followed her into what was both a kitchen and dining room. Lydia moved from one side of the room to another, trying to collect the necessary items for a tea tray.

"I am terrible at organising tea things, and everything is new and I—"

"I do appreciate you wanting to make me comfortable, but you do not need to trouble yourself. I am not thirsty. I am just happy to see you and spend time with you. I do *not* need tea."

Lydia turned to her. "Are you sure?" She was blinking rapidly, and her eyes were welling with moisture.

"I am sure."

They returned to the sitting room. Their silence was a dark cavern; if they were not careful, they could fall and injure themselves.

Mary wished that she was better at this. She considered what more she could say and remembered that Lady Trafford always recommended asking people about themselves.

"How do you like Brussels? Have you done anything interesting?"

"I have mostly stayed inside. Though I did stop by a market and buy a few things. It is a very pretty city, small compared to London, but nice."

"The air seems cleaner in Brussels than in London."

"You are right."

They fell into silence again.

Kitty had been the sister who was closest to Lydia. What would Kitty do if she were here? Likely ply her with gossip or interesting stories.

"I met the Prince of Orange."

Lydia's eyes were fixed on the door. She shook her head and asked, "What did you say again? I am horrid at paying attention."

"I met the Prince of Orange."

"Really? You met a prince. Now I am famous by association. What is he like?"

"He is young."

"As a prince should be," said Lydia. "What else?"

"He is quite handsome, very slender. And he seems to pay attention to everyone. From our brief interaction, it seems he does not treat people as inferior, even when he is their better. Of course, almost everyone is inferior when you are royalty."

"He sounds quite princely," said Lydia, and she seemed to regain the vigour from her younger years. "Maybe I will have the chance to meet a prince as well. If the three of us are at the same event, would you introduce me?"

"Of course," said Mary. "Are you attending the military inspection in the park on Monday? It should be a sort of parade."

"My husband expects me to be there, so I will attend." Lydia did not seem as enthusiastic as Mary might expect. An entire event full of officers and soldiers would have made fifteen-year-old Lydia ecstatic, but of course Lydia had spent years attending such events. Perhaps it was not appropriate for a married woman to be excited about such things, though it had never stopped their mother, Mrs. Bennet.

If their sister Jane were here, she would invite Lydia to join her at the parade, in the hopes that familial company would buoy Lydia's spirits. Of course, there was no reason Mary could not do the same.

"I am planning to attend with Lady Trafford. I would love if you would join our party."

"Really?"

"Yes, of course. It would bring me great pleasure to spend more time with you."

"Thank you. I think I will."

Mary immediately regretted extending the invitation. How could she do any spy work with Lydia present? But it was too late to retract. She would manage somehow.

"We can bring you in the carriage. I will send a note with the time so you are prepared."

There was creaking in the hall. Once again, Lydia's entire body tensed.

"Thank you for visiting me," said Lydia. "I do not want to be rude, but unfortunately, I have…things I need to attend to."

Mary was not always the best at recognizing conversational cues, but this one was so apparent it would be impossible to miss. "Of course," said Mary, standing. "I will leave you to your tasks."

"I do appreciate you visiting me," said Lydia. "And I look forward to seeing you at the parade."

"I do as well."

Mary left and began the walk back to her residence, trying to avoid the mud and the carts and the horses. She was successful in the avoidance of a lurching cart, but she was defeated by the mud, which inched up her boots and her skirts.

Something was different about Lydia—different in a way that left Mary feeling uncertain, even worried. Mary had never known Lydia well—they were opposites in every single way. Yet Lydia had always possessed an exuberance, an energy, a joy in even ordinary things. It was natural for her to mature and become more serious-minded. But today Lydia had also been jumpy, and apologetic about minor things. The only time Mary had ever heard Lydia apologise was when she committed a transgression and Elizabeth forced an apology from her.

In the past several years, Mary had changed, changed in ways that helped her be more aware of other people, and in general gave her more fulfilment. But Lydia's changes…Lydia did not seem as happy as she had once been, and despite the vast distance between them, this gave Mary sorrow.

Chapter Seven

"They say, that if [Bonaparte's] army be but faithful to him, he will find himself sufficiently strong to oppose any invading force."
—*The Public Ledger and Daily Advertiser*, London,
June 5, 1815

STATUES OF MARBLE and stone, and busts of Roman emperors stood guard in the Park of Brussels, or, in French, the *Parc Public*. The goddess Diana held a sheath of arrows and was accompanied by her hunting hound. Nearby, a scantily clad Narcissus rested his foot on a dolphin; his face was filled with admiration and desire as he looked down, as if at his reflection in a pool of water. The statues and hundreds of assembled spectators would greet the Allied army as they marched through the park.

A light breeze rustled Mary's skirts. She wore a peach-coloured dress embroidered with small summer flowers and a matching cream hat adorned with fake flowers, and she felt very seasonably appropriate.

Lydia, on the other hand, was not dressed for the occasion. Her dress was of a thick material; it had a high collar and sleeves that extended all the way to her wrists. It could certainly not be comfortable in the June heat, and Lydia kept scratching an itch on her neck.

"Come," said Lady Trafford, gesturing for Mary and Lydia to follow her. "I would like to speak to Mrs. Oldfield."

Mary tugged on Lydia's arm, and they stepped through the crowds, offering endless apologies, until they reached Mrs. Oldfield. Mrs. Oldfield introduced them to her children—Miss Oldfield, age seventeen, Matthew, age fourteen, Mark, age nine, Luke, age six, and Priscilla, age four. While using Biblical names was common, the ordering of the boys' names seemed rather structurally adherent to the New Testament. If only there were a fourth son so they could complete the gospels.

In disguise, Mary and Mr. Withrow had interviewed Mrs. and Mr. Oldfield, who had dined with Leon before his murder. Fortunately, Mrs. Oldfield did not recognize Mary. Mary and Mr. Withrow had fully briefed Lady Trafford on what they had learned—there had not been much of significance—but Lady Trafford must believe that she could discover more.

Before they could begin the conversation in earnest, trumpets sounded. A grand wooden entranceway, covered with flowers, had been constructed, and the Duke of Wellington rode through on his horse. He was accompanied by the Prince of Orange and General Blücher, the commander of the Prussian Army.

Following Wellington, the Prince of Orange, and General Blücher were the staffs and aides-de-camp of Wellington and the prince. The men rode up the walkway and through the park, amidst cheers by the many who had come to watch the inspection. The Oldfield children threw flowers onto the path in front of Wellington, and Luke whined when his flower was trampled by a horse.

Little Priscilla attempted to run into the parade path, but

her sister, Miss Oldfield, lifted her up. "Never run out in front of horses," she chided. Priscilla fussed, but Miss Oldfield said, "Look, you can see better now. How many horses are there?"

Priscilla counted the horses until she used up all the numbers she knew.

Their area of the park was empty for a moment, and Miss Oldfield occupied her sister by pointing out clouds in interesting shapes. Mary joined in, noting a cloud that looked rather like a horse, though Priscilla insisted it appeared more like a cow. Then Wellington and the others rode back, once again to wild cheers.

The leaders positioned themselves in an area which had been prepared for them, near the entryway, where they could best inspect the troops. After the signal of another trumpet, the troops began their march. The officers led their soldiers, marching in perfect unison, left right left right. They each carried their muskets, and Mary reminded herself that despite all this pomp and regalia, the task of each of these men was to kill the enemy.

The troops were not divided, with all the soldiers from a particular country together, but rather, they were intermixed. A regiment of smartly dressed British soldiers in red uniforms were followed by a group of German soldiers in orange uniforms, from one of the small German princedoms. They were followed by another regiment of British soldiers, this time in blue, and then by the King's German Legion in green, which was actually an English regiment, despite being populated with German soldiers. Each regiment wore a different shako—a cylindrical military hat—some with plumes, some with tassels, and many with a badge representing their unit. A unit from Brunswick in black wore a skull and crossbones on their shakos. Next came a large contingent of soldiers from the United Netherlands, with mismatched uniforms in red, blue, green, and black, not even consistent among each regiment. Some of the blue uniforms looked suspiciously like those of Napoleon's French armies.

These troops seemed nothing like the troops she had seen in Ostend. While the removal of troops from the boats had been characterized by disorderly chaos, these troops—especially the British troops—were orderly, disciplined, and experienced. The Duke of Wellington was creating an army that could face Napoleon Bonaparte's best. Yet that would only be possible if the Allies could continue to work together—so many of these groups represented in the parade had their own histories of conflict, their own ongoing squabbles over borders and trade and policy.

Lydia was subdued, but any time a group of British soldiers in red uniforms approached, she peered intently at the officers. She must be looking for her husband. Mr. Wickham, through the financial assistance of Mr. Darcy, had been promoted to the rank of captain. Captain Wickham. It had a good sound to it. Lydia must be pleased.

"I heard that the Duke of Wellington called our troops the scum of the earth," said Mrs. Oldfield.

It was a shocking thing to say—both Wellington's original statement, assuming it were true, and Mrs. Oldfield's recounting. Of course, Lady Trafford always cultivated friendships with people who enjoyed gossip. It was a proven method for gathering information.

"Not the officers, surely?" asked Lady Trafford.

"Not the officers," Mrs. Oldfield agreed. "But the men themselves. What sort of man becomes a common soldier, after all? Drunks and thieves and the dregs of the earth.

Wellington is quite right—they are scum."

"But they are willing to fight for our country," said Lady Trafford.

"As long as we supply them with enough money and beer."

Miss Oldfield coloured at her mother's words. "Mother, the troops can hear you."

"Not with all this hubbub, they cannot."

"Speaking of officers, I heard that Major General Leon had dinner at your house," said Lady Trafford.

"The day he was—" said Mrs. Oldfield, and then stopped, noticing her seven-year-old tugging on her dress. "We did not bring our governess with us from England. I have been trying to find one here, but with no success."

"It must be quite trying for you," said Lady Trafford. "As must have been hearing the news about the major general."

"Incredibly so."

"I have heard some very interesting things about what Leon did that day."

"I would be interested to hear it," said Mrs. Oldfield. "But we had best talk more privately. Tabitha, you are in charge of the children."

Miss Oldfield seemed like she wanted to protest and then thought better of it. As Mrs. Oldfield and Lady Trafford stepped away, little Priscilla flailed in Miss Oldfield's arms, Mark jostled a man in the crowd, and Luke complained that his head hurt.

"Do not fear," said Mary, "we will help you. Lydia, Lydia." But Lydia did not seem to hear. "Fine. I will help you." Mary took Priscilla from Miss Oldfield's arms so she could attend to the other children.

Mary's arms instantly felt the strain of holding a writhing

four-year-old. She had some experience holding children—her sister Jane's baby was now over a year old, and Elizabeth's baby was now seven months—but a baby weighed significantly less than this child and did not protest being held. Miss Oldfield must be much stronger than she looked.

Mary tried, still, to watch the march, but it was more difficult. However, she did notice Mr. Wickham. His shako was black with a brass bugle horn badge. "There is your husband, Lydia."

"Where?" asked Lydia, standing very upright.

Mary pointed, almost losing little Priscilla in the process.

Lydia waved enthusiastically and called out to her husband. "Captain Wickham, Captain Wickham!" This was the same enthusiasm Mary remembered from her, but there was a desperate edge to it now.

Mr. Wickham winked at a woman in the crowd. Lydia continued to call out to him, and as he passed their position, he must have seen them—he could not have done otherwise—but he did not wink at Lydia, or quirk his mouth into a smile, or acknowledge her in any way.

A flicker of disappointment showed on Lydia's face, but then she composed herself. While her sister was only disappointed, Mary was surprised to discover that she herself was angry.

When Mr. Wickham had first come to Meryton as part of the militia, he had charmed everyone with his conversational skills and drawn their sympathy with his stories of past hardship. He had known exactly what to say to everyone at exactly the right time, and for a time, Mary's older sister Elizabeth had seemed quite in love with him, as had half the eligible young ladies in Meryton.

Everyone had loved Mr. Wickham until everyone hated

him. When Lydia ran away with him, it had not only irreversibly shattered Lydia's own virtue, but almost damaged the prospects of the entire family. At the time, Mary had judged Lydia harshly, but over the years, Mary's views softened. Lydia had only been fifteen, in many ways still a girl, young and impressionable and easily manipulated, and Mr. Wickham, much older and more experienced in the ways of the world, had clearly taken advantage of her.

Fortunately, Mary's uncle, Mr. Gardiner, had forced Lydia and Mr. Wickham to marry, which had largely recovered Lydia's reputation and saved the family. There had also been rumours about Mr. Wickham's gambling and extensive debts in Meryton, but someone must have paid them because soon Meryton became quiet on the matter.

Since then, Lydia had been gone, in Newcastle, so far away as to be practically out of reach of the entire family. Not that the distance was a true barrier. Both Jane and Elizabeth could afford that sort of trip, but there must have been some sort of lingering resentment, and a hesitancy to make the journey. And so Lydia had been alone with Mr. Wickham, isolated from her family and childhood friends. Surely this could not have been a barrier for Lydia, who had always been able to make friends. Yet something had changed in Lydia in these years, something had clearly been lost.

Lydia crossed her arms and raised her head stiffly, still looking out at the oncoming soldiers, but not seeming to see them. Mary shifted little Priscilla to her left arm in order to more easily practise one of her newer skills, which proved to be quite useful in moments like this: comforting physical gestures. She set her hand on Lydia's back. Instantly, Lydia let out a gasp and arched as if in pain.

Mary withdrew her hand with such suddenness that she

almost dropped Priscilla.

"I am sorry."

"There is no reason to be sorry," said Lydia, but she would not quite meet Mary's eyes. "Nothing is wrong."

"Clearly, my hand hurt you."

"Oh, that," said Lydia. "I fell yesterday, on my back."

"I am sorry to hear that," said Mary. "But how did you manage to fall on your back?"

Lydia glared at her. "Just because you cannot conceive of it, that does not mean it did not occur."

"I believe you." She still could not imagine how someone could fall on their back, but it was better to not to pursue that point. "Have you sought medical attention?"

"No," said Lydia. "I will be fine. It is my own fault. I am so very clumsy. I brought it on myself."

"But that does not mean—"

Priscilla escaped from Mary's arms, forcing Mary to lunge to keep her from running into the procession.

Miss Oldfield took her sister's hand. "You cannot do that, please." Her eyes searched the crowd behind them. "When will my mother return?"

"They must have much to talk about."

"Yes, and everyone cares what my parents think. No one cares what I think, or what I might know."

"It is an unfortunate part of being a young lady," agreed Mary. "I take it that you were there at the dinner with Major General Leon."

"Yes," said Miss Oldfield.

"I met him briefly at the Hôtel de Ville," said Mary, "but only spoke to him for a minute."

"I should not speak poorly of the dead," said Miss Oldfield, "but he was not a very interesting man."

"What did he speak about?"

"Oh, various things," said Miss Oldfield. "Watch the parade," she said to Matthew, who was poking Mark in the side.

It was hard for an informant to feel comfortable talking when they had so many other responsibilities. Mary looked around, trying to find something that would help. There was a vendor, selling French pastries. She removed some coins from her pocket. "Can they have sweets?"

"Yes," said Miss Oldfield.

Mary held out the money to the boys. "Can the three of you buy some treats?"

The boys greedily grabbed the money out of Mary's hands.

"You must share," said Miss Oldfield. "Go straight there, and come straight back. And take Priscilla with you."

She seemed to relax as soon as all her siblings were gone. Mary felt a little guilty, but they could watch the children from here as they bought themselves food.

"Were all your siblings at the dinner too?" asked Mary.

"Yes, so I do not see why my mother insists that we cannot talk about it in front of them. They know he is dead."

"So strange that no one knows why, or who did it."

"Well, I certainly do not know," said Miss Oldfield. "He did not declare who was about to murder him."

"I wonder who else he spent time with, that last day. Maybe one of them knows something."

"Well, he was at the Hôtel de Ville. Everyone knows that. He said there were some concerns by several officers appointed by the government that the duke would not employ their skills. And he mentioned—no… I cannot remember."

"Remember what?" said Mary. "I apologise for the questions. I know it is not my place. Do not tell Lady Trafford or your mother, but sometimes I have a rather morbid curiosity."

"Me as well. I do love a good Gothic novel."

Miss Oldfield's siblings had purchased a number of pastries and were headed back in their direction. Mary despaired of learning anything useful from her.

"Everyone seems to think it was a British or a Dutch officer who killed him," said Miss Oldfield. "But I will have you know that the major general met with a Prussian before coming for dinner. I cannot remember who, but it was about some piece of art."

"How strange," said Mary.

"Indeed," said Miss Oldfield.

Miss Oldfield was the first to mention a Prussian, and the first to account for part of the two-hour gap. Finding out which Prussian officers knew Major General Leon could be very useful indeed.

Chapter Eight

"Brussels—An urgent dispatch reveals that one of Wellington's officers was found dead in the canal on the night of June 2nd. The report did not include the identity of the deceased officer or the murderer."

—*The Morning Post*, London, June 7, 1814

For this disguise, Mary wore spectacles. A girl in Meryton had worn spectacles, and Lydia always said it made her look dowdy, but to Mary, her own spectacles did not have this effect. There was something sophisticated about them, as if Mary could see more than the rest of the world, and should not everyone be interested in her for that?

She had used different creams and faint colourings to alter the appearance of her facial structure. She was not nearly as skilled as her friend Fanny Cramer at this, but Fanny had taught her enough techniques to achieve a workable result.

Mary's dress had a lower neckline than she preferred, and Lady Trafford insisted she wear a long, rather large necklace, which drew attention to her bosom. But she had to admit it was a good disguise, so much so that when Mr. Withrow entered the room he stopped in place, had a confused expression, then shook his head.

Mr. Withrow had also donned a disguise, as her supposed cousin. He wore shoes that made him several inches taller, and longer pants that deemphasized the shoes. His clothes were fine, but well-worn, and were cut in a style that did not look quite British. Perhaps they were a Belgian cut. This time, he had given himself a moustache and a short beard. He scratched at his chin; he must also find the glue itchy.

Through various inquiries, Lady Trafford had discovered the identity of the Belgian officer who had argued with Leon: his name was Serrurier. Lady Trafford had also spoken with the contact provided by the Prince of Orange's grandmother, who had found out that Serrurier regularly dined at a certain inn.

Mary and Mr. Withrow made their way to the inn. "It is better not to seem too forward or to push too hard for an introduction," said Mr. Withrow as they sat in the carriage. "I would rather spend the hour observing, than be too obvious and raise his suspicions."

"I understand your strategy," said Mary. It seemed a little cautious, but Mr. Withrow was pretending to be a native Belgian, which was a task in and of itself. "However, if possible, should we not speak to him?"

"Of course."

As soon as they entered the inn, Mary spotted Serrurier, who she recognized from the confrontation at the Hôtel de Ville. Serrurier had dark brown skin and curly black hair. He sat with two other men who were also in uniform. As was the case for many members of the Prince of Orange's army, all three still wore Napoleon Bonaparte's French uniforms, simply with several coloured strips of fabric denoting that they actually belonged to the Dutch army. Mary had learned that the King of Orange did not have the funds, the resources, or even the seamstresses to make all new uniforms for his armies, and so instead, they wore the uniforms of their enemies—

former friends—with a token representation of their new loyalties. Hopefully their new loyalties were larger than their signifier.

With a few choice words to the hostess, Withrow managed to obtain the table directly next to the officers. Mr. Withrow and Mary spoke only in French as the hostess poured them wine and told them she would be back shortly with their food.

Mr. Withrow began a slow monologue about the day's news that he had read in the local paper, making sure to complain about the British. Despite her actual interest, as she had not yet read the paper, she feigned only partial interest to better fit tonight's persona.

The officers' conversation grew a little louder and more robust, and then they said, *"Vive Bruxelles!"* Long live Brussels.

Mr. Withrow lifted his cup in their direction. *"Vive Bruxelles!"*

They gave him a little cheer, and then turned back to their conversation.

"C'est ton tour," Mr. Withrow said quietly to Mary as the hostess returned with their food. *Your turn.*

"I have a question," Mary said in French to the woman. *"Who are those officers at that table next to us?"* She lowered her voice, but not so much that it could not be overheard. One of the officers in question seemed to sense that she was talking about them. She caught his eye and smiled. *"They are very handsome."*

This was the sort of thing women like Lydia were in the habit of saying, though Mary thought it rather ridiculous. She would never say such a thing, especially if she actually found a man to be handsome. But the hostess responded as if it were a normal, expected question.

"*They are some of Brussels' finest,*" she said. "*The one who is looking at you is Capitaine Lemoine.*"

"*Capitaine,*" said Mary. "*That is impressive.*"

"*My cousin,*" said Mr. Withrow, "*has been absent from our land for far too long. She is looking forward to meeting its inhabitants.*"

"*My establishment is a good place to start,*" said the hostess. "*How long have you been here?*"

"*I normally live in Asse, with my wife and two children, but my mother asked me to come and welcome my cousin, Mademoiselle Portier.*" They did not want anyone to think that Mr. Withrow and Mary were a couple, or soon to be a couple, because that eliminated certain avenues of conversation. "*She has spent the last decade living with foreign relations and is glad to finally be home.*"

"*You speak well, for having been gone so long,*" said the hostess to Mary. "*Let me know if there is anything more you need.*"

She turned away from their table, but Captain Lemoine called her to speak to him.

"*Pretend you are not watching,*" whispered Mr. Withrow, and Mary did as directed.

Not a minute later, Captain Lemoine came to their table and bowed. "*Excusez-moi, I am Capitaine Lemoine. I could not help overhearing a bit of your conversation, and we wondered if you would join us.*"

"*That would be a pleasure,*" said Mr. Withrow, standing. "*If my cousin, Mademoiselle Portier, agrees.*"

"*It would suit me well.*" She attempted to not look overly self-pleased. Mr. Withrow thought that getting an introduction might be difficult, but they had achieved their initial goal already. Now she wanted to learn as much as possible.

"And what is your name?" asked Captain Lemoine.

"I am Monsieur Raoult," said Mr. Withrow.

Without obtaining the hostess's permission, the men pushed together the tables. Captain Lemoine held Mary's chair for her as she took her seat, and his hand brushed her shoulder in a way that was clearly calculated as he returned to his seat.

Lemoine introduced his fellows. *"This is Colonel Serrurier and Colonel Voland. And this is Monsieur Raoult and his lovely cousin, Mademoiselle Portier."*

The conversation was warm, the drinks plentiful, and the food high quality. She could see why the officers ate here time and time again.

"Quel repas! J'en ai assez—"

Everyone stared at her, so she did not finish her statement. She only meant to compliment the food, but she must have said something wrong.

Withrow began to laugh. *"Can you believe my cousin's accent? And the things she says? J'en ai assez!"*

The others laughed as well, and for a moment, Mary was dragged back to her youth, and the sensation of being laughed at by the others in Meryton. It was an idiotic mistake, a basic problem with French gendering, and she deserved to be laughed at for it.

Yet Mr. Withrow had no malicious intent: his calling attention to an error would help protect her from suspicions. Besides, she did not have to react to this situation as Mary Bennet would—she was not Mary, not at the moment at least. She was Mademoiselle Portier, who would respond to this quite differently.

"I will not stand for your ridicule," said Mary. *"It is not my fault my relatives raised me the way that they did. If you are*

going to laugh at me, I will not speak."

"I would not want that," said Lemoine. *"Your lips are too beautiful. You must be allowed to use them as often as you desire."*

Lemoine's eyes were locked on her lips, and then they lowered, lingering on the necklace and the low neckline of her dress. Then they returned to her face. If she was here socially, she might be irritated at him—she had no interest in this sort of man, who placed his personal interest as more important than the bounds of propriety. But in this situation, she might be able to use his interest to their advantage.

"My poor cousin," said Mr. Withrow. *"She was raised by distant relatives in England, which is quite the injustice. She was very mistreated. For years they would not even allow her to speak French with the other French speakers in the village."*

"I am grateful to be home," said Mary. *"I will never return to England again!"*

"Those English," said Serrurier. *"They are all the same. Conards, jusqu'au dernier. If only they were not here in Bruxelles."*

Someone's foot brushed against hers under the table. It must be Lemoine. She pretended not to notice.

Mr. Withrow leaned in a little and lowered his voice. *"I heard that a British officer was killed. Good riddance, I say."*

"To the common cause!" said Voland.

Serrurier glanced around the rest of the room. *"You should take care what you say in mixed company. You never know who might be listening."*

"You worry too much," said Voland.

Lemoine's foot once again brushed against Mary's. Clearly, he would continue with this until she responded to him, so she gave him a flirtatious, Kitty-like smile.

"It is good advice," said Mr. Withrow.

Mary feared that the conversation would move past the death, so she tried to force them to keep the discussion on it. "Was he really murdered?" she asked. "My maid said it was an accident."

"It was definitely a murder," said Lemoine. "He was shot twice, and that sort of thing does not happen by accident."

"I think I saw him once, on the street," said Mr. Withrow. "Had any of you met him?"

Lemoine and Voland both shook their heads.

"He was quite a bastard," said Serrurier. "I am not surprised someone had a problem with him."

"Was he an unpleasant sort?" asked Mr. Withrow.

"I only interacted with him briefly, but he seemed to think that British soldiers were superior to Belgian and Dutch, and he felt like his oversight was necessary to resolve difficulties between members of the Allied army."

It was impossible to tell if Serrurier was telling the truth. Had he known Leon as little as he claimed? Yet they could not push too far. One simply could not expect a new acquaintance to confess to murder.

"It is rather strange," said Mr. Withrow, "that we are being told to fear a French invasion—we, who speak French and share much with France—when we clearly already have a British one. Why, you cannot walk a single block without running into one of those fools."

"It would seem that way," said Serrurier. "But it is not up to us to change things."

"There are ways—" began Lemoine.

Serrurier shook his head, silencing Lemoine. Clearly Lemoine had wanted to say more, perhaps even something useful. Why else would Serrurier have stopped him?

The conversation did not return to the subject, instead moving on to the upcoming horse races and various social events. While these officers were engaged in preparing their troops for war, they seemed to have plenty of time to participate in social activities.

Throughout the meal, she kept stealing glances with Lemoine. If only she could get him alone, then maybe she could encourage him to share more details. What would Lydia do? Well, Lydia before. Not Lydia now. As the meal neared its end, she excused herself, as if to use a ladies' room, but before entering the hallway, she paused. Mary turned, caught Lemoine's eye, raised her eyebrows, and gave what she hoped was a pouty expression.

Then she slipped into the hall, leaned against the wall, and waited.

After a minute, she thought that perhaps she had been unclear, but then Lemoine entered the hall and smiled.

"You came," she said.

"We are of one mind." He leaned against the wall next to her and held out his hand. *"May I?"*

At least he was a gentleman. Or perhaps not a true gentleman, but gentlemanly enough to ask permission before touching her.

"I suppose," she said, and she slipped her hand into his.

He held her hand, rubbing his thumb against the back of it, and gazed into her eyes, in a rather stereotypical French way that was meant to seduce women.

Personally, Mary did not find it appealing, though she could see how some women would find it so. She had no intention of being seduced. But Lemoine wanted something between them, and she wanted information. It would be an exchange, if she could arrange it properly.

"Earlier, you were going to say something, about actions that a man could take to change things, if he wanted."

"We have but a minute to ourselves, and you want to discuss politics?"

Here she was, bungling things already by being far too direct, and by breaking with the persona of a woman disinterested in the news. Yet there was no moving back now, only forward. *"I find political men attractive, especially if they have the* correct *politics."*

"I suspect we are once again of the same mind," he said. *"What do you think of the Dutch, and the Flemish?"*

"It is strange that they should rule over us," said Mary. *"Many of them do not even speak French."*

"You are right, Mademoiselle. When you speak about politics it is very attractive." He used his other hand to trace her face. *"I wish I could do more than speak with you."*

For the first time with Lemoine, Mary felt a bit of fear. He was certainly stronger than her, and while he had asked permission to hold her hand, she was well aware—despite not having any personal experience in the matter—that men did not always stop when you asked. She did not think the captain was that kind of man. But if he was, she would yell, and it was likely that Mr. Withrow would come and save her. Besides, did not one of Heywood's proverbs say that he who never undertook anything did not gain anything?

"I would like to see change. I would like it if our people felt safe and secure and independent," she said, as if this was a discussion in a respectable parlour.

"I do not just want *change,"* he said, *"I do what I must to obtain it, and I act without hesitation."* He leaned a little closer. Clearly, he wanted to kiss her.

"Are you really doing something that makes a difference?" she

said, trying to project a playful, yet almost taunting tone that Lydia—or at least Lydia at fifteen—would have used. *"So many people claim they are, and then what they are doing makes no real difference."*

He leaned closer to her, and she could feel the air from his breath on her face. *"I would tell you, but I am worried that you are a stuffy Englishwoman."*

"Me? A stuffy Englishwoman? I am French to the tips off my nails."

She knew exactly what Mrs. Ford would do in this situation. She would kiss him. And Mr. Withrow had been right in suggesting that kissing someone was a more moral option than killing them, because in general, it was much harder to obtain information from someone if they were dead.

"Do not tell my cousin," she said, looking up into his eyes. *"This will be our secret."*

She tilted her head slightly, pushing her lips towards his as he leaned down to kiss her.

Mechanically, kissing Monsieur Lemoine was similar to kissing Mr. Withrow. She had learned certain techniques which she could execute, even with a stranger. Yet there was no spark, no rush of sensation. Lemoine did not seem to have the same observation—he wrapped his arm around her back and pulled her to him.

After at least a minute, by which time she was starting to feel rather bored, the kiss ended. *"Now you see where I keep my loyalties,"* she said, as if she had enjoyed that. He had better give her what she wanted in exchange.

"You are definitely not English," he said. *"Maybe I can tell you, if you promise to keep a secret."*

A promise made as a spy, to gain crucial information from an informant… That was no promise at all. Was he about to confess that he had a hand in Leon's demise?

"I can keep a secret," she said.

"I am sure you can." He leaned so close that his lips touched her ear. *"I have been gathering information on the preparations of the Allied troops and sending it on to France."*

Her heart grew still—he was acting as a spy, just as she was, except for Napoleon Bonaparte. She pushed past her shock. She could not let her true feelings show.

"Incredible," said Mary. *"Now have you done this once or—"*

"Every few weeks," he said. *"We about have enough for another letter. We send it by courier."*

Mary tried to imitate Mrs. Ford's seductive smile. *"I am sure the emperor will reward you for your actions."*

"I do not need a reward from the emperor."

Clearly, he wanted a reward from *her*. Despite Rahab's Biblical example, Mary was starting to drift back towards her original stance—kissing was a terrible way to gain information, because the informant always wanted more. But she did not want Lemoine to doubt her disguise, so she obliged him with a second kiss.

She almost could not believe that it had worked, that for a kiss—well, two kisses—she had managed to extract information. Apparently, every Samson did in fact have a Delilah, but Mary would never give up her secrets so easily—she would never be so easily led.

"I should return, before my cousin begins to worry."

"Of course, Mademoiselle," he said, and then he took her hand. *"But I want to see you again."*

"Do you come here often?" she asked.

"Yes."

"Then maybe I will be able to slip away from my cousin and come on my own."

He let go of her hand, and she returned to the dining area of the inn, as if nothing had happened. Except Captain Lemoine did not even have the sense to wait thirty seconds to follow her back. He was practically tripping on her heels, and she did not even want to see what expression he wore on his face.

If she was actually Mademoiselle Portier, she would be concerned if her cousin saw her return from the hallway with a man. But fortunately, this was all a pretence.

Mr. Withrow pretended not to notice. *"Ah, Marie..."*

Lemoine gave her occasional glances, which she pretended not to notice, though her aloofness seemed to make him more interested.

The conversation did not last much longer before Withrow announced, *"Well, we must be on our way, or my mother will worry about Marie."*

They all stood and said their farewells, and Serrurier clapped Withrow on the back.

Each of the men bowed to Mary and thanked her for her company, and then Lemoine kissed her hand.

Withrow held the door open to the carriage. Once he joined her inside the carriage, he shut its door with a bit more force than necessary.

"I learned something useful," she said.

"Shh." He gestured his head in the direction of the carriage driver, who likely could not hear them through the carriage walls. They had not used their own carriage or their driver, Mr. Parker, for that could ruin the pretence. "We should wait until we get back."

"Very well."

He was silent—almost sullen—the entire ride. The carriage stopped a few blocks from the house, and they took a roundabout path back to the house, making sure they were not seen.

Finally, once they were inside, they made their way to the library, which was not much of a library, though a token number of books gave some justification for its name.

Mr. Withrow shut the door, then sat sideways in a chair, his legs hanging over the arm. "You certainly seemed to be enjoying yourself."

"Excuse me?" She took a seat across from him, though she sat in a ladylike position, her legs crossed at the ankles.

"A quarter of the people at the inn knew that you kissed Lemoine. By now, everyone does. You have officially ruined the reputation of your alias, which limits your ability to use it again in the future and limits my ability to act as Monsieur Raoult."

"You are being ridiculous."

"You did kiss him though."

"Yes, I kissed him, but regardless of what you think, I did not enjoy it. I was working."

"If you can call it work."

"You are such a hypocrite," declared Mary. "You are the one who insisted that kissing could be an acceptable means to gain information. Tell me truthfully, have you ever kissed an informant?"

"Yes," he said. "But only twice, in all of my years doing this work. Kissing anyone who crosses your path, left and right, in the hopes it might lead to something useful… That is not what I was suggesting at all."

She stood and marched towards the door. "Do you even want to know what I learned? Maybe it would be better if I woke Lady Trafford and told her. At least she would care."

"What did you learn, Miss Bennet?"

"Lemoine and the others have been gathering information on the troops and on Wellington's preparations, and then sending it via courier to Bonaparte. They will be sending another letter soon, maybe even tomorrow."

He swung his legs off the side of the chair and placed them solidly on the floor.

"You got all of that out of him?"

"Well, he enjoyed the kiss...and my promises—false ones, of course—of future kisses. Personally, I was satisfied with the exchange rate."

She opened the door and left in a huff. She wanted him to apologise, but he was Mr. Withrow. He was not the sort to apologise or admit his hypocrisy.

She had almost reached her room when she heard his voice.

"Miss Bennet."

She turned, and even though she knew it made her look sullen, she crossed her arms and glared at him. "Yes, Mr. Withrow?"

"Do you mind if I contact the Prince of Orange immediately? We need someone to follow them until they send their next letter, so it can be intercepted."

He was right—the information should be acted on immediately, and his plan was a sound one.

"I do not mind at all. Go ahead."

"Would you like to come with me?"

"No," she said, a little too forcefully, so she repeated it with a more polite delivery. "No, thank you."

She turned back towards her door.

"I am sorry for criticizing you. Your judgment on the matter was clearly correct."

She looked over her shoulder and held his eyes for a moment. He seemed sincere. And then he left, off on his errand, which would not have been possible without the methods she had used to gather information.

Chapter Nine

"A few plain, simple Questions, addressed to the Common Sense of England, if any such quality or commodity be left in it.

With infinite risk and trouble you at last succeeded in catching a royal tiger and shutting him up in a cage. Q. Why did you not keep him there?....

Q. What right had you, in the first instance, to lock him up in the said cage[?]....

Q. Is France, and probably a great part of Europe, to be laid waste, for the single purpose not only of depriving the French of the Sovereign of their choice, but of the only leader capable of defending their country in that very crisis and case of necessity, which you, England, force upon them?....

Q. Do you know that [the] expense [of the war] abroad cannot be liquidated in Bank paper, but must be provided for in gold or silver?

Q. Do you know, that at the present price of gold and silver, a million in specie or bullion will cost a million and a half in the paper currency of this country?"

—*Liverpool Mercury*, Liverpool, England, June 9, 1815

MARY AND MR. Withrow stepped into General Blücher's ball as Mr. Fothergill and Mr. Pike, set on unravelling the mystery of the Prussian art connection. The mysterious Prussian was one of their primary leads, though their suspects still included the three Belgians they had dined with at the inn, General Tippert, who they had not yet spoken to, and perhaps Colonel Kitsell. As Mr. Pike, Withrow had spoken to Kitsell's carriage driver, who had insisted that he had brought Kitsell straight home after the dinner with the Oldfields and Leon, but Withrow did not believe the driver had been entirely truthful. Kitsell, Tippert, and a number of Prussians would be at the ball, so Mary hoped it would be a fruitful evening.

Before their departure for the ball, Lady Trafford had briefed them thoroughly on General Blücher. He was in his seventies, not educated and barely literate, yet he had risen through the ranks of the Prussian military until he became the commander of the Prussian army.

Mary had only seen him at the military inspection, and then only briefly and from a distance. Now, she could better evaluate him. Blücher might be in his seventies, but he was fit and spry, with muscles which looked like they could win a tavern brawl with someone a third his age. He had a discerning look in his eye, and he greeted them in German as they approached.

"Willkommen," he said.

Mary had to fight the urge to curtsy, and bowed, only a moment after Mr. Withrow.

A man next to Blücher said, "Are you English?"

"Yes," said Mary, keeping her voice low and gravelly.

"Welcome, then," said the translator.

"Wie heißen Sie?" said General Blücher.

"What are your names?" said the translator.

"Mr. Pike and Mr. Fothergill," said Mr. Withrow.

"Die Ermittler. Ich hoffe Sie finden den verdammten Bastard," said Blücher.

"He hopes that you…find the party responsible for the murder," said the translator.

Something about the way the translator said it made her think he had modified Blücher's words slightly. Maybe it was the fact that Blücher's final word was bastard, which must be the same in both German and English.

To Mary's surprise, Mr. Withrow spoke in German. *"Es ist mir eine Freude, Sie kennenzulernen, General."*

Fortunately, the translator saw the confusion on her face and translated for her. "It is a pleasure to meet you, General."

"Ein böses Geschäft," said General Blücher. *"Gibt es eine Möglichkeit, wie ich Sie bei Ihren Ermittlungen unterstützen kann?"*

"A nasty matter. How can I help?"

"Kennen Sie jemanden, der Kunst liebt?" said Mr. Withrow. *"Es kann sein für uns nützlich."*

"Do you know anyone with an interest in art?"

Blücher provided Withrow with a list of names and then turned to enthusiastically greet the next guest, a well-decorated Prussian officer.

"I did not know you spoke German," observed Mary as they walked farther into the ball.

"I have a limited vocabulary, and my accent is terrible."

"But it should still be useful to us."

"Perhaps." He did not seem inclined to speak much to her. In fact, he had not spoken to her much at all since she had kissed the Belgian officer, and at times even seemed to avoid her. Yet he could not avoid her now, not when they must work together at the ball.

It was strange, attending a ball as a man. People always watched each other at balls, but now, it seemed as if people, especially the women, watched her differently. If she were here to dance as Mr. Fothergill, she would be taking initiative instead of waiting and hoping for partners as women were forced to do.

The wrappings around her chest were a little tight, and she had an itch under her left arm, but she did not scratch it. That might not be considered a gentlemanly thing to do.

Before they could meet any of the Prussians who General Blücher had mentioned, the Prince of Orange approached.

"Come with me, dear sirs," he said, putting his hands on their shoulders and steering them across the room to the Duke of Wellington.

An officer was speaking, in a concerned tone, to the duke. "Lord Uxbridge is attempting to seduce everyone he sees."

If Mary remembered correctly, Lord Uxbridge was the handsome officer who had criticised the duke for not giving them an assignment.

"I will take good care he does not run away with me," said Wellington with a laugh. "I do not care about anyone else." And then he turned to Mary and Mr. Withrow. "If it is not some of the most important people of the moment. I received your update."

"I think we should discuss it further," said the Prince of Orange, and something in his tone made Mary think he had discovered something more.

The Duke of Wellington gestured for them and a few of his officers to follow and entered a parlour, where he promptly asked everyone to leave. The fancy ladies and gentlemen did so without complaint, and Wellington himself closed one of the doors while the other officers secured the others.

"As recommended by Mr. Pike and Mr. Fothergill," said the prince, treating their fake identities as if they were real, "I assigned men to trail the officers in questions. A few minutes ago, they intercepted a letter that was meant to pass information across the border, to Napoleon Bonaparte himself."

The prince withdrew a letter from his pocket. It had once had a complicated seal, with a paper trap inside to reveal if it had been opened. Clearly the prince had no intention of resealing it and sending it.

The Duke of Wellington took the letter, read it, then passed it around the room.

It contained detailed information about the number of troops, officer promotions, and Wellington's plan to strike against France as soon as the Russian and the Austrian troops had prepared for their own two-pronged offensive from the other side. The details were such that Mary wondered if the Belgians had gathered all the information on their own, or if they had help from someone close to Wellington.

"Good work," said the duke. "I am glad this information did not fall into enemy hands. Is there a connection between them and the murder?"

"We have nothing conclusive supporting that conjecture," said Mr. Withrow, "though they should still be considered suspects."

"Very good, very good," said Wellington. "Keep investigating any leads on the murder case. It is of the utmost importance to unveil the truth."

"What do you plan to do about the spies?" asked the prince.

"Billy," said the Duke of Wellington, as if a father speaking to his son. Billy must be a nickname Prince Willem had earned while serving as Wellington's aide-de-camp in the Peninsula. "You must understand. Every single person in this city is a possible spy for Bonaparte. Many of those here in Bruxelles are French at heart. Every single person has friends or family on the other side of the border. Anyone you pass in the street could pass on information.

"Yet to me, this is not a matter of undue concern. Even if Bonaparte knows our plans, even if he knows the names of our officers, and the strength of our troops, it will not change the results of this upcoming conflict. Our numbers are superior, everyone in Europe stands with us, and we will crush Bonaparte before he quiets the opposition in his own country."

"I just feel—" said the Prince of Orange, but then he amended his sentence. "Yes, sir. I understand, sir."

"They are your officers, Your Highness. While I lead the Allied armies, you are still in charge of your own armies. You and your father may do with them as you please."

"Thank you, sir."

"Now I should return to the ball and visit with Commander Blücher," said the duke. "Where is my German translator?"

One of his officers rushed off to find the man in question, barely managing to leave before Wellington. The prince gestured for Mary and Mr. Withrow to stay, and Leon's former aide, Colonel Kitsell, also remained.

"You should have your officers investigated further," said Colonel Kitsell to the prince. The scars on Kitsell's chin were very pronounced in the candlelight. "Search their things. I am sure you will find a connection to Major General Leon."

"Do you know something which makes you think they are responsible for murder, instead of treason?" asked Prince

Willem. Though he was half Colonel Kitsell's age, he spoke with authority, like the prince he was.

"No, I simply—"

"I will not allow blame to be placed on my men without cause. I will keep an open mind, but I believe it is much more likely that a British officer is responsible. Now if you will excuse us, I would like to speak to Mr. Fothergill and Mr. Pike."

"Of course, Your Highness," said Colonel Kitsell with a bow.

Once he had left the room, shutting the door behind him, Prince Willem turned to them. "He has never liked me. I did pull a prank on him once, on the Peninsula. Interrupted him bathing. He yelled at me for close to an hour. But I was young—what can you expect?"

Mr. Withrow chuckled, but Mary did not. She had never pulled pranks on anyone and had never understood why people like her sister Lydia found pleasure in it.

"What do you know about Colonel Kitsell and his past?" asked Mary.

"He is one of the hardest working men in the army, with a distinguished career," said the prince. "Are you investigating him?"

"Perhaps," said Mr. Withrow.

The prince thought for a moment. "I heard an interesting story about his childhood. He was the bastard son of Mr. Kitsell, raised and educated far from the rest of the family. Shortly after the death of the elder Kitsells, Caroline Kitsell discovered a new will, leaving a portion of the inheritance to a brother she had never before met. Some questioned the matter, but Robert looks exactly like the rest of the family. He used part of his inheritance to purchase a commission as an officer. I think he has always felt he has something to prove, as he started later than most of his peers."

"I see," said Mary. It was an interesting story, yet it was not out of the ordinary for an illegitimate male son to receive a partial inheritance.

"Personally, I do not believe Colonel Kitsell is involved in the murder." The Prince of Orange gestured with the intercepted letter. "I do not believe the Belgian officers are either, however, I will ensure that they are never in a position to pass on information to the enemy again."

Mary swallowed. It felt as if something was stuck in her throat. What would he do to them—how would they be punished? But they had committed treason. Something must be done.

"Have you had any reports from Lady Trafford's spies in Paris?" asked the prince.

"No," said Mr. Withrow. "We have not heard from them yet, but we have only been here a week."

"Miss Tagore is most capable," said Mary. "She will send us word." She did not have the same confidence in Mr. Matthews, but only because she did not know him well.

Mary wondered what Miss Tagore was doing at this moment. How close was she to Bonaparte, and was she in danger?

"As the Duke of Wellington said at our first meeting, please keep me updated as well about anything you learn."

It almost seemed that the prince feared that Wellington would not keep him informed.

"Are your own spies still gathering information in France?" asked Mary.

"They are more my grandmother's spies than mine, but yes." He almost seemed to shiver, and he looked younger than he had when talking to Colonel Kitsell. "I think something will happen soon. There have been movements of troops, and one of my spies believes that Bonaparte may strike first. But Wellington's spies disagree. There is much evidence showing that Bonaparte is fully occupied by internal affairs."

"When you have only fragments of a tapestry, it is hard to make out the image," said Mr. Withrow.

"Yes, exactly," said Prince Willem.

Mary liked Mr. Withrow's turn of phrase so much that she fixed his statement in her memory. She would write it down later, when they returned to the house.

"If we hear anything, we will make sure you know of it, Your Highness," said Mary.

"Thank you both." Prince Willem smiled at her. "You are very talented at disguises."

"I had help," she said, glancing at Mr. Withrow. Unfortunately, he had not tied her cravat this evening. Instead, he had demonstrated on himself, and she had followed along, step by step. Then he had undone his own cravat and tied it in a different fashion.

"Would you do me the honour of dancing with me, the next time you are dressed as yourself at a ball?" asked the prince.

"Yes," she said, for that was what she had been trained by her mother to say anytime anyone asked for a dance. And then she added, "It would be an honour, Your Highness," for he was a prince, and, from everything she had seen, quite charming.

"Good luck with your investigations," said the prince. "Let me know if there is anything you need, anything at all."

Mary watched Prince Willem as he left the room.

Had she really just agreed to dance with a prince? How

very unusual. She supposed she should feel giddy or excited, but she was not a giddy person generally, and even a prince could not change that. But if the dance did indeed happen, it would certainly be a memorable event.

Mr. Withrow breathed out loudly.

"What is wrong, Mr. Withrow?"

"This case, the prince…it frustrates me."

"Do you not trust him?"

"I trust him to do what is best for himself and his new country. And because our country is giving his so much money and so many troops, he is, for now, our ally."

"Did I do the right thing in agreeing to dance with him?"

"That is for you to decide."

"But what is *your* opinion on the matter?"

He shrugged. "You cannot turn down a prince, unless you have a strong reason to do so. And his behaviour, as a prince…well, it is better than the behaviour of most of *our* princes."

Mr. Withrow still did not seem happy, but at least he did not disapprove of her behaviour. Not that she needed his approval—by no means did she require it—but she did value his thoughts and perspective.

They left the room and began seeking out Prussian officers who had any connection to art. Mr. Withrow kept becoming frustrated with the inadequacies of his German, yet he wanted to question people on his own, without a translator. He also seemed increasingly frustrated by Mary's presence; he alternated between occasionally translating a few words for her to not translating at all during a conversation and only afterwards giving a hasty summary in English.

The tenor of the ball felt different than others Mary had attended, and it was not just that there were multiple languages and a higher percentage of military officers. There was a heightened intensity, as if everyone present knew that the entire world watched them, for the outcomes of the coming months would shift the direction of history in one way or another.

Wellington, Blücher, the Prince of Orange, and the dozens of officers beneath them—these were the men who would make history, and Mary would witness it. Perhaps she would make an impact on history herself.

The Duke of Wellington was speaking with General Blücher, and suddenly Blücher made a very loud declaration in German, which caused the heads of nearly everyone in the room to turn in his direction. It seemed, as he said his statement, that Blücher was looking directly at her and Mr. Withrow.

"What did he say?" Mary asked Mr. Withrow.

"He wishes that our investigations into the murder would conclude quickly, so they can focus on the war."

General Blücher must already believe they were failing, despite working on this investigation for only a few days. Yet they were following every lead and had even exposed several traitors in the process. She had no reason to be ashamed of their efforts so far.

Still, she felt a weight on her chest that had nothing to do with the fabric wrapped tightly around it.

Withrow shook his head. "He is not going to help us any by complaining. But it would be best for us to ignore it."

"Agreed," said Mary.

Withrow pointed at a man who was speaking with Mrs. Graham. "I believe that is General Tippert. We need to find out why he is still in Brussels, when everyone else who has been transferred has already left."

General Tippert looked familiar to her, and she realised that she had seen him in Ostend on the day they had arrived in the Netherlands. He had stood by himself, and then handed something to an officer who boarded a boat back to England. She wondered if that had been before or after he had found out his services were not needed by Wellington.

"We can speak with him after we speak with the rest of the Prussians," said Mary.

"I meant that it might be useful for *you* to speak to him now."

"Then why did you say *we*?"

He shook his head exasperatedly.

"Never mind," said Mary. "I will do it." It was true that she was not much use in a conversation in German, and they could cover more ground if they split the tasks.

She walked off, in what she hoped was a masculine way. His request was a reasonable one, yet something seemed…broken between her and Mr. Withrow. Ever since she had kissed Captain Lemoine, Mr. Withrow had kept a greater distance between them. She had managed to set her own irritation with Mr. Withrow aside—why could he not do the same?

Because of Napoleon Bonaparte's invasion, Lady Trafford had never actually held the training on morality and ethics in spy work. She could justify kissing Captain Lemoine, especially in light of what she had learned, but even if she had not learned such valuable information, there had been a high enough chance of valuable information to make it worth it. Yet the fact that the behaviour was justified did not negate the real, continuing consequences in her normal life. It was as if you threw a stone down a hill in an attempt to hit a target, but could not stop your stone from hitting a number of other things before and after the target.

She wanted to fix things between her and Mr. Withrow, but she did not know how. And now he was speaking, in German with a smattering of French, to yet another Prussian officer.

As she walked towards General Tippert, she almost ran directly into her brother-in-law, Mr. Wickham.

"Pardon me," she said.

"Pardon," he said with a smile and a bow. "Are you one of the investigators?"

"Yes, I am Mr. Fothergill," said Mary, trying to lower her voice even a little lower than usual for her Mr. Fothergill disguise, which had the result of making it even scratchier.

"I am Captain Wickham. I heard that the death was quite the nasty business."

Mary nodded.

"It must be rather interesting," he said, and then looked at her expectantly.

It seemed that he wanted her to speak about the case, but Mary had no need or desire to provide him with details. "Do you know anything that could be of use to me in my investigation?"

"Unfortunately not," said Mr. Wickham. "Well, I might know something, if I knew who you were investigating."

His line of reasoning made her uncomfortable. "I cannot provide that, though if you know something of use, you should report it to me immediately."

Wickham was distracted by a woman walking past, and his eyes followed her in a very ungentlemanly way.

"I have heard you are married," said Mary. "Is your wife here?" She had seen no sign of Lydia at the ball.

"No, she despises all social gatherings," said Wickham.

"Now if you will excuse me, I have matters to attend to." Without waiting for a reply, he followed after the woman.

Mary almost stopped Wickham and confronted him as a liar. Lydia, despising all social gatherings? Even in her changed state, she still savoured company. Yet what would Mr. Fothergill know of the matter? Nothing, absolutely nothing. She would save this problem for another time and focus on the task at hand.

Mary approached General Tippert's position indirectly. She wanted to develop a sense for him and his personality before she spoke with him, so she stood nearby and listened to his conversation with Mrs. Graham. What she heard did not lead to a positive impression of his character.

"My dear Mrs. Graham," he said condescendingly, "your brother takes issue with the cost of the war. Yet there is a more vital question: what is the cost of *not* fighting? What is the cost of isolation, and not taking a stand? It was only through our assistance—our money, our troops, our vision—that the rest of Europe was able to rise from the tyranny and oppression wrought by Bonaparte. If we had not interfered, if we had not taken the necessary precautions and been consistent in our actions, we ourselves would have been overrun, we ourselves would have lost our country and our freedoms. I am sure you have not read your brother's tracts, but if you did, I assure you that you would see the flaws in his arguments and come to a proper view of things."

"I *have* read my brother's pronouncements on the legality and the purpose of this war, and I understand—"

"War has been an economic boon for our nation, and it has unified us like nothing else. Now I am not proposing that we continue to engage in conflicts, simply to assist the economy. Yet we should be willing to proffer our resources, and even our men's lives, should the circumstances demand it."

"I do not fully agree with my brother's views," said Mrs. Graham, her voice more raised than Mary had ever heard it, "however, you misrepresent them. My brother's point is that after the Duke of Wellington heard of Bonaparte's escape from Elba, he did not even attempt to contact Parliament before signing a proclamation that in essence was a declaration of war for all of Europe. My brother's concern is how many lives will be lost because of a single piece of paper, and—"

General Tippert interrupted her again and went into a long monologue on the virtues and necessities of war, which was coupled with a diatribe against those members of Parliament—including Mrs. Graham's brother—who opposed it. Mrs. Graham's jaw was clenched tight, and her right hand gripped her reticule as if doing so was the only way to prevent herself from shouting at the general. She did not seem to have difficulty discussing politics, but rather, she seemed to find it difficult to discuss them with someone who believed he knew everything while she knew nothing.

If Mary was dressed as herself, she would simply join the conversation, Mrs. Graham would provide the standard introductions, and then she would find a way to extract Mrs. Graham from General Tippert's presence. Friends, after all, did not allow their friends to suffer from the affliction of having a man explain something that they already knew, often with more accuracy and greater detail.

Yet she was not dressed as Mary Bennet. Of course, even dressed as an investigator, she could interrupt. She was assigned to a murder investigation, after all, and would be justified in speaking to anyone without an introduction. Yet she thought General Tippert might be more amenable to discussion if she garnered a proper introduction. She found Colonel Kitsell and asked him to introduce her to Tippert.

"General Tippert," said Colonel Kitsell, bowing. "Mrs. Graham. This is Mr. Fothergill, one of the two civilian investigators that the Duke of Wellington has assigned to the murder."

"Mr. Fothergill, a pleasure." General Tippert shook Mary's hand with such strength that it felt like the bones in her hand were being squeezed together.

"I have a few matters I must speak to you about, General Tippert," said Mary. It came out a little deeper and more gruffly than she had intended, but it sufficed.

"I should leave you two to your conversation," said Mrs. Graham.

"I apologise, Mrs. Graham," said General Tippert. "I hate to cut our discussion short."

"It is no trouble at all," said Mrs. Graham. "I completely understand, and I am quite parched, so I will excuse myself to find a drink."

The farewells somehow extended for a full additional minute, and Mrs. Graham looked quite relieved when she finally managed to escape from General Tippert's presence. She practically flew across the room. Colonel Kitsell followed Mrs. Graham, leaving Mary alone with Tippert.

Before Mary had a chance to say anything, General Tippert began.

"First, I suspect that you will want to know my relationship with Major General Leon."

"Yes, in fact, that would be—"

"I did not know him well," he said. "Throughout the last few years of Napoleonic conflict, he was stationed in the

Peninsula, in Spain and Portugal, while I was in Eastern Europe, near Russia. We had gotten to know each other a little, on the rare occasions our paths crossed. He was a congenial man, and I felt comfortable with him."

"What did—" began Mary.

"Major General Leon was, of course, the man who delivered the news to me of my reassignment, but he was simply the messenger. It was the Duke of Wellington's decision, and I respect it. If I had a deadline such as this, as Wellington does, I would do the same. There is no time for us to learn the styles of each other or how he can best utilize my skills. Also, Wellington does not give his generals as much…independence as I am used to. He likes to run out on the battlefield and lead small groups of troops himself. His approach would likely clash with my own on the battlefield."

Mary did not like the fact that Tippert had taken control of the conversation—he held the reins of the horse; he determined their direction. Mary did not know how to wrest control from him, or if doing so would even be wise.

"You will ask, next, where I was on the evening of the murder." He waited for Mary to nod. "I do not know when Leon was killed—I am not privy to that information—but I dined with my family and a few guests in my house, from seven thirty in the evening until a little past midnight. Then I retired to my rooms. You are welcome to question my servants, guests, my wife, and my children."

"Thank you," said Mary. "That is very helpful." Of course, Tippert gave details so willingly that he could easily hide something beneath them.

From the corner of her eye, she noticed Mr. Withrow dancing with a Prussian woman, large jewels hanging from her neck and arms. Likely, she knew something about art, but despite that, Mary felt—no, not jealousy. She did not feel possessive of him, nor did she feel that other women should not benefit from the positive results of his company. So it was not jealousy she felt, but rather, longing. She wished she could dance in his arms. Clearly that could not happen tonight, as she was dressed as a man, but perhaps sometime in the future, sometime soon. She had never danced with Mr. Withrow before.

"Any other questions?" said General Tippert.

Mary swallowed and tried to focus. She would not let Tippert intimidate or control her. She would ask questions which would open up the truth, petal by petal. She searched his face, and then she remembered what made him different than the other men who had been transferred by Wellington.

"Why are you still here, in Brussels?" asked Mary. "Everyone else who was transferred has left already."

"That is a very good question." He gave her a calculating smile. "Fortunately, it is an easy one." His eyes turned to the dancers, and after a moment, he pointed. "See that young lady, in blue? That is my daughter. She is soon to be engaged, perhaps even tonight. I could not leave when my daughter and my wife were so close to securing victory."

He treated love as if it were a battle to be won. Of course, so did many others, even if they did not overtly state the parallel.

There was a ringing, a loud ringing, and everyone turned to the sound. Even the dancers stopped in their places, and the orchestra stopped like a flower wilting in the sun. A Prussian officer was hitting a wine goblet with a metal spoon.

"*Aufmerksamkeit bitte, aufmerksamkeit bitte,*" he said.

A sense of foreboding struck Mary. This was not one of the officers that either she or Withrow had talked to, but she had seen him throughout the evening, lingering near General Blücher and watching the Duke of Wellington. She should have paid him more attention, but everyone was drawn to those two great men.

"Ich muss etwas sagen. Ich bin für den Mord des englischen Generalmajors verantwortlich." There was a gasp from about half the room—likely from all the German speakers. Mary's eyes locked with Withrow's across the room, and she could see his shock.

The Prussian soldier hit his spoon against the goblet again, and then in broken, slurred English he said, "I did it. I killed zee English major general."

Chapter Ten

"The army of...Blucher has been lately again reinforced by a corps of 10,000 men...and it makes now the finest body of men that Prussia ever had under arms."

—*The Star*, London, June 9, 1815

MARY'S EYES DARTED around the room, taking in the tableau of shocked faces, the entire company frozen by the revelation. This man, this Prussian officer who they had never spoken to, never suspected, had killed Major General Leon. How neat, how quick, how simple this resolution, after such an initial tangle.

General Blücher gestured. Immediately, two other Prussian officers sprang forward and seized the man. He went with them willingly.

General Blücher spoke with a voice clearly accustomed to command. *"Bitte machen Sie weiter, machen Sie mit dem Tanz weiter."*

Then the Prince of Orange spoke, his voice much younger, and not as commanding, but still sure. "General Blücher asks that we all carry on and continue the dance. *S'il vous plait continue, continue la danse,*" he said in French. And then the prince switched to what must be Dutch. *"Ga voort, ga voort met dansen als het u belieft."*

"It would appear that you have no further need to interview me," said General Tippert.

"It would appear that way," agreed Mary. "Thank you for your time."

The musicians began the music anew, and the dancers returned to their formation. Mary made her way across the room, towards the hallway where they had led the Prussian officer. Mr. Withrow reached it at the same time and gestured for her to go first. Yet when they attempted to join Wellington, Blücher, Prince Willem, and the guilty Prussian officer, they were asked to wait, in a small room, until they were needed.

Mr. Withrow crossed his arms.

"You would think *we* were the ones who had committed the crime, and now they have shut us up," said Mary.

Mr. Withrow did not respond.

"Are you still angry with me?"

"What makes you think I am angry with you, or have been angry with you?"

"You have been cold and taciturn and generally opposed to conversing with me both yesterday and today. Thus, it is logical for me to conclude that you are still angry with me about"—she almost said *the kiss* but then stopped herself just in time—"our investigations at the inn."

"I apologise for my behaviour. I admit, I was unjustifiably irritated with you, but I should not have allowed that to impact my behaviour."

"Your apology is accepted," said Mary. She looked to the door and sighed. Apparently, now that the murderer had confessed, those with real power had no need of her and Withrow's assistance.

They sat for several minutes in silence, until Mary began to fear that Mr. Withrow's second apology would do nothing to mend the discomfort between them. Yet though she wracked her mind for possibilities, she did not know how to mend this any better than she knew how to mend a rip on a fashionable dress. Finally, she blurted out the first thing that came to mind.

"Can we argue?"

"What?" said Mr. Withrow.

"Would you be willing to argue with me?" said Mary. "A good discussion would be an agreeable way to pass the time."

"That would be...fine. What would you like to argue about?"

"Anything," said Mary. "I will take the contrary position."

"Anything?" He gave a sly smile. Something about it made her heart beat more rapidly in her chest. Could he really disarm her with just a smile?

"Am I right in assuming you will put me at a disadvantage?"

"It improves the sport if I do."

"Very well."

Mr. Withrow thought for a moment. "I have been reading a translation of *The Art of War* by Sun Tzu. He makes the argument—and I will take his argument as my own—that there is no benefit to prolonged warfare."

"I have not read *The Art of War*," said Mary. "What are the primary reasons for your claim on avoiding prolonged warfare?"

"A slow victory drains the ardour of the troops, as well as the resources necessary for war, including money, food, horses, and weapons. This also allows time for the enemy to rally their forces and target your weaknesses. Thus, the fighting should be carried out, from start to finish, as quickly as possible."

"Yet surely undue haste could be just as problematic," said Mary, her mind racing for counterarguments. "An unprepared army, not properly trained, supplied, or positioned, risks taking great losses which could be avoided if one were not trying to rush towards victory."

"On that I would agree," said Mr. Withrow. "But as long as one avoids undue haste and can adequately prepare, a swift fight will always be advantageous over a protracted venture."

"Perhaps we should take into consideration the circumstances and goals of the conflict," said Mary, "for this could make a swift campaign unwise."

He leaned closer to her. "For instance?"

"Well," she said, warming to her subject, "if your own forces are much weaker or smaller in number than the enemy's, then there may be no path to a swift victory—swiftness may lead only to a swift defeat."

"Perhaps one should avoid the conflict entirely then," said Mr. Withrow.

"Yet it is not always possible to avoid. For example, in our current—"

The door to the room was pushed open by the Prince of Orange. "Am I interrupting anything?"

"Just an argument," said Mary, at the exact same moment that Mr. Withrow said, "Not at all."

"We are ready for you," said the prince. "The confession was witnessed by the Duke of Wellington, General Blücher, and myself, as well as a number of our staff members. Now we would like you to interview him in order for you to create a full accounting of the events that led to the murder of Major General Leon."

"Understood," said Mr. Withrow. "Will anyone else be in attendance?"

"We have a German translator, several officers who will serve as guards, and secretaries to take notes of the proceedings in both English and German."

"Thank you, Prince Willem," said Mary.

"No, thank you," said the prince. "Your work has been invaluable in bringing this to a conclusion."

The thanks the prince offered was unearned: while they had discovered several spies, they had not done anything that had led to this confession, besides, perhaps, stirring the pot until the murderer felt a need to confess.

They followed the prince down the hallway and into another room that appeared to be a small library. Several people stood near the side of the room—clearly the secretaries and the translator that Prince Willem had mentioned—as well as four guards, but all the attention of the room focused on the Prussian murderer.

The man's feet had been chained to each other, and to the chair, and his hands had been chained together. Yet despite the chains, he looked quite comfortable, even relaxed. He gave them a devilish smile, the kind that her sister Lydia had always found particularly appealing, but which always made Mary a little nervous. Out of habit, she attempted to twist her skirts in her fingers, but then she realised she was still wearing pants, so she placed her hands in her pockets. Convenient things, men's pockets.

Why *was* the man smiling? It did not make sense, unless the murderer wanted to be intentionally unnerving. Of course, Mary had never known someone to confess to a murder in this manner, under no pressure or duress. Most individuals tried to hide their guilt, but this man had no fear of punishment, though the penalty for murder was generally death. Of course, maybe drink has loosened his inhibitions and stripped away any self-preservation.

Mr. Withrow and Mary sat down in chairs facing the murderer.

A woman in a sedate dark dress approached. "I am Mrs. Barz," she said with a trace of a German accent. "I will be translating for you today."

"Thank you," said Mary, and shook her hand.

Mrs. Barz stood near them.

"Shall we begin?" asked Mr. Withrow, turning to the secretaries. They both nodded.

"What is your full name and your rank?" asked Mr. Withrow, and Mrs. Barz translated his words to German.

"Uwe Schmidt." He was a colonel in Blücher's army.

"Tell us about what happened," said Mary.

Though she did not speak a word of German, Mary watched Mr. Schmidt carefully as he spoke. His eyes wandered a little, and when he looked directly at the light, he paused and blinked. His cadence made it clear that he had drunk more than was polite for a ball.

At the end of each sentence, Mrs. Barz translated his words. If Mrs. Barz was providing an accurate translation, Mr. Schmidt's description was anything but extensive. "I was at a public house with some friends, and the Englishman was there. He was full of himself, and we got in an argument. The patroness asked us to take our words outside. We did, and the Englishman said something insulting, and I shot him twice and threw his body in the canal."

"What was the name of the public house?" asked Mary, and Mrs. Barz repeated her words in German.

Schmidt shook his head. *"Ich erinnere mich nicht. Ich habe getrunken."*

"I do not remember," said Mrs. Barz. "I was drinking."

"How much English do you speak?" asked Mr. Withrow.

Schmidt seemed to recognize at least some of Withrow's words but did not respond until Mrs. Barz translated.

"Nur sehr wenig."

"Only a very little."

"But you had an argument with him?" asked Mr. Withrow, and then Mrs. Barz.

"Es gibt zwei universelle Sprachen: Zorn und Hass," said Schmidt, with a certain firmness that made Mary think he had said this statement many times before, probably even when he had not been drinking.

Mrs. Barz cleared her throat. "There are two universal languages. Anger and hate."

It was a pessimistic view of reality. Music had oft been said to be the universal language, and there was something hopeful and beautiful about considering an art to be the element which would transcend all borders and boundaries, physical and ideological and linguistic. Yet anger and hate, as well as accompanying motivators like misunderstanding, fear, and greed were also shared by all humans.

"Where in the canal did you put the body?" asked Mary.

He paused before speaking. Once he did, Mrs. Barz translated.

"One of the basins."

He did not mention the bridge.

"Was that your first time meeting Leon, or had you met him before?" asked Mary.

Schmidt hesitated again after the translation, but then said, *"Es war unser erstes Treffen."*

"It was our first meeting."

Mary had wondered, perhaps, if Schmidt might have been the Prussian interested in art, but if so, it would be logical to explain the connection. His pauses made it clear that he had something to hide. But why hide things if you were willingly confessing to a murder?

There was a noise from outside, or maybe the direction of the ballroom, like someone had knocked over a table.

"Who were those with you at the public house?" asked Mr. Withrow. "What were their names?" It was a good question. She and Mr. Withrow's approach seemed aligned—their questions complemented each other's and kept a logical progression. She was glad they had argued, as it seemed to have brought them back into alignment.

There was another noise from outside the room. Had someone knocked over a second table?

After Mr. Withrow's question was translated, Schmidt thought for a moment, then shook his head. *"Ich erinnere mich nicht."*

"I do not remember."

"Are you sure you cannot remember the public house?" asked Mary.

Mrs. Barz paused a little before translating his response. "He says, 'I don't remember. Those stupid French names. Impossible to keep track of.'"

Mr. Withrow nodded. That is what he had understood from Schmidt's statement as well.

"What street was it on? What part of the city?" she asked.

Once again, he did not remember.

Mary scratched her neck, careful not to scratch too high or she might dislodge the wig. While one should not dislike a confession, she disliked Schmidt's. No motive besides hate, no memory of the public house, the area of the city, or those he was with. Yes, he claimed to have been drunk at the time…but if she did not know better, she would think he had not committed the crime.

She turned to Mr. Withrow, and she did not need to say anything, for she could see that he felt the same concerns as she did. She turned back to Mr. Schmidt.

"I want you to describe to me exactly how you killed Major General Leon, and what you did with the weapon."

Mrs. Barz translated her statement, and then translated the response. This time, Schmidt did not hesitate.

"We were yelling, and we were outside. The English officer hit me in the face. I withdrew my pistol and shot him. I reloaded the pistol and shot him a second time. We were close to the canal, and I dragged his body to it. And then I threw my gun into the canal."

This was a more detailed response. However, everyone by now must know the basic details of Leon's murder, that he had been shot twice and found in the water.

"Why have you confessed?" asked Mr. Withrow.

"Es ist das Richtige und ich wollte Papa Blücher glücklich machen."

"It is the correct thing to do," said Mrs. Barz, "and I wanted to make General Blücher happy."

"He did not say the word general," said Mr. Withrow.

"You are right," said Mrs. Barz. "He called him Papa Blücher—Father Blücher. Many of the soldiers and the officers refer to our general in that manner."

"I see," said Mr. Withrow, and he stood. "We need to converse privately, but we will return momentarily."

Mary followed him into the hallway.

"I am not satisfied with the confession," said Mr. Withrow.

"I do not think he committed the murder," said Mary. "But why confess to a crime that was not your own?"

"Perhaps if we draw out more details from him, he will contradict his own testimony."

"Or we might discover the real motive for his confession," said Mary. "Perhaps he is protecting someone."

But they did not have a chance to return to the interrogation room, for at that moment, a British officer came running down the hall. Mary feared, suddenly, that the noises she had heard had not been furniture.

"Come quickly!" he shouted. "The duke needs you. Another officer has been killed."

Chapter Eleven

"There are sufficiently strong symptoms of a [French political] party against Bonaparte. His titles are sneered at, and liberty and equality are called for, even before his House of Representatives has constituted itself."

—*The Courier*, London, June 9, 1815

EVEN FROM A distance, it was clear that the dead officer was not British.

The man, who wore a French uniform, lay crumpled on the ground in the garden, right next to the house. Mary found it difficult to see the deceased gentleman properly, surrounded as he was by the Duke of Wellington, Prince Willem, General Blücher, half their staffs, a mixture of officers from their respective armies, as well as ladies young and old, a young child, and a small yapping dog.

Mr. Withrow shoved through the crowd, and Mary tried to stay close behind while not stepping on any ball gowns. She noted that the house had no windows in this section, though there were several about twenty feet ahead on the path. Even if someone had stood at one of the windows and looked in this particular direction, with the darkness of the evening and the bright lights inside, visibility would have been poor. Unless someone besides the murderer and the victim had been in the garden, it was unlikely that anyone had witnessed the event.

Several elbows jostled Mary, but she pushed forward. It was difficult to believe that a few moments before, these individuals had danced and talked to the sound of violins and flutes. There was no music anymore, only raised voices and concerned chaperones and a child—a British girl about the age of six—who seemed a little too interested in the dead body.

The dead man must have heard the earlier frivolity as he had been shot. Had his ears been filled with the lilting laughter of the ballroom as he fell to the ground?

"We are here," said Mr. Withrow, when they finally reached the front of the throng.

"Thank God," said the duke. "Go ahead, take a look."

Mary swallowed and stepped forward to the body. Her stomach did not particularly like this aspect of her occupation, and she felt a little dizzy, but it was a touch easier, this time, to look upon a horrific death, in part because she had expected it, but also because she was gaining the skill of seeing a person without truly allowing herself to see a person, for if she allowed herself to truly see an individual with hopes and dreams, it would be too tragic to bear.

They crouched down next to the form. While his face masked his emotions, Mr. Withrow seemed a little hesitant in his movements.

"Are you all right?" asked Mary, keeping her voice low and gravelly. She was, after all, still dressed as a man.

"Yes, I just—this entire affair troubles me."

Mary nodded. It was troubling—a second murder in a matter of days.

The victim had been shot twice. His head was…no longer quite a head. Blood ran from it and into a clump of yellow, orange, and white flowers. These flowers were common to Brussels and normally had a robust, hopeful look to them, but now were crumpled and covered with not only blood but pieces of matter, perhaps part of the man's brain. Blood also seeped from the man's side. The location of that bullet wound, if she were correct in her understanding of anatomy, was not far below his heart.

Two injuries, made by two bullets, in almost the exact same locations as the injuries on Leon's body. Like the uniforms of Lemoine, Serrurier, and Voland, his uniform had tassels, marking that he was now fighting for Prince Willem and the new United Netherlands.

Mr. Withrow took a handkerchief and wiped blood off what remained of the slain officer's face.

The face was one Mary recognized. She generally had a knack for remembering faces, so while she had never met this man, she knew that he had been present at the Hôtel de Ville. He had stood apart, seemingly uninterested in the conflict between his fellow Belgian officers and the British officers. He had also been at the ball, dancing with a woman she believed was Prussian.

"What was his name?" she asked those standing nearby, and then, in French, *"Qui était-il?"*

"Colonel Ouvrard," said one of Prince Willem's men.

"Merci," she said.

"Was he at the ball?" asked Mr. Withrow.

"Yes," said Mary. "He was alive before Schmidt confessed. He stood in the crowd, staring as Schmidt was taken away."

They had already suspected that Schmidt was not the murderer, and while it was still theoretically possible for him to have murdered Leon, he had certainly not murdered Ouvrard. He had been in custody from the moment he had declared his guilt, wearing chains and surrounded by watching eyes.

"We should check his pockets, as we did for Leon," said Mr. Withrow.

"Good idea," said Mary. It was disturbing to rummage through his pockets, with his body cooling yet still warm, and discomfiting to do so with so many people looking on. It was even possible that the murderer could be among the crowd.

All of the expected items that might be in an officer's pockets were still there. He even had a pistol strapped around his waist. Why had he not fired it? There had been time between the first gunshot and the second: why had he not defended himself and fought back against his attacker?

The Prince of Orange sent one of his men to collect the items. Mary was unsure of what they should do next—surely there was more they should do—but Mary found it difficult to think sequentially with such noise and attention on them.

For a moment, Mr. Withrow seemed to experience a similar indecisiveness, but then he said, "We should learn about Ouvrard from the other officers. They are all present, after all."

They asked Prince Willem who they should speak to, and he gathered a handful of his officers. "Everyone here speaks French," he said, and then he himself switched to French to provide introductions.

The prince remained part of the conversation, interjecting occasionally and guiding the conversation in a manner which surely was meant to be helpful, but also meant that Mr. Withrow and Mary kept needing to bring the conversation back to certain points so they could obtain the information they needed.

They learned that the dead officer's full name was Henri

Frances Ouvrard. He was twenty-eight years old, a native of Brussels, and in addition to French spoke Dutch. He had risen through the ranks in Napoleon Bonaparte's army, serving under him from 1807 until Napoleon Bonaparte's defeat in 1814. From 1808 to 1814, Ouvrard had been stationed in the Iberian Peninsula. Every single one of the officers they spoke to had first met Ouvrard during his Napoleonic service; every single one of these Belgian and Dutch officers had served under Bonaparte. And now they prepared to fight against their former emperor. Hopefully, unlike officers Lemoine and Serrurier and Voland, these men's loyalties were to their prince and their new country.

It would be useful to question each of them individually, to see what could be learned when it was an individual conversation rather than a group discussion moderated by the Prince of Orange.

Suddenly, the crowd surged forward, people at the back attempting to reach the body and everyone else caught up as if in a wave. The little girl screamed, and Mrs. Graham looked as if she might be crushed.

"Stand back, stand back!" yelled Mr. Withrow, and the prince started shouting in all of his languages, but they did not heed them.

Mary positioned herself in front of the body—if the crowd continued to push in such a manner, then the body and all the evidence could be trampled. As those near the front pressed closer and closer, she regretted her positioning. She had read, once, of individuals being crushed or trampled to death, and while Ouvrard was already dead, she was not dead, and she preferred to keep it that way.

"Halten!" bellowed General Blücher, with such force that the entire crowd froze in their places.

"We will have order," said the Duke of Wellington, now that the crowd had quieted. "Everyone that is not in conversation with us, please, go back to the ballroom or depart in your carriages."

Prince Willem repeated the words in German, Dutch, and French, and the crowd melted away, funnelling like water back into the ballroom. One of the officers tried to shepherd Lord Uxbridge to the ballroom, but he said, quietly but sternly, "My place is here."

Mary realised that her hands and arms were trembling, and though the risk to self was gone, her breath felt laboured and short.

"I do not understand the public fascination with viewing the dead," said Mr. Withrow to her.

"Nor do I," said Mary. "And if they insist upon it, it would be better if they did it in an orderly manner, perhaps by age or rank."

Mr. Withrow smiled, but he did not seem to be laughing at her.

"Quite right. Shall we get back to our work?"

"That is a good proposal," said Mary.

The officers with whom they had been conversing had remained, so they began anew their conversation, though this time, it was without the Prince of Orange, for he was speaking with a pair of very official-looking messengers.

"Did Colonel Ouvrard know Major General Leon?" asked Mary, for this seemed to be the most pressing question. They needed to discover what, if anything, the two victims had in common, for that knowledge might help them find the true murderer.

The officers seemed puzzled by that question.

After a minute, one said, *"They were at the same events sev-*

eral times, but I never saw them converse together."

"I do not think Ouvrard ever mentioned Leon. It is hard to be certain—perhaps we could check Ouvrard's papers."

One of the other officers had opened his mouth to speak when Prince Willem interrupted them. "I have an urgent matter to discuss, Mr. Pike and Mr. Fothergill. *The rest of you, please, go and enjoy the ball. I will contact you if I have further questions concerning Ouvrard and his death.*"

It was strange for him to dismiss the officers during the middle of a conversation. Why could they not stay to answer additional questions after Mary and Mr. Withrow discussed the urgent matter with the prince?

The prince led them to the Duke of Wellington and General Blücher.

"Clearly, Schmidt did not murder Colonel Ouvrard," said Mr. Withrow, "and we have strong doubts about his connection to Leon's death—he had no real motives and could give only sparse details."

"I am sure you are right," said Wellington. "We got caught up in what would have been a very convenient solution."

Prince Willem nodded. "That is an important conclusion, but not the reason I needed to speak with all of you. I apologise for any trouble this may cause, but I sent a messenger to my father, as was only proper, and the messenger has brought me a reply."

At this, he frowned.

"What did he say?" asked the duke.

Not quite looking at anyone, Prince Willem said, "The king has decided that as the murder victim was one of our officers, it is not appropriate for British individuals to investigate the murder."

Mary squinted at him. Had he really said they were being removed from the case? She glanced at Mr. Withrow, whose eyebrows were drawn together.

The prince held out a paper towards the Duke of Wellington.

Wellington glanced at the words but did not take the paper.

"Of course," said the duke. "That is to be expected. Why, I would not expect your men to investigate the murder of one of my own people in London—that would be preposterous. This is perfectly in the right. I apologise for overstepping my bounds by inviting Mr. Fothergill and Mr. Pike to view the body. I hope you do not hold it against them."

"Of course not," said Prince Willem, "and I know this must frustrate you—"

"No, Billy, not at all," said Wellington. "Please, go ahead with your investigation."

"Thank you," said the prince, and he gave a short bow to Wellington and Blücher.

Wellington and Blücher both gave deeper bows in return.

"Prince Willem," said Mary. Even though it was not her place to give advice to a prince on an investigation that was no longer her own, she could not help herself. It was difficult, after all, to relinquish a fitting line of inquiry. "It may be useful if your investigators inquire into whether Ouvrard and Leon knew each other or had any communication."

"Of course."

"If your investigators discover anything during that inquiry, or if they learn of anyone who might have been upset or angry or had any prior disagreements with Ouvrard, we would appreciate you giving us word," said Mr. Withrow. "We have no intention of going against the word of you or your father, but such knowledge may help us in our own investigation into the death of Major General Leon."

"I will update you as often as possible," said the prince. "I hope you will share any of your discoveries with my investigators as well."

Several men stepped forward, Dutch and Belgian officers that Mary could only assume were tasked with the case. The prince began to converse with them, giving them rapid directions in both French and Dutch.

"We had best be on our way," said Wellington, and they followed him away from the scene of the crime. He and Blücher stopped about thirty feet away, and Wellington looked back, peering towards the lights illuminating the body.

"Politik," said General Blücher softly, and his translator unnecessarily provided the English cognate: "Politics."

"Well, that is damn inconvenient," said Wellington. "Apologies for the language," he said, glancing at Mary. Even though she was dressed as a man, he did not fully treat her like one—she suspected he would not apologise to a man for swearing. Not that she wanted to hear that sort of language. But it did not offend her as much as she might have supposed it would.

"May we speak to you for a moment more?" asked Mr. Withrow.

"Of course."

"Even prior to this incident," said Mr. Withrow quietly, "we suspected that Schmidt did not murder Leon. I fear that he is protecting someone."

"Can we speak to Schmidt again?" asked Mary.

"Of course," said the Duke of Wellington. "That, at least, is still in our jurisdiction, and General Blücher has no objections to us continuing our investigation." He leaned in and lowered his voice. "Despite what has been said, I do need you to investigate this murder as well. However, you will need to go about it in a more discreet manner, rather than in your role as official investigators."

The Duke of Wellington would have them directly defy the orders of a king. Wellington truly considered himself, as head of the British forces and commander of the Allied armies, as having more authority than the King of the Netherlands. True, the king had only been king for a short time, and British influence had been a contributing factor in making the appointment possible, but he was still a king. Of course, Mary's loyalty was not to a foreign king, but to her own country and her own leaders, including the Duke of Wellington. And the murders were clearly connected; not investigating the second would only hamper their investigation of the first.

"We understand," said Mary. "We will do as you request."

"Excellent," said the Duke of Wellington. "You are dismissed."

Together, Mary and Mr. Withrow walked back into the house. Somehow, the ball appeared almost as it had been before, people dancing and conversing, though there was an undertone of unease, and lines of worry on some people's faces.

They made their way down the hallway and towards the doorway, behind which sat the Prussian. As they walked, Mr. Withrow seemed to slow.

Mary turned to him, and he looked as if he had something sour or distasteful within his mouth.

"What is wrong?" she asked.

"I keep trying to convince myself that people possess some

level of inherent goodness. But then things keep proving to me that *everyone* is horrible."

It reminded her of a conversation they had had long ago, when Mr. Withrow had said that all actions were motivated by money—both actions positive and negative. The more time that she spent as a spy, the more she could understand this cynical perspective, yet she refused to entirely believe it.

"I believe that everyone has the capacity to be horrible, and that everyone makes choices that are horrible at one point or another. We must only hope that our own are not too large or damaging to others. However, I refuse to believe that these negative traits are the essence of what it is to be human."

He looked at her intently, and she decided that she would not mind terribly if he looked at her more often. But that was not the matter at hand.

"Besides, you have fallen into the fallacy of making an absolute statement, which is almost impossible to defend. I would say that it *is* impossible, but then I would make the same error."

"You are right," he said. "Not everyone is horrible. You are one of the few people that I know who is not horrible at all."

She was not sure what to make of this statement; was it a compliment for him to say that, unlike the rest of humanity, she was not horrible? But before she had time to truly consider his words, let alone formulate a response, he pushed open the door to their interrogation room.

"Another officer was killed," Mr. Withrow announced, to the shock of the secretaries and the guards. "We know, for a fact, that you did not commit the crime, as it occurred while we were in this room together."

The translator stepped forward, and, after a large breath

of air, translated Mr. Withrow's words to German.

"Your story is lacking," said Mr. Withrow. "You are unwilling to commit to any details about the murder, and in fact you are wrong about a number of details." He paused dramatically after each sentence to allow Mrs. Barz time to translate, and, Mary thought, to intimidate the officer. "You have no motive and could not have killed the second officer."

There was a sheen of sweat on Schmidt's forehead.

"Did you do it?" asked Mary. "Did you, in fact, kill Leon?"

Mrs. Barz translated her question.

Schmidt was very still for a moment. He looked back and forth between them, then to the translator, then to the transcribers, and then to the soldiers with their guns.

"Nein, ich habe es nicht gemacht."

"No, I did not do it," said Mrs. Barz.

"If you did not kill him, then why on earth did you admit to it?" asked Mr. Withrow.

Mrs. Barz translated the question without raising her voice as Mr. Withrow had.

Schmidt provided a rather lengthy and emotional response in German, which Mrs. Barz translated to English, once again without the same level of emotion. "Papa Blücher was upset. Papa Blücher was worried that this was distracting from the war, so I wanted to end the distraction to make him happy. I only did it to solve a problem, not to create more."

Mr. Withrow shook his head, and Mary sighed. What a ridiculous plan. It had brought them no closer to the truth, and now they had two murders to solve.

Chapter Twelve

"Widow Welch's Pills, For Female Complaints. Widow Welch's Pills are particularly serviceable to all females, from the age of 14 or 16 years of age and upwards. Their celebrity [is] as a Tonic...for removing all obstructions in the Female system, [and] curing what is vulgarly called the Green Sickness."

—*The York Herald*, York, England, June 10, 1815

AFTER TWO HOURS and twenty-three minutes visiting British women in Brussels, Mary determined that social calls on mere acquaintances were the most respectable form of torture ever formulated. In theory, visiting so many seemingly important women should have helped her acquire knowledge of import on the two murders, but mostly she had gained a headache and lost her patience.

Mary would rather have donned the itchy moustache and smelly wig and spent the morning with Mr. Withrow, consulting with the Belgian detective, Monsieur Jacobs, but Lady Trafford had insisted that, in light of the second murder, it would be best to separate so they could cover more ground. Lady Trafford herself was meeting with the Belgian woman mentioned by the Prince of Orange's grandmother, which left Mary to sift through troughs of gossip in the hopes of finding something—anything—meaningful. Yet how could one discern, with certainty, which of endless details and facts were relevant? So often, relevance was only discerned in retrospect.

Mary looked at her list. She had only two women left to visit, Miss Oldfield and Mrs. Graham. She rode to the home of the Oldfields, but they were out, so she instructed her driver, Mr. Parker, to take her outside of Brussels in order to call upon Mrs. Graham at the Capels. Yet as they were leaving the city, they were hailed by a carriage going the opposite direction.

Both carriages stopped, and from the other carriage stepped Mrs. Graham.

"My dear Mary, I thought it was you!" exclaimed Mrs. Graham. "What is your destination? Did you find something to visit in the beautiful Belgian countryside?"

"No," said Mary. "I had planned to call upon you."

"You were going to call upon me?" asked Mrs. Graham, rather too surprised for the situation.

"Of course," said Mary. "Why would I not? But since you are clearly not home, I will call upon you another day."

"Or you could join me on my errands," said Mrs. Graham. "I need to stop for a new pair of gloves, but it is not far from a very good bookseller, and I know finding a bookseller was one of your goals for this trip."

Mary had forgotten that she had told Mrs. Graham. She had a very good memory. "Thank you," said Mary. "I would love to join you."

Mary joined Mrs. Graham in her carriage, and they made their way to the glove shop.

"I met your Mr. Withrow the other day," said Mrs. Graham.

"He is not *my* Mr. Withrow, and you should stop using

inaccurate pronouns when describing the men of my acquaintance."

Mrs. Graham laughed. "But I do enjoy tormenting you. Mr. Withrow said that you have stayed with him and Lady Trafford *several times* at their castle in Sussex."

"Yes," said Mary, for she would not deny a fact.

"Between your time at the castle and here, surely there have been moments when the two of you have been together…unsupervised."

Immediately, she recalled Mr. Withrow coming to her bedroom, in the middle of the night, to wake her. She felt an instant flash of heat to her cheeks.

"Please, do not assume that—"

"Do not worry, my dear Mary. One, while I like gossip, I have absolutely no reason to ruin your reputation. And two, I cannot believe that you would do anything untoward. But making you blush does bring me great pleasure."

"I—" began Mary, but she did not know what to say.

"I think you and Mr. Withrow would make a fine match."

"He does not have any feelings for me."

"Do not be so sure," said Mrs. Graham. "I would like you to know that I have amended my previous recommendation. Before, I insisted that you not marry for love, as doing so can only bring pain and loss. And while I would not wish any possibility of pain on you, now that I have met Mr. Withrow, I think that as long as Lady Trafford does not object, you could be very happy together."

"I—uh—well… If there is ever a possibility of something between Mr. Withrow and myself, I will consider your recommendation."

Mrs. Graham smiled magnanimously. "What is Mr.

Withrow's given name?"

"Henry."

"A strong name. My husband's name was Frederick, which is very regal. He was like your Mr. Withrow. Intelligent and well-spoken. He loved agricultural tracts and the poetry of Erasmus Darwin."

"Did you read together?" Mary had heard of some couples doing that, though her own parents had not.

"Yes, we did. And we talked about politics and went riding with the hounds and played cricket. My husband had no interest in excluding me from any activities, even ones traditionally seen as masculine."

"He sounds wonderful."

"He was," said Mrs. Graham, wistfully.

They arrived at the glovemakers and stepped inside.

"One can never have too many gloves," said Mrs. Graham, and then, more quietly, as if it were a state secret, "or at least, that is what I claim. The truth is I treat them terribly—I am always spilling something on them or staining them in one way or another, so I constantly must buy new ones."

As Mrs. Graham tried on gloves both casual and formal, she said, "I missed seeing you last night at the ball. Were you or Lady Trafford feeling ill?"

"We were both well," said Mary, and then she used the excuse she had used during every social call this morning. "There was simply a misunderstanding with our invitations."

"A misunderstanding?" said Mrs. Graham, her interest clearly piqued.

"We were not invited," she said flatly, hoping she had sold the story properly. "But Lady Trafford has already spoken to several rather important individuals, and she feels confident that this will not occur for the next ball."

"I would love to know who was responsible for such a slight. For General Blücher clearly did not make his own invitation list. There must be someone, someone important, who holds a grudge against Lady Trafford."

"It does not matter to me how or why it happened," said Mary. "Lapses in judgment occur even in the very best of people with the very best of intentions."

"That is rather dull compared to an intentional slight. You have a red spot, just above your lip."

"Oh," said Mary. Her skin must still be irritated from the moustache glue. "I was bit by a mosquito and did not resist the impulse to scratch."

"How unpleasant," said Mrs. Graham, and she brought her new gloves to the counter and paid for them. "Have you been bit there before? It was a little red above your lip the other day as well."

"I do not recall," said Mary. She feared that Mrs. Graham's intelligence and good memory and insatiable curiosity would lead her to seek for the truth. Mrs. Graham had seen her, last night, dressed as Mr. Fothergill. It was one of Mary's best disguises, but no disguise was perfect.

Mary was quite relieved that Mrs. Graham did not pursue the subject as they exited the shop and walked down the street.

Suddenly, Mrs. Graham tugged on Mary's arm, pulling her backwards. Liquid splashed onto the cobblestone right where Mary would have been standing, were it not for Mrs. Graham. Mary looked up to see a maid with a chamber pot.

"That is disgusting," said Mary.

"Rather too close for comfort," agreed Mrs. Graham.

"Should we report it to the authorities?"

"There is nothing to be done," said Mrs. Graham. "I have

seen it at least three times during my stay already, and I have heard it is quite the norm. Despite having less crime, in my opinion, these streets are even more hazardous than those in London. Can you imagine if it had fallen on us? I should not tell you, but, well, I must. I heard that Captain Kitsell walked straight into it a few weeks ago, but because he had a pressing engagement he decided not to change until afterwards."

"It must have been quite uncomfortable."

"For more than just him. Ah, here we are."

They entered the bookseller's shop, and Mrs. Graham pointed out the sections that she found most interesting. Mary much preferred to peruse the shelves by herself, in silence, because the act of discovery gave almost as much pleasure as the content of the books themselves, yet she would not be rude to her friend, and she still needed to ask the questions she had asked of every other woman she had called on this morning.

"What was the ball like?" asked Mary. "With the Belgian's death, I mean."

"It was not what I was expecting, to be sure. Of course, no one expects a murder at a ball."

"Was it frightening?"

"After the fact, yes. If anyone had known what was going to happen, I am sure we would have all been frightened before."

"What happened, exactly?"

Mrs. Graham smiled and raised her eyebrows. "I was hoping you would ask—you have proven that you have a bit of a gossip in you as well."

"It is not gossip," said Mary. "It is facts and information that I am seeking."

"What is gossip if not facts and information? Gossip is the

most honest facts and information, and yet it is called gossip because it is largely engaged in by women, and anything which gives women information is seen as dangerous."

It was an interesting theory, not one that Mary was sure she entirely agreed with, but before she could discuss this definition of gossip, Mrs. Graham began on the subject of the ball. "First, a Prussian officer confessed to the murder of Major General Leon. I am sure you heard about that."

"Yes, I did."

"They dragged him away. Your prince was running around joyfully as if he were the one who had solved the crime. He is a prince, and a handsome one at that, so he may take credit for apprehending a murderer if he chooses.

"That incident would have made the evening shocking and memorable on its own. Everyone seemed relieved to have that matter cleared up at last, though it did take a few minutes for the music to begin again. I was not in the mood to dance, so I was speaking with the Bandelins, a lovely Prussian couple. There was a loud noise, which I later learned was a gunshot. Colonel Bandelin reassured us that there was nothing to be alarmed about, and that he would return after he investigated. He had barely left when there was a second noise—another gunshot.

"I am not sure who discovered the body in the garden—one of the many officers, I am sure—but then everyone rushed from the ballroom, as if there were a fire. I was almost trampled, and because of the general exodus, I was pushed out onto the lawn with everyone else. I did not want to see the body, but I did see a little of it. No one deserves to have their body treated as spectacle, especially when they are dead."

"That must have been very unpleasant."

"Indeed."

Mrs. Graham's account had not offered any details that Mary did not already know.

"What is everyone saying about the murder? Who do they think did it?"

"They say endless things, each as nonsensical as the last. Mrs. Oldfield claimed that when she looked out the window a few minutes before the gunshots, she saw half a dozen French soldiers, with guns drawn, and that they intended to kill us all. Of course, if that had been the case, why did they not carry out their work? Someone else said it was a ghost." She gave a little laugh. "Some people believe that the Prussian officer who committed the first murder snuck out, shot the man, and then came back inside. I trust *our* officers too much to believe they would allow such a thing to occur. The only rumour that seems reasonable is that of a man in a dark cloak in the garden."

"That does seem more reasonable," said Mary, "though it is not a very distinctive description."

"No," agreed Mrs. Graham. "I cannot see that helping the investigators much."

Mrs. Graham took a book off a shelf, opened it, and then paused. "It does make me wonder if I should return to England, where it is safe."

"I would hate to see you leave," said Mary, surprised by the truth of it as she said it. "But if you do leave, I completely understand. Personal comfort, and, even more, one's own safety, is paramount."

"You are not afraid?"

"No," said Mary. "Though maybe I should be. It seems that the murderer is targeting officers. I wonder—"

"What do you wonder?"

"It was a disturbing thought. But I wonder if the murderer has more victims in mind."

"That is disturbing." Mrs. Graham shivered. "Murder is not good gossip."

"No, it is not," Mary agreed.

They went back to looking at the books, and while Mary did not select anything—she would prefer to return later, by herself—Mrs. Graham settled on a book of poetry, *The Bride of Abydos* by Lord Byron.

As Mrs. Graham purchased the book, she opened her rather large reticule. Near the top was a handkerchief with the initials A.M. She seemed almost embarrassed by it and shoved it back down into the bag.

"What is that?" asked Mary, realising that the question might sound rude, but asking it anyway.

"What do you mean?"

"That handkerchief. It does not look like yours."

"Oh, the handkerchief." Mrs. Graham smiled. "Last night, at the ball, I was conversing with a rather unpleasant gentlemen, General Tippert, when Colonel Kitsell and one of the investigators, Mr. Fothergill, interrupted us. Have you met either of the investigators?"

"No, I have not."

"They were both at the ball. Mr. Fothergill was quite handsome. He looks a little like you. Perhaps he is a distant cousin."

"Not one that I have heard of," Mary managed to say, though her heart pounded in her chest, and she could feel her pulse against her temples. Mrs. Graham was too clever for her own good, and shrewd. She could solve the puzzle in an instant, and if Mary accidentally gave something away—

"To come to the conclusion of what is becoming quite unnecessarily a long story—for it does not even have any scandal, and only scandalous tales deserve a lengthy telling—Mr. Fothergill needed to converse privately with General Tippert, so Colonel Kitsell escorted me to procure a drink. I spilled a bit of wine on my glove, and he lent me his handkerchief, and then, when I turned to return it, he was gone. Then there was the confession and then the murder, and throughout it all, I spent the entire evening searching for him, trying to return the handkerchief. I learned later that he had left the ball early and never returned. Now I am in the uncomfortable position of possessing a man's handkerchief."

"It is only a handkerchief," said Mary.

"It is not *only* a handkerchief with a man like Colonel Kitsell," said Mrs. Graham. "I have it on good authority that he has no interest in marriage, and I do not need my reputation ruined if something happened between us. I have no desire to be shunned by society, while a man stays in its good graces."

"Surely a man would also be shunned for his participation in an affair."

Mrs. Graham laughed. "You are so innocent, Mary. It is delightful. Unfortunately, that is not the case. Surely you heard what happened to Lord Uxbridge and Lady Charlotte?"

Mary shook her head.

"Well, you may know that Lord Uxbridge—Henry Paget as he was known in his younger years—is the brother of Mrs. Capel, my friend and host here in Brussels. Lord Uxbridge is the head of the cavalry for the Allied forces, and he *was* married to Lady Caroline Villiers. But then Lord Uxbridge ran off and had quite a public affair with Lady Charlotte Cadogan, who was married to Henry Wellesley, the Duke of Wellington's brother. There was a duel and much drama, and both Lord Uxbridge and Lady Charlotte ended up divorcing their spouses and marrying each other. I hear they are both happy, but Lord Uxbridge is welcome in polite society, while Lady Charlotte is never invited anywhere, and if she were to attend a social event, it would cause a scandal."

"In this situation, no one's behaviour seems to be of repute," said Mary. It seemed, though, that Uxbridge had not changed his ways—there had been the remark at Blücher's ball about Uxbridge trying to seduce everyone.

"True, but is not the treatment of Lady Charlotte unjust? And all because she sought love."

"It does seem unjust," said Mary. "They should both be shunned."

"Shun Lord Uxbridge?" said Mrs. Graham. "No one would dare. The cavalry would be in shambles without him, and despite the fact that he ran off with the Duke of Wellington's sister-in-law, they must work together."

"That must be difficult for them," said Mary. It explained the tension between them when at the Hôtel de Ville.

"I understand that they have managed to set their differences aside." They left the shop, and Mrs. Graham shivered at a slight breeze. "I should simply discard the handkerchief, and if Colonel Kitsell asks for it, I shall say I lost it."

"That is a good plan," said Mary. "He should not have given it to you and then disappeared."

But where had he disappeared to? Now that Mary reflected on it, she did not recall seeing Colonel Kitsell at all after he and Mrs. Graham left General Tippert's company. Colonel Kitsell would have been expected to be among those dealing with the confession, examining the body, and speaking with the Duke of Wellington. But he had not been present. If he had committed the murder, it would have been easy enough for him to leave the ball and not return.

Chapter Thirteen

"A third proclamation orders all aliens who...have arrived in England since April the 1st, to register themselves.... Every alien not having obtained such license...[is] liable to six months imprisonment."

—*The Antigallican Monitor*, London, June 11, 1815

MARY DID NOT believe that Lydia would have further information beyond what Mrs. Graham and all the other gossips in Brussels had provided, for Lydia had not even attended the ball, but because she was worried about her sister, she had sent a note and then been invited to visit.

"Mary, it is so good to see you," said Lydia. "I am afraid I was not very good company at the parade. I was feeling unwell, and very much not myself."

"I am glad that you feel better now," said Mary, and indeed, Lydia's transformation was extraordinary.

"You must see my new bracelet. Let me go put it on—you wait here."

She dashed to her bedroom before Mary had the chance to say a word. Soon she was back, prancing like a pony and holding out her arm as if it held the queen's jewels.

"My dear Wickham gave it to me. It was made by a local craftsman, and it is to commemorate our time here in Brussels. Isn't it lovely?"

"Yes, it—"

"It is actual gold, with an actual amethyst, symbolising the vibrancy of our love and our ability to overcome any obstacle that we face."

"That is a very generous gift."

And indeed it was quite lovely, though it appeared, to Mary's eye, to be a low-carat gold, and the amethyst was quite small. However, it was, as Lydia had said, vibrant.

"Wickham is so skilled at choosing gifts," said Lydia. "Why, I do not even need to visit a store for him to know what I would like."

"I thought you enjoyed choosing things and looking at the items in the windows."

"Well, I do, but—but it is nice to have a husband who will buy things for me even when I am not there to choose them for myself. And then I am prevented from buying things which are too expensive and which I do not actually need."

"When we were younger, you *did* buy many a bonnet which you did not even like."

"Yes, and it was such fun to do them up in a new style." She gave a little sigh, and then smiled. "I hope you will stay for dinner, Mary," said Lydia. "My dear Wickham would like to see you. It has been years since we have seen anyone in the family, after all. No one ever visited me, and I was only able to visit anyone else a few times, and only within a few months of my marriage."

She seemed sad, suddenly. But it was not as if Lydia had not had opportunities—she could have visited if she had chosen to.

"If you wanted to see everyone, you should have come to Father's funeral."

Lydia looked down at the floor. "I wanted to come. I really did." She tugged at her new bracelet. "I have regretted that I was unable to attend, every single day since then."

What a strange thing to say—Lydia had used the money sent so she could attend the funeral to buy a fashionable *burgundy* mourning gown. In fact, it might even be the burgundy gown that Lydia wore at this very moment. It had dark burgundy embroidery on the bodice, and a series of parallel black ribbons were sewed to the dress, stretching from the waist all the way down to the hem. Lydia *would* justify this as a mourning gown, but it seemed highly inappropriate to do so, and especially to continue wearing it after mourning, as if it was just another fashionable gown.

"If you are going to stay, you must help me cook," said Lydia.

"Of course," said Mary, a little reluctantly, and followed Lydia into the kitchen. Her strongest memory of the kitchen was from when the cook had scolded her as a child for spilling food on the floor.

Lydia immediately began removing ingredients and supplies. "We have never been able to keep a cook, and only once were we able to hire a full-time maid, so I have become quite proficient in the kitchen. I actually enjoy cooking, as long as I have ample supplies, and I am rather skilled at making do even when I do not."

It made sense, if one were tight on funds, that one would need to create their own meals, but Mary had never once assisted in a kitchen.

Lydia endlessly punctuated the meal preparation with pointed comments like, "You mustn't cut a potato like *that*" and "Have you truly never chopped an onion before? Please, let me do it."

Mr. Wickham returned just as Lydia and Mary were setting the food on the table.

"My dear George," said Lydia. "Look, I managed to time everything properly tonight."

"Well done," he said with a charming smile.

"And my sister Mary will be staying with us for dinner."

"Excellent." He smiled at Mary. "It has been too long. I very much miss our discussions about books, and your many aphorisms."

"Thank you." She did not remember ever discussing books with Mr. Wickham, but surely she had talked about them with him, and the fact that he missed her aphorisms gave her great pleasure. Hopefully they had helped steer him to better paths.

"You wore your new bracelet while cooking?"

Lydia's face fell. "I should not have. I was showing it to Mary and forgot to take it off."

There was a pause as Mr. Wickham seemed to consider his words. "It is not something you should trouble yourself with, my dear," he said, rather more magnanimously than the occasion required. "Let us eat, before the food grows cold."

They each served their own food.

Mary sensed that it would be appropriate for her to say something. "It was a dreadful thing, Bonaparte escaping."

"If they had asked me, I would have told them that Elba was far too close," said Mr. Wickham. "This sort of thing was guaranteed to happen."

A great many people, with much more authority and credibility, had expressed that concern.

"You are a captain, is that correct?"

"If Montgomery had not interfered, I could be a colonel. Instead, I am a lonely captain, of the 64th company."

"Surely there is someone who can help you."

"General Tippert was going to help," said Lydia.

"General Tippert?" asked Mary, suddenly much more interested in the conversation.

"General Tippert promised me a promotion, but he has been reassigned. Now he is in no position to help me at all."

"Was he very upset at the news?"

"It does make things a bit more complicated for him, but I really should not say more."

"I understand that his daughter is soon to be engaged, or perhaps she is engaged already," said Mary. "Is that why he stayed even after being dismissed?"

"It is one of the reasons. The less scandalous perhaps."

"Really?" said Lydia. "General Tippert involved in a scandal? I have only met him once, but he was so refined and proper, I cannot imagine him being involved in any sort of scandal."

Mr. Wickham pretended that he did not want to tell them, but he clearly did, for within a minute he said, "General Tippert is a gambler. He gambles on everything, not just the normal horses and cards. He owes many people money—he even owes me a little. He cannot leave Brussels until he resolves his debts. Fortunately for him, his debts are a little lighter than they were before."

Wickham seemed to like the attention that came to him as a storyteller, and he liked pausing at strategic places to force the listener to show investment and ask a question. Mary did not find this sort of mannerism particularly endearing, but because she wanted information, she would do as he desired.

"Typically debts do not become lighter on their own, without outside assistance."

"You are correct about that, Miss Bennet. General Tippert is quite lucky, quite lucky indeed. From what I heard, he owed Major General Leon over a thousand pounds."

Wickham wanted a reaction, so Mary gave it to him. "A thousand pounds? But Leon is dead."

"No one is happy to see a superior die in those sorts of circumstances—with honour on the battlefield is preferable—but I would not say that General Tippert is sorry. A number of people owed Leon money, but it seems that he did not keep clear records, so it is unlikely that the family will be able to insist the debts be repaid."

Mr. Wickham, too, seemed quite pleased. Mary remembered his debts in Meryton and wondered if Mr. Wickham had also owed Leon money. Would that make him a suspect as well?

Mary shook her head—no, her brother-in-law could not possibly be involved in the murders.

Lydia seized the moment of silence to draw attention to herself, a habit she had maintained since childhood.

"I am not invited to events often," she said, "but once, when we were at Newcastle, a colonel insisted that all the wives of the officers attend a ball. Do you remember, George, how wonderful it was?"

"Of course, my dear," he said lazily.

"Now George had business to attend to, and I did not know anyone, and I was standing alone, and several officers began to speak to me—without introductions. They thought I was unmarried and wanted to spend time with me. Can you guess what my dear Wickham did?"

"No," Mary said flatly. She hated when people insisted that she guess something that could have a thousand possible answers.

"He ran up to me, lifted me up in the middle of the room, spun me around, and kissed me. Everyone gasped, thinking they had witnessed such a scandal, and then you said... What did you say, George?"

"This is Mrs. Wickham, my dear wife, and I will have no one steal her from me."

"It was quite memorable." Lydia rotated the bracelet on her wrist and smiled.

The rest of dinner, Lydia and Mr. Wickham told stories, making jokes at the expense of others in the regiment and Mr. Wickham's superiors. They did not inquire after Mary or her life or give her space to speak beyond responding to their stories, but Mary did not mind.

She did not completely understand her sister, the way she had been so reserved and not herself their past few times meeting, but it was clear from this evening that Lydia was happy. Perhaps she could only be her full, happy self with her husband.

Once dinner was finished, Lydia and Mary returned to the kitchen, and Lydia instructed Mary on the proper method of cleaning dishes. This was not an accomplishment Mary had heretofore developed—their mother had wanted each of them to marry in such a manner that they would not need to perform this sort of labour.

"Everything has been perfect tonight," said Lydia. "I do not want it to end."

"We are both in Brussels. There is no reason why there will not be plenty of opportunities for us to do this again."

"I know, it's just—"

Lydia lowered her voice and spoke in a whisper, occasionally glancing to the door. "We hardly ever have anyone for dinner, and we are never invited anywhere, and sometimes my dear Wickham does events with the other officers, but most of the time wives are not invited. I had so many, many preconceptions about marriage, but I never thought that it would be so lonely."

She scrubbed a dish with such fierceness that there would surely not be a smidgen of food left on it. "I keep having this dream that someone is travelling, and there is an awful storm, and Mr. Wickham and I own the only house in the area, and we have a grand house, and because of the storm, a fine lady or gentleman is forced to knock on our door, and we take them in, and we feed them and let them stay and…" She shook her head. "It is a silly dream."

Mary rarely remembered her dreams, so she did not have strong thoughts on the significance of dreams, but Lydia had said she was lonely, and she dreamed that someone would spend the night.

"I would like to spend the night with you," said Mary. Lydia's face filled with surprise. "I hope that me asking is not seen as inconvenient or inappropriate for the situation, but you are my sister, and you do have a second bedroom. I could easily send for my things."

Lydia was quiet for so long that Mary was certain she had made a mistake.

Then Lydia splashed the bubbles up in the air. "I have never heard of anything so wonderful. Of course you can stay. I shall be a proper hostess and make sure you are comfortable. Oh, my dear George—" she called, and Mr. Wickham entered the room.

"Yes, my love?"

"Mary will be spending the night with us."

"No."

He said it as if it was final, as if there were no chance at negotiation. But why could she not spend the night? Lydia should have just as much a say in the decision as her husband.

"I am very much looking forward to spending more time with Lydia," said Mary.

"I know you would like to stay," said Mr. Wickham, "but unfortunately, it is impossible."

"I do not mean to be an inconvenience," said Mary.

"I invited her," said Lydia, and then she stepped closer to her husband and dropped her voice, but Mary could still hear her words. "It would not be proper for us to rescind the invitation now, especially as Mary is staying with *Lady Trafford*, who knows everyone, and has connections with high-ranking military officers, even, they say, with the Duke of Wellington himself."

For a moment, Mr. Wickham appeared angry, but then his face smoothed. "You are right my dear, of course we should have your sister. It is the proper thing to do."

MARY DID NOT know for how long she slept before she was awoken by some sort of disturbance.

She sat straight up in the bed, and it took a moment for her to place herself in the darkness between the threadbare sheets.

The noises were coming through the wall, the wall between her room and the one in which Lydia and Mr. Wickham slept. Clearly it was a thin wall, without proper insulation.

"Please, stop!" said a woman in pain.

That had been Lydia, pleading. Mary's pulse raced. She stood and made her way to the wall, against which she pressed her ear.

"I'm sorry," said Lydia, "I will not go against what you say again. I promise."

"Quiet, you wench," said Mr. Wickham. There was the sound of a hand hitting a body.

Then came a gasp of pain. "I won't invite her again."

"I said be quiet," said Mr. Wickham. "The walls are thin." Another slap, another gasp of pain, this one quieter.

A silent terror seized Mary. Mr. Wickham was a violent man, and he was harming her sister.

She did not have a plan, but she rushed to her door, for she must do something to intervene. But as she tried to open the door, she discovered she could not.

It was locked.

The door was locked, and she had not been given a key. Someone had locked her in.

Mary continued to push at the door handle, but to no avail. Maybe if she could see better, she could find a way. She found a candle, but had no way to light it, for there was no fireplace in this room, and no fire-making supplies.

There was silence from Lydia's room for a moment, and then, another quiet cry of pain.

Mary flung open the curtain covering the small windowpane, which let in a little light from a streetlamp. She searched desperately around the room for a key, or something else she could use to open the door, despite the fact that even if she found an item that would fit in the lock, she did not have the knowledge requisite to pick it.

Finally, she decided to knock on her own door. "Please, let me out of my room! Please let me out!"

But no one came, and soon she heard another cry of pain from Lydia, louder this time.

Tears streamed down Mary's face. She pounded on her door. "Please, let me out!"

But Mr. Wickham did not release her from her prison. Instead, she only heard Lydia crying out, and then Mr. Wickham yelling at her, and the sound of something hitting the floor.

Mary bit her lip, stifling her own cry. What if her own actions were causing him to hurt Lydia more? She could not ask for her own release if it caused more harm to her sister.

And maybe she had caused all this harm. Mr. Wickham was angered by Mary's presence and—

No.

Mary would not take any blame for Mr. Wickham's behaviour. Irritations of any sort did not justify harmful behaviour. Her own father, Mr. Bennet, had been plagued by Mrs. Bennet's complaints, and suffered many irritations and travails throughout his life, but he had never retaliated, he had never caused physical harm.

She rushed to the window and pushed against it with all her might, but it was not designed to open. There was no latch; it was simply a pane of glass. Despite the knowledge that it would do no good, she continued to press on it. Perhaps she could break it. She found a heavy vase and was about to smash it against the window when she realised that even if she broke the window, she might not fit through it. Using the vase, she measured the size of the window and compared it to the size of her body, concluding that it was rather unlikely that she would fit. If she did fit, it would require much pushing and squeezing, a rather dangerous proposition when on the third story of a building. Falling from a window would not help her or Lydia any.

Mary sank to the floor against the wall. Her poor sister.

Lydia, a girl full of energy and enthusiasm, a girl who loved spending time with other people, who had been so excited to be a married woman, with all of the associated benefits and prestige. What benefits did she have now? When did her marital bliss end and this horror begin?

There was no noise, now, but Lydia must still be in pain.

Mary's arms shook. She wrapped them around her legs, but it did nothing to stop the shaking. Tears continued to fall, the warm, salty water seeping into her mouth. She was angry at Mr. Wickham, but she was also angry at her sisters and their husbands. Why did they insist on purchasing Mr. Wickham a commission so very far away? Why had Elizabeth and Jane, despite their extremely fortunate financial positions, never visited Lydia to make sure her life was…well, as it should be. Satisfactory at least, though happy and fulfilled would have been better.

Lydia had not written to Mary, never responded to her letters, but she had written to Elizabeth and Jane. Had they never noticed anything amiss? Surely there must have been a sign, some sort of sign, that they should have recognized.

But Mary could not simply reserve her anger for her sisters and their husbands: she saved some of her anger for herself. She had thought it unusual that Lydia had worn a dress with long sleeves to the parade, and Lydia had cried out in pain and then provided an illogical explanation for her injury. Yet Mary had dismissed her own concerns, and now, she had come to Lydia's home, with no means of helping herself or Lydia. She had been fooled, once again, by Wickham's easy manners.

It was not simply her present decisions that caused a festering self-loathing, but also, her entire past relationship with her sister.

They had never shared any degree of congeniality, not really. They had never understood each other, ever, and Lydia had been cruel to her at times, saying unkind things and stealing her writing paper and mocking her openly in front of company.

But Mary had never been kind to Lydia either. If she were honest, she had treated her youngest sister as if she were incompetent, immoral, idiotic, overwhelmingly silly, and undesirable as a companion. Not only had she treated Lydia that way, she had truly believed it. Even since her arrival in Brussels, she had indulged in dozens of negative thoughts towards her sister.

Mr. Wickham should be held responsible for his mistreatment of Lydia, but Mary also needed to hold herself responsible. The way she had mistreated her sister was much less severe, but it was damaging and harmful all the same.

There was another sound, not through the wall this time, but through the door. A gentle knocking, and Mr. Wickham's voice, so soft and gentle. "Miss Bennet?"

A chill encompassed her entire body. What would Mr. Wickham do to *her*, who had overheard his behaviour, when he opened the door? She wished she had her pistol. She wished that she had it, and that Mr. Wickham *would* attack her, so she would be justified in defending herself.

Mary shivered. No. She could not wish death on anyone. She did not wish to *kill*. But to protect her sister—there was much she would be willing to do to protect Lydia.

Metal scraped against the lock of the door. The key, he had the key. But now, she did not want him to open it.

Like a rabbit fleeing, by impulse, from a fox, she leaped back into her bed. She pulled the sheets all the way over her head and tried to stop her trembling, tried to pretend, as best she could, that she was asleep.

The door creaked open, slow and sure. Footsteps, light

and gentle, as if they did not foretell evil, made their way to her. She shut her eyes fast, willing herself not to move, anticipating pain. She could hear Mr. Wickham's breath; she could sense his body inches away from her own.

She could not stand this fear, so she counted in her mind, desperately hoping that he would leave. *One, two, three, four.* Her heart pounded so loud she could hardly hear her own thoughts and she was certain he must know she was not asleep, but still she counted, number after number after number. Finally, when she hit *seventy-six*, Mr. Wickham stepped away from the bed. His footsteps retreated. The door closed, and she heard the sound of the key within the lock. For another minute she kept her head covered with her sheet, then she slowly pulled it off her head. She was alone, alone at last, alone but not safe.

Filled with fear and worry, she found it impossible to sleep. Instead her mind twisted in knots as she considered everything she knew about Lydia's situation. Finally she concluded that while ultimately it needed to be Lydia's decision, from a rational, reasonable perspective Lydia needed to leave Mr. Wickham.

It was almost impossible to obtain a divorce as a woman—only a handful of women had ever done it, and it required great wealth and an actual act of Parliament. Divorce was for people like Lord Uxbridge and Lady Charlotte, not for people like the Wickhams. But perhaps Lydia could obtain a separation.

For Lydia could *not* be treated in such a manner. If their father were alive, he would put a stop to it. Perhaps the husbands of her eldest sisters, Mr. Darcy and Mr. Bingley, could help. But they were in England, and she was here, with Lydia, in Brussels. She would find a way to help her sister immediately, whether through a separation or other means.

MARY MUST HAVE eventually fallen asleep. When she woke in the morning, her limbs were heavy and she prepared slowly. Hesitantly, she turned her door handle. It was unlocked, and she pushed the door open.

"Ah, Miss Bennet," said Mr. Wickham pleasantly. "It sounded, last night, as if you were having a nightmare. I hope you are feeling better today."

"I am quite fine," said Mary, "but I—"

"There is no need for you to tell anyone about your dream. Women's dreams are always such silly, trivial things and their minds frequently become confused. There is no use troubling anyone with it."

Mary straightened a little. "I am quite capable of making my own choices."

His voice became harder. "As you make your choices, you should consider what is best for you, and for your sister." Then he reverted to his normal charming manner. "I am afraid that we have quite a busy day ahead of us, so it would best if you would attend to your other responsibilities."

"I would like to see Lydia before I leave."

"Unfortunately, your sister is feeling indisposed. She expressed her regrets at being unable to say farewell to you, but she was happy to see you and hopes that you have a marvellous day."

"Why did you lock me in my room last night?"

There was a flash of anger on his face, and Mary felt a sudden fear, but then Mr. Wickham said smoothly, "Surely you locked your room yourself, and then lost the key. It is fortunate that I had a second key and was able to open it for you this morning."

She knew that she should be afraid of Mr. Wickham, but instead, she found herself growing angry, her breathing growing heavy, her hands, clenching, as if by impulse, into fists.

"If you know what is best for yourself, then you will leave, as I have already requested. Nosiness only results in noses getting hurt."

In this moment, Mary realised that she hated her brother-in-law, truly and absolutely hated. How could he be so cruel, so abusive, to Lydia? How could he not even allow Mary to see her? She tried to calm her breathing and think rationally. She did not know what she could do here at this moment, and she remembered last night, when her banging had only resulted in more pain for her sister.

It was better to pretend to acquiesce than to continue this confrontation.

"I will gather my things and then I will go."

"Very good," said Mr. Wickham with his sickening, charming smile.

She entered the room and shut the door, as if nothing were amiss. She did not actually need to gather anything—the few things that she had sent for from Lady Trafford's yesterday evening were already organised. But she was not ready to leave. If Mr. Wickham would not allow her to speak to Lydia, she would find another way to communicate with her sister.

From her bag, she took a pencil, and then she ripped a page from her drawing pad.

My dear sister Lydia,

I know that something is wrong, very terribly wrong, for

I heard everything through the wall last night.

You deserve better than this. You should never be treated by anyone in the manner in which Mr. Wickham is treating you. I am worried that you are not safe. If you do not feel safe, if you are, as I suspect, being treated in a horrendous manner, then there must be a change.

I have included five pounds. I would leave more, but it is all that I brought with me. Spend it however you need to. If you need help, please, come to Lady Trafford's house, and we will take you in.

I am sorry that we are not better friends, but I hope that you will still listen to me when I say that we can figure out a resolution to this problem together.

She paused, lifting her pencil.

"Are you almost ready to leave, my dear sister Mary?" asked Mr. Wickham from the other side of the door. She worried that he would open the door and see the letter and that all would be lost.

"Yes, very nearly." She almost closed the letter then, but she knew she needed to end it properly. Endings were as important, if not more so, than beginnings.

You are strong and brave, Lydia. Trust in yourself, and in God.

With love, faithfully your sister,
Mary Bennet

She folded the paper into a note, inserted the five-pound bank note inside, and wrote Lydia's name on the outside. Then she disordered the bed a little more and slipped the letter under the sheet. She could not imagine Mr. Wickham cleaning the room, so either Lydia would make it, or the maid who came once a week. Hopefully it would be Lydia, and hopefully she would notice the note today.

But if not, it would not matter, for Mary would find another way to help her sister.

Chapter Fourteen

"The people of the British Empire know that the war is solely against one man.... The question is, whether we chuse to have war now with all of Europe united with us, or whether we shall have it in two years' time without that union."

—*The Courier*, London, June 12, 1815

WHEN MARY RETURNED to Lady Trafford's, she discovered that Lady Trafford and Mr. Withrow had already left for the morning. Mrs. Boughton informed Mary that she should be prepared for waltzing lessons at two in the afternoon and handed her a letter from Lady Trafford about the murders.

Yet Mary could not think about the murders. She paced back and forth in the drawing room, wishing that Lady Trafford and Mr. Withrow were here. She knew she could trust them with her family's affairs, and they might have useful advice on how to help Lydia.

After thirteen minutes of fruitlessly pacing, a messenger arrived with a letter. Mary ripped open the seal.

Dear Mary,

I have snuck out to send this letter. My husband knows nothing of it.

I am sure you are concerned about what you heard last night, but I am fine. Nothing serious occurred. I will let you know if I need anything. Please do not make this public or do anything that would bring shame to me.

Your sister,
Lydia

Lydia did not want help.

The realisation took Mary's breath away. Why would she not want help?

The letter was, without a doubt, written by Lydia's hand—Mary recognized the fanciful loops, the way the capitals were majestically oversized.

She did not believe Lydia, she could not believe her, when she said "nothing serious occurred." She had heard something happening through the walls, and while Lydia might not consider it serious, Mary did. There was no reference to the note that Mary had left or the money, but maybe she had not yet cleaned that room, or had read the note and chosen not to mention it.

But what of the request that Mary do nothing? Mary must do something, she must interfere, she must tell a few select individuals so they could help her rescue Lydia—

Yet that was exactly what Lydia had requested that she not do.

Mary returned to her room and forced herself to focus on the letter from Lady Trafford. Apparently, the King of the Netherlands would not even allow them to read the transcripts of the interviews with Ouvrard's wife and others who knew him well. Monsieur Jacobs insisted that there was no connection between the deaths of Ouvrard and Leon, and, to make matters even worse, Prince Willem had not removed

Serrurier, Lemoine, or Voland from their positions or punished them in any way for spying for Bonaparte. In Mary's opinion, this might be reason to add Prince Willem or Monsieur Jacobs to the suspect list. The other information of note was that Lady Trafford had discovered where Colonel Kitsell had gone on the nights of the two murders, after the Oldfield dinner and during Blücher's ball: both times he had met with a group of officers and soldiers outside of Brussels. Each of the men were in different regiments, and each of the men swore to Colonel Kitsell's presence. Apparently they met regularly to discuss Shakespearean characters—those in attendance had given detailed descriptions of Kitsell's contributions to their discussions of Portia on the first night and Rosalind on the second.

It sounded suspicious—why would the group meet out of the city, and late at night?—yet Mary could not focus on the case for long, for her thoughts were too filled with her sister. She removed a plain sheet of paper and began to brainstorm possibilities to rescue her sister Lydia.

Mrs. Boughton slammed open the door to Mary's room. "Miss Bennet, you are needed in the drawing room. Immediately."

Mrs. Boughton did not even attempt to explain before rushing back down the hallway. Mary followed her. "What is it?"

"It is your sister. She came to the door… A man was chasing her, but he said he was her husband, and I let them both in. Now I am wondering if I should not have let him in or left her alone." She paused on the staircase and turned to look at Mary. "She is in quite a state, I warn you."

They descended the stairs and reached the doorway to the drawing room.

Lydia's face was dominated by a massive black eye. Tears flowed down her cheeks, which were red and puffy, and she was cradling her arm in front of her body. Lydia looked as if she were a glass figurine about to break—

No. Lydia was a glass figurine that had already been broken.

"Stop crying, my dearest Lydia," said Mr. Wickham. He placed his hands on her arms and shook her a little. She gasped. "Mary is happy to see us, happy to help us in our time of need. But you *must stop crying*."

Slowly, Mary walked across the room. If only she had done something; if only she had interfered, despite the note from her sister. For clearly the letter had been a lie. Now she was here, alone with Lydia and Wickham and Mrs. Boughton.

Mary stopped a few feet in front of Lydia and Mr. Wickham, unsure of what to say. "Lydia, are you—"

This would be much easier without Mr. Wickham present. What could she say, what could she do with him here? How could she possibly prevent him from harming Lydia further? How could she stop this man who had evil wrapped around his heart like a vine?

"I fell," said Lydia, her voice shaking. "I fell, and I hurt myself."

"My poor Lydia," said Wickham, his voice like silk, as deceptive as a snake. "It is so terrible, that she fell immediately before she wanted to come and stay with you."

Lydia's eyes seemed to plead with Mary.

"Yes," said Mary slowly. "I need time with my sister." If she could get Lydia away from him, then—well, she did not know what she could do, but it was an essential step.

"Unfortunately, we have several debts, and while I am

occupied with them it is absolutely impossible for me to spare Lydia. She does so much to make our home a place of comfort and security, I do not even think I can spare her for an hour."

"I am sure you can spare her for an hour, Mr. Wickham," Mary said coldly. Her eyes darted around the room, searching for something, anything, that could help her. Mrs. Boughton stood in the doorway, as if unsure what to do, yet also afraid to leave. There was a fire poker in the grate; Mary had attempted to use one as a weapon once, but it had not gone well. There was a porcelain teapot, and she had once managed to use a teapot as a weapon, but that one had been filled with boiling water, and this one hung empty next to the empty fireplace, and she did not know how she could reach it without Mr. Wickham stopping her. There were several chairs she could lift and possibly use in her defence, but she feared that if she did anything against Mr. Wickham, he would do more to harm her sister. She must play his game, at least for a little longer, until she could remove Lydia from harm's way.

"Mrs. Boughton, perhaps you could *prepare some refreshments*," said Mary.

"Of course, Miss Bennet," said Mrs. Boughton, stepping quickly out of the room.

Mary did not need refreshments; she needed assistance. But Mrs. Boughton was an intelligent woman, and hopefully she would procure Mr. Withrow or a constable or anything rather than chilled hors d'oeuvres.

"Surely there is something I can do which would make it possible for you to spare her," said Mary.

Mr. Wickham nodded. "An interesting proposition. You already gave us five pounds, which is useful, but does not cover our needs. Perhaps with another forty pounds I would be able to spare her, for a few days."

Forty pounds—she did not even have forty pounds with her in Brussels. It was a huge sum. She could buy a pianoforte with forty pounds. Working as a spy, she only made seventy pounds a year.

"I do not know if I can accommodate that sort of request," said Mary.

"Mary—" pleaded Lydia.

"Well, surely I *can* figure something out," said Mary. "I *will*," she added for Lydia's benefit. "But in order to do so, I *must* speak to my sister first. Alone."

"What could you possibly have to say to your sister that you cannot say in front of me?" asked Mr. Wickham, as if Mary had just proposed the most illogical thing in the world.

"I need a word with her, that is all," said Mary, crossing her arms. "I cannot do as you demand without a word with her."

"I am not demanding anything," said Mr. Wickham, standing. He stepped close to Mary, inches away, forcing her to look up at him. "It was Lydia who said you might be able to assist us."

"Please, Mr. Wickham," said Mary, aware of Mr. Wickham's strength and his military training. "I would be very much obliged to you." She prayed that Mrs. Boughton found someone quickly.

Mr. Wickham fingered the hilt of the sword that hung at his waist. "Very well. You may have a moment with her." He strode and stood next to the door, blocking them in, and not truly giving them space or privacy.

Mary went and sat next to her sister's side. "Lydia," she whispered.

Lydia leaned in, embracing her with only one arm, keeping the other arm cradled against her body. "I am sorry," she whispered. "So sorry."

"Do not be sorry," whispered Mary. "I will find a way to help you."

"I need you to give him forty pounds. I told him you would give him money if he would let me stay here. I am sorry, but I cannot go back. I cannot. I would rather die than go back."

"I will make sure that does not happen." And if she needed to pay Wickham forty pounds—forty pounds!—then she would find a way to do so.

Mr. Wickham suddenly stepped towards them. "You have had enough time," he said. "Now I recommend you go and procure the money that you have agreed upon."

"Come, Lydia, we will—"

"No," said Mr. Wickham. "Lydia will stay with me, while we wait for you."

She did not want to leave Mr. Wickham alone with Lydia, but standing here and arguing with him would not help anyone. She rushed up the stairs to her room. Including coins, she had a little over seven pounds left, and about the same in the currency of the Netherlands, nowhere near the forty Wickham demanded. But neither Lady Trafford nor Mr. Withrow were here to lend her money. Hopefully Mrs. Boughton would return soon, with help, but as there was no guarantee of that… Mary opened the hidden compartment at the bottom of her clothing press. She removed a dull scarf and found, underneath, her pistol.

Mary had requested weapons training—she had wanted to learn to shoot to protect herself and others. But now that it came to it, would she be willing to wield a pistol to protect herself and her sister? Would she be willing to take a life? Was it worth killing to save lives?

On an abstract level, the answer had to at least sometimes be yes, or every single war would be unjustified. Yet the thought of picking up her gun, cocking it, aiming and firing at a human being…this seemed a separate matter entirely.

There had to be another way besides violence—surely, there was another alternative. Perhaps the mere presence of the weapon would be enough to shift the balance. But she could not assume that. You could not bring a weapon into a dangerous situation unless you were prepared to use it.

She thought of the black and purple bruise around Lydia's eye, the way Lydia cradled her arm, the way Lydia had pleaded for help. Lydia would rather die than stay with her husband.

Mary picked up the gun. The metal felt cold and lifeless. She put in a bullet and poured in gunpowder, though she did not cock the gun. She placed the gun, along with a bag of gunpowder and extra bullets, inside her pocket and began to walk down the stairs. Her pocket felt heavy in her hand, but she held it close. She would not turn back now.

The front door opened, and in stepped Mrs. Boughton and Mr. Withrow. His eyes instantly went to her, and she rushed down the last few steps. It was no small thing to share your family's shame with another, but she trusted Mr. Withrow completely.

Speaking quietly, so Mr. Wickham could not overhear, she said, "My sister has been hurt by her husband and is trying to run away from him. She wants to stay here. They are both in the sitting room. He demands that I give him forty pounds if I want him to allow Lydia to stay here, but I only have seven with me, and I was hoping that I could borrow—"

"I will take care of this," said Mr. Withrow, and without

another word he stepped into the room, Mary close behind.

Mr. Withrow stood for a moment, taking in the situation, and then he strode towards Mr. Wickham.

"It is my understanding," he said, "that Mrs. Wickham would like to visit her sister, and that you are preventing that."

"She wants no such thing," said Mr. Wickham. "In fact, we were just leaving." He yanked Lydia to her feet, and she gasped, once again, in pain.

"Lydia already told me she wants to stay," said Mary.

Lydia nodded her head, fear in her eyes.

"It is not her decision." Mr. Wickham pulled Lydia closer to his left side. "She is my wife, and it is within my rights to make decisions for her."

"Not in my house," said Mr. Withrow. "I have no respect for those who harm or subjugate others."

Mr. Wickham's left hand tightened even further on Lydia's arm. He reached with his right arm across to draw his sword, which hung on his left side. What did he plan to do with his sword? Mary knew she should remove her gun from her pocket, but she felt paralyzed by fear.

Mr. Withrow moved without hesitation, slamming his left hand into the upper portion of Wickham's right arm, effectively pinning it against his body. Wickham could not draw his sword if he could not move his arm. A fraction of a second later, Mr. Withrow bumped his body against Mr. Wickham's, knocking him off balance. At the same moment, Mr. Withrow swung his right arm around the back of Wickham's neck and used the momentum to twist Wickham away from Lydia. Wickham began to trip, and Mr. Withrow slammed him towards the ground. Wickham's back hit the edge of a table and then he fell to the floor. Mr. Withrow was immediately on top of him. Not heeding Wickham's punches, Mr. Withrow yanked at the sword's scabbard, using such force that he tore the scabbard's binding. Mr. Withrow flung the sword, still in the scabbard, across the room, then punched Wickham in the ribs.

There was a crack—the crack of bone—and Wickham gasped in pain. But the fight was over. Wickham was pinned down by Mr. Withrow—he could not move, he could not resist any longer.

"If you hurt me," said Wickham, "the law will be on my side."

"Will you tell everyone that you were trounced by a civilian?" asked Mr. Withrow.

The hesitation on Wickham's face said that he would not. But then, he spoke again. "Mrs. Wickham is my wife, and by law, I can do with her as I please. If I want her back, you are obligated to give her back. If she is stupid as she always is, then it is within my rights to beat her."

"You have no right to hurt my sister," said Mary. She picked up the sword and scabbard from the ground.

"What do you think that *you* can do, Miss Bennet?" said Mr. Wickham. "The middle sister, the one everyone mocks. Do you know how many times, over the course of my marriage, I have been subjected to tales of the stupid things you have said, and the embarrassment you were to all of Meryton? Your sister has never once said a kind word about you. She has shown you no mercy. You owe her nothing."

Lydia began to bawl. Mr. Withrow tightened his grip on Mr. Wickham.

Mary blinked away tears. Mr. Wickham knew exactly what to say to hurt her. He knew to say something that she would know with certainty was true. Of course her sister had mocked her. Yet learning this still hurt.

She shook her head. It did not matter. She loved Lydia, regardless, and she would help her despite their personal history.

The rage in Mr. Withrow's face was clear—he was more than willing to hurt Mr. Wickham, and he might even be willing to kill him. But if Mr. Withrow killed Wickham, Mr. Withrow could be hanged for the offence. Surely there must be another way to save Lydia.

"Mr. Withrow," said Mary. He did not turn to look at her, and he did not loosen his grip on Mr. Wickham. "Henry," she said, saying Mr. Withrow's first name. He turned his head, ever so slightly, towards her. "My sister needs us. And I think we must let Mr. Wickham go."

He breathed deeply then nodded. "You will never hurt Lydia Bennet again."

"Why would I hurt my dear Mrs. Wickham?" Wickham's voice was sticky and saccharine.

Mr. Withrow's hands tightened on Wickham's body, and then, after a few seconds, they loosened. Mr. Withrow stood, but he kept his arms in an attack position.

Wickham stood warily, his hand on his rib. Mr. Withrow pushed him towards the door.

Mr. Wickham held out his hand. "Forty pounds or my wife. It is your choice."

Before Mary could retrieve what money she had from her pocket, Mr. Withrow handed Mr. Wickham a pile of five-pound notes.

Mr. Wickham counted out the money, then smiled. "It appears to be in order." He gave a pointed look at Lydia. "I do believe I have gotten the better end of the bargain. Have a nice visit, my dear. I'll be back for you soon."

He glanced, for a moment, at his sword with its broken scabbard, but then turned and left without it.

Mr. Withrow instructed Mrs. Boughton to keep the front door and all the other entrances to the house locked at all times, and to instruct all the other servants to not, in any circumstance, allow Mr. Wickham to enter.

"I am so sorry," said Lydia with a shudder. "I am so sorry, I should never have come, I should never have—"

"I am glad you are here, Lydia," said Mary. "I am glad you trust me to help you."

"I do not deserve your help," she said. "I do not deserve anyone's help."

"That is not true," said Mary. "Of course you deserve help."

But Lydia would not listen; she would not be consoled.

Mr. Withrow gestured to Mary, who approached him. "We need to ascertain the extent of her injuries," he said in a low voice. "I can send for a doctor, if necessary."

Mary nodded. He was right, of course, and she should have thought of it herself.

She returned to her sister. "How did he hurt you? What hurts the most?"

"I am fine," said Lydia. "He did not hurt me."

"But you are hurt, and—"

"I fell," she said. "I brought this on myself. I deserve what has happened to me."

"No, you do not."

"Mr. Wickham is a good man, inside. He just needs patience and time and love, and if I was better at giving it, if I were a better wife—"

Mr. Withrow crouched on the floor near her, though he seemed careful to give her plenty of space. "Even if you were to give everything, it would never be enough. No one would ever be enough for him. He has probably harmed others as well. You might see something good in him, but that does not redeem him, or his vile actions against you. You do not need to protect him—we know that you have suffered these injuries at his hand."

Lydia shook her head.

"Please, Lydia," said Mary. "We need to know how you are hurt."

Again, she shook her head.

Mr. Withrow spoke gently, as if speaking to a wild kitten. "It is not your fault, even if you blame yourself, even if you think you could have done more. I was hurt...many times, very violently, when I was a child. I know at least a little of how you feel right now, so I know that you do need help, and I hope you are brave enough to take it. You were brave enough to come here today. Where do you have the most pain? Is it your arm?"

Lydia gave a quick nod.

"Can we look at it?" asked Mr. Withrow. "We want to help you, but we need to know what sort of help you need."

In a motion that appeared rather painful, Lydia held her arm out a little from her body.

Hands open and towards the ceiling, Mr. Withrow leaned towards her.

"I would like to touch your arm, very softly," he said, "so I can examine it. Depending on your injury, it may hurt a little, but I will touch it as minimally as I can. Do I have your permission?"

She gave a little nod.

He tenderly, gently, pulled back the sleeve on her lower arm, and Mary was so grateful that Mr. Withrow was such a man as he was, that it was him, and not anyone else, who was here to help her sister.

The skin on Lydia's arm was so bruised it was mottled with colour, and there was an unnatural angle to it, and an abnormal bulge underneath the skin.

"It is broken," said Mr. Withrow, "though the bone has not broken through the skin, which I believe is a good thing."

"We need a doctor," said Mary. "I will go and—"

"Please, do not leave me, Mary," said Lydia.

"I will send Mrs. Boughton for a doctor," said Mr. Withrow.

"If it is not an inconvenience, may I make Lydia comfortable in one of the guest rooms while we wait for the doctor's arrival?"

"Of course," said Mr. Withrow. "Yes, to whatever you need."

Mary helped her sister up the stairs to a spare room, while Mr. Withrow gathered supplies that the doctor might need.

Rather glumly, Lydia said, "If a doctor is coming, I suspect I will need this dress off, so he can…examine me."

"I suspect you are right," Mary agreed.

"Will you help me, Mary?"

"Yes, Lydia."

Carefully, Mary helped remove Lydia's dress. Lydia did not cry or whimper, not even as the fabric tugged, for a moment, against her broken arm. She was a rag doll, limp and pliable. When Lydia was wearing only a threadbare chemise, Mary helped her back into the bed and pulled a sheet over her body, but not before seeing the bruises.

Lydia's body was a journal, a journal of Mr. Wickham's treatment of her. Some of the bruises looked several weeks old, faint remnants of discoloration, almost back to normal skin colour. Other bruises were large, others small, some purple, some blue, some black and fresh. There was hardly an area of her body without bruises, and while Lydia's body held only a record of the past few weeks, it was likely a recurring journal: as soon as a patch of skin became clear and free, a page of the book of her life became empty, open, ready for more pain, more bruises.

"I am sorry," said Mary. The words felt inadequate. "I am sorry" was for spilt cider or a lame horse or a leaky roof. Not for—for this.

"It is not as bad as it looks," said Lydia, turning her face away.

"I suspect it is worse," said Mary. "When did he break your arm? Was it last night?"

"No," she said. "It was this morning. After you left. After he forced me to write the letter. After I cleaned your room and found your note."

Mary could not forgive herself for leaving—leaving her sister with Mr. Wickham. She should have insisted, she should have brought some means to protect Lydia from him, she should have immediately returned with help, despite Lydia's letter.

She sat on a chair which she pulled as close to the bed as she could, and they waited. She had so much she wanted to say, so much she wanted to ask, so much concern for her sister and guilt over her own behaviour and thoughts towards her sister, that she could not formulate anything to say at all. They waited in silence until Mr. Withrow arrived with the doctor.

The doctor was a small man, Belgian, who did not speak very much English. He examined Lydia, asked her questions, and then gave her a sleeping draft which would last for the rest of the day. Once she was fully asleep, he set her arm and bound it in a sling.

The doctor left, and Mr. Withrow and Mrs. Boughton left the room to discuss hiring a nurse to assist with Lydia's needs. Mary stayed with her sister, keeping vigil, the way she had watched over her father's body after he had died. Lydia was not dead—though how much more would it have taken for Wickham to kill her?—yet she was a husk of her old self.

Mary was grateful that she had not needed to use her pistol, grateful that Mrs. Boughton had been able to find Mr. Withrow so quickly, grateful for the way he had handled things, grateful that a doctor had been able to fix Lydia's arm. But Wickham had broken more than her arm; Wickham had bruised more than her skin. Who could fix the injuries to her soul? One of his worst crimes was convincing Lydia that it was her own fault, that *she* was the one to blame.

Mary wanted Mr. Wickham to be punished, but she did not know how. Unless he killed Lydia, little legal recourse could be taken. Lydia belonged to Wickham. She was, in the law, an object he could mistreat as he pleased, unless she managed to obtain a separation.

There was a light knock at the door.

"Come in," said Mary.

Mr. Withrow stepped into the room, closing the door quietly behind him. He shifted a chair next to Mary's own.

"Have you been carrying your pistol with you?" he asked.

"Not regularly," said Mary. It was large enough that it took up most of her pocket, and, to be honest, she still felt uncomfortable with it.

"It does not do you any good to know how to use a weapon if you do not carry it with you. Between Wickham and the murderer, there is risk to you, and to others, at all times. You should bring it with you, regardless of whether you are dressed as yourself or as Fothergill."

She nodded. "I will carry it with me."

"Good," he said.

"I do not know how best to help Lydia," Mary admitted.

"A private separation would provide Lydia the protection she needs, but I do not know if Wickham would agree to it—it limits the amount of money that a man must pay to support his separated wife, which the man normally likes, but in this case, it would prevent him from getting further money from your family. The other option is a judicial separation. If we brought the doctor to London, he could testify of the severity of Lydia's injuries, or a private investigator might be able to find something else against Wickham. Yet a judicial separation would drag your entire family, very publicly, through the courts."

"There are no good options," said Mary. "I fear that any sort of separation would take too long. She cannot go back to him—not for another day. He will only hurt her further and—and she told me she would rather die than go back."

"My aunt may have other ideas, when she returns," he said.

"She may," said Mary. "Or...perhaps Elizabeth and Mr. Darcy could pay Wickham in exchange for him agreeing to a private separation, though he may ask for an unreasonable amount. If I write to them, at least they can provide funds so that I can pay my debt to you."

"That is unnecessary, Miss Bennet. I have helped many a stranger in this sort of position, and I am more than willing to help your sister." He paused. "We are not so very different. I am a third son, and...not my parents' favourite. If Lady Trafford had not chosen me as her heir, I would be in a similar financial position as you." He was silent for a moment. "I loved my cousins full-heartedly. Their loss was devastating, especially to Lady Trafford. Every time I think of my inheritance, I feel…uncomfortable. I still feel pain at their passing, and to that is added guilt, that I will receive what should have been theirs."

"I am sorry," said Mary. She wished she could say more but did not know what she could say. When she was younger, she had thought that an aphorism or a passage of scripture could assist in any situation, but now she was not so sure.

Lydia stirred, and then cried out. Mary took her hand again and Lydia stilled, but she did not have the calm, peaceful expression that often accompanied sleep.

"I hate men and women like Mr. Wickham," said Mr. Withrow, his hands in fists. His eyes were filled with pain, pain she wished she could remove.

"You told Lydia that you had suffered violence. What happened to you?" Immediately she regretted the question—who was she to question him about past pain? "I apologise. I should not have asked."

"Do not apologise," he said, and then he was silent for long enough that she thought he would not say more. Finally he spoke. "My parents were strong believers in corporal punishment. I received many beatings, even when I was three and four years old. Then, when I was seven, the heir of the neighbouring estate, who was three years my elder, began giving me regular injuries, sometimes severe. My parents did nothing to stop it. That is why I learned how to fight—so no one could hurt me, ever again. So I would never again feel helpless." He traced a thin scar on his left palm that she had never noticed before. A scar that must be a constant reminder of when he had felt helpless. He cleared his throat. "As I grew older, I realised I could also use my skills to protect others."

"Thank you for sharing your story with me." He must trust her greatly to be so open about his past and his struggles. "You are very good at protecting others."

"Thank you for not allowing me to do permanent harm to Wickham," said Mr. Withrow. "I wanted to, but I would have regretted the consequences. I am sure we will find another way to resolve this matter."

She liked that he said *we*, that he intended to be her partner in the resolution of this problem. She reached out her hand to him, and he took it in his own.

Chapter Fifteen

"PAYNE'S WALTZ and COTILLION ACADEMY, No. 32, Foley-street, Cavendish-square.—The Russian, German, French, and the most fashionable style of Waltzing, expeditiously taught with ease and elegance."
—*The Courier*, London, June [12], 1815

"THERE WAS WALTZING at the Congress of Vienna," said Lady Trafford as she led them to the largest room in the house, which had been cleared of most of its furniture. "And there will be waltzing at the Duchess of Richmond's ball. I am not as spry as I once was, but I shall at least attempt to learn the dance."

"If you plan to dance," said Mr. Withrow to his aunt, "it would be an honour to be your partner."

"Thank you, Henry," said Lady Trafford. "And Miss Bennet shall dance with the instructor."

For a brief moment, Mary felt disappointment: why could she not dance with Mr. Withrow? But of course, it was proper and honourable for him to dance with his aunt, and there would be nothing remarkable about dancing with him.

A part of Mary wished she could skip the lesson and stay by Lydia's side, but Lady Trafford insisted that she attend. With the sleeping draft she had been given, Lydia would be asleep for hours, and Mrs. Boughton watched over her. At least now she was safe.

After a minute or two, the dancing master and a lone violinist joined them.

The dancing master was British, a Mr. Thomas Wilson, who appeared to be about forty years old. He was visiting Brussels for several months, but normally he trained the dancers at the king's theatre and opera house in London. He mentioned that he had authored several books on dancing, which they were welcome to purchase at most reputable booksellers, and that he was in fact in the process of writing a book on today's subject, the French and German waltzes. He began, not with actual dance instruction, but with a bit of a lecture.

"The waltz, which owes its origin to the Germans, is one of the most fashionable and agreeable species of dancing. In England, there are many prejudices against the waltz, but you need not fear—waltzing is much more chaste than most of our country dances, and certainly more chaste than cotillions. When danced properly, waltzing is a beautiful, graceful, and pleasing union of attitudes and movements."

From what Mary had seen at General Blücher's ball, waltzing involved more physical contact with your partner than any of the English dances. Rather than moving up and down a line, and interacting with nearby ladies and gentlemen, you interacted only with your partner for the entirety of the dance. It was little wonder that people had made moral judgments against the dance, but Mary was determined to keep an open mind.

"First, we will review the five positions. You each know them, of course?"

"Yes," said Lady Trafford and Mr. Withrow.

Mary pushed aside unpleasant memories of learning the

five positions and said, with as much confidence as she could muster, "Yes."

Unfortunately it soon became clear that Mr. Wilson was exactly like her first dance master, always focusing on *her* flaws and comparing her to everyone else.

"Quite impressive, Lady Trafford, quite impressive," said Mr. Wilson when they reached the fifth position. He gave a polite nod at Mr. Withrow's form, and then he turned to Mary. "Clearly, you are not a finished dancer. You must be sufficiently turned at the hips! Please, touch your heels to the opposite toes. Further, further."

Mary grit her teeth, trying and trying to improve her fifth position. She hated, she abhorred, she despised fifth position. Her sisters Lydia and Jane had been the best at it, and Elizabeth and Kitty had been close to their level. But she had never been as flexible as her sisters, nor had she possessed any interest in becoming this flexible.

Finally, Mr. Wilson said, "That is sufficient."

Mary stepped out of fifth position and looked at the floor. She did not want to see Mr. Withrow and Lady Trafford's faces. She did not need their judgment as well. Why did dancing in a ballroom *always* require ballet techniques?

"Now, we shall begin with the French waltz, as it is more popular in Brussels than the German waltz. First, I will provide an overall picture of the French waltz. I expect each of you to pay close attention."

He looked at each of them in turn, but his eyes lingered for longer on Mary. She sniffed. The fact that she found fifth position more difficult did not mean that she was any less capable at listening to instructions.

He gestured to the violinist, who played music in three-eight as Mr. Wilson spoke.

"The French Waltz consists of three parts, which are performed sequentially, without a pause in the music, though the progression is signalled by a change in the tempo of the music. First, there is a short march—only four steps—of the couples around the circle"—he demonstrated with an imaginary partner—"and then the slow waltz begins. This is characterized by slow pirouettes and the pas de bourée, the timing of which are offset between the ladies and the gentlemen to produce a smooth, flowing movement. Once this portion of the dance is completed, this is followed by the sauteuse waltz, which is characterized by springing movements. This includes a modified pas de bourée, performed more rapidly and with the first step transformed into a spring."

This movement was much quicker than the first section of the waltz, and it was, indeed, filled with springs. Mary questioned the choices which had led her to this moment—while she found her life as a spy fulfilling and of great worth, she did not know if she would be able to learn this dance, or even if she wanted to. She pictured herself writing a note of apology to the prince, excusing herself from dancing with him. Lady Trafford would look down on the action, and Mr. Withrow—well, she did not know what he would think. At least she had, years ago, learned the pas de bourée.

"Then comes the third section of the French waltz: the jetté, also known as the quick sauteuse waltz."

Mary could not resist a small groan. The sauteuse was already a quick waltz, and yet this would be even quicker?

"As apparent by the word jetté, this section incorporates leaps or jumps in the movements. In a company of good waltzers, it has the most beautiful and enchanting effect, and produces an impression of the most complete gratification on the minds of both the dancers and the spectators."

It was a good turn of phrase, and she was certain this waltz was lovely, but it would be much more strenuous as a dancer than as a spectator.

Then, the truly difficult part of the lesson began, as they learned each of the sections. For now, they practised separately, without a partner, which was just as well, for imitating Mr. Wilson's movements was difficult enough without anyone blocking her vision. He would give out a long series of instructions, which were extremely technical and difficult to follow. And of course, he frequently dispensed criticism.

"When you perform the pas de bourée," he told Mary, "you must avoid the rising and sinking of the body. You do not want to appear like a children's puppet, popping up and down without form or beauty."

At one point, exasperated, he declared, "How can you even perform a country dance without being able to do a proper fifth position? The very notion is absurd."

Mary tried to come up with a response, she tried to summon some sort of defence in her favour, but she had none. It did seem like a great failure when stated in such a manner.

After a few minutes of failing to improve her fifth position, Mr. Wilson decided that in some cases, she would be able to substitute the third position for the fifth. "It is not a bad substitution, really," he mused. "I shall put it in my book. It is useful to provide variations for dancers who are…less advanced."

This was a great relief to Mary, and it did not bother her that he had called her a *less advanced* dancer. It was true, and much kinder than he probably felt.

Fortunately for Mary, the sauteuse waltz was not quite as difficult as she had thought it would be; the overall movement matched that of the slow waltz, which she was able to keep in her mind as she transformed her steps into springs. The jetté did prove more difficult, but by the time two hours had passed, she could adequately perform the basic footwork for all three sections of the dance.

They had a ten-minute break, and Mary savoured the opportunity to sit and drink tea. As always occurred during dance lessons, her entire body was exhausted.

"Are you enjoying the lesson, Miss Bennet?" asked Mr. Withrow.

"As you can see, I am not a very good dancer."

"Mr. Wilson is used to teaching professional dancers. He cannot expect the same of us, and you should not expect the same of yourself." He paused. "You sidestepped my question. Are you enjoying the lesson?"

"To be honest, I feel conflicted. I do not like being inadequate, yet I do enjoy learning new things. This creates internal tension and can make gaining new knowledge and skills quite uncomfortable."

"Yet you still push forward."

"I try."

Mr. Wilson called them back to the dance floor.

"Now," he said, "it is time to address the movements of the arms, head, and body, as well as the formation of the attitudes for the French waltz."

"What do you mean by the attitudes?" asked Mary.

"The attitudes are the overall positionings formed by a combination of the arms and the body in particular configurations."

This did not really answer her question, but she had no chance to ask for a better explanation, for he began, once again, on one of his lectures. Soon she became lost in his descriptions of posture, avoiding upper body movement, and the proper arm holds.

"Now, come, Miss Bennet, help me demonstrate. Please stand here, on my right."

She swallowed and stepped forward. It was not fair to make her demonstrate something she had never seen herself, yet he had not brought an assistant so she supposed she must assist.

"No, Miss Bennet, do not face me, face forward. It is a march, after all."

She breathed out heavily and turned so she did not face Mr. Wilson.

"My dear Lady Trafford, and Mr. Withrow, if you could imitate our movements. First, we will begin the attitude for the march. Using our inner arms, our hands will touch the back of each other's shoulders." He placed his hand on Mary's back. "And now, Miss Bennet, please raise your arm, just in front of mine, and place your hand, on my shoulder."

She tentatively placed her hand.

"No!"

His sudden vehemence startled her. She dropped her arm and stepped away.

Mr. Wilson glared at her. "Come back, Miss Bennet."

Mary sniffed.

Lady Trafford looked a little sympathetic, but Mr. Withrow looked...bored, perhaps. Despite how much time she had spent in his company, she could not always determine his mood.

Reluctantly, she returned to Mr. Wilson's side.

"It is important to note that rather than using the entire hand, in the waltz only the thumb and the forefinger need touch your partner—that is both sufficient and proper."

"Plenty of country dances use the entire hand," said Mary.

"That is true, and the use of the entire hand is appropriate for country dances, but in the waltz, that would be obscene."

Generally, Mary weighed moral arguments highly, yet this made no sense to her. Why would the same action be perfectly acceptable in most dances, yet obscene in the context of the waltz? True, the waltz required the man and the woman to be closer to each other, and for the entirety of the dance, yet to her this did not justify a ban on three entire fingers.

Mary was about to say as much but Lady Trafford cleared her throat and gave a little shake of the head. She could guess what Mary wanted to say and did not approve of it.

Fine. Mary would not protest, and she would abstain from touching Mr. Wilson with her three dreadfully obscene fingers. But that did not mean she would find any pleasure in it.

She delicately placed her and thumb and her forefinger on the back of his shoulder.

"Better," said Mr. Wilson. "Now, we take our opposite hands and hold them together in the front, creating an easy curve."

Mary took his hand, once again, careful to only use two of fingers—this entire lesson was ridiculous—and then the truly difficult part of the instruction began.

Mr. Wilson would not simply teach one of the new attitudes. He insisted on them learning a new attitude while doing the footwork. Yet the footwork of the men and the footwork of the women were offset—she did not understand how they were meant to integrate—and she was expected to perform the steps perfectly while using new arm movements and learning to transition between the various attitudes. In short, it was a disaster.

Or, better put, *Mary* was a disaster. Mr. Withrow and Lady Trafford were performing commendably.

She frequently performed the same steps at the same time as Mr. Wilson, tripped on her feet, forgot the steps entirely, used the wrong fingers, and once even managed to hit Mr. Wilson in the face with her hand as she attempted to transition between attitudes.

Mary had always considered herself as more of an intellectual person than a physical one. Since becoming a spy, she had learned to enjoy running, and sometimes she wore a dress which allowed for optimal movement and ran in a secluded area for twenty or thirty minutes. Yet clearly, this did not translate into making her a better dancer. Nor were the numerous country dances she knew doing much to assist her at learning the waltz. She wished she possessed a fragment of the dancing skill of her fellow spy, Miss Tagore. Miss Tagore probably already knew both the German and French waltzes. Was she dancing now, in Paris, to obtain information?

Mary forced her focus back to the dance, but a directed focus was insufficient to prevent additional criticism.

"*No!*" said Mr. Wilson, echoing his frequent refrain. "You cannot, due to your own lack of balance, rely on support from me to pull you around the room. That is not waltzing. Hold your own body."

She raised her jaw and crossed her arms.

"You must move your feet and your arms with ease and confidence, for this will give you balance. And above all, you must obtain a *feeling* of the performance, for this *feeling* matters more than anything else."

Her only feeling was frustration, which was certainly not the intended feeling of the waltz. She blinked rapidly, but she refused to cry in front of Mr. Wilson.

Mr. Withrow whispered something to Lady Trafford. She nodded, and then Mr. Withrow approached the dance master.

"Mr. Wilson," said Mr. Withrow with a small bow. "Would it be possible for us to switch partners? Lady Trafford would appreciate your technical expertise and guided mentorship on the transition between attitudes three and four, and I would be more than willing to dance with Miss Bennet."

"Of course," said Mr. Wilson, walking to Lady Trafford and giving a deep bow. He could not very well turn down the woman holding the purse strings.

"I hope you do not mind being my partner," said Mr. Withrow quietly.

"Not at all," said Mary. Though she was just as likely to be dreadful, she would rather be dreadful while dancing with Mr. Withrow than dance with Mr. Wilson for even one more minute.

"I have never attempted to learn an entirely new dance in one day," he said. "I have always had lessons spread across several days or weeks."

"It is exhausting," said Mary.

"Only a few minutes more and it will be over, I am sure."

She nodded. "I will persevere."

Mr. Wilson instructed them to begin again in the third attitude. Both she and Mr. Withrow placed one hand on each other's waist. The other hand hung to the side. The violinist began the music, and she focused on the dance.

"If you look up, rather than watching your feet, it might be easier," said Mr. Withrow. "I always stumble when I am watching my feet."

She looked up, which naturally led her eyes to Mr. Withrow's face. She considered the shape of his jaw, his nose, his eyes, and suddenly she found that her feet's movements came more naturally. Gazing at Mr. Withrow like this, and having him consider her in return, almost took her breath away. Theoretically this should distract her and make the footwork more challenging, yet this sort of distraction actually allowed her feet to move more naturally, more in the way in which her fingers moved unconsciously over practised scales and chords on the pianoforte.

"Now switch to the fourth attitude," said Mr. Wilson.

For the first time, she transitioned between the third and fourth attitudes with ease. She and Mr. Withrow raised their left arms and joined their hands above their heads, with their right arms at each other's waists. After several measures, they raised their right arms above their heads and placed their left arms on each other's waists. They were spinning, waltzing around the room, and Mary felt almost giddy.

Mr. Wilson requested that the violinist pause her performance. "You are well suited for each other," he told them. Mary felt a small blush rise on her cheeks, and then Mr. Wilson continued, "Since you are very close in height, it makes you ideal partners."

He continued his instruction, teaching them the remaining attitudes. He was still critical and exacting, but Mary did not mind as much now that she danced with Mr. Withrow.

When the lesson finished, they said polite farewells to Mr. Wilson, and Lady Trafford gave him generous thanks. "I shall tell all of my friends of your great skill."

"It has been an honour, Lady Trafford." He gave her a deep bow.

Then Lady Trafford excused herself so she could rest in her room. "This takes more out of me than it used to."

Yet Mr. Withrow did not immediately follow the others

from the room, so Mary took the opportunity of the private moment to ask, "Did you propose the switch in partners, or did Lady Trafford?"

"Which would you rather have occurred, Miss Bennet?"

"My preference has nothing to do with it. I am requesting a simple fact."

"You have a preference, even if you will not admit it to me. But I will tell you the truth. I proposed it."

"Thank you." She wished she could say more, but how could she express what a difference it had made to dance with him? She swallowed. Her throat was dry, but she tried to ignore it. "Mr. Withrow, would you be willing to assist me in additional practice of the waltz?"

"Are you concerned that you will not be ready to dance with the prince?"

"I do not care about the prince. I—"

Mary almost took the coward's route. It would be so much simpler to lie, to not tell him why she wanted to dance with him. But she did not want to be a coward, both out of principle and because if she were brave, it might open future possibilities. As she looked into Mr. Withrow's eyes, she wanted to be brave.

"You said, a few days ago, that you enjoy my company," said Mary. "I enjoy yours as well. I have never had the opportunity to dance with you before today, and I would…like to dance with you more."

"The violinist left," he said.

This did not seem like a true difficulty; while music was helpful, it was not absolutely required. But then she remembered something Lady Trafford had taught her. This was the sort of statement people said to politely decline an invitation. He clearly had no interest. Why would he possibly want to dance with her? It was incredibly silly of her to think that he might.

"I...forgot she had left," she said, trying to keep her disappointment from her voice. She turned away and began to flee from the room.

"Miss Bennet," said Mr. Withrow.

She stopped, but she did not turn around. She did not want his pity.

"Could you count a beat for us?" he asked.

"I thought you did not want to dance."

"I did not intend to give you that impression," he said. "It would be a great honour to dance with you again."

She turned back to him, almost expecting that she had imagined his last words. But his hand was outstretched.

She took the few steps back to him and slipped her hand into his.

"You dare to use more than just the thumb and the index finger to touch my hand?"

"I apologise," said Mary, "I—"

"I jest," said Mr. Withrow. "I prefer it this way as well, though if Mr. Wilson returns, he will be thoroughly scandalized and likely refuse to teach us dancing again."

"Would that be such a terrible thing?" asked Mary.

"Perhaps not," said Mr. Withrow. "Shall we begin with the march?"

They did the four steps forward, and Mary actually managed to do the fifth position properly. Then they moved into the waltz. Mary counted aloud as they danced, "One, two, three, one, two, three, one, two, three, one, two, three."

After a minute or two she stopped counting, but they did not stop dancing.

"Shall we move to the jetté?" he asked.

"And skip the sauteuse? That sounds almost criminal."

He laughed, which was gratifying, because her jest had been intentional.

"Besides, my leaps are not graceful," she said.

"Nonsense."

"Very well."

On the third leap she stumbled. His immediate reaction was to catch her.

"I told you my leaps were not graceful."

"Maybe not the most graceful if you insist on technicalities. But I think they are excellent."

They returned to the normal waltz, and for a while danced in the seventh attitude, with his hands on her waist and her own held behind her back. Then she moved her arms to his waist—the eighth attitude—and their movements slowed. They were dancing slower even than the slow waltz, and if Mr. Wilson were here, he would surely criticise them. They were not in time, they were using their full hands rather than their thumbs and index fingers, they had ceased the proper footsteps, and in truth they were simply spinning around each other in circular movements across the floor. Mary could not imagine anything better.

Finally, they stopped dancing altogether, but Mary did not drop her arms, and neither did Mr. Withrow. They stood there, arms on each other's waists, and Mary never wanted to let go.

She felt especially daring, and being daring had led to this moment, so it clearly was an attribute to be indulged. "Mr. Withrow, would you dance with me at the Duchess of Richmond's ball?" It was customary for men to ask women to dance, but at this moment, she did not care.

"Yes, of course."

Never before had she attended a ball with a dance reserved in advance, yet for this ball, she now had two reserved dances, one with a prince, and one with Mr. Withrow. Her sister Kitty would call this quite the conquest, but she only cared about one of the two planned dances.

Mr. Withrow let go of her, and immediately she felt the loss of his hands on her waist, but then he reached his left hand up and touched the side of her face.

"Miss Bennet, you are quite extraordinary."

This would be a fine compliment from anyone, but from Mr. Withrow, critical, cynical Mr. Withrow, this was a fine compliment indeed.

His face leaned in towards her own. Her lips tingled with anticipation, and then he kissed her.

It was as if someone had managed to capture a year of happiness, put it in a jar, and then dispensed it all at once. It was one of those rare, transcendent moments, like stepping in front of a painting and having it speak to your soul, or hearing, for the first time, the tune that would become your favourite melody.

Yet when the kiss ended, he stepped back, away from her.

Rather stiffly, he said, "I apologise, Miss Bennet."

Why was he apologising? Maybe he feared where such a kiss could lead, maybe he regretted it already, maybe he did not want any sort of commitment or relationship with her. Or maybe he simply felt unsure as to whether or not she had wanted to be kissed.

"Do not apologise, Mr. Withrow. I found the kiss appropriate—for my sentiments, at least. I cannot speak for yours."

He smiled. "Yes, the kiss matched my sentiments as well."

They stood there, looking at each other, and the gap between them seemed both infinitesimal and infinite—the distance could be crossed in a moment, or might never be crossed.

Mr. Withrow cleared his throat. "Neither of us are apt to make impetuous decisions, particularly for matters of import."

She nodded.

"If it is agreeable to you, I propose that we both spend time on private reflection and contemplation, about future possibilities. And then we can return to this...conversation."

Mary's heart felt torn in different directions: she wanted to converse—or contemplate the future—or kiss—or all of the above—immediately. Yet he was right. The implications of a kiss between them were of great, long-lasting import.

"That is agreeable," said Mary. "But I will hold you to a future conversation."

"Of course." He bowed to her, and she curtsied—perhaps the best curtsy she had ever given in her life. As Mr. Withrow left the room, he stopped for a moment and turned back to her. And then he was gone.

Mary sat down at the pianoforte and, from memory, played the tune of the waltz. As she did, her lips still felt warm.

Chapter Sixteen

> *"Tho' I have given some pretty good reasons for supposing that hostilities will soon commence, yet no one would suppose it judging by the Duke of Wellington. He appears to be thinking of anything else in the world, gives a ball every week, attends every party and partakes of every amusement that offers."*
>
> —A letter written by Spencer Madan from Brussels to England on June 13, 1815

CHANGING HER APPAREL in a carriage was officially one of the most uncomfortable and awkward things Mary had ever done. She could not fully stand, and she tried not to bump the curtains, or everyone outside would see her half-dressed. She had thought it likely, for visiting the horse races, that she would only need her Mr. Fothergill costume, but after she and Mr. Withrow had met with Lord Uxbridge, the head of the cavalry and the man who coordinated the weekly horse races, she had spotted Lemoine, Serrurier, and Voland. They had decided that Mr. Withrow would question Mr. Hayes, the man whom Uxbridge had informed them coordinated much of the gambling, while Mary transformed into Mademoiselle Portier to interrogate the Belgians.

Once Mary had finished putting on the dress, she removed the wig and the moustache, then, using a small mirror, hastily applied some creams and colour to transform the appearance of her face. Finally, she donned the spectacles to complete the look.

She hesitated, but then she transferred the pistol from a holster on the belt of her Mr. Fothergill outfit to a large reticule that could be added to the Mademoiselle Portier costume. None of the three Belgian officers had attended Blücher's ball, but it would have been possible for one of them to have committed the crime without entering the ballroom.

Once her disguise was ready, she peeked out of the carriage to make sure no one was watching: it would be a shame if someone saw her enter the carriage as Mr. Fothergill and exit as Mademoiselle Portier. Unless, of course, they thought that Fothergill and Portier were separate people and engaged in a tryst, in which case it would not damage her own reputation, just the reputation of her fake identities.

She found the Belgian officers watching a race around a lake. Trees and bushes surrounded large sections of the lake, and the narrow path used as a racetrack contained fallen logs and other obstacles. It did not seem the safest racetrack for the people or the horses, but who was she to judge? Several boys—maybe only twelve or thirteen years of age, but with military uniforms—competed against full-grown men.

She greeted the Belgians in French. *"What a pleasure to meet you here. My cousin brought me to see the races, but he has stepped away for a moment."*

"I have not seen you at the inn," said Captain Lemoine.

"I have been quite busy, unfortunately." She realised her delivery must seem cold—it was hard to channel the flirtation she had used the last time, but she needed at least a little of it, or how would she gain any information? She smiled the way

Kitty might, at a moment like this. *"You have missed me, then?"*

"Of course, mademoiselle."

On the far side of the lake, one of the boys flew off his horse and landed in the lake. When his head came back above the water, everyone in the crowd cheered. Lydia would have found the incident amusing...the old Lydia, not the current Lydia who largely refused to leave her room in Lady Trafford's house.

There was a small leaf on Lemoine's uniform. While Mary would normally ignore it or comment on it, Mademoiselle Portier would remove it herself, so she very deliberately reached out to Lemoine's uniform and took the leaf. She twirled it between her fingers before letting it fall to the ground.

Lemoine smiled, but Colonel Serrurier and Colonel Voland looked as if they were about to step away. She wanted all three of them there for this conversation—as she and the other spies had not been allowed to question anyone on Ouvrard's death, this was an opportunity.

"I have heard the most shocking news, that a Belgian officer, Colonel Ouvrard, was also killed."

This statement created quite the reaction. Colonel Serrurier said something in French that Mary did not understand. Lemoine glared at him, and he apologised, so it must have been a profanity.

"Ouvrard was a friend," said Voland apologetically.

"I am very sorry for your loss," said Mary. *"He must have been a great man."*

Lemoine nodded.

"We were in the same regiment together, until we were both promoted to colonel, and he was transferred to a different

regiment," said Colonel Serrurier. *"It was close, intense fighting on the Peninsula, so we still saw a lot of each other."*

"Who would have wanted to kill him?" asked Mary.

"It does not make any sense," said Voland. *"They have interviewed us, but we cannot think of anyone."*

Their anger and frustration at Ouvrard's death seemed genuine. Of course, many murders were committed by friends and relations, so she could not simply eliminate them as suspects. And if they were innocent, they might unknowingly possess information of use.

"I heard that the Englishman was a gambler. Did Ouvrard gamble?"

They shook their heads. A pity. That would have been a convenient connection between the two deceased men.

Mary knew that if she asked further questions, it might raise their suspicions. These men were traitors, sending messages to Bonaparte, and had somehow managed to avoid any consequences for their actions. A chill travelled down her spine, but she ignored it and raised her next line of inquiry.

"I heard a Prussian might have been the murderer."

Serrurier and Voland laughed, and even though Mary was playing a part, even though this woman in a low-cut dress was not her, it stung, and she felt her cheeks burn in shame. Lemoine put his hand on her arm in a comforting gesture.

"I do not mean the Prussian who lied about killing the Englishman." It was now common knowledge that Schmidt was not the murderer. *"I mean someone else."*

"Someone else?" said Serrurier slowly. "Who would that be?"

"I heard that the dead Englishman met with a Prussian about art the same day he was killed, and I thought that if that art person killed the Englishman, he could have also killed Ouvrard." It was a stretch—it was not even a fully fleshed out

theory, and as she said it, she knew it did not make sense. But perhaps that fit in the nature of the character she had constructed as Mademoiselle Portier.

Serrurier and even Lemoine looked at her with scepticism, but Voland looked thoughtful.

"*The Prussian involved in art,*" he said slowly. "*Was it a man or a woman?*"

"*I thought a man, but I could be wrong,*" said Mary truthfully.

"*There is an artist,*" said Voland. "*A Prussian artist, who lives here in Brussels. She has lived here and done art for the past thirty years, so most do not know she is Prussian. I cannot see her having a reason to kill, but if she did meet with the Englishman before he died, she may know something that can help us solve Ouvrard's murder.*"

"*Come,*" said Serrurier, tugging on Voland's arm. "*Let us find someone to talk to about this.*"

"*Thank you, Mademoiselle Portier, for your help,*" said Voland, and before Mary could respond, Serrurier and Voland were gone, and Mary was alone with Lemoine.

Well, as alone as one could be at a horse race.

Unfortunately, Voland had left before Mary could ask him the name of the Prussian artist.

"*I did not know there were any Prussian artists in Brussels,*" said Mary.

"*Neither did I,*" said Lemoine.

So he would be of no use. But maybe, with this extra piece of knowledge, she would be able to find the woman.

"*May I take your arm?*" asked Lemoine.

"*Of course,*" said Mary, and he took her arm in his and they began to walk through the crowd. At one point Lemoine stopped and drew his face closer to hers. She suspected, based on their previous interactions at the inn, that he wanted to kiss her again.

She did not want to kiss him—she did not want to kiss anyone but Mr. Withrow. When she and Mr. Withrow had parted a few minutes ago, he had encouraged her to use whatever means necessary to extract information from the Belgians. She suspected he was making a concerted effort to behave differently than he had after their visit to the inn. Yet, if possible, she still wanted to avoid kissing Lemoine.

"My cousin was quite upset with me last time, leaving the table and being gone for so long. He wants to make certain there are no rumours about my marriageability."

"There are thousands of people here," said Lemoine. "No one would notice us."

"There are thousands of people here," said Mary, "which means someone is watching us, even if we do not know it."

Perhaps that had been too harsh, so Mary sighed archly, or at least, she tried to approximate the way in which other women sighed archly. *"I do not like following his advice, but I must think about my future prospects. Perhaps you should think about your future prospects as well. Not now, of course,"* she added quickly, for receiving a proposal from Lemoine today would be most inconvenient. *"But do give it some thought."*

"I will give it all the thought in the world, ma chérie."

Oh dear. Hopefully she did not have to don this disguise again, for it seemed distinctly wrong to allow a fake persona to become engaged. Now she worried that her words today, while preventing a kiss, would cause Lemoine heartbreak. She had no business tormenting respectable—or partially respectable—men, even if they were spies for Bonaparte.

There were cheers. The race around the lake was complete, and Lord Uxbridge awarded a medal to an enthusiastic

British officer in his twenties. Uxbridge had expressed a concern, when she and Withrow had spoken to him a few minutes before, that Wellington would not use him or the cavalry when hostilities began with France. He did not show any of that concern now, as he spoke to the jovial crowd.

Mary was supposed to meet Mr. Withrow after an hour, but she dared not check her pocket watch to see how much time had passed.

"*Do you plan to participate in the races yourself?*" asked Mary.

"*No. It is mostly the cavalry who compete. Yet I ride very well.*"

His smile and his tone made Mary suspect that there was innuendo in the statement—innuendo that Mrs. Graham or Mademoiselle Portier would recognize. But it was hard to respond properly to something you did not understand, so instead she smiled and asked, "*Have you written another letter? To…your friend south of here.*"

Lemoine shook his head. "*No, I have decided to stop.*"

"*To stop? You surprise me.*"

"*I may not like the Dutch, and I certainly despise the English, but there are good things to be had from independence from France's rule. I spoke with the Prince of Orange, and he has a vision for the future of the United Netherlands that has a place at the table—a very good place at the table—for the Belgians.*"

"*That make sense,*" said Mary. So the Prince of Orange, instead of dismissing or punishing the spies, had attempted to win them to his side. But who was to judge if a man had actually switched loyalties? Lemoine could simply be playing a part. It was a risky game the Prince of Orange played, a risky game indeed.

She played a risky game as well. Lemoine could easily suspect her—he might wonder why the prince had suddenly chosen to talk to him, so shortly after he had revealed his actions to Mary. He might wonder why she cared so much about the murders and the war.

"I had better go find my cousin, but I am so happy to have seen you today."

"The pleasure was mine," said Lemoine, and he raised her hand and kissed it. At least, though, he had not kissed her on the lips, or encouraged her to reciprocate affections. However, to maintain the disguise, Mary gave him a quick kiss on the cheek.

Once he was gone, she headed towards the planned meeting place, but then she saw General Tippert walking hurriedly, so she followed him.

"But you just arrived, sir," said a lad at Tippert's side. "Won't you place just one bet? The odds are—"

"I have a feeling that gambling is not the activity for today," said General Tippert. "Give my regrets to Hayes."

What would cause Tippert to arrive at the horse races with the intention of gambling and then leave almost immediately?

He must have seen Mr. Withrow, dressed as Mr. Pike, speaking to Mr. Hayes. He did not want to be questioned about his gambling, or his debts to Major General Leon.

Yet she could not question him as Mademoiselle Portier—she had no authority to do so, and he no reason to answer her questions—and if he really was leaving, there was no time to change back to her Mr. Fothergill disguise.

There was nothing she could do but stall General Tippert and hope that Mr. Withrow noticed her. It must be nearing the time they were to meet, and theoretically close enough to the meeting spot that Withrow might see her.

She made her way around the side of the crowd, pushing through so she was moving faster than General Tippert, and then cut in front of him so as to intercept him.

"Please, sir," she said, attempting to add a French accent to her English. "I am looking for my brother. I cannot find him. Please, sir."

"I am sorry," he said, pushing past her. "Surely someone else can help you."

"But he is only six years old."

General Tippert stopped and turned around, giving her his full attention. "Six years old. What does he look like, and where did you last see him?"

Haltingly, Mary described an imaginary six-year-old brother, trying to use as many details as possible to prolong their conversation. She had just begun to describe the last time she had seen him when Mr. Withrow arrived.

"General Tippert," he said. "I would like to speak to you. My partner Mr. Fothergill spoke to you the other night, at Blücher's ball."

"I would, but I am helping this local woman, and then unfortunately I have an appointment in Brussels."

"Oh, I see my little brother in the crowd!" said Mary, gesturing towards a particularly dense spot. "Thank you, sir, for being kind enough to help me."

She stepped away.

"If you are leaving, perhaps I can walk you to your carriage," said Mr. Withrow.

"That is acceptable," said General Tippert.

Instead of walking farther into the crowd, Mary followed Mr. Withrow and General Tippert. She wanted to hear their conversation, and to be there in case she needed to feign the loss of a brother again.

"I suspect that I have nothing more to tell you that I have not already told your partner," said General Tippert, "but I will begin, again, at the beginning. Major General Leon—"

"Actually," said Mr. Withrow, "I do not need to hear your story. Instead, I would like to discuss your gambling debts."

"Gambling debts? What do you mean?"

They began walking along the line of carriages. Mary stepped to the other side of the carriages and stayed back a little, so she could hear without being seen.

"Several people have mentioned your gambling debts, most recently, Mr. Hayes. He only answered my questions when...encouraged. But beyond him, it seems that you have not managed to keep your debts as much of a secret as you might have liked."

"I always discharge my debts honourably, and I do not see how they concern you."

"What about your debts that were left unwritten, and acknowledged only verbally? What about an amount said to surpass four thousand pounds, to a man who is now dead? It must be very convenient to not have to pay your debts to Leon."

Four thousand pounds? Wickham had said Tippert owed Leon one thousand pounds, but he must have been mistaken.

There was silence for a moment. Mary could glimpse Withrow and General Tippert through the carriages ahead. She stepped back a little, but not before she saw that Tippert was very red in the face.

"Despite Leon's death, which I had nothing to do with, I still consider my debt as a debt. I sent a letter to my bank in London requesting five hundred pounds to be transferred to Mrs. Leon. It is my first instalment, and there is documentation to prove it. Write to the bank, write to Mrs. Leon. You will see that it has arrived."

"The fact that you have given her money does not prove your innocence," said Mr. Withrow.

"Of course it does," said General Tippert. "Why else would I pay back the debt when there is no record of it?"

"If a man such as yourself felt guilty for creating a widow, would he not want to find some way to assist her?"

"I am done here," said General Tippert, stomping away.

"Do not leave Brussels," Mr. Withrow called after him.

"You have no authority to prevent me from doing so."

"I can have Wellington's signature on a paper by the end of the day. I will have it sent to you."

The general stalked off to his carriage, and Mary joined Mr. Withrow as they walked back towards the races, standing a little apart in case someone thought it strange for an investigator and a Belgian woman to be walking to each other.

"Thank you for preventing him from leaving," said Mr. Withrow.

"You are welcome," said Mary.

Later, they took their own carriage back to Brussels. She told him about her conversation with the Belgian officers, and he told her about the conversation with Hayes. In addition to General Tippert, there were three men that he knew of who had owed Leon debts, but they were all less than five hundred pounds. Yet plenty of people killed for less.

From memory, Mary drew a sketch of General Tippert and then a sketch of the three Belgian officers together.

"You have captured them," said Mr. Withrow. "You have captured them all. But Lemoine has a little more hair in front of his ears."

"I never noticed," said Mary, and added a little hair to

Lemoine. Mr. Withrow was watching her very intently. "I have drawn many people, but I have never once drawn you. Would you sit for me?"

"Most certainly. However, I should remove my disguise first."

He removed the wig, the mould on his nose, and the wads of fabric in his cheeks. Then he did several rather silly poses which made her laugh.

"I cannot possibly draw you like that, practically falling over."

"Fine," he said. "How about this?"

He sat upright, his hands folded together. He did not smile, but there was something pleasant and composed about his expression, and the way he looked at her, the expression in his eyes—

"I will try to draw quickly," said Mary. "I know that it is difficult to sit in one position for an extended period of time." She also knew that as the carriage ride progressed he would begin to feel ill, and wanted to finish before then.

"Do not rush yourself, Miss Bennet. I can sit like this for as long as you need."

Despite the occasional bumps of the carriage, he was quite good at holding the pose. He had very good facial features, which she had grown to appreciate as she had gotten to know him better.

As she drew him, she thought about their dance the day before, and their conversation after. Mentally, she formulated a list of reasons for marrying Mr. Withrow. It was quite the lengthy list, ranging from analytical reasons to emotional ones to small items that made them compatible. Then she attempted to mentally create a list of reasons against marrying Mr. Withrow. Yet despite applying herself for several minutes to the task, she could not formulate a single item for that list.

She drew his eyes, attempting to capture their intensity, their kindness, their insight, their shape. Clearly, she should be able to come up with legitimate reasons to not marry him. For example, she did value independence, and marriage required the sacrifice of some independence in order to create a partnership. Yet that was not a true detractor, in her mind, if one married the right person.

Mary continued to consider the matter as she finished the portrait, and by the time she was done, she felt like she had devoted enough mental, rational, and emotional energy to come to her final conclusion: she wanted to marry Mr. Withrow.

The very thought made her feel buoyant, the cushions softer, and the sun brighter. They could be happy, together, and make a difference in the world.

She showed him the portrait.

"It is very good. You have surpassed yourself."

"Thank you," said Mary. "You do not find it deficient in any way?"

"Not at all." He paused. "You have given a number of your portraits to their subjects. May I have this?"

"No."

"Why not?"

"It is the only drawing I have ever made of you, and I would like to keep it, so I can look upon it even when you are not present." She felt herself blush. She had become almost reckless in the way that she spoke to him—but was it not merited? "I will try, later, to make a copy, and I will give that to you."

"Do not trouble yourself," he said.

"It is no trouble at all." She was certain that it would

cause her no suffering to draw even twenty portraits of Mr. Withrow.

Chapter Seventeen

> "30,000,000 musket ball-cartridges, and 30,000 barrels of powder, of 90lb. each, have been embarked at Woolwich for the Duke of Wellington's army in the Netherlands, since the army has been there."
>
> —*Kentish Chronicle*, Canterbury, England, June 13, 1815

MADAME BAUER'S FRONT room was filled with oil paintings, mostly historicals and portraits. While some of the portraits represented the upper classes, the majority featured ordinary people with a full range of skin tones: workers and shopkeepers and beggars and musicians. In each painting, the Prussian artist captured personality and insight on the canvas, and while the space was not necessarily comforting—art was not always meant to give comfort—Mary did feel comfortable. Like Mary, Madame Bauer was an observer of human nature, and hopefully she would act as a useful informant and not become a prime suspect.

"Can I paint while we talk?" asked Madame Bauer in French.

Mary agreed and followed the woman into a back room where a half-completed painting sat on an easel. When Mary and Mr. Withrow had returned to Brussels after the horse races, Lady Trafford had used Mary's information and her own connections to discover the identity and location of the mysterious Prussian artist, and Mary had gone immediately to pay her a call.

Madame Bauer looked to be in her sixties. She had brown skin and dark black hair, and wore a frock flecked with paint over her dress. Her fingers, too, were stained by oil paints.

Mary knew that she should broach the subject matter, but suddenly she felt uncomfortable doing so. She scratched at her fake moustache and watched the painter at her work, applying layers of colour to a girl's face.

"This painting was to be for Major General Leon," said Madame Bauer.

"Who is the subject?" asked Mary.

"His daughter. I have never met her, which makes painting her more difficult, but I do have a detailed sketch he provided." She applied more paint to the canvas. "It is unusual for even the rich to commission paintings of their daughters, until the time they wed. But I am not one to complain about a commission."

"It is my understanding that Leon came to talk to you about this painting on the second of June, the day he died."

"Oui. He came to see my progress."

"You had met with him before?" asked Mary.

"Oui. About a week before."

"How did you make his acquaintance?"

"He had seen one of my paintings here in Brussels and wanted to commission me to paint her portrait. Previously, he had hired an artist in England to paint her but did not feel like it captured her essence." She paused, her paintbrush raised. "I think he trusted me to paint her properly, because I have brown skin, and I have painted many people with a similar skin tone."

"It is a fine painting so far," said Mary.

Madame Bauer shrugged. "We will see. Once I am satisfied

with it, I will send it to England to his wife."

"Did Leon pay you for the work in advance?"

"He paid two-thirds in advance, and the last third was meant to be paid on completion."

"So you will finish it, even knowing that you will not receive the final payment?"

"Two-thirds is enough, and I do not like to leave a work unfinished. Besides, it would seem heartless to not finish the commission of a deceased man."

"During your second meeting, what time did Leon arrive, and what time did he leave?"

"I did not check the time. It was in the afternoon, and he was not here for more than an hour."

"Can you describe the visit? What did you talk about?"

"We talked about the painting, and he helped me adjust her facial features—the sketch did not contain all the necessary details. I also wanted to understand his daughter Martha and her character, for I always try to provide a window to someone's inner being. Of course, the painting is naturally as much about Leon and his connection to Martha as it is about Martha herself. It is also a portrait about a time and a place, and future generations may use this painting to try to understand us. In some ways, this painting is also a self-portrait: every one of my paintings is about me and the way I see the world."

It was a different perspective on art, not one Mary had ever considered.

"You talked about nothing else besides the painting?"

"I am sure we spoke of other things." Madame Bauer cleaned her brush in a strong-smelling turpentine oil, and then dipped it in a maroon and added more colour to the dress.

"Did he seem agitated or worried in any way?"

"No, but he was rather nostalgic. He mentioned missing many years with his wife and his children because of war." She stopped painting suddenly and turned to Mary. "At one point he apologised for not being more attentive. Earlier in the day, he had spoken to someone who reminded him about a particular Peninsular battle—he did not say which one. He seemed rather unsettled. That is useful to you, I hope."

"Yes, I believe it is." Mary asked Madame Bauer about Ouvrard, but while she had heard of him and his death, she knew nothing about him. She also inquired into Madame Bauer's whereabouts on the night of the murder. She had been at home, painting, as always. Nothing about Madame Bauer's speech or mannerisms seemed suspicious in any way—Mary truly believed the artist's only connection to Leon was the painting. After a few minutes more of conversation, Mary left the shop.

Perhaps the most important part of the conversation was the unnamed person who had spoken to Leon and reminded him of an event on the Peninsula. This seemed to be the key. But who had served with Leon in the Peninsular Wars? Colonel Kitsell and the Prince of Orange, the Duke of Wellington and Lord Uxbridge. General Tippert had not served on the peninsula, but he still could have referenced an event that had occurred there.

Mary felt like she was missing some key piece of information. Or perhaps she had gathered all the information she needed and simply interpreted it wrong.

Maybe the case was like Madame Bauer's paintings. It was about the murdered men, yes, and it clearly was about the murderer, but it was also about the war more generally and about the Duke of Wellington and Napoleon Bonaparte. And finally, it was about her and Mr. Withrow and Lady Trafford, their ability to see and interpret a situation, and then to display their discoveries to the world.

ANOTHER MAN HAD been murdered, in his cottage several miles outside of Brussels.

The Duke of Wellington had used one of his contacts to get them fifteen minutes with the body—any longer and the Prince of Orange and the King of the Netherlands would need to know.

"The victim is a Monsieur Marsal," said the duke as Mary, Mr. Withrow, and Lady Trafford stepped into the cottage. "Age forty-five, he lived alone. The body was discovered early this morning by the woman who delivers milk."

The body had taken a single gunshot to the head and was crumpled on the kitchen floor. Mary should be used to the appearance of a brain blown to pieces, but even after two men killed in this manner, it still shocked her.

"The Dutch do not believe the crimes to be connected," said the Duke of Wellington. "Marsal was not an officer, and he was not shot twice."

"There appears to have been struggle, unlike in the previous murders," said Mr. Withrow. He pointed at papers spread across the floor and the askew chairs. Then he acted out the scene, moving from spot to spot, as if he were the dead man, and pointing at where he thought the murderer had stood. "If Marsal raised the chair and stepped towards the attacker, the attacker could have shot him once, in the head, instead of the normal two shots."

"Marsal has only one leg," said Mary. "It is common to lose limbs in battle. Could he have previously been an officer or a soldier, even if he is not now?" There had to be a connection to the war—or the previous wars.

"If we ask, the Dutch government will find out," said Wellington. "We must find our own evidence for that or another connection—and quickly."

They used the rest of their time in earnest, scouring the house while attempting to leave no trace. It was strange to see the Duke of Wellington himself searching through papers, as if he were not the commander of the entire Allied forces, preparing for an impending war with Bonaparte. She had heard it said that the Duke of Wellington often kept himself in the midst of the battlefield—he liked to manage things from the heart of the action. To him, this investigation and the continuing murders were yet another battle.

Mr. Withrow gave Mary several encouraging smiles as they worked. It was quite strange: encouraging smiles were not part of Mr. Withrow's normal repertoire. But she liked it very much.

"I found something," Lady Trafford announced. "Discharge papers. Monsieur Marsal was an ensign, the lowest rank of officer in the French army. He served in the peninsula, under Ouvrard."

This was the peninsular connection. "Ouvrard and Marsal served together in the peninsula," said Mary, "and the Prussian artist said that Leon was troubled because someone had told him something about an event in the peninsula. Could the connection between the murder victims be that they fought on opposing sides of the same battle?"

The Duke of Wellington considered for a moment. "I will ask Colonel Kitsell to check the records, but according to my memory of events, Leon and Ouvrard would have fought against each other several times."

Something must have happened in those battles, something that had led to the current murders. But why were the murders occurring now, rather than closer to the events? There must also be some connection to the current conflict.

Chapter Eighteen

"If Napoleon were really that 'blockhead' which some would represent him, what ought those to be called whom he has so egregiously outwitted?"

—*The Correspondent and Public Cause*, London,
June 14, 1815

THE LAST PERSON Mary had expected to arrive at their doorstep was Miss Tagore.

Truth be told, she was not the *last* person. There were plenty of people who would be less likely to arrive at their abode in Brussels seeking entry: Napoleon Bonaparte, random Americans…even Mary's mother, Mrs. Bennet, would have been more surprising. Yet still, Miss Tagore was in Paris—or had been, for clearly she was now in Brussels.

Miss Tagore wore a wrinkled men's suit, yet she had not disguised herself as a man—she had done nothing to flatten her chest or disguise her hair, which was braided and wrapped in a coil on the top of her head. Some of the black strands had come loose, and there was a sheen of sweat on Miss Tagore's brow.

She had travelled non-stop from Paris in a period of fifty hours. Her first horse—a horse trained for traversing long distances—had almost died, and then she had managed to find a new horse to purchase, and then she had abandoned the second horse on the road and walked the last ten miles to Brussels on foot.

Mrs. Boughton gave Miss Tagore a second cup of black tea as they waited for the Duke of Wellington and the Prince of Orange to arrive. Miss Tagore drank the tea in a few seconds and then began pacing, once again, back and forth across the room.

"Watching you is making me tired, Miss Tagore," said Lady Trafford.

Miss Tagore smiled. "How could I possibly make you tired? You always have endless energy."

"Now I must moderate it," said Lady Trafford. "I danced rather too much French waltz two days ago, and I have yet to recover."

"Would that I could have taken your place." Miss Tagore sighed, and her body began to droop, but she forced herself upright and paced faster than ever. She must have urgent news indeed, for her to leave her post in Paris and ride for days to bring them word. Something dreadful must have happened, or, perhaps, something dreadful was about to happen, but she thought it best to only tell them once the Duke of Wellington arrived.

"Have you spoken to Mr. Matthews?" asked Lady Trafford. He was the other spy she sent to Paris.

"He went missing a week and a half ago," she said. "I fear something has happened to him."

"A disturbing thought," said Lady Trafford.

It was disturbing indeed.

After finishing her first cup of black tea, Mary sat down on a sofa. A few seconds later, Mr. Withrow made his way across the room and sat next to her. Of course, she should not read too much into that, but when he glanced at her, she smiled. He gave her a quick nod and then turned back to the others. Her heart palpitated wildly. Amazing the effect of a simple nod from the correct person. Had he taken the time to consider the possibility of a future between them? It had only been two days, but now that Mary had decided what she wanted, she was impatient for him to come to a conclusion. How long would be reasonable to give him? Perhaps tomorrow night, at the ball, she could ask him while they danced.

The Duke of Wellington and the Prince of Orange entered the room with Lady Trafford's carriage driver, Mr. Parker. Everyone stood. Immediately, Mrs. Boughton looked up and down the hallway, closed the door, and then locked it. No one could disturb them—Lydia and her Belgian nurse must be shut out. Lydia was shut out of so many areas of Mary's life, many of which could never be opened to her. Perhaps they could find something to share, yet it was difficult. Even now, Lydia's words were not always kind, and they had never much liked each other's company.

"I know your time is extremely valuable," said Lady Trafford, opening the meeting, "so I would like to thank you for coming so quickly. This is Miss Madhabika Tagore. Miss Tagore, this is the Duke of Wellington and the Prince of Orange."

Miss Tagore did a rather marvellous curtsy. How could she perform such a fine curtsy when she was not even wearing a dress? Some things were simply unjust.

"It is a great pleasure," said the Duke of Wellington. "I met your parents once, in India. They are fine people."

"Yes, they told me about meeting you."

"I thought you were in Paris."

"I had a message that was too urgent and too important to pass through any other messenger."

"Then please, share it with us."

"Napoleon Bonaparte has left Paris to join his troops. From what I was able to gather, there are seventy to eighty thousand men, headed in this direction, likely with the intent of taking Brussels and breaking the Allies."

Mary felt as if her heart stopped for a moment, and there was a faint yet audible reaction of surprise from Lady Trafford and Mr. Withrow. The Prince of Orange clutched the edge of his chair, closed his eyes, and whispered something, perhaps a prayer. Yet the Duke of Wellington did not seem surprised or worried in any way.

"Explain further, if you will," said the duke.

"Napoleon Bonaparte will not wait for the Allies to gather troops and prepare for an offensive. He knows that he cannot put up a good defence, especially with his own people in the west revolting."

"It is the revolts in western France that make me question your information," said the duke. "Bonaparte has had trouble procuring horses and rations, and only yesterday I received word that he is focusing on quelling the uprisings in western France."

"I saw Bonaparte, with my own two eyes," said Miss Tagore impatiently. "He packed his jewels into his carriage. He sent word ahead to his troops, and, out of desperation, he gave Ney a command. I know for a fact that there are at least seventy thousand men in northern France, near the border. The officers I spoke to know that their orders are to break the Allies. If Russia and Austria can ready themselves and unite with the Prussians and the Allied troops, he will fail. But if he can gain a quick victory against the Allied forces or the Prussians, then he can rally France to his cause."

The Duke of Wellington put his hand on his chin, as if

posing for a portrait. "Bonaparte is a master strategist. There have been dozens of times when he has outwitted an enemy by leading them to believe he was doing one thing with his troops, causing them to overcommit, and then doing something else entirely." Wellington unrolled a map he had brought with them. "I need you to show me the exact locations, movement, and numbers of the French forces, the last time you saw them."

They all gathered around the map, giving Miss Tagore, the Duke of Wellington, and Prince Willem precedence. Miss Tagore showed her understanding of the troops and their positions. There were a number of roads they could take to attack the Prussians and the Allies, assuming they used roads, which were easier for the troops and wagons and artillery to navigate. Miss Tagore did not know which path they planned to take, or if Bonaparte planned to divide his troops and attack from multiple locations.

"We must act, immediately," said Prince Willem. "If you were to send additional Allied troops to supplement—"

"No," said the duke. "Assuming that this intelligence is correct, and that Bonaparte has indeed decided to take the offensive, I must wait until I am certain of the path he has chosen and his strategy. If I deploy too early, he will divide and distract and subvert us—if I allow him to outwit me, the Netherlands will fall within a week."

"Very well, sir," said Prince Willem.

"However," said the duke, "do as you will with your own troops. I trust you and the preparations you make."

"Thank you, sir."

"Thank you for bringing me word," said the duke. He asked Miss Tagore a few more questions about her observations in Paris, and then inquired as to the health of her family.

Then he said his farewells, but Prince Willem did not leave with him.

"Miss Tagore, it truly is a great pleasure to make your acquaintance, although it be in trying circumstances. I do hope you will be attending the Duchess of Richmond's ball?"

Miss Tagore glanced at Lady Trafford, who nodded. "I believe so."

"I look forward to seeing you there. And thank you for your service."

"Wellington said that you are welcome to act on the information," said Miss Tagore. "What precisely do you plan to do?"

"Your intelligence matches other reports I have received. I will adjust the placement of troops in a few minor ways, but mostly, I plan to have large contingents of troops ready for a fight at any moment across the entire border with France. I will also send out spies to see if they can ascertain which road will be taken."

"I hope that is enough," said Miss Tagore.

"I apologise for changing the subject," said Mr. Withrow, "but why have you not arrested Serrurier, Lemoine, and Voland, or at the very least removed them from their positions?" Though Mary had told him of Lemoine's professed change of heart, he had not been convinced.

The prince shifted uncomfortably. "My father and I decided it was best to leave them in their positions, so as not to cause disruption, and to see if any others are engaged in similar behaviour. We will, of course, intercept further communications and prevent any news from being passed to France."

"I wonder if that is wise."

"History will judge. It always does." He turned to Mary.

"Miss Bennet, I hope you have not forgotten about our dance."

"It would be a rather unusual thing to forget," said Mary.

"I am looking forward to it." He bowed to each of them, thanked Miss Tagore again for her information, and left.

"Dancing with a prince?" said Miss Tagore. "Good work, Miss Bennet. But Mr. Withrow, you do not need to seem so put out."

"I am not put out," said Mr. Withrow, "especially as Miss Bennet has also promised *me* a dance."

Ideally, their dance would be a waltz, for Mary wanted to repeat the proximity between them.

"I hope that Miss Bennet leaves at least one dance partner for me," said Miss Tagore with a teasing smile.

"Unlike balls in England," said Mary, "balls in Brussels have an excess number of gentlemen, due largely to the number of officers. Also, you are known by many to be a skilled dancer and a pleasant conversationalist. I am sure you will have plenty of partners."

"I hope so, for I do love dancing." She paused. "Yet the thought of attending a ball, knowing the death and destruction that is coming…it is a little unsettling."

It was a sobering thought. For over every frivolity, every hope and dream for the future, hung the cloud of war.

Chapter Nineteen

"Why ask so oft, with fond alarms
 If constant I'll remain?
And o'er my heart how long thy charms
 Will hold their wonted reign?

No more these questions let me hear,
 Since I cannot reply;—
I do not know, my Sylvia dear,
 The day when I shall die."

—R.A. Davenport, *Cheltenham Chronicle*,
Gloucestershire, England, June 15, 1815

For Mary, the Duchess of Richmond's ball was a guessing game: who knew of the events occurring hours to the south, and who was completely oblivious? Wellington had received word that Napoleon Bonaparte had, indeed, attacked. Miss Tagore felt quite vindicated, for she had known it was coming. However, while messengers had scurried around Brussels this way and that, there had been a lack of messengers from the battlefield, and Wellington did not know where the battle had occurred, how many men had been lost, or the size and positioning of Bonaparte's forces. Without this information, he could not act, and so he had not only allowed the Duchess to have her ball, but required his superior officers to attend.

It was clear that the Duchess of Richmond had absolutely no knowledge of the hostilities. She had told Lady Trafford and Mary, "I checked with the Duke of Wellington this morning, and he gave me full permission to have my ball. Is it not delightful? But I do not understand why some of the attendees have not yet arrived." Normally, one with wealth and rank did not need permission to hold a ball, but due to the tension in Brussels and the fact that she wanted the officers to attend, the Duchess had clearly felt it expedient to obtain Wellington's blessing.

The Duke of Richmond chatted amiably with his peers, tousling the hair of his nine-year-old son. Despite being an officer, he also seemed to have no knowledge of greater events. Mrs. Graham had informed Mary that he had reluctantly paid for the ball in an attempt to appease his wife for his affair—and he had paid handsomely. New rose-trellis wallpaper covered the walls, there were piles of fresh lilies and roses, and red and gold fabric hung in fanciful patterns throughout the room. Of course, Mrs. Graham had also informed Mary that there were rumours of some sort of liaison between the Duchess of Richmond and the Duke of Wellington. It would be easier if everyone was simply loyal to their own spouses and treated them well. Doing so would improve not only individual morality, but the overall moral tenor of society.

The Scottish Highlanders in their kilts did not seem to know. They performed a dance with bagpipes to great applause. Many of the officers did not seem to know, particularly colonels and others of a lower rank. Some of the women danced without care, yet some seemed fearful, and Mary overheard Mrs. Oldfield telling her daughter, "Do not commit your heart, as girls are wont to do at balls. Tonight of all nights is not the night for it."

Lord Uxbridge was busy wooing various women, as his wife was too scandalous to be invited to a ball. He acted as if he had no concerns other than the beauty of those around him, yet there seemed to be an edge to him, and his eyes often lingered on some of the other officers, especially on the Duke of Wellington.

The Prince of Orange was in quite a state, rushing around the room, anxiously peering out the windows for messengers, and attempting to speak to the Duke of Wellington whenever he had the opportunity. He clearly knew everything there was to know and had approached Mary with a gallant bow. "I apologise, Miss Bennet, but I must withdraw from my dance. There is too much occupying me tonight."

"I completely understand," said Mary. "There are much more important matters than dancing at a ball."

"Thank you for understanding, Miss Bennet. You look very beautiful, tonight."

And then the prince was gone, off to fill everyone he spoke to with unease.

"You do look very beautiful," said Mr. Withrow from behind her.

She turned.

"Of course, you always look beautiful."

Heat rose in her cheeks. "You do not normally bestow this sort of compliment."

"Sometimes realising what matters to you makes you willing to say those things that are normally left unsaid."

It was a very pretty statement, and Mary was about to seize the opportunity and demand his thoughts on a future between them, yet the opportunity was stolen from her by Miss Oldfield and a gaggle of other younger girls. They approached Mary and began a rather too enthusiastic conversation, which drove Mr. Withrow away. It seemed an unusual bestowal of attention until one of them said, "Oh do tell us of the Prince of Orange!"

She had a rapt audience, and it seemed to be a serious request, so she decided to oblige. "The Prince of Orange is a man at a pivotal moment in history, in a pivotal country. In many ways, he is a child of a European experiment: his father was the prince of a region which has long sought its independence, his grandmother hails from the kingdom of Prussia, and he has spent most of his life raised in England, and as such has a true understanding of our sense of democracy and other ideals."

"But is he very clever?" asked a girl who could be no more than sixteen. "And what is it like to gaze into his eyes?"

So that is what they actually wanted. "I am not one to gaze into the eyes of a prince. But he is clever and kind, and he does all he can to make good decisions for his people."

This explanation only partially satisfied them, but Mary had no desire to indulge them with the types of descriptions they wanted. She was trying to find a way to extract herself from the situation when she saw an officer she recognized from the day she had landed in the Netherlands.

Amidst the chaos of unloading soldiers and horses from the boats, this young officer had spoken with General Tippert. The general had given him papers or other materials, and then the officer had returned to one of the boats. Mary had completely forgotten about the incident until now.

"Do any of you know that officer over there?" asked Mary. "I recognize him, and I would like an introduction if any of you could provide one."

"Oh!" exclaimed one of the girls. "Did you see him and instantly fall in love with him? That is what happened with me and the prince."

Mary rolled her eyes. The question did not even merit a response.

"I could introduce you," said Miss Oldfield. And then, to her friends, she added, "But I do think Miss Bennet would appreciate speaking to him *alone*."

The others giggled and then dispersed, many to their partners for the next dance.

"I apologise," said Miss Oldfield. "Some of my friends become rather excited by the possible prospects of others."

"It is good that they are finding joy in these times." For who knew what death and devastation the coming days would bring?

She wished she could bring her sister Lydia some sort of joy, but Lydia had refused to join their party at the ball, despite the fact that Lady Trafford had verified that Wickham would not be in attendance.

Miss Oldfield led the way in the direction of the officer but did not walk directly towards him, or look at him exactly, which led his eye precisely to her. Miss Oldfield had a certain amount of cunning and awareness of situations that was enviable, and, much sooner than Mary expected, the officer approached them.

"Miss Oldfield," he said, with a bow. "What a pleasure to see you again. And who is your charming friend?"

"This is Miss Bennet," said Miss Oldfield. "She is friends with the Prince of Orange. And this," she said, gesturing towards the officer, "is Colonel Tippert."

"Colonel Tippert?"

"Yes," said the man. "General Tippert is my father."

"I did not know he had a son, stationed here, who was also in the military," said Mary.

"I was not on the continent before, but I recently was transferred. I arrived yesterday."

The lie was so blatant it made her scalp itch. But what was the purpose for such a deception?

"It must be so exciting, to be here, before the Duke of Wellington takes his offensive," said Miss Oldfield.

Clearly, Miss Oldfield did not know that the British forces were already on the defensive.

"Quite exciting," said Colonel Tippert. "I look forward to performing my duty to God and country."

"You said you just arrived," said Mary, "but I saw you several weeks ago."

"Are you certain it was me?"

She was certain—she had a good memory for faces—but she did not want to come across as accusatory.

"I might be mistaken, but I thought I saw you the day that I arrived in Ostend," said Mary. "You were assisting as the military boats were unloaded, and you spoke with your father, the general. He gave you something, and you returned to the boat."

Colonel Tippert was quiet for a second, maybe two, but he seemed to come to a conclusion. "You did in fact see me, Miss Bennet. I assisted, for a few weeks, with the movement of the military officers, but I was stationed in Dover."

"Your father must have been quite happy to see you." This was the sort of statement that could make someone feel uncomfortable in an official interview but felt more natural in a conversation at a ball when one did not know he was being interrogated.

"Yes, he was," agreed Colonel Tippert. "He gave me several things for his sister, in Dover."

"It must be much nicer, now that you are here permanently, and not going back and forth every day," said Miss Oldfield with a smile.

"It is, indeed."

"The Netherlands is so beautiful," said Miss Oldfield, "and Brussels is quite charming."

"I am certainly enjoying it so far," said Colonel Tippert, and he seemed to mean it as a personal compliment to Miss Oldfield rather than a general one to Brussels.

Miss Oldfield gave an attractive blush. Unlike Mary, whose face sometimes went extremely red in unflattering ways, Miss Oldfield looked like a woman in a painting.

"Is it your first time in Brussels?" asked Mary.

"My first time in quite some time," said Colonel Tippert. "My grandmother on my father's side is from Brussels, so I have visited before. Now my grandmother lives in Paris, which is unfortunate, as I cannot see her."

A grandmother in Paris—General Tippert's mother lived in Paris and was originally from Brussels. General Tippert had given something to his son. The elder Tippert was engaged in gambling and owed substantial debts to Major General Leon. But what if there was more to it than that? She had already uncovered one set of spies reporting to Napoleon Bonaparte: might there not be more? And if the spy were a top member of the military, even if not assigned to Brussels…well, it would provide an extra reason for him to remain in Brussels.

Mary was about to ask another question—perhaps more about Grand-mère Tippert, or something about General Tippert—but then someone caught her eye, a messenger entering the ballroom from the outside door.

The messenger walked straight through the room, ignoring anyone and everyone, and headed towards the Duke of Wellington. Prince Willem darted in that direction. Unless

Mary was very much mistaken, this was the messenger the duke had been waiting for, the message that would determine the duke's next actions.

"I hope you will excuse me," said Mary. "I have...other matters to attend to."

"I hope nothing is wrong," said Miss Oldfield.

"Not at all." She could think of no proper excuse, and the truth would not do, so she curtsied, not quite as prettily as she would have liked.

"It was a pleasure to meet you," said Colonel Tippert.

"It was a pleasure to meet you as well," said Mary, and then, trying not to make it too apparent that she was following the messenger, she made her way around the ballroom. In this situation, dressing as Mr. Fothergill would have been easier. She had brought that disguise in the carriage, in case she needed to change into it, but if she left to change now, she might entirely miss the upcoming events.

The Duke of Wellington called to the Duke of Richmond. "Do you have a map? I need a map of the region."

"Yes, I do."

Both dukes, the prince, Lord Uxbridge, and a number of other officers stuffed themselves into a library, presumably with a map, and Mary was left outside, wishing she could be within. It seemed that Mr. Withrow had the same thought, for he approached.

Outside the library, Miss Kitsell tugged on her brother's arm.

"I know, my dear, that you would like me to talk with you and your friends," said Colonel Kitsell. "But if I do not attend to the duke, what chance of promotion do I have?"

"You should worry more about our country than your promotion."

"But think what the promotion would mean—what a triumph it would be for me. For us."

"Of course," said Miss Kitsell. "Go ahead."

Colonel Kitsell entered the library, and the façade on Miss Kitsell's face dropped, revealing a stark sadness. She covered her face with a handkerchief and feigned a cough.

It must have been difficult for Miss Kitsell to lose a sister, and have that sister replaced by a brother she had never known.

Mary approached. "Miss Kitsell, is anything the matter?"

"I am quite fine, Miss Bennet."

"You seem distressed." It was not the most tactful statement, and rather too direct, but Miss Kitsell did respond.

"My brother...he used to be good at seeing to me and my needs. Sometimes now he forgets." She brought her handkerchief again to her face. "I apologise. I must go."

She hurried off.

Mary returned to Mr. Withrow, who stood next to the library.

"I wish we could know what was happening," said Mr. Withrow.

"We have fooled ourselves, these past weeks, into thinking we are important," said Mary. "Yet we are not meant to take part in any truly important conversations."

"At least, then, the fate of nations does not lie within our hands. It is comforting that I cannot destroy any countries, or ruin the prospects of an entire continent by my decisions tonight."

"It is comforting indeed." Mary looked out at the couples waltzing. Would she even have a chance to dance with Mr. Withrow tonight?

He seemed to have the same thought. "Will you dance

with me—now, rather than later?"

Mary felt a strange sort of thrill rise within her chest, a sensation that was such that it felt like her feet might lift off the floor. Truly, what a strange creature was the human body and the ways it responded to emotion.

"Yes, I would like that."

They joined the dance.

"Only using two fingers?" Mr. Withrow asked.

"It is an inferior method of dancing, but it is best not to be obscene in public."

He chuckled.

Mary would give anything to have him hold her like this every single day. She could imagine dancing with him like this in thirty years, in forty years, in fifty years.

She wanted him so much that it hurt. Mrs. Graham had told her that love caused pain, and she was right. Mary knew what she wanted, and he must know what he wanted. It had been three days—surely that was enough time to decide.

Lady Trafford was also waltzing. She looked perfectly serene as she caught Mary's eye and smiled.

"I hope you understand," said Mr. Withrow, "but I cannot abandon my aunt or go against her wishes. She has had too many losses, and I will not cause her pain."

"Of course," said Mary. "I would not want you to, I—"

And then she realised what must lie beneath this statement. A few years ago, she would not have picked up on any of the cue in his words, but now, she understood it. Either he had no true interest in her, or Lady Trafford did not approve of the match. It was enough to make her wish that she had not learned to read people. Ignorance was preferable to this— is this how he told her he did not want to marry her?

It would have been better if he had told her at once, after

the kiss.

She broke away from him. They were close to the library, back where they had started.

"I have hurt you, Miss Bennet, and I do not want to. I want, more than anything, for you to have every joy and happiness. Please understand that I simply need a little more time before I can give you my response."

It was not a complete closing of a door, then, but she still felt a shattering—her mind tried to grasp onto fragments—pain and love and disappointment and hope, and she almost wished she could feel none of it, but she also wanted to feel it all. She wanted to feel his eyes on her, even if it caused her pain.

She diverted her focus to those exiting the library. Considering Mr. Withrow and a possible future or lack thereof was too much right now, so she was happy to have a distraction.

Lord Uxbridge leaned very close to the Duke of Wellington and whispered into his ear.

"Let them finish their dance," the duke told his officers.

"I will be leaving immediately," said the Prince of Orange.

"May your horse have the speed you desire," said the duke. "I will retire for a few hours, and then go."

Prince Willem nodded, and, without a word to a single other person, he left the ball.

While the Duke of Wellington had declared that his men could finish their dance, not everyone did. Word of the upcoming march south to meet Bonaparte's armies spread even among those who had previously known nothing of the attack. Some couples stopped dancing in the middle of the dance, and officers said touching farewells to their partners, using great emotion even when speaking to a new acquaintance. One officer moved to one knee and attempted to take Mrs. Graham's hand, but she pulled it away and did not permit him to say anything foolhardy. Miss Tagore's partner left the dance early, and so she sought out as many officers as possible and wished them luck in the upcoming conflict.

As the remaining couples finished the dance and the officers moved in mass to the doors, the Duchess of Richmond stood in the middle of the ballroom.

"Please, do not leave!" The duchess sank to the floor, in a manner that both somehow managed to feel both overly dramatic and genuine.

This great duchess, one of the central figures of Brussels, had been brought to her knees by this war. No one approached her, no one knew what to say, though the eyes of the entire ballroom were drawn to the spectacle.

Mary pitied her, and she understood her despair. The very thing the Duchess of Richmond wanted, to throw a memorable, meaningful ball, had been wrenched from her grasp, and in such a public manner. The duchess felt shame, and everyone knew it.

Of course, the ball might be made even more memorable by the fact that it had been interrupted in such a manner.

There was a loud bang.

A gunshot.

Mary's head turned.

A woman in a fine gown fell to the floor.

Mary could not make out her identity from this distance. The Duke of Wellington was at her side, helping her. He must have been next to her when she was shot.

Another victim. Why would this pointless violence not cease? Why could they not have peace and security, at least off the battlefield?

Mary, and everyone else it seemed, rushed to the scene. As she approached, she realised that she should not be running to the scene: she should be looking for the murderer. Her eyes darted around the room, searching for anyone or anything out of place, yet she had no notion of who had fired the shot.

"She is not dead," yelled the Duke of Wellington, which caused a flurry of relief. "Give us space!" Everyone heeded him—he was, after all, *the* commander of their times.

A doctor rushed forward to assist. Colonel Kitsell and other officers who had not already left for the battle took over the ballroom, organising everyone present into groups, questioning them in case they had seen anyone, writing down notes on anything and everything, and then, once a ball guest was cleared, sending them home.

Once their party had given the sparse details of what they knew, they were sent out of the ballroom into the night. Rather than departing in their carriage, Lady Trafford requisitioned a small servant's cottage next to the Richmonds' house. She stood watch as Mary and Mr. Withrow used separate rooms to change into their Fothergill and Pike costumes.

Dressed as detectives, Mary and Mr. Withrow returned to the ballroom. Colonel Kitsell and other officers were still in the midst of interviewing those present.

It was only now that Mary saw the woman who had been shot. It was Miss Oldfield. Mary's throat felt dry and itchy and full of fear. Miss Oldfield—a young and vibrant girl, newly out in society, had been shot, and now lay, unconscious, on the floor of a ballroom. What did the murderer have against her?

Mrs. Oldfield sat, weeping and wailing, by her daughter's side.

The doctor had cleaned the injury from the bullet wound. "How is she?" asked Mary in her Mr. Fothergill voice.

"The bullet went mostly through the arm, though a shard is lodged in the bone of her arm which I cannot remove. She has not injured anything essential and should likely recover."

"Did you see from whence the bullet came?" Mr. Withrow was asking the Duke of Wellington.

"Over there." He pointed, then walked in that direction. "The shooter would have been behind one of these four potted shrubs."

Mary and Mr. Withrow examined them. Each pot was positioned against the wall, and each bush was large enough to hide a person.

"I found gunpowder," said Mr. Withrow. Mary and the duke went to Mr. Withrow's side. There was indeed a bit of gunpowder on the branch of one of the bushes.

"When I have shot a pistol," said Mary, "sometimes a small puff of gunpowder comes out the side."

"That is likely what happened here," said the duke.

"It is a good thing they did not miss," said Colonel Kitsell to the Duke of Wellington. "It could have been you who was shot."

"Or perhaps they did miss," said Mary, a sinking feeling in her stomach. "They might have been aiming for the Duke of Wellington."

Mr. Withrow and the duke nodded in agreement. Colonel Kitsell expressed his doubts—but what reason would he have to disagree, unless he had been involved in some way?

There were many who might have reason to shoot the Duke of Wellington. She did not believe that General Tippert had been in attendance, and, to her knowledge, neither had any of the Belgian officers who had been acting as spies for

Bonaparte. Of course, any of them could have sneaked into the ballroom, and exited during the immediate moments of chaos after firing the gun. The Prince of Orange had left—theoretically—and was he even a suspect? Or it could be any of the individuals who had been questioned before leaving the ballroom.

Regardless of who the killer was, this attempted murder was different than each of the successful murders before. In the past, the killer and the victim had been alone: there had been no witnesses. Yet now, the killer had taken a shot in a crowded ballroom with over a hundred witnesses. To Mary, this meant only one thing.

The killer was becoming desperate.

Chapter Twenty

Excerpts from the journal of Mary Bennet:

June 16, 1815: All the officers and soldiers are off to war. Brussels is gripped with fear, and some residents and visitors have fled to the north.

Miss Oldfield is recovering, and as of yet, no infection has set in. Mr. Withrow and I dressed as investigators and interviewed her and members of her family. Nothing we learned makes me think that the killer intended to harm her. Lady Trafford agrees that the target was the Duke of Wellington.

Lydia often stares vacantly at the wall. I read to her and try to provide stimulating conversation, but I am afraid that we are ill-suited as conversational partners.

Later:

Two battles occurred today. The Prince of Orange and his Dutch and Belgian forces held Quatre Bras—they fought valiantly and were victorious against Ney's French armies, though they lost five thousand men in the process. They were assisted by the Duke of Wellington and the rest of the Allied forces.

The other battle was held farther east, at Ligny, between Napoleon and the Prussians. Blücher fell in the battle, and the Prussians lost. Over ten thousand Prus-

sians were killed. The rest of the army is fleeing back to Prussia.

June 17, 1815: Blücher was not killed in battle. He was crushed by his horse, but his aides bathed him in brandy and he regained consciousness. Blücher directed that his troops change directions and join with those of the Duke of Wellington. It is not known if the Prussians can march so many miles in time.

Lady Trafford received word that the Duke of Wellington and the Allied forces are marching to a spot near the hamlet of Waterloo, where Wellington plans to fight Bonaparte. The duke has directed that he wants Withrow and me to join him at Waterloo as Pike and Fothergill. A number of civilians have been watching the battles as spectators, and several were behaving suspiciously at the Battle of Quatre Bras. He fears that the murderer may be among them.

I do not want to leave Lydia to go off to the battle. Last night I heard crying from her bedroom, and when I joined her there, she told me things that made my heart break. The first time Mr. Wickham hurt her badly, she ran to the parsonage, but they told her to go home and do her duty to her husband. Mr. Wickham would not allow her to go anywhere without his permission—he told her she could not attend our father's funeral, so she took the money Jane and Elizabeth had sent and bought a mourning gown, for she would not have Mr. Wickham waste it on gambling.

Why did we do nothing? Why did we cast her out? Why did I treat her as if her transgressions were more important than her as a person? I do not know if I will ever be able to forgive myself.

I told Lydia that I must leave for at least a day to call upon an acquaintance in the countryside. Lady Trafford and the nurse have promised to look after her.

I have never witnessed a battle before—I do not want to witness a battle. Yet forces much larger than myself are at play.

Chapter Twenty-One

> "*The Duke of Wellington exposed himself as usual to eminent danger: the bullets, says our informant, were whizzing about him in every direction.*"
>
> —*The Times*, London, written about the events occurring on June 18, 1815

THE BATTLEFIELD WAS a tapestry of chaos and death. The red, blue, white, gold, black, green, orange, and grey uniforms of the Allies clashing with the uniforms of the French, many of which were blue, but some which were red, white, gold, green, and brown.

Men screamed—screamed as they charged, screamed as they bled. Other men waited—waited to fight, waited to die.

To Mary's inexperienced eye, it did not seem like the French were winning. However, it did not seem like the Allies were winning either.

"We will never find or stop a murderer in the midst of a battle," she told Mr. Withrow. "There is too much enemy fire, too many people dying."

"I agree," said Mr. Withrow. "If I had wanted to participate in a battle, I would have become an officer."

They could not very well abandon the Duke of Wellington's orders, so they continued to make their way behind the line, occasionally talking to officers and having reports forced into their hands to deliver to Wellington and the other leading officers. She had thought they would spend their time watching the civilians, most of whom were a little farther back from the battlefield, but apparently this was how they were currently needed.

The Duke of Richmond saluted them from his horse. The Duke of Richmond was officially in command of the reserve force which had stayed in Brussels to protect the city, yet he was clearly not in Brussels. He wore plain clothes, not those of an officer, and was chatting with various officers and pointing out the military operations to one of his sons, who was astride his own horse. This son looked to be about fourteen or fifteen and was dressed in military uniform, but his arm was in a sling and his eye appeared wounded. He must have been absolved from duty for this battle, yet he was still here as a spectator, with his father, taking rather more pleasure in the events than was merited.

Mary and Mr. Withrow passed rather close to Captain Wickham and his regiment, the 64th. Wickham recognized her as Fothergill from Blücher's ball and gave her a brief nod, which she returned, though it pained her to treat him with any civility. How could a man hurt his wife in such a manner, and then carry on as if nothing was amiss? He had found a new sword, less expensive than the one he had left at Lady Trafford's, and did not seem to be greatly impeded by his broken rib.

Mr. Withrow had informed her that he had broken a rib once, and while it had been painful for several weeks, he had been able to carry on without much trouble. She almost wished that Wickham's rib was giving him more trouble—an unfamiliar part of her wanted him to experience great pain. She wanted him to suffer for all that he had done to Lydia.

Yet vengeance belonged to God and to the law, and even if the law was unlikely to do anything to help Lydia, vengeance did not belong to Mary.

The Prince of Orange rode along the line, translating commands between French and German and Dutch and English. He was dressed in a black top, the front covered with strips of gold fabric and gold buttons. Everyone he passed, everyone he interacted with, seemed to stand a little taller. Last night, the prince had offered to relinquish command of his troops and have them spread amongst the rest of the Allied troops. Wellington had initially protested, explaining that if the prince did so, he would not receive the credit he deserved for the battle. The prince said he cared not about credit, but rather about protecting his country, and the duke had agreed that it was a good strategy. Mary found the prince's actions admirable—giving up a focal position for the greater good.

"We are being hailed," said Mr. Withrow, tugging on her arm. "They must want the reports."

Mary had expected that the Duke of Wellington would have a command tent, removed from the battle where he could see the field and direct the events. While he had such a tent, he did not use it, instead staying close to the line—close to the danger, where he could easily be struck by a stray bullet. He was a man of action, a man of the moment, a man who, for the first time, Mary was seeing in his element: a commander who constantly shouted off insights, who could guess at Bonaparte's strategy before it played out, who was heeded with exactness by his men.

"Where is Tinney? Where is Harthwright?" asked the Duke of Wellington. He wore a dark blue cloak, almost black, with a white neckcloth and a black cocked hat.

"Both dead, sir," said one of the officers.

"I do not want to lose any more aide de camps," said the duke. "Take watch over yourselves, please."

Mary and Mr. Withrow delivered the messages to an officer. No one immediately gave them another task, so Mary hoped that they would be allowed to join the civilian spectators a little farther from the action. After all, that was why they were here—because there might be a murderer, and it might be one of the civilians.

"Someone must know which troops are currently positioned near that line," growled the Duke of Wellington, pointing at a spot near the barn on a large hand-drawn map of the battlefield.

None of the officers volunteered information, and the officer with all the reports hastily sifted through them. Mary and Mr. Withrow had passed that position on their way here, but she did not feel it her place to give an answer.

"Well?" asked the Duke of Wellington. "Do I need to gather the information myself?"

"The 64th," said Mary. It was Wickham's regiment. Then quickly, she added, "The 110th were also nearby, as was the 15th."

The Duke of Wellington nodded. "Send the 64th and the 15th," he told one of the officers, and then he outlined the strategy they must use.

Mary stepped back, away from the decision makers. It was not her role to push men's lives around on a chess board, yet by volunteering a list of regiments, that is exactly what she had done. Of course, these men would have gone into battle today even without her interference. Wickham would have been sent to a position of peril even without her. But it would not have been at her hand. She rubbed her hands against each other, as if to remove a stain.

Mr. Withrow followed her. "You did no wrong."

"I know." He meant to comfort her, and he spoke with sincerity, yet Mary could not help but remember his words at the ball and the new distance between them.

"Come. There will be time to stew over it later. We have been instructed to first walk towards that fencing, to see if anything looks suspicious, and then to join the spectators and see if anyone looks like they might be a murderer."

"I suspect that most murderers do not look like murderers." She had only known two murderers—*only*, that was laughable, would that she had not known any—but neither of them had looked like a murderer. "If Wellington truly thinks it might be one of the civilians, why not ban them from the battlefield?"

"I thought the same," said Withrow. "But with this chaos, it would be difficult, and Wellington needs his troops to fight, not to enforce a civilian ban."

As they hurried towards their destination, she contemplated her surroundings. It was strange to think that yesterday, this entire area had been a farm. But the farmers had been removed—hopefully they would be compensated for the loss of their livelihood—and now the barn and the fencing and the other structures were being used for defence, and the corn, the beautiful corn, was being trampled by soldiers and artillery and cavalry alike. Blood, endless blood, watered the soil. This farm would produce no crops this year, and it might never produce crops again.

The ground shook.

A whizzing sound.

Metal and rock and fire flew close to her face.

For a moment, Mary could not breathe.

She found herself on the ground.

Now there were screams and wails of pain. Of course, not all the men were screaming; some of the men could no longer scream. One man had lost his head entirely—literally lost his head.

Why was she here on this battlefield, in a man's outfit, with only a pistol? Her weapon was of no use at all, unless the French came so close that it would be unlikely for her to survive the encounter.

Mary wiped blood and other unpleasant substances—none of it her own—from her fake moustache, then turned and saw Mr. Withrow, fifteen or twenty feet away. His face was pale, and he stood apart, blood dripping from his hand.

She ran to his side.

"Are you injured?"

He did not reply, but clearly, he was. On his left hand, his second finger—well, it was no longer fully attached. She swallowed back bile, hoping she did not lose her stomach, and tried to consider the situation rationally.

Mr. Withrow needed assistance, but he was in some sort of daze from his injury, so he would not seek it himself. She would do it for him.

In this case, women's clothing would be much more useful than men's apparel: in stories, women always ripped off part of a skirt and used it as a bandage. Instead, she used a pocketknife to cut off part of her shirt sleeve, which she wrapped around his hand. "Come with me, to the surgery."

He shook his head. "No. We were told to go to the fencing, and then to join the civilians."

"We are not actually needed," said Mary, tugging on his unwounded arm. "In the heat of the battle, the Duke of Wellington is much more likely to be killed by an enemy bullet or a piece of shrapnel than by our murderer. We must get you care."

"I cannot draw the surgeon's attention away from those who truly matter."

"Stop being ridiculous. You are as important as any soldier."

For the first few feet, she was practically dragging him, but then he gave in to her insistence. It was unnerving to have the battle behind her, unnerving to know that they would not see a bullet coming, and she found herself turning her head back towards the horror behind them, and then, just as quickly, turning to face forward. She could do nothing to protect herself, and she could do nothing to protect Mr. Withrow from further injury, except remove them from the scene of battle as quickly as possible.

The field hospital tents were a quarter or a half mile behind the battlefield. As they walked, Mr. Withrow's bandage grew redder and the tents seemed to get no closer. When they finally arrived, she led Mr. Withrow to the back of a line of at least forty-five men who waited for assistance.

After a few minutes, a soldier with a medical badge approached her. "You are the duke's investigators, are you not? Trying to solve those murders, correct?"

"Yes, we are," she said.

"Come this way."

She felt guilty as they were moved to a shorter line filled with officers rather than ordinary soldiers, but at the same time, she did not protest that Mr. Withrow would receive care earlier rather than later.

When it was finally their turn, Mr. Withrow was seated in an open-air tent. There were buckets of blood and other filth and Mary fought to keep the contents of her stomach.

The surgeon examined Mr. Withrow's hand. "There is no

way to repair the finger," he said immediately. "It will have to be removed."

A chill ran down Mary's spine. Mr. Withrow took the news with stoic silence, or maybe it was simply shock.

The surgeon directed Mr. Withrow to lie down on a table. The surgeon lifted a knife, bloody from another patient, and wiped it clean on an old cloth.

Mr. Withrow began to tremble. "Please," he said, and he reached out his uninjured hand.

Mary went to him instantly, and, despite the fact that she was dressed as a man, the surgeon did not say anything or act surprised when she held Mr. Withrow's hand in her own. The surgeon's assistant held down Mr. Withrow's arm that had been maimed.

"I am ready," said the assistant.

The surgeon cut off the remains of the finger, just below the first knuckle, and Mr. Withrow let out an involuntary, inhuman cry, and he gripped her hand with such intensity that it hurt. Then the surgeon took a hot iron and pressed it to the remains of Mr. Withrow's finger, and he once again cried out and clenched her hand. Mary held onto him with all her might.

Mary helped transfer Mr. Withrow to a field tent where he collapsed into slumber. It was not long before she was cast out of the tent by one of the nurses. While she could not see the battle, she could hear it, the roar and rumbling and death and destruction. The number of wounded men, many of them wounded grievously, seemed to be increasing. They poured towards the tents, desperate for help. Several collapsed on the way, and, despite the attempts of others to help them, did not get back up.

Two of the injured men were from Mr. Wickham's regiment—they had been standing next to him when she passed. One of them had taken a bullet to the arm, and the other had a head injury. Blood poured down his face.

"How did your charge fare?" Mary asked them.

"Poorly," said one of the men. "We lost our captain before it started."

Lost their captain.

"Captain Wickham?" said Mary, almost choking on the words.

"Yes."

"Is he dead? What happened to him?"

"We were making our way into position, and he was hit by a stray bullet. He went down. And the second in command led the charge and died during it."

"Are you sure that Wickham is dead?"

"Yes. We checked on our way back, and he is completely dead. Were you friends with him?"

"No," said Mary. "I...I had asked him some questions during the course of my investigation."

"Good luck," they told her.

"Good luck to you," she said.

She stood there, dazed, as messengers and nurses and injured men rushed past her, all with a purpose, all with a clean conscience.

Mr. Wickham was dead. He was *dead*. She felt awash in shock and guilt—for she had given his regiment's number to Wellington. Yet amidst the shock and guilt, she also felt relief—this solved all of Lydia's problems. Lydia no longer needed to obtain a separation, and because she was a widow, she could remarry, if she desired, rather than spend the rest of her life alone. But then, Mary felt guilt again, guilt at her relief, guilt that she felt happy that Wickham was dead, even if it meant that he could no longer hurt her sister.

Someone bumped into Mary, she did not even see who, but it jostled her from her stupor. She needed to move, she needed to do something. She was supposed to keep watch on the civilians and see if any of them looked suspicious.

A number of the civilians were quite close to the troops and the battle, or stood among the battle itself. The Duke of Richmond still rode behind the troops with his son. A woman in trousers rode on a pony just behind a regiment of men. Mary recognized her—she was the wife of an officer, and it appeared that she had acquired a rifle and was prepared to use it.

Mary made her way to a group of civilians that was farther from the action. A number of them were the wives of officers, watching the battle. Two of them appeared to be in the family way. There was also a button seller from London, several traders from Brussels, a gaggle of young boys, a number of impoverished women who assisted the regiments with various tasks, and some of the villagers from Waterloo, all watching anxiously. None of the civilians appeared suspicious, most of them said they had not been at the Battle of Quatre Bras, and it seemed unlikely that any of them were the murderer.

One smartly dressed woman had an opera glass, a sort of telescope covered in paintings of an operatic scene. Mary asked if she could borrow it. She used the opera glass to look, first, at where Wickham's regiment had originally stood, then followed the path they would have taken. There, lying on the field, was his body.

Thousands of dead bodies lay on the field, yet the battle was still in its height, so no one moved them. Sometimes soldiers and horses marched around the bodies, but at times they marched on top of them. Mary lowered the glass.

One of the women nearby cried out in horror. She grabbed the opera glass from Mary's hand, trained it on a spot on the field, and then shoved the glass back into Mary's hand. She ran across the field, her hands clutched around her belly, which was great with child.

"By God," said one of the other women. "She is going to get herself killed."

They took turns using the opera glass, watching as the woman made her way to her husband, an officer who had at least two severely injured limbs.

"I would do it," said one of the women. "Getting your husband to the hospital now, instead of hours later, can be the difference between life and death."

"She has been hit! In the leg!" said the woman currently holding the opera glass.

Mary took the opera glass and looked. The woman's leg had indeed been hit, and she had collapsed on the field, next to her husband.

Mary could not save Wickham. Wickham was dead, and she could not erase her part in it. But she could attempt to save this woman.

Keeping her voice low and masculine as her disguise, Mary said, "I will get her to safety."

"And her husband?" asked one of the women, her voice a desperate plea, as if saving this woman and her husband were essential to keeping her own husband safe.

"Yes, I will get him to safety as well," said Mary.

Swallowing her nervousness, she made her way across the field, not running, as the woman had, but moving carefully, aware of her surroundings.

In the distance she saw the woman. She had stood and was limping across the field, somehow still helping her husband to safety, despite her own injury.

Mary felt her mortality very deeply. She could die at any moment—one could always die at any time, but she had never felt that truth as she did now, as she walked through a churning, roaring, screaming field of death and bullets and metal and blood, blood, blood.

She reached the woman and her husband. With the woman's limp and the blood running down her skirts from the bullet wound, it was incredible that she could even walk. She refused to be brought to the hospital first, on her own—"You are a man, you would not understand why I can't leave him," she told Mary—so Mary helped them both to the field tents.

"Thank you," said the woman, in tears. "Thank you."

"It is nothing," said Mary. There was some small comfort to acting in opposition to the battle, to bringing life instead of death. "Are you feeling well?"

The woman patted her stomach. "Yes, I am well. My child will have a father, because of you."

Mary left so the woman and her husband could be treated, but there was no escaping the wounded, dead, and dying. The world was mad. This battle was madness. She checked on Mr. Withrow, who was still asleep, and then returned to the civilians.

The button seller had been recruited to send messages for the Duke of Wellington, and the camp women did their best to help the wounded. The position of the remaining civilians grew more precarious as the French advanced, so they moved to the church in Waterloo and watched the battle from one of the top windows.

For hour after hour, Wellington and Bonaparte used brilliant strategies that she did not have the knowledge to understand. The French general Ney brought his cavalry against the British line, charging again and again and again, taking suicidal losses. At one point, as she took her turn with the opera glass, she spotted Napoleon Bonaparte on his horse, majestic with his three-pointed hat, a man whose charisma and intelligence and strategy had transfixed and bewildered and dominated an entire continent for almost two decades.

It seemed, for a time, that the Allied forces might lose, but then Blücher and the Prussian army arrived from the east, in their earthy green, sky blue, dark blue, and black uniforms. They drew a huge swathe of the French forces to fight against them on the road.

How many miles had the Prussian army travelled since losing the Battle of Vigny? It must have been at least twenty miles marched on muddy roads in less than twenty-four hours—and this after a crushing defeat and a hasty retreat. Yet these were some of Prussia's best men, and they acted the part.

The battle seemed not like a single battle, but a hundred battles being fought simultaneously in the same vicinity, each with its own triumphs and tragedies. The fighting went on for hours, and afternoon turned to evening, and evening to night. There was not an exact moment when the battle was certain, not an exact command of retreat from the French officers, but then the French soldiers were fleeing, running over the dead bodies, away from the battle, back towards France.

Mary and the others exited the church and ran outside.

Soldiers everywhere shouted, *"Sieg!"* "Victory!" *"Victoire!" "Zege!"* A number of regiments pursued the French army while others remained and helped the wounded.

"This battle will end the war," one officer told another. "This could be the battle to end all wars."

She hoped the first statement was true—maybe Bonaparte

had truly and finally been defeated. Yet it seemed implausible to assume that human nature would suddenly change as a result of a single battle, that countries and individuals would learn to live with each other in harmony. After all, she still needed to find a murderer.

Chapter Twenty-Two

"The Mayor of Brussels announces...that the grand hospitals of the Allied Army are established at Brussels, and calls upon the inhabitants to send old linen and...as many mattresses, sheets, quilts, &c, as they can spare, for which he relies on their humanity and patriotism...[He] shall be obliged...to send sick or wounded to the rich citizens who disregard this appeal."

—*The Times*, London, written about a proclamation given around June 19, 1815

Still dressed as Fothergill and Pike, Mary and Mr. Withrow rode back to Brussels on a horse that had managed to escape injury in the battle. Mr. Withrow sat behind her on the horse, his arms around her waist.

This would have been wonderful, in other circumstances. It would have been thrilling, had it not been for his laboured breathing, the excessive heat of his face, and the way, when she turned to look at him, his eyes did not quite focus on her own.

As the horse's feet hit the dark road beneath them, she tried not to think about how many fewer people would return to Brussels than had left—how many fewer people would return to England's shores. And some of these deaths—some of these deaths would weigh on her more heavily than others.

She wished she could feel greater joy at the British victory, but the fatigue of the battle had set in, as had the weight of death. And the dread—the dread of speaking to Lydia.

It was well past midnight when she and Mr. Withrow entered Brussels through the gate of Namur. Some of the city was still awake, celebrating the news. Lady Trafford immediately called for a doctor—the same doctor who had treated Lydia. The nurse who had been caring for Lydia had left to assist with the wounded on the battlefield.

"The surgeon did good work," said the doctor. *"He has a light fever, and a little redness in the hand. The next twenty-four hours will determine whether an infection takes hold or not."*

The doctor applied leeches to Mr. Withrow's hand and chest. After a few minutes he removed them, promising to return in the morning.

"Let me know when Lydia wakes," Mary told Mrs. Boughton, for Lydia had been asleep since they arrived, and she did not want to wake her to tell her the news.

Mary went to her room, cleaned herself, and changed into fresh clothing. Using a small candle for illumination, she stared at herself in a small mirror. She looked different than she had before the battle. Even now that she had removed all the dirt, the grime, and the dried blood splatter, she did not see the same woman she had been before.

She returned to the room where Mr. Withrow slept and knocked lightly on the door.

"You may enter," said Lady Trafford softly.

Mary stepped into the room.

Lady Trafford sat on the bed next to her nephew. Tenderly, she brushed a lock of hair from his forehead. Lady Trafford had always seemed so in control, so confident with her position in life, but now, she seemed vulnerable. She had lost her husband and her daughter and her son to death a few years before, and her nephew had acted as a son to her since then—perhaps had even begun to act as a son before then.

It was only then that it struck Mary: Mr. Withrow could die. There was no rhyme or reason for when infection set in on a wound, but if it did, losing a finger could turn into the loss of life.

Mary sank into a chair, overcome by sorrow for the possibility of loss and what that would mean to Lady Trafford. But it was not simply sorrow for Lady Trafford—Mary felt sorrow and fear of what the loss of Mr. Withrow would mean to her. For Mary loved him, truly and fully. She respected him and understood him. She wanted only the best for him, and the thought of him made her heart leap and her spirit soar. What would it mean to lose him now? Despite the Duchess of Richmond's ball, she still hoped they might have a future together. And even if he did not want that future, he deserved a long and happy life.

"I am worried that his forehead is too hot," said Lady Trafford. "Can you gather a basin of water and fresh cloths?"

"Of course," said Mary.

She was glad to have a task with which to occupy herself. After she returned with the items, she and Lady Trafford took turns wetting a cloth and placing it on Mr. Withrow's forehead and chest, trying to cool his fever.

After a while, Lady Trafford sat down in a chair. "That is enough, I think. I hope."

"I hope so as well," said Mary, also taking a seat.

They were silent for a few minutes, and Mary wished there was more she could do. She did not like inaction, and she did not like waiting, powerless over how events would unfold. Yet all she could do now was to wait and hope and pray.

"Did Henry tell you he had spoken to me?" asked Lady Trafford.

"What do you mean?"

"He spoke to me about the possibility of marriage."

"He did not tell me that," said Mary, her heart quickening. "He only told me he would not abandon you."

"He asked me for permission to marry you. He went on, quite elegantly, about how he loves, respects, and admires you."

"I...I see." Had he really told that to Lady Trafford? Did he really feel that way?

"Secretly, I was pleased. For the last few months, I have been a bit of a matchmaker, leaving you two alone at times, hoping you would see how suited you are for each other. But when Henry asked for my approval, I did not tell him this.

"Instead, I requested that, as you have no fortune, he create a thirty-year plan for Castle Durrington, its prospects, and our investments. I did so because I want to ensure his happiness, and I know that happiness is very hard to achieve without security. I also do not wish to see all the labour lost that my husband and I put into Castle Durrington and the estate. I want it to endure and mean something."

"That is very logical," said Mary. It also explained his behaviour at the ball.

"Logical? Yes, yes I suppose it is," said Lady Trafford. "But I have changed my mind. I will make no demands of my nephew. I will not stand in the way of what he wants. If both you and Henry desire it, I will give you my approval and my blessing."

"Thank you," said Mary. To have Lady Trafford's approval *and* blessing—that was no small matter.

"I admire you, Miss Bennet," said Lady Trafford. "You possess many admirable traits, and, more importantly, you are a good person. It truly would be an honour to have you join my family."

"Thank you." Mary wished she could say more, but she was not sure of what to say. Should she praise Lady Trafford or reciprocate Lady Trafford's sentiments? Should she reassure Lady Trafford of her feelings for Mr. Withrow? Should she make promises concerning the attention she would bestow on Castle Durrington? Yet none of those statements quite made sense, none of them felt like the right thing to say, in part, because she feared that Mr. Withrow would change his mind. They had not become engaged; Mr. Withrow had not told her the things he had told his aunt.

Mr. Withrow's eyes blinked open.

"Aunty," he said, as if he were a child. He held out his uninjured hand to Lady Trafford, and she grasped it.

"I will stay here for you, my child. Please, stay with me, Henry."

"I will do anything for you, Aunty."

It was a tender moment, and a private one. Mary stood quietly and turned to leave so as not to intrude.

"Please, Miss Bennet, stay," said Mr. Withrow.

She nodded, and sat down in her chair. He smiled at her and then closed his eyes again, holding onto his aunt's hand as if onto life itself. Eventually he fell asleep, and his body relaxed.

After an hour, perhaps longer, Lady Trafford fell asleep in her chair, which made it all the more important that Mary stay awake. Someone needed to keep the vigil and make certain that Mr. Withrow's condition did not worsen.

She tried to blink away her fatigue, to focus instead on the weight in her stomach, the guilt she felt at Mr. Wickham's death. Yet she could not force away her exhaustion. Her back felt tight, and her posterior stiff from all the time spent on a horse. She yanked out a few strands of her own hair to keep herself awake.

The door opened and in stepped Miss Tagore. Her eyes took in Mr. Withrow and Lady Trafford, both asleep, and then settled on Mary.

"My turn," said Miss Tagore. "You should sleep, and I will watch over him."

"I can—"

"No," said Miss Tagore firmly. "I will not dismiss the attachment between the two of you. But I am also Mr. Withrow's friend. We have been friends for almost a decade, and I would like to do what I can to assist him."

Mary wanted to protest, but had not Miss Tagore admitted that they both had claims to him? Miss Tagore's willingness to sacrifice sleep for a friend was admirable. And Mary did need sleep, so, with only a little guilt, she left Mr. Withrow's bedside and fell asleep in her own room.

※

MARY WAS WOKEN in the morning by Mrs. Boughton. "Your sister is awake, and she has heard of our great victory. Per your request, I did not tell her the other news."

"Thank you." Mary attempted to dress in a hurry, but she struggled with the fabric and the fastenings. She knew what she needed to say, but she did not know how to say it. For though a part of her knew that it was not her fault that Mr. Wickham had died—she had not aimed the gun and pulled the trigger—she felt a sense of deep responsibility. If she had not, someone else could and eventually would have given the same information. But the fact remained that she had done it, and listed Wickham's regiment first. And Wickham had died.

In the Old Testament, David was a righteous king, a good person, but he had desired Bathsheba and sinned with her. To hide his guilt, he had sent Bathsheba's husband, Uriah, to the front lines of battle, where he had been killed. After, the prophet Nathan had spoken to David and condemned his behaviour. What he had done was murder.

Mary did not need a prophet to tell her that she should feel guilt—she felt it aplenty. And part of the guilt came from the fact that she was glad Mr. Wickham had been killed. It freed her sister and solved the impossible problem.

In the moment when she had told the duke the number of Wickham's regiment, she had not taken the time to think about her actions. She had not consciously thought that she was giving him Wickham's regiment. She had simply replied to a question with the answer she knew. And yet, a part of her had known. A part of her had supplied that regiment more easily than the others. A part of her had wanted Wickham to be placed in harm's way.

In many ways, Mary's motives were better than King David's. Her actions had not been to commit adultery or to hide her own sins. She had been angry at a vile, despicable human being. He had mistreated Lydia, and, if allowed to, would have continued to do so. He could have easily killed her in a rage. Yet did that give her the right to play God or general? What right did she have to be a messenger, a carrier of information, when even a single word could cause death?

When she could dawdle in her room no longer, she found Lydia at the breakfast table.

"Sit," said Lydia, gesturing to the chair across from her.

Mary sat but did not meet her sister's eyes.

"My husband is dead, isn't he?"

Lydia had known—she had made the correct assumption, for why else would Mary need to speak to her on a matter of import? Or perhaps Lydia had felt her freedom burn within her.

"Yes," said Mary. "Captain Wickham was killed yesterday, during the battle."

"How did he die?" asked Lydia. "Was it bravely? Did he redeem himself of all his faults in his final moments?" She seemed almost bitter about it.

Mary had planned to lie to her sister, to claim he had died heroically, in the hopes that it might comfort her. Yet even if one died in a heroic manner, it could not undo the harm and the injury they had done throughout their life. It did not make them a good person.

"Well, I was not there, clearly. However, I went with my acquaintance, after the battle, and spoke with a number of officers and soldiers. Two regiments, including his, were sent to a different part of the conflict. But he did not die while engaged in fighting. While they were moving towards their new position, he was hit by a stray bullet."

"I see." Lydia intertwined her fingers, looking at them as if they were the most interesting thing in the world.

"He did not die with a glorious charge. He did not die dishonourably. He simply died."

"I should be sad," said Lydia. "Shouldn't I? I should be able to mourn. I was married to him, for years. But I am relieved, and I am angry, and I am happy. And I am broken. But I am not sad. Or maybe I am sad, about a great many things, but not the things a widow should be sad about."

"Do not feel obligated to feel a certain way. This is…a

complex matter, and you will feel many things."

Lydia pulled a bracelet out from underneath the table. It was the one Mr. Wickham had given to her, to represent their time in Brussels. She handed it across the table to Mary.

"What do you want me to do with this?" asked Mary.

"Do something with it. I don't care." Lydia stood and began to rush out of the room. Mary tried to follow her, but Lydia slammed the door to the dining room as she left. "Leave me alone," said Lydia. "I need time alone."

Mary sat at the table, holding the bracelet. She ate—it should be harder to eat, given the circumstances, but her body demanded food. And still she stared at the bracelet. Mary could throw it in the River Senne or give it to a beggar. But neither felt quite right. Finally, she decided on a course of action: the bracelet, and some of the accompanying harm, should be returned to its source and placed with Wickham's body.

The decision was a good one, both symbolic and physical, yet she dreaded the thought of returning to the scene of the battle alone. She did not know if she had the strength to do what must be done. However, she did not necessarily need to do this alone. But who would go with her? She could not ask Mr. Withrow in his state, and Lady Trafford would want to remain at his side. Miss Tagore would likely be willing to go, but Mary did not feel completely comfortable asking her. They had a friendly relationship, but they were not necessarily friends.

Yet she did have a friend in Brussels, someone who might be willing to accompany her.

"I HOPE THAT it is not too much to ask, Clara," said Mary, as she and Mrs. Graham made their way, in Lady Trafford's carriage, out of Brussels.

"It is not at all," said Mrs. Graham. "No one should have to face the nightmares of life alone, especially not you, my dear Mary."

When they arrived, the driver was forced to park the carriage a ways from the battlefield, and Mary and Mrs. Graham continued at a walk. It seemed that thousands of people were there for various purposes. The hospital tents were more full than they had been the evening before, and hundreds of men lined up to receive care, many of them carried by their fellow soldiers. There were at least a hundred well-dressed women, likely seeking out their own dead.

Mrs. Graham greeted several of the more fashionable women, and then turned to Mary. "I am glad you invited me—this appears to be *the* social event today, and I would have missed it were it not for your invitation."

Someone hailed them, and they walked in his direction. It was the Prince of Orange, with a bandage on his left shoulder. "It is good to see you both. We were victorious, but as you can see, it is a sobering victory."

"Are you injured, Your Highness?" asked Mrs. Graham.

"Hardly. A bullet went straight through my upper arm last night. It did not damage the bone and should heal quickly."

He led them over a hill, and suddenly, they could see the expanse of the dead.

"By God," said Mrs. Graham as she saw the field.

Though Mary had seen it yesterday, at the end of the battle, it still managed to shock her. Life after life cast aside. It had taken a full day for all of these men to die, but it would take more, much more, for their bodies to be removed.

"Our current estimate is that there are over twenty thousand dead, and at least five thousand horses," said the Prince of Orange. "Of course, the numbers could be higher than that."

Over twenty thousand dead. It was ten times the number of the people in Meryton and the surrounding areas, where she grew up. It was as if everyone in Meryton, everyone she had grown up knowing and seeing, had died in a single day, ten times over.

"It is such a tragedy," said Mrs. Graham, her hand over her heart.

"Yes, war always is," said the prince. "Now if you will excuse me, ladies, I have tasks I must see to. Let me know if you need my assistance."

"Thank you," said Mary, and she began to lead the way to Mr. Wickham's body.

"You do not need to ask where to find your brother-in-law's body?" asked Mrs. Graham.

"No. I—I received a description from an officer this morning."

It was a simple mistake, but one she regretted. She could only hope that Mrs. Graham did not suspect anything. The skin above her lip itched, likely from wearing the moustache the entire previous day, but she did not allow herself to scratch it, for that would only draw attention to it.

The living walked among the dead. Some looked for injured family members and friends, while others looked for survivors more generally. Dozens, perhaps hundreds of scavengers searched pockets for valuables and removed rings from fingers. One man, near them, was pulling out teeth.

"What is he doing?" asked Mrs. Graham with horror.

"Probably acquiring teeth for dentures," said Mary. "Human teeth are better than wood, gold, or animal bone, and I assume that the teeth of younger individuals are better than those who died of old age."

"That's exactly right, miss," said the man.

Mrs. Graham shook her head. "The mouths of Europe will be grateful for yesterday's battle."

They continued onward, sometimes struggling to find clear ground on which to walk between the bodies. She wondered if it were possible that the murderer was among the dead, was one of the many killed. Finally, they found the spot where Mr. Wickham lay.

"This is him. Captain Wickham."

Mrs. Graham nodded and stepped away, giving her space.

Mary was glad that she had asked Mrs. Graham to accompany her. Mrs. Graham was clearly affected by the sights around them, but she was not squeamish, and she did not make Mary regret the invitation.

The bullet had hit Mr. Wickham in the chest, and blood had blossomed out onto his red uniform, staining it a deep, angry currant. She wondered how long he had bled in this field before he took his final breath. She wondered whether he had been able to see his men run towards the battle, whether he heard their screams.

She removed the bracelet from her pocket. With the sun shining on it, it looked even more dull than it had in the house, a fake imitation of something meant to be meaningful. Not that high-carat gold was an indication of value. It was the sentiment behind a gift that mattered more than the monetary expense, and that was why the bracelet was dull. Mr. Wickham had given it to Lydia as a way to control her—he beat her and then gave her gifts, gave her a hint of hope that she could survive with him another day.

Mary tried to clasp the bracelet around Mr. Wickham's wrist, but the bracelet was too small. Perhaps a pocket? But there were scavengers searching pockets and an item with this sort of history should not risk falling into the hands of another woman. This bracelet must go with him, either to be buried in earth or consumed by fire, however they disposed of all these corpses.

She slid the bracelet into his stocking. Then she paused. Mr. Wickham's shako lay next to his head, and while the hat itself was covered with blood, the brass bugle-horn badge signifying his regiment was unharmed.

Would Lydia even want it?

She did not know, but she would not come back to Mr. Wickham's body, and so it would be best to take it now. She removed the bugle horn from the shako.

Mr. Wickham's dead eyes seemed to stare at her. Mrs. Graham kneeled down next to her and gently closed his eyes. "That is better," she said.

Mary swallowed, and then tears flowed down her face. It was not better. Not better at all.

"Did you have a close relationship with him?" asked Mrs. Graham.

"No, and he was a terrible husband to my sister. It is better for all of us that he is dead, and I know that is a terrible thing to say—"

"Sometimes the truth is a terrible thing, but still, it must be faced," said Mrs. Graham.

"I cannot explain why I am crying," said Mary.

"You are crying because things have changed, and you feel lost," said Mrs. Graham, laying her hand on Mary's back.

"Yes," said Mary, nodding.

She had lost some of her innocence. She had become a spy with the belief that doing so would help her make things right. And, in many ways, she had helped make things right. At least, partially so. Yet it was like carrying buckets of water against an entire tide of wrong.

Answering the Duke of Wellington's question had been the correct thing to do. If she could go back, perhaps she would list all three of the regiments immediately, or list them in a different order. But she could not change what was done.

Before, she had possessed a sense of moral certainty, a confidence that her actions were right, that she was fighting for a just cause, that good would always prevail and evil would always perish. Yet if her weeks in Brussels had taught her anything, it was that the world was more complicated than that. There was good and there was bad, but so much of that was a matter of perspective, a matter of where you were from and which country or leader represented your views. Some things were clearly right or wrong, but so many choices that fell between these two poles. How then could one make choices?

"If there is anything I can do to relieve your burdens..." said Mrs. Graham.

Mary wanted to tell Mrs. Graham everything, the full truth, and she suspected it would help her to deal with all that had happened. She had judged Lemoine for telling her of his secret messages, but now, she was so tempted to tell Mrs. Graham. Ah, to unburden herself to a friend! Truth, as always, wanted to be revealed, but she could not allow it to spring forth. Despite being a good friend, Mrs. Graham was an incurable gossip, and would be unable to contain a secret of this size. Alas, the burden of being a spy was one she must bear alone.

Mary gave Mr. Wickham one long last look, and then she walked away.

"I wonder if someone like the Duke of Wellington feels guilt for his actions. If this"—Mary gestured at the field of death—"makes it harder for him to sleep."

"I have not read as much on ethics as I ought—do not laugh, Miss Bennet, I do sometimes read on serious matters."

"I had no intention of laughing," said Mary, and it was true.

"It is just that morality always requires a framework, and if you accept the framework and the choices it requires, you can feel comfortable within that framework. A military man like Wellington clearly has no difficulty with the military deaths of tens of thousands, yet would find the murder of a single individual repugnant. That is the only way a society like ours, with war as an almost constant, can continue with any sense of moral superiority, yet an outsider looking in might find this framework repugnant, and indeed hold a very opposite framework."

"That is very insightful," said Mary. "I wish I could write it down."

"Oh, please do not," said Mrs. Graham, "for that would quite ruin my reputation, which I must maintain until I have finished writing an entire tome of ethical analysis. Everyone will be quite in raptures at my *Six Volumes of Ethical Inquiry, Contemplation, and Reflection by a Widow of No Standing*."

Mary gave a little laugh. "I would read it."

"I am afraid even you would not have patience for my writing. I will be forced to engage in other pursuits."

They made their way back through the bodies. The path seemed longer from this direction, as they tried to leave the fields of death.

Colonel Kitsell stood with a group of other officers, making some sort of catalogue. The sun glinted on the scars on his chin. "Mrs. Graham," he said respectfully. He did not acknowledge Mary, but he only knew her as Mr. Fothergill.

As Kitsell turned back to his fellow officers, he seemed to pause on a name. "Lieutenant Gilly? I knew his family. I will take care of his body myself."

It seemed strange that Colonel Kitsell would trouble himself, but none of the other officers seemed to find it unusual, and Mary had no excuse to linger.

"Thank you for coming with me," Mary told Mrs. Graham. "It is a horrific scene, and I hope that it has not offended your sensibilities."

"Sometimes I am too caught up in trivial affairs," said Mrs. Graham. "I am glad to be a witness to the events that have occurred."

Up ahead they saw General Tippert. What was he doing here? He was lifting a body, against the objections of another officer.

"I will not have him join a mass grave," the general told him. "I will find a little church in the countryside."

If only Mary could get close enough to see the identity of the corpse.

"Where are you going?" Mrs. Graham asked Mary.

"I think we should follow him."

"You must not have spent much time with General Tippert. He is most disagreeable."

"That is why he must be followed."

"I am having a hard time grasping your logic," said Mrs. Graham, but she made no further protests.

General Tippert was strong and seemed to have no trouble carrying the body. If only Mary could see who it was, but he kept a fast pace. The distance between them and Tippert increased, but it did make it less likely he would notice them.

The general deposited the corpse into a wagon, and then walked back to the field.

Mary approached the wagon and peered over the edge.

Laying unceremoniously on the wooden slats was the general's son, Colonel Tippert.

Colonel Tippert, who had spoken with Mary and Miss Oldfield. Colonel Tippert, who had been alive and well at the Duchess of Richmond's ball.

"That is tragic," said Mrs. Graham. "Whatever is General Tippert doing now?"

The general was stepping on top of bodies now—not even bothering to go around, and increasing speed, as if focused so intently on the person in his path, a person whose back was to them, but whose uniform looked familiar.

Mary ran towards the scene, her hands fumbling to open the pocket in which she kept her pistol. The general was close, close now, and he was drawing his sword.

"Watch out!" Mary shouted, but not loudly enough.

"Prince Willem, watch out!" yelled Mrs. Graham.

Mary hoped that their cries were not too late.

Chapter Twenty-Three

"Your Lordship will observe, that such a desperate action could not be fought, and such advantages could not be gained, without great loss; and I am sorry to add, that ours has been immense."

—Excerpt from a letter written by the Duke of Wellington at Waterloo, on June 19, 1815, after the victory of the preceding day

THE PRINCE OF Orange spun around, drawing his sword as he did so, raising it just in time to block the general's sword.

Though the prince was slender, he was fit and skilled and faster than the general, and his eyes were not clouded with anger. With a few quick moves he managed to disarm his attacker.

The prince held his sword at the general's throat, and the general visibly shook with anger.

Other officers ran to them. They tackled General Tippert and tied his hands behind his back.

Only now did Mary manage to open her pocket, now that the pistol was not needed.

"I am going to kill you!" shouted the general. "And the duke!"

"Good heavens," said Mrs. Graham. "I wonder if he is the

murderer."

"It is possible," said Mary. However, attempting to kill the prince in a fit of rage did not mean that Tippert had deliberately murdered three other men.

"Can you believe that I just saved the prince's life?" said Mrs. Graham. "I will be the subject of everyone's gossip for at least thirty-six hours. Do not worry, Mary. I will include your *small* part in the telling as well."

"You are welcome to take all the credit. I do not need any."

"I was joking," said Mrs. Graham. "Of course you will be in the story—without you, we would not have followed him. What insight, what perceptiveness you had! Everyone will be talking about us, Mary. Everyone."

This was not the sort of attention Mary wanted, not the sort at all, and indeed, once they returned to Brussels she received an excess amount of attention. It was a lesson in the risk of friendship as a spy: though she had managed to resist the temptation of telling Mrs. Graham her secrets, there were still consequences to their friendship.

The next day, General Tippert apologised for his behaviour. He said he had been overcome by emotion, and that his attempt to strike down the prince was unconscionable. He also insisted that he had nothing to do with the murders.

Mary, dressed as Mr. Fothergill, assisted the officers in a thorough two-day search of Tippert's house and possessions. He did own a set of duelling pistols, but there was no evidence that they had been used for murder. He seemed like an ideal candidate: angry at his reassignment, in debt to Major General Leon, with a French mother who lived in Paris, yet he had no motive for murdering Colonel Ouvrard and Monsieur Marsal.

As Mr. Fothergill, Mary requested and received a set of papers from Colonel Kitsell. The papers included a complete list of everyone who had served with Major General Leon in the Peninsula. He had also included a list of everyone who had served with Ouvrard. She read through the complete lists twice and then spread the pages out on the table.

"I would love your insights, Mr. Withrow, if you have a moment."

Mr. Withrow's fever had passed and the doctor declared that he had fully recovered from the loss of his finger. Of course, being fully recovered did not have the effect of returning his finger to his hand, and further, he seemed to have lost his normal temperament and his enthusiasm for any sort of company.

"I am sure you are quite capable on your own," he said, not looking up from his book. He held his left hand—his injured hand—to the side of his body, pressed between his leg and the chair, almost invisible.

"The trouble is I am not seeing any connections between these lists and our case."

He stood, rather reluctantly, and walked over to the table, his injured hand behind his back. He picked up a few sheets of paper and then set them down. "I do not see any connections either."

Of course he did not—he had not taken the time to read them.

He returned to his chair and again picked up his book. She had never seen him so disinterested, but she could not tell if he was disinterested in the case or if he was disinterested in her.

"Are you feeling unwell, Mr. Withrow?"

"I am in good health."

"Then what is wrong?"

"Nothing," he said, snapping the book closed.

"This is not *my* case. It is *our* case. And we are not finished."

"The case may not be finished, but I am finished."

"But why?" said Mary.

"The battle made it clear that no true progress can be made."

"Please, tell me what is wrong, and I can help you."

She reached out her arm to him, but as she did so, he abruptly stood.

"I apologise, Miss Bennet, but I cannot work with you or spend time with you. It is for your own good."

He left the drawing room.

Mary sank to the floor. She had been shunned and snubbed and scorned so many times in her life, that it was not difficult to recognize. Mr. Withrow was distancing himself from her.

He had considered the possibility of a future between them and decided he did not want it. He did not want her.

What had happened? Why had he changed his mind? They had shared pleasant interactions at the ball, even with their minor misunderstanding. Did he judge her for giving the number of Wickham's regiment to the Duke of Wellington? Did he look down on her behaviour, the way she had helped him after the loss of his finger, the way she had convinced him to seek medical care? None of it made sense.

He had called for her in his feverish night. But that was the last time he seemed to have cared, and now he seemed so distressed by his hand and so distant.

If only he had not lost his finger. If only she had not made a choice that had led to her brother-in-law's death, no matter how convenient that consequence. If only—if only the occupation of a spy did not ask so much of them, did not change them and compromise them and break them.

What more must she lose for her work, for her country? She had lost her sense of innocence. She had lost, somehow, her connection to Mr. Withrow. She had lost the confidence that she always knew the right thing to do. She had lost parts of herself that she did not think she could regain.

The things she had lost seemed too great to bear.

※

MARY LET HERSELF wallow in self-pity on the floor for twelve minutes, and a miserable twelve minutes it was.

Then she stood. Her loss did not change the fact that she had work to do, and she might have time to meet with Colonel Kitsell again and then change back into her own clothes before the afternoon's victory celebrations.

She dressed, once again, as a man. Doing so felt easy now, natural, and not quite as scandalous as it once had. She glued the moustache onto her face, managing to suppress the emotions she did not want to think about. But as she tied her cravat, they all came back. She remembered when Mr. Withrow had tied it for her, the way his fingers had brushed her skin, the way that they had stood so close together.

She finished tying the cravat and walked away from the mirror. She gathered her papers, ready for her visit with Colonel Kitsell.

※

"YOU MEAN TO tell me that you only included *half* of the men who served with Major General Leon?" asked Mary as Mr. Fothergill.

"I eliminated everyone who had been killed, to make it easier," said Colonel Kitsell.

"I need the *original* list. The murders may be connected to someone who died, rather than someone who survived."

"There is not exactly a list," said Kitsell. "That is why I did not give it to you."

Mary pursed her lips and felt her moustache twitch. What an unpleasant sensation, and a good reason not to wear a moustache, except when absolutely necessary.

"What do you mean there is not a list?"

"There were dozens of reports and journals and other papers, and I compiled the information I thought you would find necessary."

"I must decide what information is relevant and necessary. Not you." Was he intentionally sabotaging the investigation?

"I understand," said Colonel Kitsell, seemingly chastised. "I have work to do for the celebration. However, as soon as it is finished, I will gather all of the papers for you."

He waited, but Mary did not leave. Instead, she thought about the question of who had died—those who had been murdered over the past weeks, those who had died on the Peninsula. Who else had died? Lieutenant Gilly, and Kitsell's sister.

"It was reported to me that you took care of Lieutenant Gilly's body after Waterloo. You said that you knew Gilly's family. When? Before you received your miraculous inheritance, or after?"

He seemed to be thinking quickly.

"You have never met his family," said Mary sharply.

"You are right. I knew him from our discussions of Shakespeare. Mr. Pike can attest to that—he interviewed him."

"You knew dozens of men who died at Waterloo, if not hundreds. Why care for Gilly's body?"

"I—I felt it was expedient."

"What is your Shakespeare group really?"

He did not have a ready reply, and he seemed, for the first time, afraid.

Mary stared at him. She considered the scars on his chin, and then looked at the bookshelf, where well-worn copies of *The Merchant of Venice* and *As You Like It* stood in a prominent position.

Suddenly, everything fell into place. Kitsell had been perfectly clean-shaven the morning after Waterloo, when everyone, even the prince, had stubble on their chins. The prince had once interrupted Kitsell bathing and been yelled at for an hour. Mary scratched her fake moustache—Kitsell's pretense should have been obvious to her before, for it was the same as her own.

"In *The Merchant of Venice*, Portia dresses as a man to gain freedom, and so does Rosalind in *As You Like It*."

Colonel Kitsell's face grew very pale. "I don't know what you mean."

"After your parents and Susan died, Caroline conveniently found a will which gave an inheritance to a bastard son. I think that Susan did not die, at least not in the traditional sense. You are Susan, or you were. You probably always wanted to fight, and you realised that you could if you became someone new."

Colonel Kitsell swallowed. "You have no proof."

"You needed to dispose of Private Gilly's body so no one else would discover Gilly's own deception."

"Please, do not say a word," said Colonel Kitsell. "You

will ruin us, ruin us all." He did not wait for Mary to reply. "Haven't you ever wanted something that was completely out of your reach? And what if it became a possibility? Wouldn't you take it?"

"I have no interest in revealing your secrets," said Mary. "I am simply trying to find a murderer."

"I had nothing to do with the murders, and neither did anyone else in the Shakespeare group."

Perhaps Leon had discovered the truth, and Kitsell had killed him for it…but what about the two Belgian officers who had been killed, or the attempted murder of Wellington? Wellington had said that he took action only if a female soldier's identity became publicly known.

"We are innocent, all of us," said Colonel Kitsell. He looked at his pocket watch. "I am willing to undergo further questioning, but for now, I have tasks which *must* be completed before the celebration."

Mary thought for a minute, and then agreed. She had used her entire arsenal of insight and accusations and had nothing further to press him with.

She asked one of the other officers to discreetly keep an eye on Kitsell and made her way back to Lady Trafford's to prepare for the grand celebration. There were a number of celebrations planned for the coming weeks—dinners and parades and such. Some of them seemed to focus entirely on the contributions of Britain, erasing the essential roles played by their allies. Today's event was a formal affair, with speeches and awards in the Grand Square. She considered staying in her Mr. Fothergill disguise, but Lydia would be attending, and she needed to be with her sister. She could only imagine how difficult the event would be for Lydia, hearing the endless praise for the dead and their sacrifices. And so she prepared herself in a gown and joined Lady Trafford, Miss Tagore, and Lydia in a carriage.

"Is Mr. Withrow not joining us?" asked Mary.

"I have bullied him into coming," said Lady Trafford, "but he insists on walking."

"I am worried about him," said Miss Tagore. "He is more standoffish than usual."

At least it was not only Mary who had found this to be the case.

When they reached the square, Lady Trafford led them to seats which she had had reserved for them. They were facing not the Hôtel de Ville, but some of the other buildings in the square. Mary looked for each of her suspects. She spotted Lemoine and Serrurier. Voland had perished, fighting valiantly against the French at Waterloo. Fortunately, neither Lemoine nor Serrurier noticed her, or if they did, they did not recognize her. General Tippert was sitting in the back row with his wife and remaining children, surrounded by guards that Wellington had assigned to accompany him. Yet look as she might, she did not see Colonel Kitsell—not on the stand or in the crowd. He had said that he would be here. He had said he had preparations. Had he fled, or did he now intend to retaliate?

Mr. Withrow slipped into their row, but he sat on the far side of Lady Trafford, forcing all of them to shift seats. This put him as far away from Mary as possible, which was rather unfair. If he wanted to avoid her, he should not have come.

The audience simmered with excitement. Everyone was certain that this had been Bonaparte's last defeat: he could not come back from this, and forces had pursued him all the way to Paris. Yet Mary could not shake her feeling of unease, as if something was about to go wrong.

Lord Uxbridge, head of the cavalry for the Allied armies, approached, using crutches to walk. He had indeed been allowed to play an important part in the battle—the cavalry had been instrumental at multiple points, and eight horses had been killed beneath him, yet he had kept fighting until he lost his leg and an aide pulled him to safety.

"Lady Trafford, a pleasure. You are looking very fine today."

"Why thank you, Lord Uxbridge. I cannot believe that you are here, so soon after such an injury. And looking quite well, given the circumstances. How are you feeling?"

"Excellent, truly. In a few weeks, I should be fitted for a wooden leg. I heard they kept my old leg, and they plan to build a shrine to it. It is a little pagan, if you ask me."

"You played a key part in helping the Allies to victory," said Lady Trafford. "Preserving your leg may be extreme, but you do deserve your fair share of admirers."

"I do not have as many admirers as I would like," said Lord Uxbridge with a mischievous smile. Did he intend to seduce Lady Trafford? It seemed unlikely that he would be successful. "But perhaps it is good that I lost my leg—time to give the younger gentlemen a chance with the ladies." He turned to Mr. Withrow. "I heard you lost your finger in an accident with a horse." That was the story that they had spread, though Lord Uxbridge knew the true cause.

"Yes, it was an unfortunate incident," said Mr. Withrow.

"Of course, a finger should not stop you from wooing ladies—you still have nine, and fingers are not the most important body part."

Mr. Withrow did not say anything in response, and Mary found herself looking at her hands.

"Perhaps we should depart from bawdy humour, with

young unwed females present," said Lady Trafford.

"Bawdy—body—I see what you are saying," said Lord Uxbridge. "I hope you all have a wonderful afternoon."

Lord Uxbridge departed, but Mary found herself still looking at her hands, wishing that things were better between her and Mr. Withrow. And then, she saw Mrs. Graham, a little ways off.

"Mrs. Graham, would you like to join us?" She thought that she might tell Mrs. Graham of her heartbreak. She had not told Lady Trafford or Lydia or Miss Tagore. But Mrs. Graham would understand, she would sympathise and give advice.

Mrs. Graham stopped and turned. She reached out with her lacy gloves and took Mary's hands in her own. "I apologise. I committed to attend to Lady Capel and the Oldfields. But we must speak after the celebration—hopefully I will gather some interesting gossip."

Her eyes looked tired, as if she had not slept well.

"Of course," said Mary. "After is fine. Is—is anything the matter?"

"No," said Mrs. Graham, a little too quickly. And then her voice softened. "Is it not rather ridiculous to have this sort of spectacle and celebration? Thousands of bodies still decay on the fields of Waterloo, and yet here we are, commemorating our greatness."

"It is rather absurd," agreed Mary, "but I do think spectacle is often a societal approach to dealing with great emotion, and perhaps celebrating is an attempt to give each death a purpose."

"A fair argument," said Mrs. Graham. "Now, I must go, but I expect you will keep your word and find me after the event. Otherwise I will be quite put out."

"Of course."

Mary tried to settle in her seat, but she felt unsettled again when she saw the Prince of Orange dart across the stage towards the Duke of Wellington. He stopped, of course, and whispered something in the duke's ear. She need not be so jumpy. The Prince of Orange was not a threat to the Duke of Wellington, and if he was, he would not take action against the duke in front of a crowd. Such behaviour would rip the new kingdom of the Netherlands apart and cause another war, one that England would easily win.

Yet, if the guilty party were not the prince, a public murder could be the perfect opportunity.

Mary turned around in her seat, looking for a spot where a murderer could secure themselves, like the ornamental plants at the ball. She still did not see Colonel Kitsell anywhere. She turned back to the front. There were two rather official stone buildings behind the stand, three stories each. One of them even had stone crenellations, in the style that you might commonly find on a castle or a rampart. If someone climbed to the roof, they could remain concealed and yet have a clear shot to the podium.

"I may be mistaken," whispered Mary to Miss Tagore, "but I fear there may be a danger of another…incident occurring."

"Then we must act," said Miss Tagore. She whispered to Lady Trafford, who whispered to Mr. Withrow.

Mary turned to Lydia. "I will be back in a moment. I must…talk to a friend."

Lydia gave a little nod and wrapped her arms around herself as if cold, even though it was a warm day. The bugle horn that Mary had taken from Wickham's shako sat on top of her skirts.

Mary exited the row and walked along the edge of the crowd. Someone tapped her shoulder and she turned. It was Miss Tagore, accompanied by Mr. Withrow.

"What would you have us do?" asked Miss Tagore.

"I will climb to the roof of that building," said Mary, pointing surreptitiously. "If one of you could discreetly alert someone on the stage, and someone else could climb the other roof."

"I will do the stage," said Miss Tagore.

"Then I will do the roof," said Mr. Withrow. "I—I am sorry, Miss Bennet, for these past days." He rushed off before she could say anything in reply.

She hurried as well, opening the door to the building—government offices—and racing up the stairs. She undid the clasp to her pocket and removed her pistol. It took a minute, but she found a closet with a ladder that led to the roof. As she climbed the ladder, keeping hold of her pistol with her right hand, she realised she had chosen what might be the most dangerous building. This was the roof which would provide the best position to shoot at someone on the stage, this was the roof that looked like a rampart. Why had she chosen this, the most dangerous spot, for herself?

She reflected on this question, and she realised that it was because she had solved the mystery. She knew the identity of the murderer, and she needed to be the one to confront her.

If she was right, it was not Colonel Kitsell or any of the other suspects.

A man had died during the Peninsular conflicts, a man who likely had served with and under Major General Leon, something she would be able to prove once she received the full records. The murderer had placed the blame for this beloved man's death on Leon, on Ouvrard, on Marsal, and on the Duke of Wellington. The murderer blamed them all, and was now trying, by her own estimation, to right the wrongs which had been done to her.

It all came down to the gloves. The puff of gunpowder that escaped from the murderer's gun, that they had found on the tree. The gloves that needed to be replaced. This woman had often tried to change the subject when Leon's death was mentioned. She had fled at Blücher's ball, not from the presence of General Tippert, as Mary had originally supposed, but from the presence of Mary as the detective, Mr. Fothergill. She had received a surprise, unwanted proposal from an officer at the Duchess of Richmond's ball, and then, just a few minutes later, had attempted to kill the Duke of Wellington.

As Mary pushed open the door to the roof, she could hear, faintly, the Duke of Wellington's voice. He had begun his speech.

At the edge of the roof, on the side overlooking the stage, stood a woman with a long blue dress, a finely tailored blue and white hat, and smartly arranged brownish-blond hair.

"Clara," Mary shouted.

Mrs. Graham turned to face her, for a moment, but then she turned back to the front, lifted her gun, and aimed down towards the stage. "Turn around and go down the ladder."

"No." Mary cocked her gun as she dashed across the platform. "You must stop, Clara."

"These wars will be done, once and for all." Mrs. Graham cocked her gun.

Mary could not make it there in time—even if she had the skills to disarm Mrs. Graham, she would not make it in time to do so. Mary stopped running. She aimed her own gun at Mrs. Graham.

There was no time to think, no time to reconsider. Mary

pulled the trigger and fired.

Bang.

A puff of black powder hit Mary's own gloves. A woody, burning smell with a hint of sulphur hit her nose.

Mrs. Graham collapsed on the ground.

Mary's hand trembled, and she dropped her gun. She looked at her hand, then at Mrs. Graham, then again at her hand. She had shot Mrs. Graham. She had shot her friend.

Mary felt as if she, too, might collapse, but instead, she ran the rest of the way across the roof to Mrs. Graham.

Mrs. Graham's body looked limp and broken, her face pale. Mary's bullet had entered her back and exited the front of her body.

Mrs. Graham gasped for breath, in and out. Only a small amount of blood came from her wounds, but the blood that welled on the front side of her body was filled with little bubbles of air.

"I am so sorry," said Mary. "So sorry." She pressed her handkerchief against Mrs. Graham's wound in an attempt to staunch the blood.

Mrs. Graham's breath wheezed in and out, and her eyes looked at the clouds. Then she turned to Mary.

"Why did you stop me?" asked Mrs. Graham. "I was going to be free, finally free."

"What do you mean?"

Before Mrs. Graham could answer, there was shouting and others joined them on the roof. Soon, they were surrounded by Mr. Withrow, the Prince of Orange, several officers, and several other spectators.

Mary looked up at Mr. Withrow. "She is the murderer," she said. "She was going to shoot the Duke of Wellington, and so I…"

Mr. Withrow nodded. He understood. He turned to the others. "We need a doctor, immediately."

They stood there, not reacting.

"Listen to this man," said the prince. "We need a doctor."

Mrs. Graham kept gasping for breath.

"It is going to be fine," Mary told her. "It will be fine."

Mrs. Graham reached out for her hand. "I did not plan to kill Colonel Hubbard."

Who was Colonel Hubbard? He was not one of the men who had been murdered, but the name did sound familiar. Had Mrs. Graham mentioned him before?

"I was so angry when Colonel Hubbard told me of my husband's death, and then, a year and a half later, I found out that his negligence was partially to blame. I only wanted to confront him about his choices. I never meant to kill him, I never—"

She struggled to breathe, her breaths shallow and rapid.

"I know, I know," said Mary. Mrs. Graham had murdered even before arriving in Brussels.

"When it happened, I felt better, for a while. I knew that justice had been served."

The Prince of Orange, Mr. Withrow, and others pressed in against them, but Clara did not seem to see them. Her eyes were fixed only on Mary, as if she were the only one present.

"After a few weeks, things went back to how they were. I was consumed by anger and pain and despair, and I knew the only way to stop it would be to bring full justice to my husband. I researched who was responsible for my husband's death—both British and French officers. I practised, improving my skills with a pistol. Then I came to Brussels, and I killed them, one by one."

The prince said something under his breath. It sounded

like a curse, probably in Dutch or German.

"I would shoot them in the side, tell them why they deserved to die—they had to know why—and then shoot them a second time."

Mary wanted to tell Mrs. Graham that killing these men had not been justice. This sort of revenge did not right any wrong. But it was too late to tell Mrs. Graham that. Mrs. Graham had fixed herself on a course and followed it to near completion.

A military doctor arrived, pushing Mary and the others out of the way. He examined Mrs. Graham for several minutes. Mary could not see what was happening, she could not do anything for her friend, her friend who was a murderer, her friend whom she had shot.

Mr. Withrow handed her the gun, and she slipped it back in her pocket.

"It may not feel like it now," he said, "but you did the right thing."

She nodded. It had been the right thing—she had needed to stop Mrs. Graham—but that did not make it any easier.

"Thank you for your assistance in this matter," said the Prince of Orange, very formally. She saw none of the playfulness of the man who had asked her to dance. "The Duke of Wellington and my father, the King of the Netherlands, will be pleased that the case is closed."

The doctor stepped away from Mrs. Graham's body and addressed the Prince of Orange. "The bullet passed through her lung," he said. "I have bound the wound in her back, but not in the front—from my observations on the battlefield, binding the front will only make her die faster. I have done everything I can, but I cannot save her."

"Mary," said Mrs. Graham, and then, once again, she

gasped.

Immediately, Mary returned to Mrs. Graham's side.

"Will you hold me, Mary, while I die?"

"Yes. Yes, Clara, I will."

The doctor and Mr. Withrow helped lift Clara into Mary's arms. Even now, Clara smelled of lavender, flowery and heady, something so light and buoyant it could carry you away.

Mary did not know how long she held her friend. There might be nothing the doctor could do for her, but that did not mean she died quickly. In between Clara's gasps for air, Mary heard the speeches and the celebrations continue beneath them in the square, complete with a military band playing triumphal tunes.

Blood saturated the bandage on Clara's back, and it slowly spread from the open wound on her front, like wine on fabric, reaching out and staining a larger and larger area.

Clara clung to Mary as if for the scraps of her life. Her breaths became more rapid and shallow. "My chest," she gasped. "It hurts so much."

Tears streamed down Mary's face. Her cheeks felt salty and dry. "I wish I could make you whole."

Clara trembled, and she blinked, as if it required a world of effort to do so. "Thank you," she whispered.

Her entire body went still.

The doctor checked, and indeed, Clara had died. The doctor moved Clara's body, laying it flat and closing her eyes.

Mary stood. Her whole body felt sticky, as if she had bathed in blood. She had no tears left, only an emptiness so deep that she could not see into it.

Mr. Withrow was crying—why was Mr. Withrow crying?—and Lady Trafford was here—when had Lady Trafford come?

Lady Trafford reached out to embrace Mary.

"I am covered in blood," Mary protested. "It will ruin your dress."

Lady Trafford pulled her close. "I do not very much like this dress anyway."

Mary shook in Lady Trafford's arms, and she watched as they took Clara's body away.

War, death, murder: they broke things, in ways that could not be mended.

Chapter Twenty-Four

"Thus has one glorious battle put an end to a war, which threatened the desolation of Europe; and though this battle cost this nation a melancholy loss of blood, it is truly soothing to the hearts of the families who have suffered, to reflect, that it is owing to British gallantry alone, that the triumph was achieved."

—*The Bath Chronicle*, Bath, England, June 29, 1815

IT HAD BEEN a week, and yet still Mary struggled to sleep. When she closed her eyes, she could see herself shooting Clara Graham, again and again and again. In her mind, Clara was suspended in the air as the shot hit her body. She could see Clara falling, see herself running to her, holding her friend as she died in her arms. It was as if she was outside herself, watching herself in a play, time and time again, and she could not make it stop.

She lay in her bed, her body shaking, wishing she could let it go, wishing she could forget for a few minutes so she could rest. All of the other nights she had eventually managed to fall asleep, but not tonight.

Among Mrs. Graham's things they had found further evidence which condemned her: notes on different officers and their movements, including those she had killed. In her fireplace they found the remnants of a journal—it was as if she had known that after shooting the Duke of Wellington, she would not be returning. Most of it had burned, but the pages that were left painted a portrait of a woman who had been broken by the loss of her husband, who had been shamed by her family for the level of her grief and had become so embittered that her rage and anger had consumed her.

Mrs. Graham—Clara—had done terrible things, and nothing could justify killing again and again. Taking a life was no small matter, no small crime. Yet Mary understood her, understood the way her pain and anger and heartbreak had become twisted, the way it had grown. Mary could understand why Clara had done what she had done, and that frightened her.

She missed her friend, yet there had been no other sensible choice. Mary would not have been able to live with herself if she had allowed Clara to murder the Duke of Wellington.

Which meant that now Mary must live with the fact that she had killed her friend.

The sermons, essays, and books that had uplifted Mary and acted as a sort of compass throughout her life—the words of Fordyce and Hannah More and others—did not address the issue of killing for your country. This sort of deadly action was not meant to be a possibility for a lady, so it was never discussed.

As Mr. Fothergill, she had received an award for Special Services Performed for the Crown. The official story had been the truth, or close to it: Mr. Fothergill had tracked down Clara Graham and shot her to save the Duke of Wellington. Yet so much was missing from the official story. The medal was very solid, very pretty, but the idea of wearing it was painful. She wondered if she would ever act the part of Mr.

Fothergill again.

From the remnants of Mrs. Graham's journal, it became clear that Mrs. Graham had realised that Mary and Mr. Fothergill were the same person—she had realised it the moment in which she told Mary that she and Mr. Fothergill looked alike. Yet despite this realisation, she had kept Mary's secret, though she had tried to throw suspicion on Colonel Kitsell through the story of the handkerchief.

Colonel Kitsell was guilty only of helping other officers and soldiers who would not be able to fight as women. Kitsell had disappeared for several days after Mary's confrontation but had returned upon concluding that Mary did not intend to reveal his secrets. General Tippert and his family had left Brussels and returned to England with his mother, who had managed to leave Paris. The Prussian artist had been significant only because of Leon's love for his daughter. There were rumours that Lemoine and Serrurier wanted Brussels and other Belgian regions to secede from the Netherlands, but that was not Mary's concern.

There was a sound from somewhere else in the house—someone crying out.

She leapt out of the bed, to her door, and into the hall, making her way to Lydia's door. After the celebration, Lydia had learned that Mary's friend had died—and that Mary had seen her shot and killed, or such was the story, and had offered heartfelt condolences.

The cry came again, but it was not from Lydia's room. It was from Mr. Withrow's.

Fearing something was wrong, she pushed open his door. He sat in a chair next to a candle, cradling his hand with the bandaged finger.

"Mr. Withrow," she said, but he did not seem to hear.

"Henry."

At this, he turned to her. There was such despair, such anguish on his face, that it almost broke her.

She wanted to run across the room to him, but that was a ridiculous idea. She could not bring herself to do so, especially with the distance that was now between them. Instead she said, "Henry, you have five minutes to prepare yourself—only five—and then you shall come with me. We are going on a walk. So be ready."

"It is the middle of the night."

"I do not care. I am getting out of the house, and you are coming with me." And then she said what he had said to her, over a year before, when their situations had been reversed. "You have no choice in the matter."

The smallest of smiles crossed his face, but it was still a smile.

A year before, she had been in a state of despair, devastated by a loss that she thought she might have been able to prevent. He had informed her that they were taking a walk, and simply getting outside of her room, of the house, had been enough to help her move forward. Perhaps the same approach would help Mr. Withrow. She did not dare to hope that it would do more; she could not hope that they could mend the rift between them, the rift that he had started. But she still cared for him and wanted to help him.

She went to her room to don more appropriate apparel, and then waited outside his door. What if he refused to come? But after a few minutes, he opened the door, and they left the house.

"Where are we going?" he asked.

"You will see."

She increased her pace and he matched it. There was

something about fast movement that was distracting, that eased her own pain and loss.

They walked about a mile through the dark, empty streets. Brussels was much quieter than London at night, and neither of them spoke, but their silence was a companionable one. They reached the staircase to the ramparts and she led the way to the top.

She leaned onto the top of the rampart wall, but while there were little prick points of light in the dark—solitary candles in the occasional house—very little of the city was visible. The moonlight was not strong enough to give definition to the edges of buildings and streets.

"I thought there would be more to see," she said, "but sunrise is not for hours."

He nodded, looked out at the darkness, and then sat down with his back against the rampart wall.

After a moment, she sat beside him. She turned to look at him. "I know that you may regret…prior conversations in which we discussed the possibility of something between us. Yet we had no agreement, we made no commitments, and I will not attempt to force anything upon you against your wishes. I do, however, hope that you will talk to me. Tell me what is wrong, tell me what is troubling you, if you can. Please."

He was quiet for a moment, then he lifted his eyes to her. "I am sorry, Miss Bennet, but I cannot be the person that you need me to be. I—I am not who I was, before the battle. Tens of thousands of people lost their lives. And thousands and thousands were injured much more severely than I. For many, there is no possible return to a normal life. And yet, despite all of this suffering, I cannot cope with the loss of a single finger."

He held up his hand and studied it.

"I have felt so depressed in spirits. It is as if there is no way forward, no light, as if nothing I used to care about matters. I keep seeing the battle, I keep feeling that I am there, and the memories grip me and will not stop hurting. Lord Uxbridge lost a leg, and he treats it like a game. I lost so little, yet I am in pieces."

It felt strange to give advice when she herself was struggling, when she herself did not have all the answers. But she must. She considered her words in advance, and thought about what Lady Trafford would say, or what one of her sisters or Mrs. Graham would say, were she still alive. But she rejected their approaches and said what she, Mary Bennet, thought it best to say in this situation.

"The full amount of suffering is unimaginable. The weight of it is enough that if any of us fully comprehended it, we could not bear it. The vastness of total suffering, and the great depths which others suffer may lead to comparisons with our own suffering or lead us to feel that our own suffering should not cause us such trouble. Yet our individual pains are valid and real in their magnitude. And the only way to get through the pain is to experience it and live with it."

He was silent for so long that she did not think he would speak. But then he said, "Thank you, Miss Bennet." He paused. "Mary."

"I am sorry about your finger."

"I know."

They lapsed into silence again. The night air was a little cold, even with Mary's cloak. It had been fine when they were moving, but now she began to feel the chill.

Her arms shook a little, and her legs, and she curled her legs up with her arms around them. She believed what she had told Mr. Withrow, but it did not make it easier.

She closed her eyes and saw Mr. Wickham's body on the battlefield. She felt Clara Graham bleeding to death in her arms. She could still smell the flowery perfume from Clara's skin. Mary's arms could feel, as if it was currently happening, Clara's blood soaking through her dress and staining her skin. She had washed off the blood, and there was no visible sign, but her skin still felt as if it were stained.

Her teeth began to chatter, and her arms and her legs began shaking with much more vigour.

Mr. Withrow placed his hand on her shoulder. "Mary?"

"I killed my friend," she said. "I killed my friend. How am I going to live with that? And though it may not be deserved, I still feel guilt at the part I played in the death of my brother-in-law. I do not feel guilt for Mrs. Graham's death, not exactly—it was the only thing to do, it was the right thing to do—yet the fact that I did it, with my own hands… When we were training with pistols, I never actually thought I would kill someone."

His hand on her shoulder felt like the only thing tethering her, his warmth the only thing providing weight, the only thing keeping her there.

"I have done many things as a spy," he said, "some of them complicated, with complicated results—things similar to the death of Mr. Wickham. But I have never had to kill for the job. It is no small thing. I can imagine that the fact that you know it was the right thing to do does little to lessen the difficulty."

Mary nodded. "Lying, pretence, deception—they become second nature as a spy. But where do we draw the line, when do we stop? How do we prevent it from seeping into our normal lives, our core identity?"

"Even if we can separate ourselves," he said slowly, "even if we can maintain a sense of morality and goodness, those negative aspects and those difficult decisions are still a part of us. Of course they will affect us."

He understood her, and she appreciated it, but still a tear leaked from her eye and trailed down her face.

"You are a good person, Miss Bennet," he said. "That is why you care, and that is why you will have this conflict within you that may never be completely reconciled."

Mary's breaths felt ragged in her chest, which reminded Mary of how Mrs. Graham had struggled to breathe as she lay dying.

Mr. Withrow ran his hand across her back. "We are both broken, but we will get through this."

We will get through this, he had said. *We.*

She turned towards him and had an overwhelming urge to embrace him. Why should she not? He had said *we*.

Mary leaned into him but almost immediately pulled away. The last thing she wanted to do was force her attentions on him, if that is not what he wanted.

"I am sorry, Mr. Withrow, I—"

"I can hold you, if you would like."

"Yes." She shifted so she was fully seated on his legs, and she leaned against his chest, tucking her head onto his shoulder. He once again smelled of leather-bound books. She could feel his heart beating, and he wrapped his arms around her, pulling her closer still. "Thank you, Henry."

"You have a light in you, Mary, and this will not put it out."

She cried into his chest for a while, cried for her friend Clara, who had become so lost and hurt that she had done unimaginable harm. Cried for her sister Lydia, who had been mistreated by the one who was supposed to treat her with respect and love. Cried for the tens of thousands of men and women who had lost their lives in this war. Cried for herself, and the decisions she had made, especially those decisions which were irreversible. Of course, most decisions were, in part, irreversible. They pushed you forward, in one direction or another, and it was impossible to go back.

Henry's embrace was warm, it was close, it was peaceful, it was everything she wanted and needed. When her tears were spent, she relaxed more fully into his arms. She wanted to stay here, in this position, for as long as possible. Hopefully he would oblige her. She closed her eyes and drifted off to sleep.

"Mary," Henry said in her ear. "Do you want to watch the sunrise?"

She blinked her eyes and realised she was still in Mr. Withrow's arms, and they were on the rampart. When she had closed her eyes, it had been dark, but now the light was beginning to illuminate the sky. "I think I fell asleep on you."

"You did. For several hours."

"I apologise," she said, trying, and failing, to climb off of him.

"Do not apologise," said Mr. Withrow. "I fell asleep as well." His lips quirked into a smile. "It is the best sleep I have had since the battle, which is surprising, seeing as I was sitting on cobblestone and leaning against a rock wall."

He helped her to her feet. When his hands touched her hand and her waist, she experienced a tingling, a rush of warmth and longing. And then, when he let go, she felt suddenly cold.

She leaned on the rampart wall, staring at the sunrise, orange with a glint of crimson, and several clouds, currently a greyish blue. Her cheeks felt a heat that reflected the redness in the sky. Had she really slept in Mr. Withrow's arms? What a remarkable and unexpected occurrence. That was certainly not part of any plan she had made for herself.

Mr. Withrow stood a few feet from her, also looking out at the sunrise. He held his hands very formally behind his back, the white wrappings still around his severed finger.

"What are you going to do once we return to England?" asked Mr. Withrow.

"I think I will take Lydia to stay with my sister Jane. If there is anyone who is complete kindness and goodness, it is Jane, and Lydia needs that right now. I should probably stay, for a time, to help her."

"Is your mother there?"

"Yes, though perhaps I shall have to persuade her to stay with the Darcys at Pemberley. My mother may be too much for Lydia right now."

Mr. Withrow seemed very intent on the sunrise, but then he turned to face her.

"Miss Bennet, may I come visit you when you are staying with your family?"

"That is very kind, but I would not want you to inconvenience yourself."

"I understand," he said. And then he—grimaced?

He took a little rock off the rampart and threw it down below. His body language would indicate that he was upset, and the look on his face...well, he seemed disappointed. But what did he have to be disappointed about? All she had said was that he did not need to visit her. Of course, that was after he had asked if her mother would be there.

"Were you wanting to speak with my mother?" she asked.

"It does not matter."

She stepped closer to him. "Mr. Withrow."

He would not turn and look at her.

"Henry, please."

Finally, he turned.

"I am rather dense...and very inexperienced. And I am not accustomed to noticing the social cues that might symbolise that a man may be showing his regard, and if that is the case, in this particular circumstance, I hope you will not stop showing such a regard, if that is indeed what you were intending to show."

"Do you feel regard for me?" He asked it as if it were the most important question in the world. And perhaps it was the most important question, for what could be more important than love?

"That would be an understatement, but yes. Of course I do. And not just regard. You...you make me feel alive. I, I—" Better to force it out, than to leave it unsaid. "I love you, Henry."

He reached out his hand and touched her face. "Truly?"

"Yes." She stepped back and crossed her arms. "But it is not fair, or just, or right for a woman to be forced to disclose her true emotions if the man will not reciprocate and share his own."

"Is that in Wollstonecraft?"

"No, but it should be."

"I—I do not know if I should express my emotions, or even if I should engage with them. I have felt such darkness and despair since the battle. I am not whole, and I do not know if I will ever be whole enough to be the man that you need by your side."

"Is that why you have pulled away from me?"

"Yes. I told myself that I would rather cause harm for a

short period of time than pretend I was whole and cause you more harm for an extended period of time."

"That is flawed logic," said Mary.

"I am sure it is."

"It also assumes that you have the right to decide what I might or might not want to face in my life."

"Which is false, certainly. I should not have made that assumption."

Mary leaned again on the wall, looking out at the light fighting with the darkness, attempting to subdue it. The light would win, day would rise, and the light would diminish, and it would be dark, but then the light would rise and vanquish the darkness again.

"Should only those who are whole have a chance at love and happiness?" asked Mary. "We both have our own darkness and despair to face. We both will have times when it seems that there is no light and no hope. But I am willing to stand with you when everything feels dark until the darkness passes."

"That is the most compelling statement anyone has ever made to me," said Mr. Withrow.

"Then you should write it down," said Mary. "If one does not make note of statements they find inspiring, they are apt to forget them, despite their compelling nature."

"That is good advice—I will write it down," said Mr. Withrow. "I hope you do not mind if I attempt to say something compelling to you."

"I do not," said Mary. "However, to be truly compelling, your words should be both thorough and expressive, yet not too drawn out. A solid organisation of thought could be indicative of good intentions, yet one would not want it to feel too contrived or scripted."

"You are more demanding than any tutor." His mouth tilted into a smile. "But I shall attempt."

"If you need time to prepare your remarks, I can give it to you."

He laughed.

"I was not joking."

"I know, but I still found it endearing. Just as I find you endearing, Miss Mary Bennet. Would a rhetorical flourish be appropriate?"

"If it is relevant."

"It is. Endear comes from two roots, en, meaning to make, and dear, which likely comes from an Old Germanic word meaning dear, or in high esteem. I have not always been the best at showing it, and I did not recognize it at the start, but you have become dear to me. I hold you in the highest esteem. You are one of the only people in this world who I trust completely. I had hoped that you would feel the same towards me, but, fool that I am, I have often despaired of it."

A warmth blossomed in Mary's chest. "So you love me?"

"Yes, I love you, Mary."

"Well, that was an adequate expression of emotion."

"Only adequate? You wound me."

"With a little additional effort, you could improve your expression."

"You have high expectations. How would you have me improve?"

"By always kissing me after making such a statement."

"I am more than willing to oblige."

Henry placed his arm around her waist and gently pulled her to him. Their first kiss was short and sublime, their second kiss, full of longing, and their third kiss, like sunlight dancing on a meadow of flowers. Their subsequent kisses increased in both duration and intensity. Mary wished she could catalogue every kiss, wished she could remember and mark each one.

They paused to gaze into each other's eyes. There was something terrifying and wonderful about knowing the way Henry felt for her, knowing that each kiss contained real meaning and passion.

Mary ran her fingertips along Henry's face, exploring.

"If someone were to come upon us, this is a rather compromising situation," he said.

"It is less compromising than it would be, were we not engaged."

"Are we engaged? I do not believe either of us actually asked it as a question."

"I would say we are engaged," said Mary. "Otherwise, what was the point of this conversation?"

"Fair," he said. "Are you certain you want to marry a man who is missing a finger?"

"Strictly speaking, you are not missing an entire finger. Only two-thirds of one. Though if you want to possess only nine fingers, I am sure a surgeon could assist you further."

"I will keep the third that I have," he said. "Could you marry a man who is missing two-thirds of a finger?"

"Yes. With no hesitations."

"I heard from my aunt that the government is rather impressed with our work as Fothergill and Pike and may want us to reprise those roles. I had numerous errors of judgment in this investigation, but I hope that you would consider working with me again."

"Yes. We make a good team."

"I like to think so."

"I hope we can sometimes dress as ourselves, and not just

as Fothergill and Pike. Of course," and then she began to blush, "I do rather like it when you tie my cravat."

"I see." He ran his finger along her collarbone, once again producing a burning sensation. "I may write that down as well."

Henry kissed her cheek, then he held out his hand to her—the hand with the bandage. Mary smiled and took his hand in her own.

Life did not offer certainties—no certainties of health or happiness, no certainties that good would triumph or that one would always choose the correct path. But of this path Mary felt certain. This was the path she wanted to take.

The End

Want more? Check out Mary's latest adventure in *The True Confessions of a London Spy*!

Join Tule Publishing's newsletter for more great reads and weekly deals!

Historical Note

As I did research for *The Lady's Guide to Death and Deception*, I found myself captivated by the real people involved in these historic events, from the Duke of Wellington to the Duchess of Richmond to General Blücher to the spies employed by the Prince of Orange. Many real historical figures make an appearance in the novel, while other historical figures inspired characters in the book.

After being injured while saving her husband at the Battle of Waterloo, Elizabeth McMullen gave birth to a healthy baby girl who was christened Frederica McMullen of Waterloo. Unfortunately, like so many other infants in the time period, Frederica died a few months after birth.

The Prince of Orange did not dance with anyone at the Duchess of Richmond's ball. He quickly recovered from his bullet wound at Waterloo. In 1840, he became the King of the Netherlands when his father abdicated. While much has been made of the British role in the Allied victory, in *Wellington's Hidden Heroes: The Dutch and the Belgians at Waterloo* Veronica Baker-Smith makes a convincing argument about the crucial roles Prince Willem and the Dutch and Belgian troops played in the Battle of Waterloo.

In 1830, Belgium fought for independence, though its independence wasn't recognized by the Netherlands until 1839.

Thomas Wilson was a real dance master at the King's

Theatre and Opera House in London. In 1816 he published a book titled *A Description of the Correct Method of Waltzing*. While there are no historical records indicating that Mr. Wilson travelled to Brussels in 1815, I made him the dance instructor in the novel. Most of his dialogue consists of quotes adapted directly from his waltzing manual.

With the exception of one, all the epigraphs are real quotes from newspapers or letters. The advertisement for waltzing classes actually appeared on June 19th rather than June 12th.

While you can still visit the Brussels-Willebroek canal, the basins leading up to St. Catherine's were eliminated during the late nineteenth century. Due to the lack of photos of the basins, a mid-eighteenth century painting ended up being extremely helpful: Andreas Martin's "Les bassins des Barques et des Marchands."

I consulted dozens of books and countless online sources, but a few of the sources that were most useful included:

- An 1820 travel guide titled *A New Picture of Brussels* by J.M. Romberg
- *Dancing into Battle: A Social History of the Battle of Waterloo* by Nick Foulkes
- *Road to Divorce: England, 1530-1987* by Lawrence Stone
- *The Duchess of Richmond's Ball* by David Miller
- The podcast *Pete and Gary's Military History*
- *Uniforms of Waterloo* by Philip J. Haythornthwaite
- *One Hundred Days: Napoleon's Road to Waterloo* by Alan Schom
- *Wellington at Waterloo* by Jac Weller

- *Wellington: Waterloo and the Fortunes of Peace 1814-1852* by Rory Muir
- The 1891 book *Waterloo letters: a selection from original and hitherto unpublished letters* edited by H.T. Siborne

It is impossible to do justice to the Battle of Waterloo in a fictional novel. I made a number of minor changes to the historical details around Waterloo, including changing the date of Blücher's ball, changing the date and using a different park for the inspection of the troops, simplifying the naming and numbering of the Allied regiments, and adding a series of murders. If you find other historical discrepancies, I assure you that they were also completely intentional, for the sake of the narrative.

Acknowledgements

While much of this book is owed to Jane Austen, the setting of the book and a few of the plot devices were inspired by William Makepeace Thackeray's *Vanity Fair*. I also took some structural inspiration from Agatha Christie's *Death on the Nile*.

The map and drawing in Chapter 6 were created by Anna Lunt, who is not only an incredible friend and artist, but also an incredible writer. The map uses the Jane Austen font, courtesy of Pia Frauss' Fonts.

I normally do not use music in any part of my writing process, however, while writing and revising this book I listened to two songs to get me into the minds of two different characters: "About Love" by Marina and "You Broke Me First" by Tate McRae.

Special thanks is owed to my Irish dance instructor at BYU, who gave me the lowest grade of my entire college career.

This is the first novel I have written in which I managed to include all the subplots *and a main plot* in the first draft. This was largely due to brainstorming sessions with my talented mother, Sarah Johnson.

I am extremely grateful for my Kalamazoo writing group, who read early versions of the chapters: Anna Lunt, Michelle Preston, and Lynn Johnson. This book would not have been possible without my amazing critique partners, who I list in the order in which they gave feedback on the book: Sarah Johnson, Jeanna Mason Stay, Pam Eaton, Emily Goldthwaite, Whitney Woodard, Rachel Josephson, Sarah Chow, and Kerry Cowley.

Many of the things I wanted to do in this book were well beyond my own areas of expertise, and I'm grateful for all the time and talents that made this story possible. In terms of languages, thanks to Rebecca Davis for assistance with French, Elayne Petterson for German, and Ruben Sosa for Dutch. Sarah Kemp was kind enough to give me emergency room medical advice. Erin and Don Brady explained the engineering behind canals and basins, as well as what dead bodies would and would not do within a canal. Gavin Johnson offered up his knowledge on historical guns, though I suspect I did not include nearly as many details about the guns as he would've liked. Richard Johnson provided multiple demonstrations of how to quickly disarm someone who is drawing their sword.

I am incredibly grateful to Tule Publishing for falling in love with this series and bringing it to the world. My editor, Sinclair Sawhney, has offered endless insight, guidance, and support. Countless others at Tule have applied their talents to my novel, including Nikki Babri in marketing, Meghan Farrell in editorial, Lee Hyat, who oversaw three amazing covers, and of course, the founder of Tule, Jane Porter, who does such a fabulous job championing her authors. Thanks also to the copyeditors and proofreaders.

Thanks to Dreamscape Audio for the audiobook versions of these books and to the incredibly talented Alison Larkin for bringing the books to life.

It is not an overstatement to say that this book—and this series—would not have been possible without my incredible literary agent, Stephany Evans. Thank you for believing in me, for mentoring me, and for inspiring me to tell stories. I look forward to working on many more books with you!

My husband, Scott Cowley, has gone above and beyond in his support for both me and my writing. He is my real-life Austenesque hero. My three daughters should also be mentioned—they read my books, cheer me on, and love watching Jane Austen adaptations with me.

I would also like to thank Jane Austen for creating the character of Mary—a character who is often underestimated, yet who has so much potential. I like to think that Jane Austen would enjoy people playing with her stories, themes, and characters. I find so much inspiration for my life through reading and rereading her words.

If you enjoyed *The Lady's Guide to Death and Deception,*
you'll love the other books in…

The Secret Life of Mary Bennet series

Book 1: *The Secret Life of Miss Mary Bennet*

Book 2: *The True Confessions of a London Spy*

Book 3: *The Lady's Guide to Death and Deception*

Available now at your favorite online retailer!

About the Author

Katherine Cowley read *Pride and Prejudice* for the first time when she was ten years old, which started a lifelong obsession with Jane Austen. She loves history, chocolate, traveling, and playing the piano, and she teaches writing classes at Western Michigan University. She lives in Kalamazoo, Michigan with her husband and three daughters. *The Secret Life of Miss Mary Bennet* is her debut novel.

Thank you for reading

The Lady's Guide to Death and Deception

If you enjoyed this book, you can find more from all our great authors at TulePublishing.com, or from your favorite online retailer.

CPSIA information can be obtained
at www.ICGtesting.com
Printed in the USA
LVHW100712230623
750517LV00002B/242

9 781957 748566